PLAY YOU FOR IT

PLAY YOU FOR IT

A NOVEL

SAMANTHA SALDIVAR

DELL
NEW YORK

Dell
An imprint of Random House
A division of Penguin Random House LLC
1745 Broadway, New York, NY 10019
randomhousebooks.com
penguinrandomhouse.com

A Dell Trade Paperback Original

Library of Congress Cataloging-in-Publication Data
Names: Saldivar, Samantha author
Title: Play you for it: a novel / Samantha Saldivar.
Description: New York, NY: Dell Books, 2025.
Identifiers: LCCN 2025032260 (print) | LCCN 2025032261 (ebook) |
ISBN 9798217092598 paperback | ISBN 9798217092604 ebook
Subjects: LCGFT: Lesbian fiction | Romance fiction |
Sports fiction | Novels | Fiction
Classification: LCC PS3619.A43428 P57 2025 (print) |
LCC PS3619.A43428 (ebook)
LC record available at https://lccn.loc.gov/2025032260
LC ebook record available at https://lccn.loc.gov/2025032261

Printed in Canada on acid-free paper

2 4 6 8 9 7 5 3 1

BOOK TEAM: Production editor: Annette Szlachta-McGinn · Managing editor: Saige Francis · Production manager: Maggie Hart · Copy editor: Megha Jain · Proofreaders: Dan Janeck, Angela Brashi, Amy J. Schneider

Book design by Caroline Cunningham
Title page background and chapter opener art: MicroOne/Adobe Stock

The authorized representative in the EU for product safety and compliance is Penguin Random House Ireland, Morrison Chambers, 32 Nassau Street, Dublin D02 YH68, Ireland. https://eu-contact.penguin.ie.

For my wife, Emily.

I didn't know how to write a love story until I met you.

PLAY YOU FOR IT

CHAPTER ONE

Damp pines and petrichor ushered in basketball season at David Douglas University as if the sport relied solely on the change of seasons to arrive. Jordan inhaled the end of autumn and the approaching winter on a ride across the quad, the tires on her ten-speed crackling through sodden leaves. The clouds broke for a dry afternoon, though Oregon's usual rain rarely deterred her from cycling to the quaint college campus nestled on the edge of the Willamette River.

Jordan biked for three reasons—fitness, the school's abhorrent parking situation, and last but certainly not least, to clear her head. And today, she most certainly needed to clear her head. Despite leaving for work with plenty of time to spare, punctuality as second nature to her as waking before the first alarm and making her bed with tight corners—habits instilled by a man who preferred she call him sergeant instead of father—she continuously checked her watch. Because somewhere, the phone rang with her future. She wondered if it was now.

Booming laughter and the flash of a familiar letterman's jacket across the courtyard prompted an unwelcome detour. She grumbled and rerouted toward a hulking young man lounging on the steps of the university's brick bell tower. A girl sat behind him, rubbing his shoulders, head thrown back in a fit of overzealous giggles that Jordan cringed at.

She pumped her brakes in front of them. "Mr. Torres, this doesn't look like study hall."

Leon Torres groaned. "We got done early."

The girl blushed and nodded as she straightened up. "Yeah, I'm, uh, tutoring him. Are you a professor?"

"No. This is Coach D'Amato." He glared. "She gets sick enjoyment out of stalking me."

"No. You're just incredibly predictable," Jordan said.

The basketball team's star forward skipped class or trudged in late for practice weekly, his excuses varying as widely as the women she stumbled upon him with. Jordan long ago accepted that a job revolving around college-aged young men required she give them the occasional nudge in the right direction. Leon, however, often required a shove.

"I'm technically not doing anything wrong," he said.

"Right. And what subject were you two studying?" Jordan rolled her eyes at Leon's self-satisfied smirk. "Don't say anatomy." She held up a finger as he opened his mouth again. "Or chemistry."

"But."

"Get to the gym and suit up."

"Relax, I have plenty of time. It's only—"

The bell tower clanged above, announcing the top of the hour.

"You were saying?" She raised an eyebrow. Leon grabbed his backpack, ignored the girl asking for his phone number, and scampered off. Jordan pedaled alongside him. "You know, study hall is for your benefit."

He shook his head. "I don't need it."

"Your grades suggest otherwise."

"It won't matter after we win a national championship and I go to the NBA."

"You need a backup plan." Jordan slowed and circled around him. "Less than two percent of college players get drafted."

"Lucky me then." He winked. "Lucky you too, if you play your cards right. Stop hounding me this season and I'll buy you a car with my signing bonus. No more pedaling around in the rain. You forget, I'm a very, very generous person."

"I appreciate the offer, Torres, but I have a better idea."

"What?"

"Beat me to the gym and I won't tell Royce you skipped study hall." She coasted ahead and smirked over her shoulder. "I suggest you run! You're going to be late!"

"No fair!" Leon started on a half-hearted jog. "Let me borrow that dumb bike and I'll make it two cars!"

The clanging campus bells matched the trill in Jordan's chest as she sped down the burgundy and gold shrouded path to the athletic facilities. The breeze flapped her windbreaker. Low-hanging clouds warned of rain. A calm before the storm and a decision she wasn't quite ready to make.

She chained up her bike and hurried into the Walton Athletic Center. After changing into practice gear, she paced outside the men's locker room, checking her watch so often that she counted seconds instead of minutes. When the door squealed open, she tensed, held her breath, and then let her shoulders collapse at the player who stumbled out like a lost puppy.

"Oh, Coach, thank God." Dominic Reed was half dressed for practice as he came at her with a mess of papers.

"What's up?" She kept her eyes on the door behind him.

"Should I take psychology or sociology next term?"

Jordan narrowed her eyes. "Don't you have an academic advisor for this?"

He shrugged. "Yeah, but it's easier to talk to you. So, which one? What's the difference?"

"Well, when you have a problem, do you think it's something wrong with you or something wrong with the system?"

Dominic's eyes stretched wide. "What?"

"It's a joke, Dom. Just take psychology." Jordan pulled at the gold chain around her neck. "Have you seen Royce?"

"I think he's on the phone in his office."

The call. His call and, by default, her call. Jordan gulped down a wave of nausea.

"Want me to get him?" Dominic asked.

"No. It's fine."

Rather than pathetically continue pacing, she left for the court. When in doubt, stressed, or bored, Jordan picked up a basketball. The grooves and bumps, its distinct beat on the hardwood, never failed to soothe her.

Practice didn't start for another fifteen minutes, but Brooks McCray Jr. was already shooting baskets. Jordan joined him, swiped a ball from the cart, and launched a shot behind the three-point line. It rattled the rim.

"Everything okay?" Brooks asked.

She grabbed another ball, dribbled between her legs, and shot again. It slipped through the net with a satisfying hiss. "Yeah, why?"

"You're usually out here before me."

Their shooting sessions had become near ritual. It started during Brooks's freshman year when he struggled to stop double clutching open shots. Jordan took him on as her personal project. Now, as a senior and team captain, poised to go in the first round of the draft, Brooks didn't need her to build his confidence on the court, but they still indulged in the one-on-one sessions.

"I was just looking for Royce," she said.

"Does this have something to do with that trip he took?" Brooks stopped shooting.

"No." Jordan turned away and glimpsed at the clock. Royce should have finished the call by now. Perhaps it wasn't happening. Perhaps she worried for nothing. "How was the visit with your parents?"

Brooks grimaced. "My mom keeps asking when I'm going to bring a girlfriend home." He fired another basket. "Dad is surprisingly supportive of my singleness, though oblivious. He keeps lecturing me about how I have to be careful now that people think I'm going to the NBA. Girls are going to be all over me. He told me these awful stories about his time on the road—how women would show up at his hotel room after games."

Jordan cringed. "I'm sorry, Brooks."

"It just never seems like it's going to be the right time to tell them." His throat bobbed as his glistening eyes met hers. "Is there ever a right time?"

She sighed. "Only you'll know when that is."

Jordan sank at Brooks's frown and the burden of his secret. One she'd shed herself nearly two decades ago, though she'd argue the timing wasn't right then either. It put the clock back in her head. The seconds she was willing away but scared to face.

"Jordan."

Royce Ortega, head coach of the David Douglas men's basketball team, stood at the edge of the hardwood like the towering legend he was. The former Olympian had won at nearly every level of the game, both on the court and sidelines. Along the way he'd brought Jordan with him, molding her into his assistant, advisor, and right hand.

After ten years, they communicated with simple looks, whether chalking up a play or making a gut decision mid-game. Today, he nodded to issue her fate. Without either of them saying a word, she knew he'd made his decision. He was leaving. And as she stood there, the basketball nearly dropping from her hands, she knew she had a decision to make too.

"What's going on?" Brooks glanced between them.

"Come on." Royce waved him over. "We need to have a team meeting."

Jordan always knew the day would come. It was only a matter of time before the NBA called Royce's name, and he'd already turned down multiple offers to join the big show, but this one was different. Jordan knew when he spoke to her about the interview that he wanted and needed this next chapter. She just hadn't expected him to offer a fresh start of her own.

Days before his last call with the Seattle Emeralds, he sat her down in his office.

"Jordan, I'll gladly bring you with me. I want to. You have the experience and basketball smarts. I don't care what anyone else thinks. You're a perfect fit on an NBA bench," Royce said. "You can come with me, *or* you could change the game on your own."

He wanted her to take over. It would make her the first woman to lead a men's NCAA Division I team. She'd technically garnered the title a few years ago when Royce ate a bad egg salad sandwich and couldn't stop vomiting before the first round of the national championship tournament. She guided the team to a convincing victory, but the sports analysts remained skeptical. They insisted the team played a much lower ranked opponent, that the talented squad hardly required coaching. A famous anchor spouted that his five-year-old could've done as good a job as Jordan. She expected crueler scrutiny ahead if she stepped into the position permanently.

But it wasn't the media or a backlash she feared. After all, growing up as a queer kid in the south taught her to care little of what others thought of her. No, what stirred her doubt was the only thing she cared about as a coach—the players. The ones she won over as Royce's assistant but worried would recoil, or worse, revolt, if she commanded the ship. A fear the team all but confirmed when Royce broke the news to them in the locker room that afternoon.

"What about us?" Brooks asked. "Who's going to be our coach?"

"I'm meeting with the athletic director tomorrow." Royce glanced at Jordan. "But I have some ideas. I wouldn't leave if I didn't think you could go all the way without me."

Leon, who'd buried his head in his hands at Royce's announcement, sniffled and abruptly stood. "This is bullshit." He slammed the door shut behind him as he stormed out.

Jordan flinched. It was just as she'd predicted: Royce's departure leaving the kids in the lurch, abandoned and bitter. It wasn't exactly the ideal situation for her to take over.

"What do you think?" Royce asked her after dismissing the team. He gave them the day to ponder, to ask questions, and swallow the news. "You're on the clock now."

"I know," she said. "I just need to talk to one more person."

Jordan returned to the hardwood. To the basketballs and the sweat and the empty stands. She ran for layups, lost her breath, wishing the coaching opportunity instilled confidence in her life's work. Instead, for the first time in her career, she balked.

She didn't balk when she walked on as a freshman at Duke or hesitate when she suited up for her first WNBA game. She didn't falter or shed a tear when injury cut her playing days short—she simply believed she'd find another way. And she did. She didn't hesitate when Royce asked her to coach with him, not even when it made her a men's assistant coach at college basketball's highest level. But those opportunities didn't put her on the front lines, didn't put a target on her back, didn't stake the team's success and failure on her.

"I think it's kind of messed up he's leaving now. He could've stayed and finished the season with us," Brooks said behind her.

Much like she knew Royce's decision with a simple nod, she knew Brooks would still practice despite it getting canceled. He needed the game as much as she did.

"He's too good of a coach. This was bound to happen." She stopped shooting and caught her breath. "Can we talk?"

He frowned. "Are you about to tell me you're going with him?"

"Actually, I'm about to tell you the opposite." Jordan chucked a basketball at his chest. "Royce wants me to take over the team."

Brooks's mouth dropped. "Wow."

"What do you think?"

"What do *I* think?"

"You're the captain now. This team looks up to you."

She nearly regretted burdening him with the news as he chewed his lip, but whether or not she stayed, Brooks stared down a challenging season. His last shot at a title with a new coach. After years of mentoring him, Jordan believed him plenty primed for the moment, which was why she refused to lead without his blessing. To let him choose the next step for his team.

"You're a good coach, and you've been with us as long as Royce has." Brooks exhaled, his cheeks puffing out as he shook his head. "It's a lot of pressure. You'd be the first woman, right?"

"Someone always has to be the first. That's not what I'm worried about."

"What are you worried about?"

"This won't work if the team isn't behind me. Not for me and not for our season." Her chest tightened, her future quietly hinging on the young man's answer.

"I can't speak for the other players or promise they'll all be happy about it," Brooks said. "But I trust you. I've got your back, Coach."

"It won't be easy," Jordan said, though she didn't know if the warning was for him or herself. All she knew was that she'd made her choice. It hummed in her bones like the lights above, fused into her like the ball in her palm.

"Since when have you done anything easy?" Brooks flashed a dimpled grin. "Let's do this."

She pounded his outstretched fist. "Let's do this."

XOXO

"You're putting me in a really shitty position here."

Mark Fellner, the athletic director, glowered when Royce and Jordan met with him after practice the next day. It thundered outside his office windows, a mirror to his indignation, not at Royce's departure but at his insistence that Jordan fill his shoes.

"I'm leaving you with my top assistant who's recruited and coached this team for six years," Royce said.

"That doesn't mean she'd be my first choice," Mark said. "No offense, Jordan."

She shrugged. "That's fine. If you don't take me, I'll go with Royce, but I'd rather coach these young men to a championship. You have three seniors who deserve a real send-off."

"This way they'll have consistency. She wrote half of our playbook." Royce chomped his gum and hunkered forward in his chair.

"Sean Reilley could do the job," Mark said.

"He has a third of the experience that Jordan does."

Royce hired Sean as an assistant coach at the behest of one of the school's boosters. He barely got drafted into the NBA and was promptly cut after summer workouts. His failed professional career did nothing to curb his arrogance, or the athletic director's fondness of him.

Mark laced his hands together on his desk. "Let me be frank. Do you think a bunch of eighteen- to twenty-two-year-old guys are going to want to play for her?"

"Are you really going to make this about gender? She's already stepped in to coach this team before," Royce said.

"Yes, and it made all the headlines and sports shows. We were a spectacle. I don't want a spectacle. I want a championship."

"We both do." Jordan's leg bounced beneath the table. For all her stress about the decision, her chance at the top now seemed unlikely to come to fruition. The endless work, the trophies and plaques she'd helped to win, the ones Mark proudly displayed in his office, didn't matter. She was a nonfactor, not even a choice.

"If Jordan was a man, we wouldn't be discussing this." Royce's eyes bulged out of his square head. Jordan sensed they hovered dangerously close to an infamous Ortega outburst. It wouldn't be the first time she witnessed him fly off the handle, but never away from the court, let alone with their boss. "I won't hesitate to share this conversation. I'm out the door. What are you going to do about it?"

"Royce." Jordan gasped. She adored him for fighting for her but hated that considering her for the job required he do so.

Mark huffed and stood. He glared at them before turning to face the windows overlooking campus. "We don't have a lot here. We don't make money off our teams, except men's basketball. That's what this sports program is."

"I know. I helped build it," Jordan said. She steeled herself for a final plea before the chance slipped from her fingers. "I want this, Mark. For the school, for the team, and for those boys. I want this, and I promise I can deliver. I promise I'll do it right."

Mark kept his back to them. "If I do this, it'll be in the interim."

"Seriously?" Royce scoffed. "You don't even have the respect to invest in her for one season? After everything she's helped do here?"

"It gives me a chance to explore other options and find a permanent solution. It's a trial run. If Jordan can't hack it, Sean can step in. We'll start a nationwide search in the meantime."

Jordan clenched her fists. "And what if I am the permanent solution?"

The athletic director shrugged. "Then we'll finally have that championship. And we can discuss a long-term contract."

Jordan nodded, despite Mark's clear lack of faith. "I'll do it."

The next step required every shred of grit she'd spent a lifetime cultivating. Another chance wasn't guaranteed. Even worse, if she fucked it up, another woman might not get a fair shot at the top again. So, she ventured forward, eyes set on her mission and what was sure to become the most important season of all.

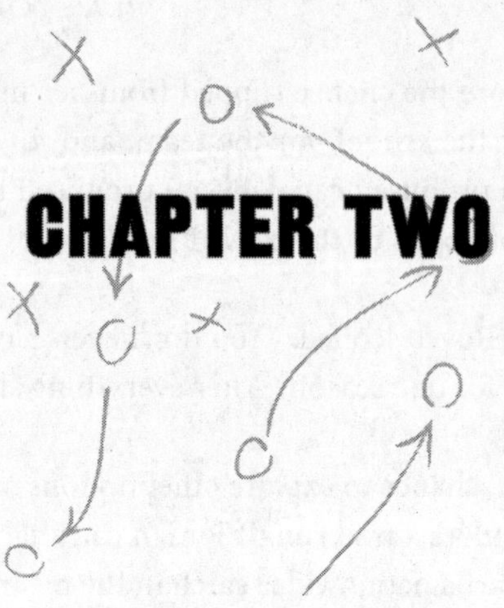

CHAPTER TWO

An emergency press conference sent Beck groaning back into the rain as quickly as she escaped it. She only managed a few steps into the Northwest Sports Network headquarters and unzipped her drenched parka when a producer blocked her path.

"Don't take that off." Nick Ruiz shoved a camera pack at her.

"Seriously?" Beck scowled.

"The Seattle Emeralds just named Royce Ortega their new head coach. We need you down at David Douglas. They're announcing his replacement."

Beck's shoulders unclenched and her eyes widened. "So, I'm top story tonight?"

He handed her another bag. "I don't know yet."

She grinned. "But you're saying it's a possibility?"

"Maybe."

"I mean, it's a great hook, Nick. I can write it now if you need help." Beck snatched up the tripod that slid off her shoulder in the frantic exchange of equipment. She puffed damp hair out of her eyeline before prattling on. "Storied head coach leaves weeks before the home opener after his team has its best preseason ever, leaving top draft pick Brooks McCray Jr. behind—"

"Okay, okay. I'll consider top story a possibility. It just depends on who they announce."

"Well, in that case, can I get a photographer?"

"I already sent a full crew to Seattle to cover Ortega." Nick grimaced. "Sorry. You're going to have to fly solo on this one."

Beck rolled her eyes as she barreled back out the door. "Don't worry. I'm used to it."

Her bosses blamed modest resources for her frequent one-man-band assignments, but Beck knew it came down to covering the scraps while her counterparts anchored at prime time and reported on the pros. She bemoaned the injustice on the drive south from Portland, belting along and beating the steering wheel to a few angry ballads on the radio. Of course, when she stomped her brakes outside the Walton Athletic Center, she put on a camera-ready face. She cleared her throat, touched up her lipstick, and flashed a fake smile at the mirror as if she hadn't been hate singing her lungs out.

In the minute it took her to unload the camera equipment from her car, Wyatt Holt appeared. He snuck up on her so often she could set a timer to it.

"You want a hand with that?" He slid in beside her and grasped the tripod in her hands.

She tugged it back. "No, that's okay, I've got it."

"Come on, let me take it."

Beck sighed and murmured thanks. Wyatt, a former college baseball player turned sports reporter, covered David Douglas University for KASE News in Portland. She might've considered his help chivalrous if it didn't come with the expectation that she would eventually accept his invitations to go out with him. Unfortunately for Wyatt, she'd dated his type too many times before. Eye candy for the camera, more ego than substance, inclined to explain shot clock violations and offsides to her despite their equal standing as sports reporters.

"Can't believe Ortega would split this close to the regular season. He's inheriting a mess up in Seattle," he said as they walked to the arena.

"Must've been a sweet deal to leave behind his best shot at a national championship." Beck held open the door for him. "Granted, that might be out the window now. Who do you think they'll announce?"

"Probably Sean Reilley or Elliott Frost while they look for someone better." Wyatt slowed. "What are you doing after this?"

"I have to get back to the station." Before Wyatt could protest, Beck spotted a smartly dressed woman hurrying for the media room. "Molly, crazy day. Who's the new coach?"

"You know better, Beck. You're just going to have to wait." Molly Liu, the team's media director, shook her head. Beck spent the last three years trying to wear her down for leads and stories, but Molly consistently stonewalled her.

"How long did you know about Royce?" she asked. "He had to have given you a heads-up. Seattle's been hunting for a head coach for what, a few weeks now? Or did he blindside you? You know you can tell me anything . . ."

"And hear you lead with it at prime time? No thanks," she said before slamming the media room door on her.

Beck shrugged at a chuckling Wyatt. "It was worth a try."

Inside the media room, a few photographers and reporters had already set up. Beck grabbed the tripod from Wyatt despite his attempts to handle it for her. She locked the legs in place, snapped the camera on top, checked the memory card, and plugged into the mult box, finishing as a side door opened and a man and a woman entered. They joined Molly behind the microphones.

"Who's with Mark?" Wyatt asked.

"Jordan D'Amato." Beck's mouth fell open. She bumped past Wyatt and the other journalists. "Excuse me."

Beck dialed Nick as she raced for an unoccupied corner, not wanting the others to beat her to the punch. Jordan had made headlines after filling in for Royce and was currently the only woman in the huddle across the Pacific Coast Conference. If the school named her head coach, it wouldn't just be a headline, but history in the making.

"What's up, Beck?" Nick answered.

"You're going to want me to go live," she whispered. "Can we cut in?"

"No. Why?"

"They're about to name Jordan D'Amato head coach."

"Are you sure?"

"I mean they haven't said it yet, but I'm looking right at her." Beck's neck flamed at Jordan's gaze crossing hers. The coach eyed her from the table at the front of the room, seemingly aware that Beck wasn't just gawking but also talking about her. Beck swallowed, diverted her stare, and shook the chill from her shoulders. "Nick, can you just trust me for once? Would it kill you?"

"Everyone all set?" Molly asked.

"Damn it." Beck hung up.

She ventured another glance at Jordan and found she hadn't shifted. The coach's chin slanted as if studying her, as if the cameras didn't exist. Beck nodded at Jordan in return and then clumsily knocked into a chair.

"Are you okay?" Wyatt asked.

"Fine." Beck scurried behind her camera and framed up her shot, thankful to hide her blush behind the lens.

Mark Fellner cleared his throat. "Thanks for being here today. As many of you know, the Seattle Emeralds have named Royce Ortega their new head coach. While we're sad to see Royce leave David Douglas, we wish him the best on his journey." Mark fiddled with his tie, the same deep navy as the team's uniforms. "In his six seasons, Royce led the Bulldogs to multiple conference championships and helped David Douglas contend for a national title. He did that, of course, with the help of a strong assistant coaching staff."

Beck observed Jordan closely. The soon-to-be head coach's knee bounced beneath the table. She sat tall and broad shouldered, jaw cutting, brown curls tied into a bun. She wore a long-sleeved shirt and joggers as if she'd just left the court and wasn't about to be named to the biggest position of her career. Despite making the news cycle a handful of times, she maintained an incredibly low profile. Beck wondered if she knew she was about to be fed to the sharks.

Mark glanced at Jordan, then delivered the announcement with the enthusiasm of a eulogy. "As we near the start of conference play and with her many years of experience, it is an easy decision for David Douglas University to name Jordan D'Amato the interim head coach of the men's basketball team."

Beck, who'd frantically drafted a post of the news, fired it across social media. In mere seconds, her phone vibrated with notifications of reposts and shares.

Mark read directly from his notes. "Jordan D'Amato was an all-American at Duke before playing two seasons in the WNBA. She then joined Royce Ortega to coach women's basketball at Atherton State College, where they won a national championship. Six years ago, she became the first woman to be an assistant coach for a Division I men's basketball team. We're proud to call her a Bulldog and have all the faith in her moving forward."

A dense lull fell over the room. Everyone swiveled to the newly minted head coach, who stared blankly at the cameras.

"You can say something, Jordan," Mark said through his teeth.

"Thank you." Jordan's raspy voice caught Beck by surprise. It scraped and crackled like she had long ago lost it from years of screaming on the sidelines. "I'm thrilled to lead this team. I've worked with a lot of these guys for years. I know what they're capable of and we trust each other. I thank the school for the opportunity."

Jordan sat back, apparently satisfied with her four-sentence speech. Before Molly gave them the okay for questions, Beck, Wyatt, and two others shouted their queries. As usual, Beck rang first and loudest.

"How does it feel to be the first woman to be named head coach of a men's basketball team at this level?" she asked.

"I take it seriously, but my priority is this team and winning. Being the first woman isn't going to change that mission. It's all basketball to me."

Jordan stared at her through the answer and Beck looked away to stop the heat in her chest from reaching her cheeks. Something about her intensity, despite Beck interviewing hulking quarterbacks, towering point guards, and crotchety male coaches, left her unusually self-conscious. Or maybe it was just the startling shade of blue shooting from her eyes that required retreat, like staring straight into the sun.

"Mark, you said that she's the interim head coach. Does that mean you're still looking for a permanent replacement?" Wyatt asked.

The athletic director shifted in his seat. "We're exploring all options. When you lose a coach this close to the regular season, it doesn't give you much time to interview all prospects."

"So, she's not your choice?"

"Jordan's a great candidate. She knows this program and has coached this team for years. It makes the most sense for a seamless transition, but we're going to test the waters."

Beck gauged Jordan for a reaction, but she didn't flinch. "How does that make you feel, Coach?" she asked.

Jordan addressed the camera this time, not missing a beat. "Like I have to win."

The answer captured everything Beck needed to know about her. Determined, unapologetic, tough. While Jordan was reticent and unpolished in front of the media, Beck found her fascinating. During the presser, her answers about strategy and players inspired confidence. She knew what she was talking about. She knew who she was. Beck was determined to know that person too.

After the questions ended and Jordan posed for a few photos with Mark in front of the school seal, Beck made her move. She ditched her camera, weaved through the other reporters, and caught Jordan before she slipped out the side door.

"Hey, Coach, wait." Beck half expected Jordan to ignore her but proceeded anyway. If she'd learned anything in her reporting career, it was to never fear hearing no. Every so often, daring to ask earned a coveted yes.

"Yeah?" Jordan paused but eyed the door as if ready to bolt.

"I'm Caroline Beck, with Northwest Sports Network." She offered a hand that Jordan slowly shook, her grip firm and controlled. Beck held on just as tight, doing her best to exude confidence, maintaining eye contact despite her skipping pulse.

Earlier, she chalked it up to the adrenaline that accompanied breaking a story, but now jitters reignited in the coach's proximity. "I would love to do a sit-down interview with you."

"No thanks."

Jordan pushed her shoulder into the door and Beck swept in to grab the handle, pulling it back with a grunt to stop her.

"Wait. A one-on-one is much better than these press conferences."

Jordan's gaze flickered, but she shook her head. "I don't want to do an interview."

Beck whipped out a business card. "Just in case you change your mind."

"Trust me, I won't," Jordan said, though she accepted the card.

"I'm sorry. Did I do something to offend you?"

"No." Jordan reddened. "No, I'm sorry. I just don't think I like talking to reporters."

"Well, you've made that abundantly clear."

Beck usually resisted abrasively cornering sources, but not today. She'd been told off, had doors slammed in her face, been called endless insults, and almost always turned the other cheek. Not because she wanted to, but because advancing in her industry required such tenacity. But here with Jordan, she pushed. She wanted this story. She wouldn't accept a simple no.

"It was nice to meet you, Caroline." Jordan started through the door again.

"You can call me Beck," she said. "Everyone just calls me Beck." Her phone rang, and she answered with a huff. "Nick, let me guess, you want me to go live? Brilliant idea."

She didn't hear his response because Jordan hadn't used the opportunity to dart off. Instead, she lingered. Lingered with her mouth quirked to one side. "Goodbye, Beck."

Beck pulled the phone from her ear and flashed a grin. Maybe she hadn't completely bungled her chance. "Bye, Coach. And good luck."

She watched Jordan until she disappeared, grimacing when she caught the coach tossing her business card in the trash before the door slammed shut.

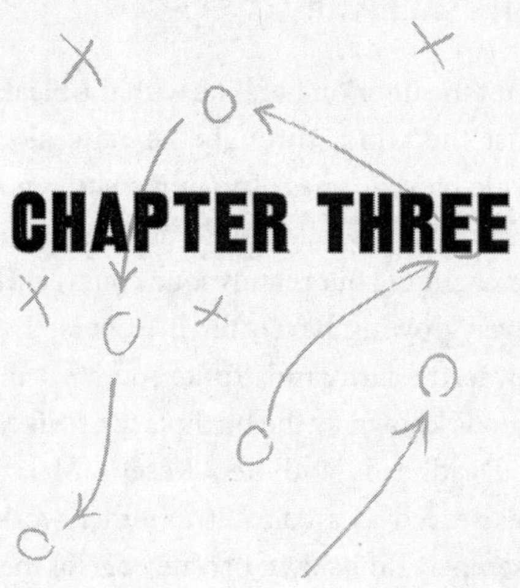

CHAPTER THREE

In the days following her ascent to head coach, Jordan's sleep deteriorated from rare to nonexistent. A mess of stat sheets and scribbled plays cluttered her kitchen table. The only time she turned on the television was for game film, and while she had enough books to open a small library, the only covers she cracked lately were on coaching.

Jordan was always committed, borderline obsessed with basketball, but now it consumed her. It wasn't just the pressure to win and prove that she could handle the top job, but the doubters roared louder each day. Reporters clogged her inbox, asking for an interview or a quote to fuel the fire. *Could she do it? How did it feel? What did it mean?* Rather than respond, she stopped opening her email altogether.

Jordan not only wanted to dodge the attention, but she didn't have an answer yet. In her manic preparation, she avoided the bigger picture. She couldn't waste time thinking about being a woman in a job that historically only went to men. She needed to concentrate on being the best head coach possible and, above all else, winning.

It sent her out the door on her bike with the bleak sunrise. She pedaled against the wind, through the rain, along tree-lined streets with wide bicycle lanes. The university's modest campus straddled the same line as much of the state of Oregon. One part rural, quiet, unchanging but picturesque country. The other part progressive, ever-growing haven for dreamers. To the college's north ran vast, fertile farmland. To its south sat the city of Eugene, a metropolis known as the birthplace of Nike, and a favorite locale for Deadheads and Ken Kesey's Merry Pranksters. David Douglas served as a conduit to either world, nestled in trees, settled serenely on its own private edge of the river.

The founders never envisioned a top ranked basketball team when the school opened before WWI. The university emphasized the humanities, literature, and environmental sciences. There wasn't Greek life or a football stadium. Alumni coached the first basketball team, slowly climbing the ranks to Division I thanks to a few star players and enthusiastic boosters.

Royce's success in the last six years lifted the team into the national conversation. Jordan joined him on every recruiting trip, crafted a playbook, and helped the Bulldogs beat a number one ranked team in one of the biggest upsets in college basketball history. Despite her time in Royce's ear building the program, it still wasn't hers. At least it didn't feel like it. Not when the athletic director waited to pull the plug on her, lurking in the corner of the gym at practice.

Jordan compensated by digging in. She studied more game film, drew out new plays, and when the lack of sleep caught up with her, she lay on her office floor, staring at the ceiling.

"Do I need to get the trainer?"

She didn't bother to move from her position on the carpet as Elliott Frost entered and shut the door behind him. He was her most trusted assistant and closest friend. One of the few people she knew had her back as the storm churned.

"No trainer necessary," Jordan said.

He squatted next to her. "Should I be worried?"

"I'm just thinking."

"About what?"

"How to beat Bader," she said. The home opener taunted Jordan as her first test at the helm.

"You sure that's it?" Frost scratched his stubble and raised a brow.

"No." Jordan sat up. "I'm thinking about everything. The big and little things I didn't expect."

The list of those unexpected things grew daily. Talking to reporters. The hateful messages and posts that spammed her and the school since the announcement. The way her once friendly relationship with the players iced over in a matter of days, the distance neatly represented by her office being down the hall from the men's locker room rather than inside it like Royce's.

"You've got this, Jay. Don't overthink it." Frost helped her up from the floor.

Jordan accepted his advice, clinging to his faith as if it might prop up her own. She swiped her clipboard before leaving her office with him in tow. "Are they decent?" she asked when they reached the locker room.

"They're dressed and ready for you, Coach," Frost said.

She barreled inside but paused when a boisterous speech rumbled around the corner.

"I didn't come here to play for a fucking woman. I came here to play for Royce Ortega."

She halted in the front hall, hushing Frost so they could eavesdrop.

"Well, too bad, Leon. He's gone. This is our team now," Brooks said. "She's our coach."

Leon scoffed. Outspoken wasn't quite the word for him. He was an artist, on the court and off, unwilling to conform for the sake of making others comfortable. He designed the two sleeves of tattoos running down his arms, wore his free-flowing dreads in a tie-dye headband, and never withheld an opinion.

"You could've spoken up, Captain," Leon said to Brooks.

"I don't have a problem with her."

"Oh, come on! You don't want to play for her. She's a nag. A glorified babysitter." Leon paused at the team's chuckles. "You're our star. You're first round. Tell them you won't play for her, and they'll drop her. Let's get your dad in here, Junior. I'd rather play for him."

"My father isn't a coach and there's no way in hell I'd want him to coach this team," Brooks said.

Jordan detected tension in the young man's voice, knew how deplorable that situation likely seemed to the point guard who lived in his namesake's shadow.

"At least he played in the league."

"So did she."

"Seriously, the WNBA? Have you ever watched a game?" Leon asked, earning more laughter from his captive audience.

"Just give her a chance."

"Why should I have to?"

"Because I'm your team captain, and I said so," Brooks said.

"Is that right? Now you want to swing your big—"

Jordan vehemently cleared her throat, steeling herself with a neutral disposition as she strode to the middle of the room. "Gentlemen, I hope I'm not interrupting something."

She leveled Leon with a knowing stare, and he turned his back to her. The other players looked down or away, but most disturbing to Jordan was Sean Reilley, twirling a whistle around his finger while he stood complacently in the corner. She shot him a glare before going to the whiteboard.

"Excellence is not an act, but a habit." Jordan scrawled the quote among the X's and O's. "Anyone know who said that?"

"Aristotle," Charlie Washington, the last piece of the team's fear-invoking senior trio, said from his locker. The nearly seven-foot center not only provided size and rebounds but wielded unrivaled intellect as the brainiest of the bunch. He intended to go to medical school, a promise that Jordan made to his parents when recruiting him from prep school.

"Gold star for Mr. Washington," Jordan said.

"Show-off." Brooks nudged Charlie's shoulder.

The rest of the players stayed silent, pelting Jordan with disdain. Or perhaps she only imagined it, feeding into the headlines and paranoia that they hated her as much as everyone claimed they must.

"Just because my door is across the hall doesn't mean it's not always open." Jordan raised an eyebrow at Leon. "You can talk to me about your concerns, and I'll always listen. Understood?"

"Yes, Coach," the team echoed. The team, minus Leon.

"Let's get going. Brooks, take them out," Jordan said. While the players and other coaches left, Jordan stopped Sean. "Coach, wait a minute."

He sighed. "What?"

She waited until the last player departed. "You're going to stand by while the team talks shit about me?"

He rolled his eyes. "He was just letting off steam."

"I need a united front, Sean. I need to know, and they need to know, that you're on my side," she said. When he didn't respond, she narrowed her gaze. "Are you?"

"I'm here, okay?"

Her eyes widened. “Mark told you that you could take over if I fuck this up, didn’t he?” she asked. Sean firmed his mouth and shrugged. Jordan clenched her jaw. “If I wasn’t trying to win these guys over and make this as painless as possible, I’d get rid of you right now.”

“If I didn’t think you were going to blow this, I’d find another program to coach at.”

“You know where the door is. I won’t miss you,” she hissed before leaving him behind.

Jordan’s head pounded as she walked to the court. She filled a paper cup with water at the sideline water cooler, trembling while she chugged. It did little to temper her frustration, especially when she turned to find the players lethargically working through shooting drills.

“Are you aware that your home opener is in five days?” Jordan’s scrappy yell reached the WAC’s rafters. In her many years on the sideline, she must’ve lost her voice dozens of times. Now it retained a permanent rasp. “Five days! So why are we out here walking around, shooting half-assed?”

“We’re warming up, Coach.” Leon sneered while he spun a ball on his pointer finger.

Jordan met the young man with force, smacking the ball out of his hands. The rest of the players cooed in surprise, and while she regretted snapping, she also didn’t dare reveal weakness. Especially not in front of Leon Torres. She glared into his defiant smirk. “This isn’t a warm-up. I’ll warm you up. Everyone on the baseline!”

The guys groaned while Jordan paced to center court. Frost blew his whistle, kicking off sprints. The players shuttled back and forth, bending to touch each line, shoes squealing with every pivot.

“We are what we repeatedly do,” Jordan recited as the team

sprinted past her to the opposite baseline. The breeze kicked up by their run ruffled her shirt and the dark flyaways from her bun. "Excellence, then, is not an act, but a habit." When the first set of sprints ended, she nodded at Frost to blow the whistle for another. "Those habits start here. We will repeat whatever is necessary for you to reach your potential, including warming up correctly. Expectations for this team are higher than ever. There's a target on your back and it's only going to get worse."

She knew the same target existed for her. Felt it in every news article and story. Felt it in Mark Fellner observing from the bleachers with Sean whispering next to him.

"We embrace that target by working hard now. By creating habits now. By creating excellence now." Jordan glanced at Frost after ten sets. "That's enough." The players stopped, hunched over, and panted. "We have ninety minutes. Give me your best. Or we'll make timed sprints a habit instead."

Jordan must have yelled more in that first week of practice as head coach than her last six seasons. She blew her whistle, shouted instructions, dragged the much larger players into position during plays, uncaring of their probable resentment. She only cared about winning. Only cared about making them the best. By the time practice ended, she was breathless.

"Rest your legs. I'll see you tomorrow," she said.

The players left without a word. A few flicked her scowls. Jordan chewed her lip, the tension headache building to a migraine.

"You okay?" Frost asked.

She glared at Sean and Mark leaving the court together. "Did you see them conspiring over there?"

"You can't let it get to you."

"Easy for you to say," she said. "You're not gunning for my job too, are you?"

"Hell no. You're making it look miserable." Frost narrowed his eyes at her. "How about you come over for dinner? Julie made lasagna. You can help me wrangle the twins. They've learned how to help each other climb out of their cribs."

"Thanks, but I'm going to stick around here, go over game film."

"You've been at it nonstop. You need to eat and sleep."

"I'm doing both, though it's a major inconvenience."

He frowned. "Listen, that shit Leon said wasn't right. But you can't burn yourself out like this."

"I can't let them down." Jordan dropped her gaze to her sneakers. "And it's not just Leon. I'm sure he's saying what everyone else is thinking. What the pundits are saying anyway."

"All the more reason for you to take a step back. Forget about this for a minute."

"I don't have a minute. I have to talk to the vultures for media availability. I'll see you tomorrow."

"See you then," Frost said, disappearing down the tunnel.

Jordan steadied herself with a breath. If practice rattled her self-confidence, the press compounded the trouble. It represented another aspect of the job that she had yet to get used to.

Rather than find the cameras in the media room, Jordan faltered when she opened the heavy double doors to the court and confronted at least a dozen reporters. With nowhere to go, she backed into the gym, and the mob followed, shoving microphones at her.

"Jordan, how are the players responding to you?"

"Are you ready for Bader University next week?"

She scanned the logos on the microphone flags. These weren't just local reporters covering a college basketball team. Every major television network surrounded her.

"Jordan, talk to us about the first week of practice as head coach," a reporter she recognized from ESPN asked, leaving her so starstruck that she couldn't answer. The journalists formed a half circle, nudging each other for the best position. She cringed when she spotted Mark in the corner, hating that she'd become just what he expected—a spectacle.

"Jordan, how much pressure is there to win the home opener?"

The reporters' jostling swelled, elbows flying in the melee to creep closer. Through the blur, Jordan spotted Caroline Beck vying for a spot in the front. The debilitating thud in Jordan's chest lessened.

Perhaps it was just the reassuring hush of someone familiar in the chaos, but Beck lured her in similar fashion at the introductory press conference. Jordan caught herself staring when she overheard Beck mention her name on the phone that day and was left bemused after she tracked her down to demand an interview. If Jordan wasn't so preoccupied with her new position, she might have thought of her again before now. Might have clutched on to the woman's number instead of tossing it in the trash.

While Jordan suctioned to her in the fray, the blonde flew to her in return. A cameraman bumped into Beck's back, knocking her off balance. Jordan caught her not a second too soon and cushioned her unsteady weight. Her heart jumped when Beck's hands clenched around her forearms.

"Are you alright?" She searched Beck's eyes, indulging in a hue that danced between olive and gold. A smile threatened to break through her lips and when she resisted, it smoldered her cheeks instead.

"I'm fine." Beck righted herself with a nod and backed out of her hold.

Jordan blinked dumbly. The hive that faded away buzzed back into focus. She covered for the lapse by scolding the rowdy journalists like she would her players. "Come on. There's no need for this. Someone's going to get hurt."

The reporters settled, including Beck, who brought her mic up to Jordan. "Sorry, Coach. Tell us about this first week of practice. How's the team responding?"

Jordan hesitated, reminded of Leon's tirade, of how she ran the guys simply to prove herself, and of the pure dread that the first conference game instilled. She refused to speak of it.

"The guys look sharp. We're ready for Bader." She held her arms across her chest in a useless shield. "We know if we can beat them out of transition, it's going to be hard to catch us."

Questions mercilessly churned from the scrum. Jordan fidgeted, staring at the floor as she pondered her responses, unconsciously twisting the gold chain around her neck, eyes landing on Beck's heels more than once, as though even in the ocean of press she'd find her like a buoy.

"That's enough for today," Molly finally said, and Jordan sighed in relief.

She rushed off with the media director while the reporters dispersed. "What the hell was that? I thought we were supposed to do that in the media room."

"I'm sorry, there were just so many. They kept trying to get into practice. I held them off as long as I could."

"A heads-up would've been nice."

"I emailed you," Molly said as they walked to the tunnel. "Speaking of which, you haven't responded to any of my other messages. The *Today* show and *SportsCenter* are both asking for exclusives."

"No."

"It's positive press for the school."

"Winning will be positive press for the school," Jordan said.

Before they reached the exit, Beck clamored behind them. "Coach, how about that sit-down interview?" she asked.

Jordan's stomach swooped, but she refused to turn. Not when

her insides swirled at their brief contact, and certainly not when she gawked at Beck in front of the national press.

"No," she said over her shoulder without breaking stride.

"You sure?" Beck asked.

Against her better judgment, Jordan stopped and let Molly stride ahead. At the very least, Beck's persistence amused her. And at the deepest, most worrisome truth of the matter, Jordan found her dangerously beautiful. The kind that left her idiotically staring and had her stopping when she had every reason to keep going. The kind of beautiful that made one blunder.

Still, Jordan drew in a breath and turned. If she resisted completely immersing herself in Beck before, she didn't resist now. The reporter wore a pencil skirt and blouse, her hair falling just past her shoulders, crescent lips shaded a subtle red, perfection for television and otherwise. Jordan felt shabby in her athletic shorts and T-shirt. She fruitlessly rubbed down her sweaty curls.

"In case you lost the last one." Beck presented a fresh business card.

Jordan's mouth dropped. "How'd you know?"

"I'm just really good at my job."

She winked and Jordan cracked the first grin she'd managed all day. Maybe all week.

"I'll hang on to this one," Jordan said.

Their gazes rooted together, and while Jordan wanted to avoid anyone with a microphone, she didn't want to leave Beck. She inhaled a little deeper, stealing a trace of citrus and flowers. It evoked a summer evening in an overgrown garden, warmed Jordan's skin, threw invisible light across her shadows. But the dose of reprieve came with a helping of wariness, and she backed away, guarding herself from indulgence, from blushing, from a distraction that she couldn't afford.

"Thanks for saving me back there. I don't think I could survive face-planting in front of half the sports media world," Beck said.

The way her eyes crinkled with a lilt of self-deprecating laughter sparked Jordan's smile once more. "Anytime. I better get going."

"I'll be waiting for your call."

"Goodbye, Beck." Jordan started on a determined walk to her office.

Beck's farewell chimed after her. "Good luck, Coach."

Jordan grimaced and cursed the pleasant churn in her stomach, a distinct shift from the unbearable sourness that roiled it as head coach. Not now, she reminded herself. No turning back. Especially not for her.

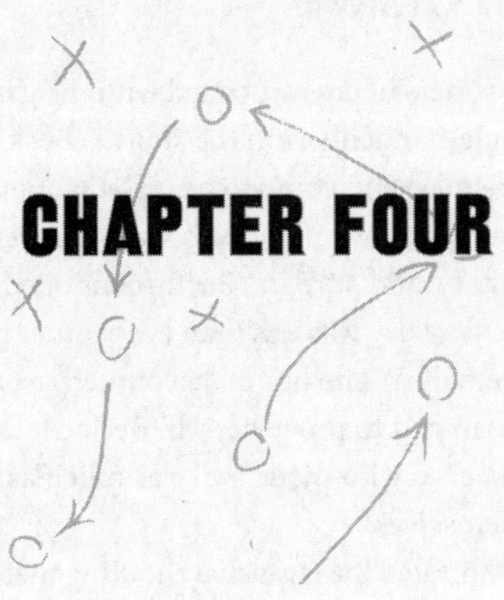

CHAPTER FOUR

"Dear Beck, please shut the fuck up. No one wants to hear your opinion. You clearly only got the job because you slept your way to the top. Do us a favor and stop running your mouth. You don't know the first thing about basketball or sports, you stupid bitch.' "

"Do you have to read those out loud?"

"Oh, I'm sorry. Is my hate mail disrupting your morning?" Beck asked as she scrolled through her email and sipped coffee. "At least that guy said please. Oh, here's a good one—'I hope Caroline Beck gets hit by a car.' "

"I thought IT was going to put in a filter, so you'd stop getting those." Nick leaned back in the desk chair across from her.

"Well, it's not working," Beck said.

In the beginning of her career, the viewer vitriol would've ruined her day. Now she read the insults unafraid, never allowing herself a tear or self-pity. Only the rare message threatening her life, suggesting she be murdered or sexually assaulted, made her shrink.

" 'Beck defending Jordan D'Amato is feminist bullshit. They

both have no business being associated with the game of basketball. They'll single-handedly ruin the sport,' " Beck read.

"I told you people were going to be pissed about that."

Beck glared at Nick. Two nights ago, during coverage of David Douglas University and Jordan, Beck mentioned that the interim head coach's salary was less than every other head coach in Division I basketball. While her male counterparts on the show argued that Jordan had to prove herself, Beck cited several other interim head coaches who made twice as much as Jordan without "proving themselves."

The segment spiraled into its usual shouting match and Beck's argument went unheard. The hate poured in online, primarily from nameless men who called her heinous words and questioned her credentials.

"You shouldn't alienate David Douglas," Nick said.

"I reported facts, backed up by numbers and public financial records," Beck said.

"Our viewers don't care about that. They only see that she's a woman," Easton Prescott said as he entered the Northwest Sports Network bullpen, twirling a wooden baseball bat.

Beck stood. "And you think that's okay?"

"It's not my place to say, but I agree she has to prove herself," Easton said.

"Giving her the job wasn't enough of a vote of confidence? She's been Ortega's right hand for a decade."

"It could still be a PR move by the school."

"And risk their season?" Beck said. "I wasn't wrong to bring it up. Look what's happened with women's soccer and the equal pay lawsuit. That's legal precedent and not to mention Title IX."

"Okay, RBG, are we talking sports or pretending to be lawyers?"

Easton lazily swung his baseball bat and Beck resisted the urge to rip it out of his hands and hit him over the head with it. Easton and Beck started at NWSN at the same time, and despite covering the same caliber of stories and games, he climbed the ranks much faster. He hosted his own talk show, *Fast Break with Easton Prescott,* and covered the NBA and NFL. Meanwhile, Beck spent her years begging for sideline reports and press conferences. She knew management assigned her David Douglas because it was a small school, but when the basketball team dominated, she refused to let go.

"I get that you want her to do well, and it's big for women, but you can't be biased," Easton said.

"You think I'm biased?" Beck scoffed. "But you questioning her because she's a woman isn't biased? I'm sorry, my little female brain can't possibly grasp it—hypocrisy is just such a big, big word."

"This is why you get hate mail. Not only is your voice like a drill to the skull, but you never know when to shut up."

"You're an asshole. While we're on hate mail, whatever you're doing for your hair isn't working. It's like your hairline is afraid of your forehead."

"You take that back." He pointed his bat at her with a glower.

"Okay, okay, guys, come on." Nick stepped between them. The producer had the unofficial duty of keeping them from killing each other. As they separated to their respective corners, Nick sighed. "Thank you. Now, which one of you is going to media availability?"

"Beck can go. I have to get ready for the show. Besides, Oprah couldn't get an interesting bite out of D'Amato."

"Maybe she just doesn't like you," Beck said.

"Like you've done much better."

"Beck, we'll have you in for five minutes at the top of the B-block. See if you can get something from McCray and Torres. Those guys have been quiet," Nick said.

"I'll see what I can do. But can I get a photographer? Last media availability, I was nearly trampled trying to juggle my own camera."

"You can take Todd with you."

Beck groaned. "Why do you do this to me?"

"Sorry. Take Todd or shoot it yourself," Nick said.

"Have a fun road trip." Easton flashed her a mocking grin.

Todd Pearson was the oldest photographer at NWSN. He constantly complained, reeked of fast food and cigarettes, and drove the satellite van so haphazardly that Beck fought car sickness. He whined about a sore back, sore feet, and swore every year that he was retiring after the season ended, but never did.

During the drive from NWSN's headquarters in Portland to David Douglas, Beck scrolled through more antagonizing posts. Whenever the harassment troubled her, whenever she couldn't laugh it off, she repeated a simple mantra. This was the dream. This was the job she'd fought tooth and nail for.

Of course, when she fantasized about sports reporting as a little girl, she never imagined it would include getting called a bitch on the regular or that people would take personal offense to her very presence on the court or field. Her father warned her, her mother never understood, and between her various moves and demanding schedule, her romantic prospects dwindled. Rather than wear her down, it motivated her to reach higher.

"I need a cigarette." Todd's coughing marked their arrival on campus. "My back is killing me. The chiropractor says I shouldn't lift anything."

She rolled her eyes. "Why do you do this job, Todd?"

"Do you think you could take the gear in for me? It'll be a quick smoke—I'll be right in."

He slammed the door before she could hiss out her answer.

"Fucking useless."

While the beer-bellied photographer moseyed away in a puff of smoke, Beck yanked their equipment out of the van, lugged the camera over her shoulder, the microphone kit and satellite pack on her back, and balanced herself out with the tripod. On her way to the WAC, she spotted a cyclist glide across the courtyard. Unmistakable ringlets poked out from the bottom of the rider's helmet, and Beck quickened her pace.

"Hey, Coach!" Beck called.

Jordan D'Amato glanced over her shoulder, eyes glimmering against the overcast sky. Beck lightened despite the camera gear's weight. Jordan's gallant catch, the gentleness of her hands when she held Beck, shot static across her skin. Just the sight of Jordan reawakened the sensation of breath-hitching closeness.

"They make you carry your own equipment?" Jordan asked.

"Oh yeah, television is incredibly glamorous. You didn't know?"

Jordan strung her helmet on her handlebars. She wore a black rain jacket and pants. Beck had seen her over the years on the sidelines, but never away from the court. She never noticed the clarity of her gaze, the chocolate speckles peppering her cheeks and sharp chin, or how she towered with the confidence of a former athlete. Beck scrambled. She didn't have time to superficially admire Jordan. She needed to form enough of a rapport with her to score an interview.

"Do you always bike to work?" Beck asked.

Jordan raised an eyebrow. "Well, you know, I can't afford a car on my salary."

Beck's mouth dropped. "I—I . . . uh, you saw that? I wasn't trying to imply that you were destitute."

"I'm kidding. I appreciated the segment, though my boss is curious about who I tipped off."

"I told you, I'm really good at my job." Beck smiled, pleased when Jordan's lips curved upward as well. She was also unexpectedly pleased by the coach watching the show, though she couldn't pinpoint why. Plenty of people saw her segments and being recognized meant little to her, but Jordan's attention had her beaming. "I'm sorry I got you in trouble. If it makes you feel any better, I caught my fair share of heat. In fact, you'd be interested to know one viewer says we're going to single-handedly ruin the sport of basketball."

"We must make a powerful pair then," Jordan said with a hoarse chuckle. "I'll see you in there."

"Yeah . . ." Beck tried to come up with something to prolong their conversation, but her breath stretched thin at that scrappy laughter. She grimaced as Jordan departed. "Damn it."

"You're still out here?" Todd said behind her.

Beck jumped and tightened her jaw. "Can you at least carry the tripod?"

"But my back."

"Unbelievable."

She ignored the schoolgirl queasiness that Jordan roused. It didn't and couldn't matter. Not when covering the Bulldogs required more concentration than ever, because Beck was no longer competing with just local reporters. Now she brushed shoulders with the big names from national networks, the anchors and reporters she long admired. Beck always intended to use NWSN as a stepping stone. Now she considered its potential as a launching pad, the storyline and season ahead primed to solidify her reputation as a serious sports journalist.

"Brooks McCray isn't available for comment today—he's stuck in a midterm. Leon Torres will answer a few questions before we get Coach out here," Molly said to the reporters waiting in the media room. Since their last tussle, the group calmed, seemingly in a truce, as the cameras set up cordially and spaced apart.

Leon entered moments later. While Brooks represented finesse, an intricate understanding of the game, unparalleled shooting and handling, Leon represented raw power. The six-foot-seven forward worked off instinct and infused the squad with energy.

He kept his hands in his pockets as he stood in front of the reporters. Beck stretched on her toes for the microphone to reach him. "Leon, how are you feeling going into tomorrow's game?"

"Fine."

"How's the transition been with Coach D'Amato?" she asked.

"Fine."

"What's your strategy going against Bader?" another reporter asked.

"I'm going to play my game."

While Leon's performance and temper bordered on unpredictable, he was a dry, stubborn interview. Beck tried again. "Leon, we haven't talked to you or any of the other players since Royce left and Jordan took over. Can you tell us how you feel about her becoming head coach?"

He paused, dark eyes flashing as he sucked on his teeth. "I came here to play for Royce Ortega. I didn't come here to play for Jordan D'Amato."

Beck unconsciously stepped forward, grasping for the next question. The other journalists tightened around Leon, knuckles white on their mics.

"Are you saying you aren't happy to be playing for Coach D'Amato?" Beck asked.

"I'm saying I would've preferred to play for Royce or maybe someone else, not that they gave us a choice."

"Do the other players feel the same?"

"I know I'm not the only guy on the team that thinks it's for show."

"How will this impact the season?"

Leon clicked his tongue. "I guess we'll see, won't we?"

"How have practices been this week?" Beck asked.

"Okay. When she's not running our asses off. I've been limping around campus like I have a stick up there."

"Alright, that's enough from Mr. Torres." Molly swiped Leon by the arm and wheeled him away, but it didn't matter. Beck and everyone else had what they needed.

An hour later, she stood outside the WAC for her live report on *Fast Break with Easton Prescott,* the hook better than anything she could've hoped for.

"Less than twenty-four hours before David Douglas University's first home game, Leon Torres cast doubt that the team supports Coach Jordan D'Amato."

While the drama worked wonders for Beck, it threatened to be detrimental for Jordan. But when asked about Leon's comments, the coach appeared entirely unbothered.

"This is a transitional period. We're feeling each other out. Not every player is going to be happy with you all the time. I've been here for six seasons, and I have strong relationships with the guys on this team," Jordan had said shortly after Molly dragged Leon away.

Despite her composure, no coach needed the public to know of infighting on their squad. The first conference game would draw interest, but questions of team loyalty turned up the heat.

Jordan assured reporters she wasn't nervous. They were prepared for their opponent. Everything else would take care of itself.

"Tomorrow night, the Bulldogs host the Bader Knights here at the Walton Athletic Center. Bader finished at the bottom of the conference last season. Meanwhile, the senior trio of Brooks McCray Jr., Leon Torres, and Charlie Washington will be hard to stop, but we'll see if this divided Bulldogs team can rally behind Coach D'Amato in her debut. Easton, back to you in the studio."

"And you're clear. Thanks, Beck." Nick's voice crackled in her earpiece.

Beck handed her microphone to Todd, who mumbled something unintelligible about needing dinner. While he edited her story for rebroadcast in the van, she wandered across the arena courtyard, checking her phone for news and scores, feigning busyness. She loitered where she'd stopped Jordan earlier, eyeing the other satellite vans lined up along the curb to be sure no one noticed her.

After twenty minutes, a bicycle chain clicked. Jordan rolled her ten-speed out, about to make a clean break, when her eyes found Beck's.

"How about that sit-down interview?" she asked.

Jordan threw her head back. "You just don't stop."

"Me and you, one-on-one, I'll even take it easy on you," Beck said.

"I've said no to ESPN, NSBC, the *Today* show—all the big ones. What makes you think I'll say yes to your little regional network?"

"Because I'm the best," she said.

"Is that so?"

"And I won't stop asking until you say yes."

"You and everyone else." Jordan clipped on her helmet.

For all her poise, Beck sensed a despondency in the woman.

Sure, most coaches guarded their personalities from the media and were acutely focused, intense individuals, but even smiles were sparse for Jordan. Beck empathized.

Whether or not she admitted it, Beck knew Jordan existed in isolation. The isolation of working in a male-dominated industry, confronting critics, and pounding on a door that was often sealed shut. Despite the professional boundaries between them, Beck wished to ask Jordan about it. Wished to tell her she understood, and that she was rooting for her, which definitely crossed said boundaries.

"Nice to see you as always, Beck." Jordan swung a long leg over her bike, but Beck stepped in front of her.

"I don't think you were honest earlier," she said. "Are you nervous about tomorrow?"

Rather than pedal around her, Jordan planted both feet on the ground. Shadows hid most of her face, but a glint caught her blue eyes. They never failed to entrance Beck. A fragile color on an otherwise gruff exterior.

"Off the record?" Jordan asked.

Beck nodded. "Of course."

"I am nervous. I can't sleep." Jordan opened her mouth to say more, but then snapped it shut and frowned.

Beck mirrored her sagging lips when she noticed bags beneath the coach's sunken gaze. Rather than push or pepper her with the many questions she wanted to ask, Beck reeled herself in. Getting ahead meant being a person first. Her parents had at least taught her that between their own newscasts and interviews. She followed their advice, even if the rest of her reporting ambitions fell short of their expectations. "You'll be great."

"I have to be," Jordan said.

The pavilion lights flickered on, and an owl cooed somewhere on campus. The gentle rush of the river accompanied their solitude. It might have been peaceful, even pleasant, if not for Jordan's grim aura.

"I'll let you go. Try to sleep," Beck said.

"I'll do my best." Jordan started to pedal, but then stopped. The gloom momentarily lifted as she smirked in Beck's direction. "I'll think about the interview, okay? Just let me get on the other side of this game."

She nodded. "We'll talk after you beat Bader."

Beck pumped a celebratory fist at her side as Jordan sped into the blackness. She felt it in her bones; the story was hers.

CHAPTER FIVE

Jordan puked so violently in the women's bathroom that it scared the cheerleaders.

"Are you okay, Coach?" one of them asked.

Jordan nodded as the stall door rattled shut behind her. "Just something I ate." She splashed water on her face after the women cleared out, hiding behind pom-poms while they whispered.

Her hands shook as she adjusted the collar beneath her jacket. She grimaced at her reflection. The suit was ten years old and out of style, one of three she bought for her first coaching job. Royce wore suits but allowed the assistant coaching staff to dress casually in team gear. Now that she was in charge, she felt compelled to better dress for the part, as if wearing the right clothes might bolster trust. While she changed in the women's locker room with the cheer squad, she knew even they pitied her.

Not that her appearance mattered. Only winning did now.

"They ready for me?" she asked Frost when they met in the hall.

"Yep. You look"—he paused and gave her outfit a once-over—"ready."

"Thanks."

She plowed into the locker room. The guys eyed her as they sat in front of their lockers. They wore crisp, white home uniforms. Leon murmured with Sean Reilley in the corner and Jordan swept past them to turn off the speaker blasting music.

"It's game day, gentlemen." She stood in front of the whiteboard while the stares of thirteen players locked on her. "This is it. Today, you set the tone for the rest of the season. The course, the first step toward a championship, starts right here."

Jordan weaved her gaze through the room. They had every tool they needed. A levelheaded and top ranked point guard in Brooks. A sharp-shooting slasher in Leon. Charlie was one of the most agile big men Jordan had ever coached. Dominic Reed was a player after Jordan's heart. The sophomore walked on and fought for every minute. Finally, there was Cooper Sloane, a lanky freshman who Jordan made several road trips to recruit. The rest of the team was just as fast, versatile, and hungry. She knew the depth and talent of their lineup should've put her at ease, but inside she felt rattled.

"Take care of the ball and run the floor early. I want constant movement. Deny them the middle and take your shots." Jordan had rehearsed her pregame speech a hundred times in her head, but she couldn't recall a single word. "You know what to do. Let's get out there and win."

The Saturday night crowd was electric. Students packed the stands, the band wailed, and cheerleaders riled up the fans. Jordan couldn't hear Frost yell last-minute notes in her ear during warm-ups, though she didn't know if it was because of the arena's noise or the shrill ring of her own anxiety. By the time the announcer called the starting lineup, she thought she might be sick again. The fans screamed for each player and then suddenly, they roared for her.

"The Bulldogs are led by head coach Jordan D'Amato," the announcer boomed.

Jordan wasn't just surprised to hear her name—not that she should've been—but that the cheers following it rivaled those of the players. A loud section of the arena caught her attention. A group of women held up signs reading, "Go Jordan!" Another waved a pride flag. She blushed and turned away.

The team huddled for a cheer, and then they were off.

The Bulldogs won tip-off, but it would be a rare bright spot. Bader scored first on a steal.

"Let's move! Quickly!" Jordan's jaw stiffened as Brooks set up their first play. He whipped the ball to Leon, who bounced it to Charlie in the low post. "Swing it!"

Rather than work the ball to the weak side where Cooper Sloane waited open for the shot, Leon demanded the ball back and fired a jump shot in double coverage. It banked off the rim.

"Rebound!" Jordan shouted.

Bader swiped the loose ball and chucked it down court, sprinting ahead in transition. Vengeful from his missed shot, Leon darted down to defend, fouling the other team's guard. Bader secured the basket and another possession.

They dropped by six, just two minutes in. When the ref blew his whistle for another foul seconds later, Jordan threw her head back.

"Time-out!" she shouted. The guys gathered around her, breathless and sweaty. "What the hell is going on?"

"Leon, fucking listen, man," Brooks barked.

"I'm taking my looks!" Leon shouted above the blaring trumpets and trombones.

Charlie wheezed. "I can't get any space."

"Listen up!" Jordan yelled. "Spread the court, work for better shots! Leon, Brooks, why are you taking a shot on the first pass? Everyone needs to be in motion—you included, Charlie. You can't just hang out flat-footed in the post. And can someone for the love of God get a rebound?"

"Yes, Coach."

Her direction provided some stability, but while they worked the ball more consistently around the perimeter, opening the lane and better shooting opportunities, they gave up easy rebounds and turnovers on errant passes. They were getting outworked. They weren't focused. And Jordan couldn't lift them above the fray.

They trailed by double digits at halftime.

"Do you want to lose?" Jordan asked in the locker room. It wasn't the most motivational start to a pep talk. When no one answered, she clapped her hands. "I asked, *do you want to lose?*"

The players shook their heads, many of them hanging low, towels dangling off their necks.

"We should be putting a body on everybody. Play physical. Not a single one of you is working for it. No one is working together. Leon, what gives? You're not even trying to play defense out there. They're burning you on the screen every time."

He stared at her blankly.

"You're making Bader look like all-stars when you beat them by twenty points last year. Someone tell me what the hell is going on!"

Deeper silence assaulted her. Jordan rested her hands on her hips. Her voice was already shot. She couldn't make them execute her plays. She couldn't make them win. There was only so much she could do from the sidelines. She turned to the whiteboard and smacked the X's and O's they'd spent weeks practicing. "These are simply plays. Focus up and run them or I'll be running you all week."

The threat landed on deaf ears.

When the Bader Knights went on an eight-point run to start the second half, Jordan knew it was over. The loss perched on her shoulders, leaked into her bones, filled her stomach with acid like a sickness. She stopped screaming for plays, demanding passes and shots. The game moved slower, and the fans faded away. She confronted her worst fears. The doubters and critics would have the confirmation they needed in one game. She couldn't hack it.

Jordan benched Leon in the final minutes.

"You're not going to let me finish?" he yelled.

"What is there for you to finish? Fouling out or screwing up our plays?" Jordan pointed a finger at his chest, and despite being ten inches shorter, roared so ferociously that he shuddered. "You're playing selfish, lazy basketball!"

"Royce would never do this!"

"Because you listened to him!"

"Put me back in."

"Sit down!" Jordan pointed at the bench. The rest of the second stringers observed them, no longer interested in the game. The cameras aimed in their direction too and soon every sportscast would air their spat. "I said sit!"

After one last sneer, Leon plopped down. Jordan glanced at the clock. They trailed by five with less than a minute left. It wasn't insurmountable. She scanned Bader's defense as Brooks dribbled up court, searching for a weakness. For a player unaware of his blind spot, for a mismatch, or a gap. When she found it, she barked the play to Brooks.

"July! July!"

It was their back door option, named after her mother.

She'd left out the back door in July, the summer before Jordan's junior year. She knew it was coming after her many nights away while her father served another tour, but it didn't hurt any less. A loss she couldn't outrun on the court, much like the one unfolding before her. She winced ever so slightly before calling the play again.

"July!"

Brooks relayed the play to the team at the top of the key. They chucked the ball around the perimeter, a flurry of movement and handoffs, until Brooks sprinted behind his man. He called for the ball and Dominic squeezed a pass through the scant opening. Brooks launched himself to a dunk. The crowd roared as he swung from the rim.

Down by three.

Bader called time-out, an easy ploy to kill their momentum.

The fans, the music, the sheer tension had Jordan straining to speak in the huddle.

"We're going to foul. Charlie, as soon as it gets to fourteen, lay it on him. He's throwing bricks." Her shaking hand barely kept up with her as she scrawled out a play. "They're not giving Brooks any space, so screen for Coop. Take the three."

The freshman met her with wide eyes but nodded.

"Let's go! We can still win this!" she shouted.

Charlie fouled after the whistle, sending Bader's big man to the line. The student section taunted him with cheers. The first free throw missed. Thirty seconds on the clock. The odds weren't great, but they were close. The next free throw swooshed in, and Bader's bench erupted.

Down by four.

The Bulldogs chucked the ball in. When it reached Cooper's hands, Jordan held her breath. Brooks expertly set up a screen. The freshman hesitated, and she squeezed her eyes shut.

"Three for Sloane! Three for the Bulldogs!" the announcer boomed.

Jordan opened her eyes to the ball dropping out of the net and the crowd cheering.

Down by one. Ten seconds.

She screamed for them to get back. The Bader Knights moved slowly, deliberately shaving seconds off the clock. Brooks and Dominic double-teamed a player in the corner. The seconds disappeared. A pass reached beyond the three-point line. A breakdown in David Douglas's defense. The kid was wide open. He put up a shot for three. Cooper swatted his wrist at the same time.

Down by four.

The ref blew his whistle.

And another free throw for Bader.

The arena deflated. Jordan's heart sank. Eight seconds on the clock.

Bader made their free throw.

Down by five.

She turned her back as the final seconds ticked away.

The loss punched her in the gut.

She shook hands with the opposing coach, resisting the urge to throw something, yell, or simply hide in the wake of such a public loss.

"Coach, what happened out there?" a network sideline reporter asked.

She tried to sneak into the tunnel, but the microphone blocked her path. "We got outworked," Jordan said. "They beat us on defense, they beat us on the boards."

As the stands cleared, a pair of students shouted at her. "You suck, Jordan!"

She gritted her teeth.

"What do you tell the team after a loss like this?" the reporter asked.

"We'll learn from it. I'll learn from it," she said. "But we won't ever feel like this again. I can promise that."

CHAPTER SIX

"For the first time in a decade, the number eight ranked David Douglas Bulldogs dropped their home opener at Walton Athletic Center. Of course, that wasn't the only history made here tonight. Jordan D'Amato debuted as the team's head coach, the first woman to lead a Division I men's basketball team. But it didn't get off to the start she or the school wanted.

"The Bulldogs lost 72–67 to Bader University tonight. Brooks McCray Jr. led both teams in scoring and freshman Cooper Sloane hit a crucial three-pointer to keep the team in the game, but it wasn't enough. Bader ran over the Bulldogs' defense, putting up their most points ever against David Douglas. Here's what D'Amato had to say about the defeat:

"We lost sight of the basics today. We didn't communicate with each other. We didn't hustle on defense. We got beat on rebounds, we gave up more turnovers, Leon got in foul trouble early. It goes back to a lack of effort and discipline. We beat ourselves tonight. The good news is those are all areas we can improve on."

"Leon Torres scored ten points, but that foul trouble D'Amato mentioned kept the forward from playing his usual minutes. Just yesterday, he told the media that he wasn't pleased when D'Amato was named coach. We saw the senior forward and coach get into it during the second half, and it seems her control over the team may have contributed to their struggles tonight.

"Now D'Amato is the interim coach, and when athletic director Mark Fellner announced she was taking over, he mentioned that a nationwide search for Royce Ortega's replacement is ongoing. We'll see if this leads to changes at the top. Meanwhile, D'Amato and the Bulldogs will get a chance to redeem themselves here when they play St. Anthony University on Thursday. Reporting for NWSN, I'm Caroline Beck."

Only the maintenance workers picking up trash remained by the time Beck finished her report in the arena. Todd packed up the camera. "You coming?" he asked.

"I'll meet you at the station," Beck said.

She'd driven down from Portland separately, the quiet drive without Todd well worth the gas money. He grunted goodbye while she scanned the buzz online. People dragged Jordan mercilessly, tearing apart everything from her play calls to her outfit.

"We're shutting down," a worker said from the top of the stands.

Beck waved, but he didn't wait to slam off the lights. Darkness veiled the court, and she felt her way to the exit. Before she reached the double doors, the faint cry of wheels on a cart squeaked behind her. The lights droned back on. The drum of a basketball hitting hardwood followed. It was a quarter to eleven and a long drive awaited her, but Beck chased the game's rhythm.

A ball hit the backboard and rattled the rim, and there, shooting from the top of the key, was Jordan. The coach dribbled, hair tied in a bun, suit replaced by joggers and a T-shirt. She pulled back for a jump shot. The ball whooshed through the net and rolled past the baseline. Beck stopped it with the heel of her stiletto.

"Hey." Jordan froze as her gaze landed on Beck.

"Hey," she said. "Tough game."

Jordan nodded. "Yeah."

"I thought you guys were going to come back for a minute."

Jordan grabbed another ball, seemingly uninterested in conversation as she sank a basket.

"You'll get the next one," Beck said, turning for the exit. "Good night, Coach."

"How bad do you think I fucked up?" Jordan asked.

Beck spun back around. Jordan awaited her answer with a ball tucked under one arm. Despite her composure, Beck detected the need for reassurance in the way her mouth wilted.

"It wasn't a blowout at least," she said. "The guys might've been a little overconfident. It happens to the best teams."

"They were so confident that they hardly listened to me," Jordan said. "Except when it was too late."

"That run at the end—when they play like that, you'll be hard to beat."

"Hopefully, I live to see the day." Jordan launched another shot. Beck grabbed the ball after it fell through the net and chucked it back to her. "What are you still doing here?"

"I was about to leave when I heard you," Beck said. "I couldn't pass up another chance to ask you about that interview."

Jordan shook her head. "You're relentless."

"I have to be." Beck shrugged. "So, what do you say?"

"No."

Jordan dribbled between her legs, fluid with the orange sphere, her hands exceptionally graceful. Beck knew little about Jordan's playing career but imagined her strong and methodical.

A poised shooter and demanding point guard when she ran the floor.

"What about you? Hasn't it been a long day? How do you have the energy to shoot around?" Beck asked.

"I'm exhausted, but I don't think I can stand my silent apartment or face what everyone is saying. Not tonight."

Jordan shot another basket, the empty arena mirroring her isolation. Beck wondered if she had anyone. If there was a loved one or family member that she leaned on when the undeniable weight of her position became too heavy.

"I'll leave you to it," Beck said. "But are you sure about that sit-down interview? I'm in high demand, and it might be too late to get me down the road."

Jordan smiled, and Beck's stomach tingled. The flash of teeth, the lift of the coach's cheeks, struck Beck as spellbinding. Sparking it made her glow like she'd accomplished something rare. Like she'd lit a fire in a rainstorm.

"How about I play you for it?" Jordan asked.

Beck nodded. She would've agreed to anything after that smile. "Okay."

Jordan's eyes widened. "I was kind of kidding."

"You're going to be out here shooting anyway and I don't have anything to lose." Beck kicked off her heels, the ground freezing beneath her bare feet. She wore a dress, and her hair was down, but she wouldn't dare pass up the opportunity. "What are we playing?"

"How about H-O-R-S-E?"

"You can go first." Beck nodded.

Jordan planted her feet on the foul line. She put up an easy shot that glided through the hoop. Beck gathered the ball and sank it from the same spot. Jordan raised a brow at her.

"Beginner's luck," Beck said. "Your shot again."

Jordan dribbled further out, shooting from the left side of the court. The ball hit the rim, and she grumbled. "Story of my night."

Beck set up outside the arc. She bounced the basketball a few times for good measure, jumping with her shot behind the three-point line. It sliced through the net with a hiss.

Jordan's mouth dropped. "Are you hustling me?"

"I never said I was bad." She tossed the ball to Jordan, who missed her shot. "H."

Her heart thumped. The competition spiked her adrenaline, even though it was a simple game of horse. That, and Jordan's stare amplified her pulse just as it did every time they crossed paths. Beck dribbled the ball between her legs before sinking another basket.

"Oh my god," Jordan said. "You played, didn't you?"

"Yeah. Ithaca College. I mean, it wasn't Duke."

"It doesn't matter. You're good." Jordan shot the ball from the same spot as Beck. It went in, and she sighed in relief. "Thank God."

"No, that's an O." Beck stopped her.

"That's an O? I made it."

"You didn't dribble between your legs before the shot," she said.

"You didn't call it." Jordan threw her arms out at her side, but a grin plastered her face.

Beck bit her lip against a too-wide grin of her own. "I'm playing barefoot against a former WNBA player and you're going to get me on a technicality?"

"Fine," Jordan said. "O."

"Thank you."

Beck scored again from behind the arc.

"How'd you get so good?" Jordan asked.

"Probably playing with three brothers," she said. "My oldest brother, Conner, played at Syracuse. And Troy played lacrosse at Bucknell. Needless to say, they were overly competitive."

"I have a feeling they weren't the only overly competitive ones." Jordan's shot rattled the rim. "This is not my best."

"Excuses, excuses, Coach." Beck chuckled. "That's an R."

"You're in my head now." Jordan winked, and Beck momentarily lost her handle on the ball.

She cleared her throat to recover. "How about you? Any siblings?"

"No," Jordan said. "Well, yes. Two half-siblings, but I wasn't raised with them. I don't really know them."

Beck waited to shoot as Jordan fiddled with the gold chain around her neck. A nervous tic she'd noticed during her first press conference.

"What about your parents? Are you close?"

Jordan grimaced. "Not really. What is this, a pre-interview?"

"I was just curious."

Beck lost concentration and missed. They plugged along in silence. Jordan locked in and made her next shots, and Beck missed in quick succession.

"Damn it." Beck chucked the ball back to Jordan. She grabbed the hair tie from her wrist and pulled her blond locks into a ponytail.

"Tie game." Jordan's mouth shifted with a faint smile. "Must be getting serious if the hair is going up."

"It's always been serious."

Jordan laughed. "Why do you want to interview me so bad?"

"Doesn't everyone?" Beck eyed Jordan as she lined up for her next shot. "It's not just a big break for me. Your story is important. It's sports history. Not everyone gets to make that."

Jordan missed and grunted. "Your shot."

"Why haven't you sat down with the big networks? They must be after you."

"They are."

"Why consider me then?" she asked.

"You've been covering the team for a while. Not like the other vultures," Jordan said.

Beck made her basket. "I didn't think you noticed me."

Jordan took the ball and dribbled away. "I mean, kind of. I'm sure you didn't pay much attention to the assistant coaches either."

"You tend to stand out on a bench."

"Well, not only have you been here for a while, but half my players have a crush on you." Jordan lined up for the shot. "Thought it could earn me some clout."

"Just the players?" Beck asked.

Jordan missed wide, a complete air ball. Her cheeks flashed scarlet and when she opened her mouth, no words came. The light tingle in Beck's chest grew to a tremble, one that stretched to the tips of her toes, stoking her with heat despite the arena's chill. She turned from a stupefied Jordan and gathered the ball, cleared her throat, and dug for her stunned voice.

"That's S." She hurried to the free throw line, with the win and her interview hanging in the balance. Enough incentive to ignore their awkward brush. "This is it." Beck deepened her tenor for dramatics. "I make this, you sit down for a one-on-one, exclusive interview with Caroline Beck on Northwest Sports Network. Any thoughts, Coach?"

"Bring it on, Beck." Jordan grinned as Beck turned her back to the hoop. "You're kidding."

"Watch how it's done." Beck palmed the ball in her left hand, bending her knees into position. She glanced over her shoulder, ensured she was lined up with the basket, and released a slow breath. "And just so there's no confusion—eyes closed, left-handed, backward shot from the foul line." Beck shut her eyes and threw the ball back. She spun around in time to witness it splice through the net without touching the backboard and threw her arms in the air. "Yes!"

"No way." Jordan shook her head.

"Your shot."

Jordan lined up with her back to the hoop, closed her eyes, and tossed the ball back with one hand. It hit the rim, rolled around the edge of the basket, and then slipped out wide. Beck released an excited yelp. "That's H-O-R-S-E! I win!"

Jordan sighed amid her celebration and offered a weak high five. "Good game."

Beck drew back, her overzealous grin zapping away. Jordan had already experienced a public loss, and here she was, rubbing in another defeat. "Hey, I'm sorry. I know it's been a rough night."

"Don't be sorry, you won fair and square." Jordan tilted her head to the side. "Plus, I should thank you."

"Thank me?"

"For taking my mind off this for a moment." Jordan glanced out at the empty court. While they shot around, Beck almost forgot about the game. When the burden returned, she swore the lightness vanished from Jordan's face.

"It's going to be okay," Beck said. She longed to reignite the coach's smile, but it drifted behind a lifeless mask, the same one that she wore for the cameras. "Teams lose. There's only so much a coach can do. You can't play for them."

"If only," Jordan said. "I'm not sure everyone else will be as forgiving."

"Don't listen to everyone else."

Beck squeezed the coach's shoulder. Grasped it on impulse. She lingered as if she might relieve Jordan's tumult through touch alone. And when Jordan's eyes settled on hers, shadows turning crystalline, the hardened edges rippling to a tepid pool, Beck thought she might have. Just as precious as sparking her smile. Only this wasn't admissible.

She withdrew her hand and retreated with a gulp. Jordan didn't break her gaze. The same intensity of their first meeting, of the many that followed, swallowed Beck whole. She staggered to where she'd abandoned her heels, busying herself by slipping them back on, leaning against the basketball hoop to support wobbling knees.

"So, when's our interview?" Jordan sauntered over with hands in her pockets.

"You don't have to. I know you have a lot going on." Beck couldn't believe what she was saying. She'd fought and begged for this chance, but the coach's defeated disposition weakened her chest, made her more human than reporter. More than that, her eyes melting for her, swooned Beck to the point of paralysis.

"Oh, I don't have to? After you asked me a million times, stalked me, humiliated me on my court—now you don't want it?" Jordan asked. "A deal is a deal."

Beck grinned. "Okay, how about Wednesday after practice?"

"You know where to find me." Jordan smiled back.

They waited across from each other for a beat. Beck almost always knew what to say. It was her job, but Jordan sucked her wordless. "Well, get some sleep and I'll see you next week."

"See you then."

Beck flushed as she departed. She'd gotten her interview. Yet something deep within her suggested she'd gotten much more from their game than a story. She wouldn't name it, but she wasn't just looking forward to sitting down for a prized interview with Jordan D'Amato. She looked forward to making the coach smile again.

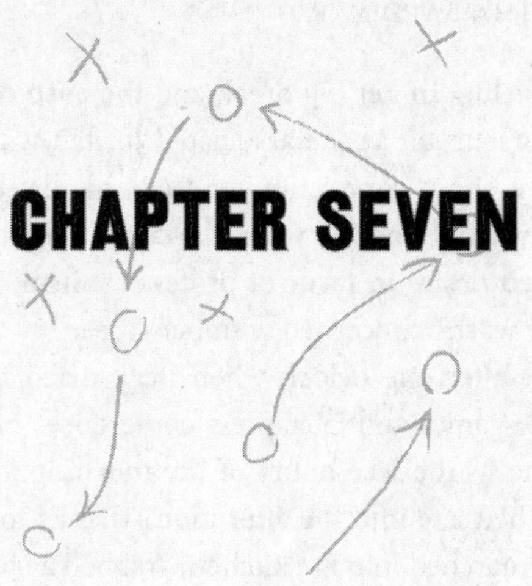

CHAPTER SEVEN

Eyes comprised of sky, nimble fingers spanning a throat, hoarse seductions vibrating her inner ear, wet lips to quivering thighs, and a pulse that pleaded for pressing jolted Beck awake on Sunday morning. She choked as she bolted up, heart hammering, body balmy and throbbing in her deepest centers and folds, on the edge of erupting without even a graze.

"Jesus." Beck sucked in a ragged breath while the remnants of the dream receded, then covered her mouth in horror as if the subject of her fantasies might be privy to her arousal. A fantasy that raged courtesy of Jordan D'Amato's gaze and rasp in her dreams.

Beck ripped the covers off and hurled herself from the bed, ignoring every urge to feed the starved screams between her legs, to shut her eyes and indulge in a few more seconds of the vision for release. Instead, she threw on the cold water, plunged into the shower, and rinsed the heat from her skin.

She assured herself that it wasn't surprising Jordan invaded her sleep. The coach eclipsed her thoughts the entire drive home as Beck blasted music, rejoicing at the interview, brainstorming questions, reveling in her big break and the cusp of something great. Of course, even as she associated Jordan with work, she drifted to the short connection of their hands, their shared laughter, the way it lit her up when the coach brightened. While she suppressed desire in favor of professionalism, her subconscious clearly wasn't concerned with her career.

It was just after one o'clock when Beck dried her hair and changed. Late games and later press conferences often had her arriving home in the wee hours of the morning, meaning she burrowed in bed late into the afternoon. Thanks to her sensual wake up, she marched into the kitchen, grabbed a cheap bottle of chardonnay from the fridge, and poured it into a coffee mug. Just as she corked the bottle, the front door swung open, and her roommate stormed inside. Without so much as a glance, Beck handed him the wine as a greeting. In return, he passed her a coffee from their favorite café down the street.

"Thank God."

"Rough morning?" she asked.

"Always. Long night?"

"The longest."

While Beck's job had her returning home at two in the morning, Kevin Weathers's work roused him from bed well before dawn. As the morning meteorologist at KASE News, he often woke up as Beck walked in. The roommates existed as passing ships in the night—an arrangement that suited them perfectly. Not only did a roommate compensate for their lacking salaries but also provided companionship that was often difficult to come by in the odd hours of their industry.

"I have some news," Beck said.

Kevin loosened the tie around his neck, kicked off his dress shoes, and shimmied out of his suit jacket. "Breaking or developing?"

"Breaking from David Douglas University—I got the interview!"

They broke into a cacophony of shrieks while they hugged and bounced around the kitchen.

"How'd you get her to agree to it?" Kevin asked when he caught his breath.

"I saw her after the game last night. We started talking, and she finally agreed." Beck hesitated to elaborate. While she didn't believe she'd done anything wrong in her pursuit of the sit-down, their exchanges teemed with an intimacy she wouldn't dare express. Flirtation sprinkled their childish game, culminating with Jordan's air ball at Beck's teasing. She worried that maybe the flirtation had been there all along and replayed the beats in her head like a highlight reel, analyzing whether they'd ever crossed a line.

"You're blushing." Kevin broke through her thoughts.

"No, I'm not."

"You look like a drag queen who just discovered rouge."

"Because I'm excited." Beck glared at his raised brows. "About the interview, nothing else."

"I didn't suggest anything else," he murmured before gulping his wine.

"Okay, I need to get to the station. I can't wait to tell Easton to suck it."

"Tell him hi for me." Kevin winked.

"Why do you have to have a crush on my nemesis? Isn't there some sort of rule for that?"

"There are no rules in love and war, baby."

"Shut up," she said, gathering her coat and bag at the door.

"Love you, Beckers."

"I hate you." She darted back to kiss his cheek. "Just kidding, love you too."

Even on Sunday, NWSN bustled with activity. Games didn't stop for the weekend, and neither did they. Beck dropped her jacket at her desk and slipped into the control room, where Nick stood with a headset on.

"How's it going?" she asked.

"Good. Nice job last night," the producer said.

Beck glanced at the wall of monitors, various camera angles on display for their Sunday Sports Hour. Easton and two other analysts sat at the main desk, sipping coffee while they discussed weekend highlights.

"This is exactly what people were saying about her," Easton said. "Even if she's coaching good X's and O's, which frankly I don't know if she was—the team isn't listening to her. You could see the disrespect on display last night."

"Take VO," Nick said to the director seated in front of the bright buttons and switches.

Video from David Douglas's game overtook the screen. The footage centered on Jordan. The coach pointing on the sidelines, barking at the team in the huddle, and then of course her argument with Leon.

"It's on her to control the team, to discipline them. I mean, if I was making the call at David Douglas, I would have some serious doubts," Easton said.

"And that raises the question—do you think her job is at risk right now?" Easton's co-host asked.

"Oh, absolutely."

"Standby for the break," Nick said to the control room. While the show rolled into commercials, he turned to Beck. "What are you doing here so early?"

"Is Vince in?"

"You know it."

"I was hoping we could meet after this. I have big news," Beck said.

Vince Holbrook hired Beck three years earlier. The aging station manager took a chance on her, and for that she owed him the highest gratitude. She spent nearly a decade scraping her way onto local sports desks and was covering high school sports in California when Vince offered her the job. He said he liked her spunk. In true Beck fashion, she submitted five reels in a single year until he finally contacted her. As always, it was a fight to prove herself, but now, sitting in his office with a coveted interview, the wait finally felt worth it.

"What's going on?" Vince asked.

"Last night I had a chance to talk to Jordan D'Amato." She stopped as the door opened behind her, and Easton entered. He leaned against the back wall of Vince's office, chomping on an apple. "Why is he here?"

"What? Is this a top secret meeting?" Easton asked between bites.

Beck's lips twitched with a smirk. "Actually, I'm glad you get to hear this. Jordan D'Amato agreed to a sit-down interview with me. Exclusive, first one-on-one since she's become head coach."

"That's amazing." Nick's eyes widened. "How'd you do it?"

"I just kept asking her," Beck said.

Vince chuckled, his leathery cheeks stretching to his ears. "That's our Beck."

She glanced over her shoulder, pleased to find Easton rolling his eyes. "D'Amato says she can do Wednesday after practice. I know *Fast Break* is our most watched slot, but maybe we make this into a thirty-minute special?"

"At least." Vince nodded. "Easton, we'll get you down there on Wednesday. We can do the show live from David Douglas."

"Easton? Why would Easton go live?" Beck asked.

"Because he's doing the interview," Vince said.

Beck edged forward, nearly pouncing across the desk. "But this is *my* interview."

"It's the station's interview. Easton is one of the faces of this network and you're—"

"Nothing?" Beck cut him off. "I've been the one building a relationship with the source. I'm the one who earned it!"

"Calm down, Beck."

"Don't tell me to calm down, Easton, or I'll shove that apple down your throat." She growled and Easton snickered, only intensifying her rage.

"Beck, I'm beyond impressed that you got D'Amato to agree to this," Vince said.

"Then give me the fucking interview!"

"We're going to be the first sports station in the nation with this sit-down." He sighed, unbothered by her response. "We can't risk it."

"You can't trust me with an interview?" She turned to Nick. "Do you feel this way too?"

"Beck . . ." Nick started with a frown.

Easton scoffed. "Quit taking it personally. The show's called *Fast Break with Easton Prescott,* not Caroline Beck."

Beck didn't know if she might cry or scream. It stopped her from opening her mouth at all. She refused to shed a tear in front of them. She bit her lip to stop it from trembling and managed a hiss. "Fine."

She stomped out of Vince's office, ignoring Easton's smug smile and Nick's weak attempts to console her, not stopping until she shoved open the station doors and charged into the rain. She took shelter in her car. Her hair hung in damp gold ropes as she flopped her head to the steering wheel.

She thought of Jordan.

Of what the coach would do. Of how she handled the loss the night before with poise and fortitude. Beck certainly wasn't like that, but she would try. She would fight for another chance. She would find another way. That's what Jordan would do. That's what Beck would do too.

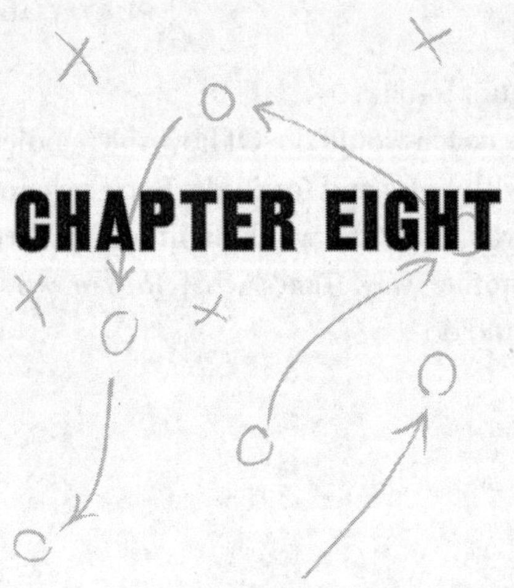

CHAPTER EIGHT

Jordan paced outside Mark Fellner's office on Monday morning, twisting her necklace, her gut fixed into knots. She knew what waited on the other side of the door wasn't good. In fact, she braced herself to say farewell to her short and laughable run as head coach when the final score glowed on the board Saturday night.

The last forty-eight hours passed torturously. The headlines deemed her a joke and the commentators scathed her, filling her head with enough doubt that she almost resigned right then. She gave the team the next day off, though she considered that a misstep too. While she ate dinner with Frost's family, word reached them that rather than rest or contemplate the defeat, the players hosted a kegger.

Instead of the usual Monday morning weight room workout, Jordan and Frost hauled trash cans to one end of the court and rounded up the hungover team at the opposite baseline. For the next hour, Jordan demanded sprints and stairs until every player hurled, sweating booze while their legs gave out.

To top off the horrible day, Mark opened the door without a

word, and for the first few minutes of their meeting they sat in silence, as though Jordan was a disobedient child. She didn't dare draw first, didn't apologize, or offer to resign. She simply waited him out.

"If you lose another game, you're done. Sean will take over until we find a replacement," Mark finally said.

"That's quite the trial run."

"You're lucky I don't just cut you loose now."

"Other coaches have lost before." Jordan wanted to cower, wanted to stare at the floor instead of his unfriendly eyes, but she held her chin up. Another lasting lesson from her father, who introduced her to harsher, more unforgiving reprimands for much less.

"You have an all-star team. If you can't get the job done with them, you don't deserve to be here."

Jordan nodded. "If I lose another game, I'm gone. You won't hear me complain. But if I win, I stay?"

He shook his head. "You're not in a place to negotiate right now. From what I can see, the team's not behind you—and honestly, I don't care if that's your fault or theirs. I just want wins. I want quiet, and I want wins."

"I don't know if I can guarantee quiet. But we'll win on Thursday."

"You better hope you do."

The days passed with more game film, relentlessly studying their mistakes against Bader. Jordan demanded the team practice defensive drills until it seared into their brains. Still, despite the training and improvements, radio silence radiated between them. Jordan coached, and the players played. No laughter, no smiles. A cold arrangement she couldn't thaw.

On Wednesday, while footage of their next opponent blared in her office, she picked at her tired copy of *The Old Man and the*

Sea. The paperback had passed through many hands, starting with her own during college. When she first joined Royce's coaching staff, she gave it to a player in need of inspiration, certain that the grit of the old man attempting to haul in a big fish with nothing but his guts and frail strength could translate to the court.

Each season, she gave it to a new student of the game. The pages were tattered and dog-eared, lines highlighted and underlined, notes scrawled in the margins in various handwritings. Everyone who read it signed the back cover. The list of names included several now on NBA and WNBA rosters.

Jordan had yet to give it to a player this year. As she flipped through the pages she nearly knew by heart, she thought maybe it was because she didn't believe in it anymore. It wasn't really a happy story. It wasn't a story of redemption. The man never got his big fish. By the end he regretted hooking it and nearly killed himself in the process. Jordan stared off as if she too rocked in a pathetic skiff surrounded by shark-infested waters.

"Hey, Coach, got a second?" Brooks stood outside her open office door.

"Of course." Jordan set the book aside.

"Figured you would've given that to someone already."

"Still deciding who needs it. What's up?"

"It's been tense." Brooks's usually buoyant eyes turned somber. "Are you doing okay?"

"I'm just trying to find a way through tomorrow."

Brooks nodded. The team captain pulled more than his weight through the transition. Jordan knew she had him to thank for avoiding a complete mutiny.

"What's going on, Brooks? How are the guys?" she asked. He shrugged, and Jordan leaned forward. "You can tell me."

"The guys are unsure about you," Brooks said.

Jordan raised a brow. "You don't have to protect my feelings. I know that I'm disliked, or as I've overheard, a 'hateful bitch.' "

"I'm sorry. I'm doing my best—"

"Don't be sorry. It's not your responsibility. Your job is to play and to enjoy your senior year. The last thing I want to do is take that away from you or any of the guys," Jordan said. For all her fighting to earn the team's respect, she also knew that she might never get there. Perhaps the noble, most helpful thing she could do if she truly cared, was unhook the big fish and paddle to shore. "Is there something I can do? What am I missing?"

Brooks bit his lip as he pondered.

"You were different before. You were more in tune with us when you were an assistant."

"The job is an adjustment for me too. More decisions, leading you guys—"

"We trusted and followed you before. This running us and screaming isn't working."

Jordan gulped as he narrowed his gaze.

"I think the reason the guys trusted you isn't because of what you showed us on the court. You showed us you cared about us. I mean, we used to talk all the time and not about basketball. Just about school and family and life."

"If I had more time—"

"You have time, but you're running us instead, making us watch twice the amount of game film. It's overwhelming." He lowered his voice. "I mean, do you know the reason Charlie is playing like shit is that he's studying for the MCAT?"

Jordan shook her head. "I didn't know."

"He's busting his ass to take the test next month, and he's pulling all-nighters every week," Brooks said. "Coop and Dom can hardly learn the playbook with everything you've added. I've tried to show Coop the ropes, but he's afraid to ask for your help. I thought you would've noticed."

"I've been preoccupied, I guess."

"Leon isn't as terrible as you think. He's just afraid of the season being over. Scared that he won't get drafted. He thinks it's the only way he can help his mom."

"And you?"

"I miss the old Coach Jay." Brooks's dejected sigh split Jordan's chest. "I don't know when the suit-wearing drill sergeant showed up, but she's not doing herself any favors."

She smirked to hide a grimace. Of all the feedback, the comparison to a drill sergeant stung most. In the wake of failure, it seemed Master Sergeant Cash D'Amato haunted her every turn. Her father was the last person she wanted to be mistaken for, and while she'd spent her adulthood outrunning him, silence existing between them for fifteen years, a secret part of her longed to prove something to the bitter old man.

"Thank you. I needed to hear that," Jordan said. Even if Brooks's assessment hurt, he was right. The players hadn't just pulled away from her. She'd pulled back from them too. Lately, she was so focused on winning, proving herself, and keeping her job that she lost sight of what she once prided herself on. Her relationships. Her ability to mold players, to support and listen. To get them to the next level in life, even if it wasn't basketball.

"I still think we can do it," Brooks said, his optimism returning with a dimpled grin.

"I needed to hear that even more."

"I know there are a lot of haters. Try not to listen."

"I'm doing my best," she said with a sigh. "You're a good captain, Brooks."

He shrugged and shifted his gaze to the floor. Jordan's brow pinched.

"How's everything else?" she asked. "School? Home?"

Brooks scrubbed a hand down his face and left it there like a shield. "Some nights I can't sleep. I come up with every excuse to put it off. After the season. Once I get drafted. Once I get a boyfriend. After my parents die." He sniffled behind his hand. "Then I wonder if it'll even get better if I do come out. I mean, what if my parents disown me like yours?"

Jordan frowned. Part of her regretted ever sharing the fact with Brooks, but when he came to her in tears his freshman year, she felt no choice but to be honest.

"Your parents love you, Brooks. I can't promise how they'll react, but turning away from you would be their biggest mistake." She kept her chin firm, though emotion threatened to breach her lower lip. "And even if they take time to come around, you have another family and home. Your team. The game. At least, that helped me."

"Yeah, but you're not really *out out*." Brooks squinted. "I don't even think most of the guys know."

"What good would that do? I doubt they care about my personal life." Jordan winked. "Maybe I'll tell them once I get a girlfriend."

Brooks laughed. "Oh, so never?"

"Ouch."

Molly knocked on the doorframe behind them. "Sorry to interrupt. NWSN is here for your interview."

Jordan's temperature shot up, much like the heartbeat rising in her throat. She yanked open her desk drawer and rifled around for lipstick.

"You have an interview?" Brooks asked.

"Yeah. With, uh, Caroline Beck."

"Oh, in that case, Coach, one more thing."

"What?"

"That is so not your color, girl." Brooks snickered on his way out of her office.

"Shit." Jordan frantically scrubbed the lipstick away with a tissue.

XOXO

The hellish week pushed her interview with Beck to the bottom of her priority list, but it never stopped glimmering in the darkness. A rare interval to look forward to. Jordan flared with longing as she followed Molly to the gym. She yearned for the banter, the prolonged glances, the hand on her shoulder, the smile lines around Beck's eyes that sprang with each shared laugh and heartened her after defeat.

She reminded herself that she was just a job to Beck. They weren't friends. They certainly weren't anything more than that. Still, Jordan tensed as the seconds drew her closer, only for disappointment to plow her over when she didn't appear.

"Jordan, it's nice to meet you. I'm Easton Prescott." A well-dressed man with slicked hair and a plastic smile offered her a hand that she warily shook.

"Where's Beck?" Jordan asked.

"I'll be doing the interview."

She furrowed her brow. "Is Beck sick?"

Easton's hollow chuckle made her recoil. "No. I'm one of the network's lead anchors, and this is a high-profile interview. I'll do the sit-down with you."

"But I agreed to do this with her."

Not only did Beck's absence upset Jordan, but she wasn't comfortable with the press or cameras. Certainly not enough to agree to a one-on-one interview with anyone who didn't put her at ease. Jordan didn't consider Beck a stranger or journalist in the crowd, but an ally. Someone she might dare to open herself to.

"I thought I emailed about this," Easton said to Molly.

"You did. Jordan, I sent you a memo about the change." Molly's jaw jutted. Jordan certainly didn't make the media director's job easy, and knew this would make it worse.

"I'm not doing this," she said.

"It will be painless," Easton insisted. "It's a great opportunity for people to hear your story."

"Yeah, and I'm not telling it to you. I'm only doing it with Beck. Period."

Easton blazed ruby red as Jordan darted off. Molly chased her down, berating her on the way to her office, but Jordan didn't slow. She plopped behind her desk, the crumpled napkin of smeared lipstick strewn across her open playbook. Jordan snatched the business card from its propped position on her computer and contemplated the number that had tempted her for the last week.

CHAPTER NINE

O'Sullivan's Bar and Grill, a musty watering hole in the middle of Portland's news outlets, was the preferred hangout for Beck and her ragtag group of local journalists. The bartenders poured heavy, games always played on TV, and peanut shells covered the concrete floor. Dim lighting and few windows made it impossible to know what time of day it was, and neon beer signs washed the space in red and yellow tints.

"I earned it, fair and square." Beck slammed down her empty glass. "Easton just swoops in. I don't know how I'm expected to get anything there."

"It's politics, Becky Boo. We've been over this." Kevin patted her hand. He'd been incredibly patient, despite Beck repeating the sob story at least a dozen times as the drinks increased.

"It's sexist," Amy Liddell, a news reporter and Kevin's co-worker, said. "Plus, Nick is a jerk for not sticking up for you."

"He just lets Easton call the shots," Beck said.

"I'm pissed too. They didn't even let me tag along," Todd said from the end of the table.

Beck rolled her eyes at the cameraman. Even when she didn't invite him, Todd always showed up.

"A refill for you." Wyatt Holt set another drink in front of her. The sports reporter squeezed himself between her and Kevin on the picnic bench.

"Sure, I'll just move." Kevin rolled his eyes.

"Thanks, bud." Wyatt clapped the meteorologist's shoulder before swiveling his attention to Beck. "I'm sorry you're upset, but at least you can say you got the interview and helped the station. Isn't that enough?"

Her eyes stretched wide. "Why should that be enough? Would that be enough for you?"

"No. No, that's not what I meant. I just think you should let it go." He sighed. "What if we tried to just forget about it and grabbed some dinner?"

The bell above the bar door chimed, and Beck thanked God for the interruption. Unleashing on Wyatt, while simultaneously rejecting his tenth offer to get dinner, would be the cherry on top of her shitty day. But the relief receded as quickly as it came when Easton stalked in.

"Oh God. Now I get to hear about it." Beck grumbled and chugged.

Easton barreled to the table at a dead heat, a vein popping out of his forehead. "What the hell did you say to her?"

"What are you talking about?" Beck asked.

"Tell me what you said to D'Amato!"

"I didn't say anything. Why? Why are you freaking out?"

"She won't do the interview with me." He glared down at her. "She said she'll only do it with you."

Beck's mouth dropped and then broke into a smile.

"Why are you smiling? It's not funny."

"I mean, it is a little for me," Beck said.

Easton's neck corded. "What did you do? Did you play the woman card?"

"No, I played horse."

"What?"

"I didn't need to play the woman card," she said. "Believe it or not, I'm good at my job. I earned her trust, and she wants to tell me her story. It's journalism 101, Easton."

"No, you did something, and this is beyond unprofessional!" Spit flew out of his mouth as he stooped over her, fists clenched at his sides. If Beck wasn't so elated, she might've worried he'd get physical.

Wyatt stepped between them. "Easton, come on, dude."

"You're being a baby," Amy said.

"Shut up, Amy. It's my interview!" Easton yelled.

"Is anyone else a little turned on right now?" Kevin whispered, a smile playing at his lips as he eyed Easton's forearms. Amy shoved Kevin, and he yelped.

"It's *my* interview," Beck said. "It always was."

Easton smacked the peanuts off the table in front of Beck, sending the shells and plastic bowl clattering to the floor.

"Can someone kick this guy out? He's out of control," Beck asked the bartenders, who glowered at the commotion and pointed to the door.

Wyatt and Todd dragged Easton out.

"Are you okay?" Amy asked.

"Are you kidding? I'm fantastic." Beck grinned.

"I know. Something about a man yelling in your face. All that bottled-up rage." Kevin shivered and blushed.

"Kev, ew, what is wrong with you?" Beck scoffed, before brightening with another smile. "I don't care about Easton. I got my interview back."

She grabbed her phone to text Nick when she spotted a message from an unknown number.

This is Jordan.
Are we still on?

Beck held her breath. She wrestled with the desire to thank her, to get in the car and do the interview right then, and the unexpected urge to call and hear her voice. To tell her exactly what it meant that she'd come to her defense. Instead, she sent a simple text.

We're still on, Coach.

CHAPTER TEN

The first and greatest victory is to conquer yourself.
—Plato

Lately, Jordan didn't know if she chose her weekly whiteboard quotes for herself or the team. As she considered Plato's wisdom, it wasn't lost on her that while she sought to conquer on the court, she barely had a grip on herself. Even after her talk with Brooks and taking it easier on the guys, the ice never melted, and for the first time in her career, she didn't know how to coach her way out of it.

At least ahead of the second game, she didn't puke.

She did, however, put on a drab gray suit, as though playing a part rather than staking her claim. She felt ill at ease and unkempt, only for it to be confirmed the minute she stepped out for warm-ups.

"Jordan, you dress like shit!"

"My mom has better suits!"

She glared up at the hecklers in the student section and bit back a retort before continuing to the sideline. The guys silently worked through pregame layups. During her pep talk, she'd again encountered blank stares. She hoped they'd be hungry after the loss, determined to prove themselves, and fired up. Instead, they smoldered quietly, leaving her uncertain if they were highly focused or hated her.

Jordan squeezed the notes in her fist, clutching the papers like a baton as she studied St. Anthony's players, searching for weaknesses. She ignored Mark hovering in the corner like the grim reaper, but his message was clear. Her fate was about to be decided in two twenty-minute halves.

"Hey, Charlie, come here." Jordan waved to him.

The towering center jogged over, beads of sweat glistening through his buzz cut and rolling down his temple. The entire team adored Charles Washington III. He had an upbeat attitude, a contagious baritone laugh, and pinned a picture of Neil deGrasse Tyson in his locker. Jordan expected him to have her back when she took over and shit inevitably hit the fan, but now knew she was understandably an afterthought.

"What's up, Coach?"

"I wanted to check in," she said. He bent down to hear, and Jordan put a hand on his back to get as close to his ear as possible. "I heard you're taking the MCAT next month."

Charlie's eyes widened. "Yes. Yes, ma'am."

The band started up in the stands, drowning out the bustle of the growing crowd sporting navy and white. Despite the team's opening loss, the Bulldog faithful overflowed. Win or lose, they were guaranteed another front-row seat to basketball history.

"I want you in my office tomorrow morning, okay?" Jordan said. "We're going to figure out a schedule so you can get your studies in before the test. No more staying up all night. We're going to make it work."

Charlie grinned, and she shrank with guilt. She'd been so out of touch that she missed an opportunity to put one of her star players at ease.

"Thank you, Coach. Really, thank you," he said.

"Have fun today and get me some damn rebounds while you're at it."

Charlie bumped her fist, and a camera flashed across the court. Jordan squinted at the media sideline, prepared to glare at the photographer, when she spotted what she spent the whole week searching for. Beck waved, her smile a meager tease from the distance, but enough to strike Jordan still. She nodded ever so slightly at her, then turned away with a blush, determined not to lose herself in the pleasant distraction.

When the announcer called her name ahead of tip-off, she was met with less fanfare. Boos echoed among the cheers, but Jordan didn't twitch or blink, because it was just noise. Nothing mattered until the first whistle when Charlie won the jump ball, and she braced to face her fate.

The first half against St. Anthony mirrored the season opener. The Bulldogs snatched more rebounds, but St. Anthony beat them physically. It was as if their opponents knew they were bleeding, fighting on the ropes, and wanted to take a piece. The Bulldogs flailed under the pressure. Rather than pass and create easy points, they threw up risky three-pointers and forced poor shots. Jordan winced at the countless balls shanking off the rim and then cursed when no one gathered the loose ball.

"Move the ball! It's that simple." Jordan growled in the huddle.

She only got more blank faces.

As the last minutes of the first half ticked away, her throat swelled. No matter what she said, what plays she called, or what she did to build the team up, they weren't responding to her.

When Dominic missed his fourth free throw to end the half, her temper finally unleashed itself. "Fuck!" Jordan turned from the cameras, though anyone could read her lips. She slammed her clipboard on the scoring table, snapping it in two as the buzzer blared for halftime.

They trailed by eight points when they entered the locker room.

It could have and should have been much worse.

Jordan put her hands on her hips while she stood in front of the whiteboard. "I'm not sure what to say right now."

A few pairs of eyes met hers, but not many. She realized this could be it. It could be her last game coaching at David Douglas. Even if they pulled out a win, a bleak road loomed ahead. A continuous tug-of-war. A team of blank faces. An athletic director who might cut her anyway. It'd been an arduous task. A risk she felt prepared to take. She knew a fall was possible, but now, surveying the drop, she wasn't ready.

"We are a mid-major, gentlemen. Do you know what that means?" She didn't have a speech planned. She offered the only thing she had left. Honest humility. "We don't have a football team. We don't have the biggest facilities or the richest boosters. For God's sake, they named this school after a guy who discovered a tree."

A few players chuckled, and more eyes found her.

"We're not the first choice for the top recruits. The big boys don't come here. But you did. You came here to hoop. You came here to fight. Because we don't do a lot of things and we don't have a lot of things that the others do, but we know how to do basketball. That's why you came here. That's why I came here too."

Jordan searched her athletes for a flicker. They straightened up as she continued.

"We're the little guy. So, we must work twice as hard even if we're twice as good. You don't think I understand that? That I don't feel that same pressure?" she said. Brooks nodded at her, and she nodded back before addressing the rest of the squad. "I'm with you. You don't have to be with me, but I think we can make it a whole hell of a lot easier for each other if you are."

Her gaze shifted to Leon.

"I know a lot of you came here to play for Royce, but he's gone. Royce trusted me. This school, this program, trusts me. If that's not enough for you, let me tell you right now—I will not let you fail. I will not let us be humiliated. I will not let you down."

She stood taller. The words formed organically. The words she should've said in the beginning.

"I can only do so much. I'm not on the court. I can't make you play with heart. I can't make you listen or trust me. It's up to you now. Will you sabotage your season to spite me?" A pit formed in her throat, one she swallowed before her last plea. "The athletic director has informed me that if we lose tonight, he'll fire me. Immediately."

A few faces dropped.

"So, it's up to you. We can end it here. Or we can win together, move forward, and live up to everything I know we are." Jordan nodded at them. "It's your decision. I'll see you out there."

She left the locker room, determined to keep her breathing even. Determined to get through the next half and everything that might be ahead, including her termination. Frost fell into step with her in the tunnel.

"I'm with you," he said.

Jordan didn't break, but her voice cracked. "Were you ever not?"

"No." Frost clapped her shoulder.

She hesitated before stepping back onto the court. "This might be it."

"I don't think so."

"How do you know?"

"Because you're a special coach, Jordan," he said. "These young men are smarter than you think."

She rolled her shoulders back and returned to the sideline with ten minutes left in the break.

"Here." Frost offered her a new clipboard. "It looks like someone broke yours."

"Shut up." She smirked.

The team returned with a minute to spare. Jordan was about to send Frost to fetch them when Brooks led the squad onto the court. The captain beelined it to her, and she got to her feet to receive his fist bump.

"I'm with you," Brooks said.

"Me too," Charlie said.

Cooper came up to her next and nodded the same. Dominic and others, including the subs and second stringers, gave her a similar nod or fist bump. Finally, Leon stood before her.

"You want to do this?" Jordan asked.

"I'll give it a shot," Leon said.

"I won't let you down."

His eyes twinkled, but the whistle for the second half blew. She nudged him onto the court in time to receive a pass from Brooks. He handled the ball at breakneck speed, dribbling behind his back, pulling up to fake a jump shot, before passing to Charlie in the paint. The burly center put a basket in off the glass.

"I told you," Frost said in her ear, above the cheering.

Jordan would never know if her speech, pity, or the fact that the guys knew they couldn't afford to lose another game without sacrificing their season spurred the second-half comeback. Whatever it was, they weren't the same team that Jordan spent the last two weeks trying to wrangle. They dominated in transition, read the options and openings that her play calls created, and moved as a cohesive unit. In the first five minutes of the half, the Bulldogs didn't let their opponents score, going on a twelve-point run that had the arena vibrating.

When St. Anthony called time-out to regroup, Jordan eased into the huddle. "Nice to see everyone again," she said. "Let's keep this going. Stay out of foul trouble. Charlie, don't let them box you out. I love that you're a nice guy, but I need you to put a body on somebody."

"Yes, ma'am." He nodded.

"Brooks, you're getting better reads than me half the time—trust your instincts. They're giving you the lane all day."

The captain nodded as he sprayed water into his mouth.

"And Leon." She paused. "Make sure you're getting your looks."

"Hell yes, Coach."

"Let's run these guys over." Jordan shouted above the band and fans. "It's time to make a statement. If we win, all the noise goes away."

The team barked "Bulldogs" when the huddle broke, the whistle blew to end the time-out, and David Douglas never let up.

Jordan remembered the game in highlights. Brooks making back-to-back threes, sending the student section into a frenzy. Charlie's insane block, trapping the ball on the backboard to stop St. Anthony's shot. Leon crashing through the key, launching himself above the defense for a behind-the-back dunk that solidified their fate. Her fate. She clapped and pointed at Leon as he ran back up court, and in a sign of progress, he pointed back before going to defend.

Jordan and Frost hugged at the final buzzer, not in celebration but relief. She high-fived the players, who for the first time in weeks sported full grins, laughing and jostling each other like kids on a sugar high. She kept her postgame talk brief to let them soak up the win.

The team blasted music as she slipped out of the locker room, the bass thudding in the hallway where she released a breath she'd been holding in for hours—maybe days. She peeled off her jacket and scrubbed a hand down her face. Thirty minutes ago, she'd been prepared to resign. Now the rest of the season and the momentum needed to sustain it stared her down.

"Jordan." Molly appeared. "They're ready for you in the media room."

"Great." She nodded and rolled up her sleeves.

"And Jordan?" Molly stopped her with a grin. "Good game."

"Thanks." She smiled.

Jordan entered the media room, still shaky with leftover adrenaline. She took the center seat at the table facing the cameras, scanned the room, and stopped when she found Beck. The urge to grin at her returned, heat ebbing from her stomach to her chest, her pulse pounding in her ears when Beck made eye contact with her. Jordan drank water to occupy herself but ended up choking instead. Before she could embarrass herself further, Brooks and Leon entered and sat at her sides.

"Coach, how does it feel to have your first conference win under your belt?" a reporter in the front asked.

"It feels good. Hopefully, this quiets some of the noise," Jordan said. "It's never been about me. This is about the team and showing what they're capable of."

"What was the difference between the first half and the second?"

"We played better."

A few chuckles rumbled in the room. She spotted Mark in the back, scowling despite the victory.

"I noticed during halftime you came out ahead of the team," Beck said. "Can you tell us what was going on there and what you said to them during the break?"

Jordan considered her answer for a beat.

"We've been through a lot these last few weeks. These guys have had to adjust to my leadership and frankly, I've been adjusting to being head coach. That's come with some growing pains.

We didn't play as a unit in our first game," Jordan said. "At the half, I left it up to them. If and how we moved forward was their decision."

She gulped as she finished, and Beck nodded encouragingly, flashing eyes that never failed to zap everything else from existence.

"Brooks, Leon, anything you want to add?" Beck asked.

"I know Coach is out there, doing what's best for us. Today we put our trust in her and in each other." Brooks smiled. "We know she's got our back and we've got hers."

"Leon?"

The dreadlocked senior leaned forward to the microphone. Jordan tensed as she awaited his answer.

"I just want to win," Leon said. "And I think we can do that with Jordan."

"I know we can," she added.

He nodded at her, and the journalists hummed with more questions.

Tucked away in Jordan's highlight reel of the day, among the incredible plays, the relief, and vote of confidence, was Beck. Jordan continually drifted to her whenever she could afford a glance. She fluttered when Beck caught her stare and grinned back.

When the press conference ended and the reporters scattered to write their stories, Jordan crept for the door. Despite usually rushing to the exit, she longed for Beck's chipper call to stop her in her tracks. To her chagrin, it never came. By the time Jordan reached for the door, she let her hand linger. She waited a second. Then another. Still nothing.

Rather than leave, Jordan turned back, rewarding herself with one more glance. If that wasn't enough to convince her of Beck's significance, Jordan's heart ballooned when they collided. Beck sought Jordan at the same moment Jordan whipped around to find her. They nearly knocked each other off balance, and Beck braced herself by gripping Jordan's forearm. While they avoided falling, it didn't leave her any steadier. Beck's fingers wrapped around her like silk, prickled her skin, and triggered a shiver that sent her unconsciously leaning closer as if seeking her warmth.

Jordan cleared her throat and drifted back before any more of their skin dared to skim despite how everything beneath demanded it. "I'm sorry," she said through the extra raspiness that followed games.

"I'm the one who snuck up on you." Beck blushed and glanced down at her hand still on Jordan and quickly withdrew it. "I just wanted to tell you congratulations."

"Thank you." She forced a smile that felt more like a grimace with how badly she wanted Beck's touch to return. Like it might assuage the anxiety that winning should have solved. Only this didn't require winning, and this wasn't anxiety. This was simple want, aching through her bones, forcing her to stand stock-still to stop the inner tremble from betraying her outwardly.

"And thank you for still wanting to do the interview with me," Beck said.

"Of course. I was—I am—excited to talk to you."

"Are you going to be able to sleep tonight?"

"What?" Jordan stared at the sweet downward crescent of her mouth so closely that she somehow missed what it parted for.

Beck smirked. "Now that you've won."

Jordan shrugged, reeling herself back in. "Maybe. Two road games next. The prep for Vardell starts now."

"You don't stop."

"You would know a thing or two about that." Jordan winked.

"Speaking of which, I'm on deadline," Beck said. "I'll see you after your road trip and we'll make some TV magic."

"Looking forward to it."

Jordan released a flustered exhale as Beck turned away, struck by the same regret she used to get from double clutching open shots. Perhaps she was out of practice when it came to infatuation. Not that practice promised reprieve. She flushed knowing only one ending might bring that about and it lived in the tantalizing tickle Beck's fingers left behind. It didn't stop her from waiting to leave until Beck disappeared, adding one last image to her highlight reel, beaming as if she chalked up a second win that night.

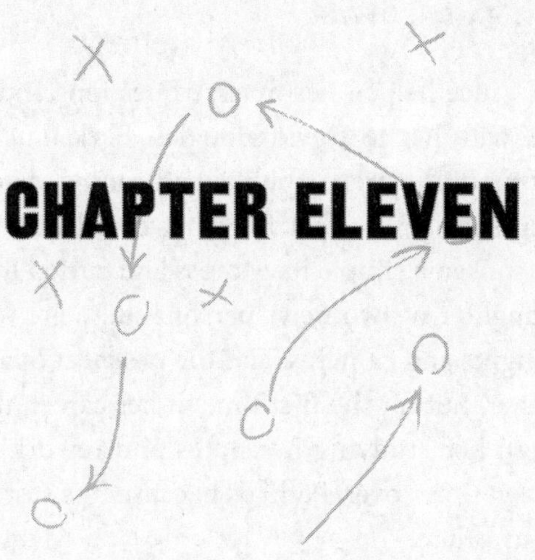

CHAPTER ELEVEN

The Bulldogs notched two more wins by the time Beck got her interview. What some initially deemed a fluke turned into a streak, and despite a shaky start, Jordan had a steady hand on the wheel. The team's up-tempo offense moved like a tide, overwhelming their opponents. Leon led the team in steals and assists, and Brooks simply couldn't be stopped, earning Player of the Week honors.

For Jordan, at least on the surface, nothing changed. During press conferences, she shared the same message of teamwork and trust. Whenever anyone prodded for a more interesting bite, the coach either ignored them or gave a half-hearted answer. It made her more intriguing to the public as the Bulldogs climbed to a sixth-place ranking.

It also heightened the anticipation for Beck's interview. She prepped all week, digging up everything she could about Jordan, from her upbringing to her playing career to her heavily guarded personal life. In fact, she'd learned so much about the coach that if it weren't for the excuse of her profession, she'd be considered a disturbed stalker.

Nick and Vince helped her finalize questions and sent a full camera crew with her to David Douglas. Beck touched up her makeup in one of the arena's public bathrooms, determined to look nothing short of perfect for what could be her national debut. She'd chosen a simple navy dress and curled her hair.

As the daughter of two news personalities, she was familiar with studio lights and cameras, and the prospect of an audience rarely fazed her. But for the first time in her career, the pressure closed in, had her studying her notes and reworking her approach a dozen times over. Perhaps because this story promised more than any other.

But when Jordan arrived, her nerves subsided. The coach's subtle smile grounded her.

"How are you?"

"I'm good. I would ask you the same, but I think the win streak speaks for itself," Beck said.

Jordan wore a polo shirt embroidered with the Bulldog logo. Her hair was tied into a bun, and she sported fresh white sneakers, as if pulled straight from the box. She seemed more comfortable like this, with her hands in the pockets of her joggers, than she did in her game-day suits.

"Todd is just going to mic you up," Beck said.

Jordan flinched when Todd clumsily came at her with the lapel mic, and Beck didn't blame her. She wouldn't want Todd's tobacco-stained fingers anywhere near her either.

"Actually, here." Beck swiped the mic out of the cameraman's hands. "Put this part under your shirt."

Jordan looped the wire through her collar before giving it to Beck. Her hand traced Jordan's neck ever so slightly as she clipped and adjusted the mic, marking her fingers with an electricity that would linger long after. The coach's sapphire eyes flashed so close that Beck's stomach plummeted, and she clutched firm to her breath, unable to move.

"Thanks," Jordan said.

Beck mumbled a response, retreated, and looked away. She reread her notes while the cameramen adjusted their shots, willing herself to not succumb to jitters. Jitters that signaled this wasn't just about an interview or a story with career-changing potential. This was a crush. More accurately, this was a problem.

While she refocused on the task at hand, the two of them sitting across from each other at the center circle, Beck noticed Jordan's foot bouncing on the hardwood. "Nervous?"

Jordan shrugged. "I've never done an interview like this. Any advice?"

"Just be yourself."

"Original."

Beck chuckled. "It's true, though. Just be genuine. People find it refreshing."

"I'll give it a try." She sighed. "You going to take it easy on me?"

"Depends on how cooperative you are."

"I'll be on my best behavior then." Jordan unleashed the sandpaper chuckle that triggered tremors down Beck's spine, but she didn't let herself smile, determined to lock in.

When the cameras settled into position, Todd gave them the nod. "Mics are hot."

Beck crossed her legs beneath her dress and addressed Jordan. "Before we start—anything off-limits?"

She knew Jordan couldn't possibly grasp the extent to which she'd researched her, and she wasn't of the belief that interviewees deserved to know questions ahead of time. It killed the authenticity, allowed for scripted and rehearsed answers that fell shallow. Still, she gave Jordan one last out. If there was something personal that she preferred to keep under wraps, Beck was giving her the chance.

Jordan rubbed her knees and shook her head. "No. Might as well be genuine."

"Great." Beck gulped, as if she might swallow the heartbeat in her throat. She gripped the notecards in her lap so tight that her tennis bracelet shook.

"In three, two, one . . ." Todd counted her in.

"Coach, thanks—thank you so much for joining me." She stumbled uneasily out of the gate. The interview would be edited later, with a full voiceover and introduction, but she inwardly cringed at her clunky delivery.

"My pleasure." Jordan nodded. The nod picked Beck back up, restoring her composure.

"Three weeks ago, you became head coach of David Douglas University's men's basketball team, making you the first woman to lead a men's Division I team. Was this always the dream?"

Jordan shook her head. "Not really. I never started my basketball career intending to end up here, but when the opportunity presented itself, I knew I had to embrace it."

"What does it mean to you to be the first woman in this position?"

"It means I need to set an example. I have to work twice as hard to make sure I'm not the last woman. This is a lot bigger than me. First, it's about the team. Second, it's about showing that anyone who wants to be in this position and has the chops should have the same opportunity, regardless of gender."

"That's a lot of pressure to put on yourself."

"I can handle it."

The coach's gaze emanated intensity in an extraordinary

shock of blue that evoked awe or fear depending on which side of it you landed. Beck hoped the camera captured everything it conveyed, but something told her its depth could only be understood in person.

"After that first loss, a lot of people doubted that you were up for the job. Now you've won three games in a row. How did you regroup and recover after that?"

"I changed my approach. I was trying to prove myself to the guys instead of being the coach they always knew. That's the biggest thing I've taken away from these last three weeks—I have to be myself. I can't be everything the fans or the media or even the school want me to be. I have to be me and that's who the team needs too."

Beck paused, allowing the statement to marinate before continuing. "Where did your love of the game come from?"

A weak smile passed over Jordan's face. "It started when I was a kid. My father was in the army, so we moved around a lot. I changed schools six times, maybe seven. I can't remember anymore. The game was a fast way for me to make friends and fit in. A rare constant," she said. "My dad also played, so it was something we bonded over. He played against Michael Jordan in high school. I'm named after him."

"Well, that seems fitting, since you're also making basketball history."

Jordan chuckled. "I would never put us in the same category."

"What does your family think about you coaching?"

"I'm not sure." Jordan's stare shifted past Beck's shoulder, landing somewhere beyond the interview. "I think, I hope, maybe happy."

Beck considered a follow-up but almost avoided the last question altogether. In her background work, she'd stumbled upon the difficult aspects of Jordan's upbringing. Her father, Cash D'Amato, spent the bulk of Jordan's childhood overseas. Beck discovered a shaky video of one of his returns home. The kind of tear-jerking story that aired at the end of local newscasts. He'd shown up in his uniform, surprising a young Jordan at a basketball game. She collapsed into his arms after years without him.

But it wasn't only happy reunions. Divorce papers came less than a year later as Cash and Jordan's mother, Annette, separated. Beck didn't know much beyond that but imagined it made for a difficult adolescence. Even now, she sensed the coach's discomfort as she reached for her necklace and then stopped, though that wasn't the only reason she avoided pressing. While those questions painted a dramatic story, it wasn't the purpose of the interview. Though a public figure, Jordan had some right to privacy.

"Let's look back on your years on the court. You played four years as a point guard at Duke where you were an all-American. Then you were the third overall draft pick in the WNBA. You spent two seasons in the league before suffering a severe ACL injury. How did those experiences impact you?"

Beck watched several of Jordan's games while gathering footage for the piece. She played almost exactly how Beck imagined. A decisive and commanding leader, a deft dribbler, and sharp three-point shooter. In her brief career, she led her team in three-pointers, assists, and steals. Then it crumbled during the playoffs. Jordan's knee gave out after a layup. The cameras caught the painful angle as she landed and the agony on her face when she cried out. The images hardened Beck's stomach, her throat constricting when Jordan insisted on limping off the court with her head held high.

"Obviously if it wasn't for those experiences, my injury in particular, I wouldn't be coaching. It was almost a year-long recovery, and I spent that time on the bench, mentoring my teammates. I became an honorary member of the staff in Chicago, and they offered me the option to either continue rehab and play the next season or stay on as an assistant."

"Why coach? Why not try to keep playing?"

Jordan chewed her lower lip for a beat. "Honestly, I got as much joy out of helping others and reading the game from the sidelines. It felt like a calling. Growing up, my coaches had the biggest impact on my life. It felt like a way to give back," Jordan said. "Plus, I think I'm alright at it."

"I think many people would agree." She smiled.

Jordan bashfully grinned back, and Beck glanced down at her notes to avoid losing herself. She'd pondered her next question deeply, gone back and forth on whether she should ask it, but prepared to dive in—even if it ran the risk of upsetting the coach.

"Off the court, you maintain a pretty private personal life. But I'd be remiss to not mention that not only are you the first woman to coach men's college basketball at this level, but also the first and only openly gay head coach."

Beck's heart thundered. Jordan wasn't closeted, but she kept a tight lid on her romantic life. She didn't have any social media accounts, no photos or statements that indicated her preference. Her apparent fan club waving a rainbow flag at home games piqued Beck's interest, and she confirmed as much in a decades-old magazine profile on queer athletes. Jordan's name was stashed away among the more renowned players, but there and out, nonetheless.

"Only gay head coach?" Jordan repeated. "Statistically, that can't be right."

The coach winked and Beck's chest unfixed itself. "I said *openly* gay."

"Right," Jordan said. "Well, why not be the first for that too?"

"What do you want your legacy to be?"

"To bring David Douglas University its first national championship."

Beck resisted laughing, not because the answer was funny but because the coach was so one-track minded. She didn't bat an eye or pause for a sentimental comment on her place in history. She just wanted to win in a steadfast, borderline ruthless fashion.

"What about the young girls who see and look up to you on the sidelines? What's your message to them?"

"This is for them too," Jordan said. "If they can play and know the game, they'll get here. It's not about gender—it's just about basketball."

After the sit-down portion, the cameras stayed for practice. They kept Jordan miked up, filming as she positioned guys for screens, walked them through new plays, and blew the whistle to pause drills. Beck couldn't stop staring. At first, she attributed it to Jordan being the subject of her story, but then found she wasn't interested in her coaching. She was infatuated with how she moved, her gravelly shouting reaching the rafters, clapping and beaming when the team got something right. Jordan's control, knowledge, and sheer determination radiated across the court, and Beck didn't want to look away.

When practice ended and the team left, she walked over to meet her.

"Is that it?" Jordan asked.

"Yes, you are officially free. Thank you so much for agreeing to this."

"Of course." She handed her the mic. "I hope you got what you needed."

"I did," Beck said. "You were amazing."

"So were you. You clearly did your research."

Beck winced. "I'm sorry."

"Don't be sorry. I have nothing to hide," Jordan said. "I'm just not a big talker. Especially not about my family or sex life."

"Well, leave it to a nosy journalist to pry you open." Heat crept up Beck's neck, but she deflected. "Plus, you have some passionate female fans at the games. Just one too many *'Marry Me, Coach'* and *'I love you, Jordan'* signs. It kind of tipped me off."

Jordan reddened. "Oh God. They're mostly just friends from the university."

Beck raised an eyebrow. "Mostly?" She meant to tease her, but the possibility of Jordan having someone shifted something inside. She used to wonder out of curiosity, but now she hoped it wasn't true. Now the prospect irked her.

"That's not what I meant."

"Hey, I'm not judging, and it's not my business."

"Oh really? I think I'm the entire focus of your business," Jordan said, quirking one side of her mouth.

Beck's chest sputtered. "Well, lucky you. After this interview, our work together is done."

"What if I don't want it to be?"

"Are you offering a follow-up?"

"No. Well, maybe." Jordan sucked in a sharp breath. "I wanted to know if you'd like to get dinner with me."

Beck's brow crinkled while she replayed the question in her head, making certain she'd heard right. "Dinner?"

"Yeah. Tonight, or whenever you're in town again."

Jordan waited with expectant baby blues, betraying her cool demeanor. Moments earlier, Beck couldn't peel her eyes off her, starving for her attention. Now that she had it, she didn't know what to do.

"I don't see sources outside of work," Beck said. It wasn't the first time a coach or player asked her out, but this was the first time she found herself flustered. Or that she considered accepting the invitation.

"Why not?"

"Because it could compromise the integrity of my reporting. I have to be objective and ask the hard questions."

Jordan smirked. "I have a feeling you still would."

Beck sighed. "If we're friends, or you know, go out to dinner together, people might think that I'm biased toward you."

"What if I play you for it?" Jordan nodded at a cart of basketballs left out from practice. "You owe me a rematch."

Beck pondered the possibility. She longed to say yes. Nearly gave in. Of course, she worried that if she agreed to the game, she might lose on purpose, because everything in her screamed for this chance. This risk. "I can't. I'm sorry."

Jordan's shoulders drooped, her playfulness dissolving in the same fall. "I understand," she said. "I'll see you at the next press conference. Let me know when the interview is going to air."

Beck gritted her teeth as Jordan turned away. She threw her head back, strangled the microphone pack, and shut her eyes in exasperation.

"One more thing," Jordan said.

Beck shot her head back up and blushed. "Hmm, yeah?"

"Do you think I dress bad?"

"What?"

"Like for games? Everyone online and in the stands says I dress bad." Jordan frowned. "I've been wearing suits to be professional, but I don't really know if it's my style. I know my sweats don't cut it either."

"You dress—" Beck stopped. She couldn't lie. As striking as Jordan was, her game-day look needed help. "Maybe you should go shopping."

"That's not really my thing. It might not be a solo mission, you know?" Jordan's cheeky gleam returned like she'd drawn up a trick play. "And you clearly know what you're doing."

Beck tilted her head to the side. "Are you asking for my help?"

Jordan kicked at the gym floor. "I mean, I wouldn't want to compromise your journalistic integrity."

"Fine," Beck said.

"Fine, what?"

"I'll help you," she said. "But it's not a date."

"Far from it." Jordan nodded.

Beck resisted glowing, determined to uphold the thin and growing thinner facade of boundaries. "Tomorrow. The mall. But that's it."

"See you then." Jordan winked before striding off. Beck chewed her inner cheek to stop a grin. For the last few weeks, she'd pursued Jordan for a story. Apparently, she wasn't the only one on a chase.

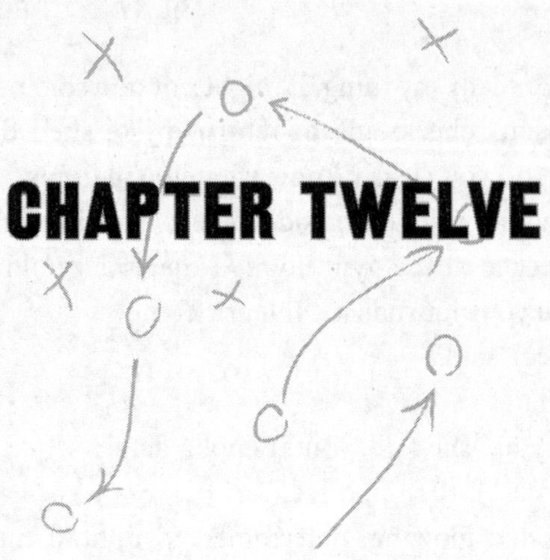

CHAPTER TWELVE

Taking risks wasn't new for Jordan. In fact, her job often required it, but said guts rarely extended beyond her area of expertise—except when it came to Caroline Beck. Jordan didn't know when she decided to ask the reporter out. It might have been when the woman's fingers traced her throat while attaching a lapel mic. Or maybe in the middle of their interview, when they spoke so effortlessly that Jordan forgot it was for television. Or perhaps when she felt Beck's eyes glued to her during practice. Of course, if she was honest with herself, Jordan knew her crush started weeks back.

On the evening of their hangout, she willed the clock to tick faster at practice, pacing the sidelines with her hands behind her back. Her relationship with the guys improved after their first win, and she vigorously built upon it. She met with each player individually, familiarizing herself with the names of everyone's parents and siblings, pets, roommates, girlfriends, hometowns, majors, and GPAs. She gained a sense of who was wary of her, who was overworked, which freshmen were homesick. Building a team wouldn't be enough. She needed to rebuild relationships.

She and Frost also took shears to the playbook. If they could execute a strong base, refine the basics, and win in transition, they would be unstoppable. And finally, she rendered Sean Reilley useless, offloading excess scouting reports and game film on him.

Mark hadn't called her into his office since their first victory. In fact, it'd been crickets after their win streak, which didn't soothe Jordan's anxiety. The critics and boos still taunted, and while the players warmed to her, it was a painstaking road. Each game she fought nausea, unsure if a loss would equate with her termination. So, she kept going, with no choice but forward.

Jordan blew her whistle to wrap up practice. "Circle up," she said, and the guys jogged over. "We're almost to winter break, but I need your focus here. I know you're also preparing for finals, so when that focus isn't here, you need to take care of your studies. If I hear of one more person missing study hall, we'll have six A.M. runs for the rest of the week."

A few players groaned and Leon rolled his eyes.

"Hey, you're basketball players, but you're also building your futures. You don't want to graduate and find you're starting at the bottom. That's not why you came to college," Jordan said. "Two more games at this court, two more wins, and you'll get a break."

She nodded at Brooks, and he counted the team out of the huddle.

"Leon, you got a minute?" she asked as the team dispersed.

"What?"

"How's your mom doing?"

Leon's scowl vanished. "She's alright."

"What are the doctors saying?"

"Gaining strength in remission."

Jordan patted his shoulder while they meandered down the tunnel. Last year, Wanda Torres beat liver cancer, but the health scare understandably affected her son. Leon wasn't the type to share his vulnerability, preferring to use any negative emotion to fuel his play. Despite his harsh edges, Jordan recognized his fear, the way he folded like a small boy at his mother's frailness, and knew he intended to take care of her financially with a professional basketball career.

"I heard she and your sister are going to be in the stands on Sunday," Jordan said. "I'd like all of us to get dinner after. Do you think she's up for that?"

"I think so," Leon said.

"Good."

"What are you going to tell her about me?"

"That you're a pain in my ass." She chuckled. Leon cracked half a smirk, which Jordan considered a win. "I want to see how she's doing and let her know I'm taking care of her boy."

"I think she'd like that." Leon nodded.

"Good," Jordan said. "Well, get out of here. And go to study hall. I mean it."

"Yes, Coach."

Jordan nearly sprinted to her office. She rarely left the WAC before midnight, and Frost gave up on encouraging her to go home. But with Beck beckoning on the other side, Jordan conveniently couldn't come up with a good reason to stay a second longer. She bounded into the December cold like a kid on Christmas, arriving at the mall nearly twenty minutes early, too impatient for her gift to exercise restraint. Her blatant eagerness would've embarrassed her if it wasn't for the lilt of amusement behind her as she locked up her bike.

"You're something else," Beck said. "You still bike in this weather?"

"It's not that bad," Jordan said.

Beck wore jeans and a turtleneck beneath her raincoat, more

casual than Jordan had ever seen her. She wasn't just effortlessly gorgeous, but Jordan found this version of her, away from the arena and not camera ready, unexpectedly intimate.

"Thanks for coming."

"No problem," Beck said.

"Shall we?" Jordan led them into the mall, concentrating on not blushing or grinning too wide as to appear impervious to Beck's charms.

"How was practice?"

"Good." Jordan nodded. "I think we'll be ready for Camden."

"What are you doing about Karsten Marks? He's making almost four threes every game," Beck said. "If you can limit him to two and disrupt Camden's pick and roll, you'll keep his average down by eight points."

Jordan's mouth dropped. "Do you want a position on our coaching staff? I'm sure I can make room."

Beck laughed. "I have to do my research, just like you."

Jordan smiled as their gazes linked, both impressed and fascinated by Beck's self-assuredness. "How long have you been reporting on sports, anyway?" she asked. While Beck knew more about her than Jordan wanted, the reporter remained a mystery.

"On sports, not near as long as I would like," Beck said. "My first job out of college was reporting news in Jonesboro, Arkansas."

"How was that?"

"Oh, what you would expect. Small-town stories, barely any equipment. I don't know how we got a newscast on the air every night. My first story was on a local 4-H competition. You would've thought I was reporting on the Super Bowl."

Jordan chuckled, imagining a ferocious Beck ankle deep in cow manure. When the laughter subsided, she struggled to find her breath. She wondered if Beck encountered the same conflicting pulls of restraint and closeness, blocking out the air. If she did, she revealed nothing, continuing her story, captivating Jordan so entirely that she hung on every word.

"I begged to report on sports but was told no. Not that there were many teams to cover in Jonesboro. So, the next job was in Erie, Pennsylvania. Bigger market, better stories, but again, no chance of getting on the sports desk. The sports anchor there was an absolute prick. He told me I'd never make it in the business."

"I'm sorry."

"No, it's okay. He called out sick once and our other sports reporter couldn't cover, so I convinced my boss to let me anchor the sportscast. I took a copy of the broadcast and sent it to every gig in the country. That's how I got my first job reporting on sports."

"So, you've always been this determined."

"Yes," Beck said. "Not that it's made life easier. I'm sure you can understand that."

She nodded. "You have no idea."

They walked through streams of shoppers as a loop of Christmas melodies filled the wide halls. Jordan wasn't a fan of the holidays, but here with Beck, it didn't strike her as cheesy or obnoxious. She understood its harmless draw at seeing an equal light among the bright colors and promise of Christmas magic.

She trailed Beck past the eye-watering perfume counter, weaved through racks of purses and shoes, and stopped when they reached women's clothing. Beck analyzed the options, her mouth pursing endearingly as she slid hangers and rifled through fabrics.

"So, what do you want your look to be?"

"My look?" Jordan repeated.

Beck sighed. "I know it's not fair, but people are always going to comment on how you look. A male coach or reporter could dress like an idiot, be overweight, have no hair, and no one would think twice. It's not the same for us."

Jordan nodded, pretending to ponder the outfits in front of her.

"Choosing a look might help. How do you feel about dresses? Or skirts? It would certainly make a statement."

"I don't need to make any more statements," Jordan said.

"Then suits it is. Just maybe something that doesn't make you look like a homicide detective."

Jordan feigned interest in the clothes, though she was never interested before and certainly wasn't now. She spent most of the search stealing glances, her heart rocking every time their eyes connected. Beck's gaze glistened more jade than gold against her olive rain jacket, the crinkles at her eyes springing when she locked onto Jordan through the forest of outfits.

She tried on various pants and blazers at the reporter's behest, complaining each time she resembled a banker, often refusing to leave the dressing room despite Beck's pleas. On the few occasions she emerged, her cheeks flamed, but Beck's attention, her requests to spin around, the slight graze on her back as she pointed something out, subdued discomfort. In fact, the easy nearness left Jordan smitten. She relished Beck's pleasure and frustration each time she shook her head, sometimes simply to get a rise out of her.

"Okay, this is it," Beck said after an hour and several stores. She stopped at a rack of colorful blazers. "This is the look."

"That's the look?"

Beck held the jacket over Jordan's torso. "Try it. And the pants."

"It's bright."

"Exactly. You could use some color."

Jordan shook her head but obeyed. Beck waited as she had for every moment of their *Pretty Woman* reenactment, chatty and unashamed just beyond the curtain. Despite the partition between them, Jordan blushed at stripping off her clothes such a short distance away.

When she revealed herself in the cerulean suit, Beck clapped her hands and grinned. "It's perfect."

She adjusted Jordan's collar, the tender brush of her hands a coax that the coach subtly leaned into. They hovered closer than they ever had before. A shiver hit Jordan's neck.

"You really like it?" she asked.

Beck stepped back. "Yeah. Yes."

Jordan whipped around to examine her reflection. The suit made her feel poised and powerful, more comfortable in her own skin than she had in weeks. She wore white sneakers with her hair in a bun, her eyes popping against the outfit's color. Jordan glanced at Beck in the mirror.

"I think I'll keep the shoes. What do you think?"

It took Beck a minute to answer. She glanced at Jordan's sneakers and nodded. "I think that could work. It says something about who you are."

A heaviness filled the dressing room, thick and sultry like a southern summer. The tight space and dim light, the carousel of mirrors, resembled a stage, where the outside world might be ignored. Jordan turned, tempted to step closer. Beck's features flickered, less friendly but otherwise unreadable. She bit her lip, and Jordan detected the slightest gasp, as if the air snagged something on its way out. And while she'd searched her for signs all night, like she did for a gap on the court, Jordan finally recognized the struggle in her too. The one against restraint and closeness.

Beck cleared her throat. "Come on, you need to buy that in every color."

She hurried back to the rack, pulling Jordan's size in multiple colors and grabbing blouses despite her protest. Jordan put down her credit card, too elated by her enthusiasm to deny her. The only thing that dampened the successful purchase was that when they left the store, multiple bags in hand, the end of their evening loomed.

"How do you do it?" Beck asked her. They'd been quiet since the dressing room, maintaining a safe distance, but ambled through the mall side by side.

"Do what?" Jordan asked.

"How do you stay so strong? You're steady through the bullshit. All the things people say about you, the doubt, and pressure to win," Beck said. "You never seem affected."

"I just focus on my mission," Jordan said before gritting her teeth. "I hate that I said that."

"Why?"

"Because I sound just like my dad." Jordan scoffed. "Maybe that's why I seem unaffected. My drill sergeant father didn't exactly encourage vulnerability. God forbid tears."

Beck frowned. "Is that why you aren't close now?"

Jordan hesitated to unload before remembering Beck's well-researched interview. Surely, this wasn't new to her. Plus, the way she listened inspired Jordan to peel back her layers.

"He came back from the war in rough shape. To make matters worse, my mom cheated during that last tour. She'd already left to shack up with the other guy. That wrecked him."

"And you?" Beck's shoulder brushed against Jordan's ever so slightly. It didn't leave as she waited for an answer.

"I was fine." Jordan avoided recalling her father's boozing, her mother's surprise pregnancy, or shuttling back and forth between two homes she absolutely loathed. That's why she leaned on basketball, and despite her strict religious upbringing, on a friendship that turned into much more. "It didn't get bad until senior year. I wasn't out then, but I was seeing a girl. Dad came home from the bar one night and found us together. I thought he might beat me to death, but I got lucky. He kicked me out instead."

Beck gasped. "I'm so sorry."

"Don't be. I really did get lucky. My mom wanted to send me to one of those camps, but my teammates that year let me couch surf instead. I had basketball and a ticket out. My teammates and coaches became my family, no matter where I went. But I never went back to see my parents after that."

"You still shouldn't have gone through it." Beck's plush lips drooped, and Jordan regretted sharing her story, especially as they stopped at the mall's main doors.

"Thanks again."

"You're going to look sharp on the sidelines," Beck said.

Jordan smiled down at her, dreading parting ways. She didn't want to return to only seeing Beck at press conferences. "I believe I owe you. How about dinner?"

She chuckled. "I would love to, but we've been over this."

"Well, someone I know showed me that if I keep asking, I might finally get the answer I want."

"She sounds extremely annoying."

"Good thing she's cute," she quipped without shame, like a bold buzzer beater, a last attempt to shoot her shot. No more double clutching. Her heart stopped while she waited to see if it hit the rim.

"Are you flirting with me?" Beck's cheeks bloomed pink, but

those crinkles around her eyes sprouted, suggesting that it didn't entirely scandalize her.

Jordan fell to a careful whisper. "I'm just trying to get you to go to dinner with me."

Beck glanced around. She scaled Jordan up and down and pursed her lips. "On one condition," she finally said.

"What?"

"You can't ride your bike in the rain like a crazy person. We'll put it in my car."

"Okay."

"And this is a onetime thing." Beck's mouth twitched with a cautious smile.

"Just this once." Jordan agreed, amazed that for the first time in a month, she would spend a night uninterested in her playbook. Not after making this precious shot.

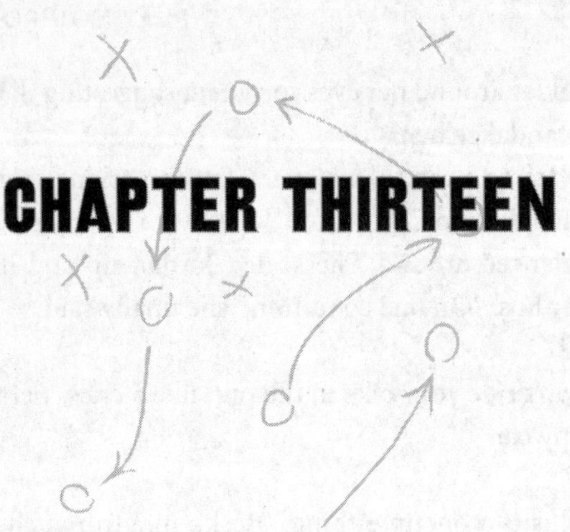

CHAPTER THIRTEEN

Eugene's Whiteaker neighborhood represented a microcosm of the city's eclectic culture. Flannel-clad artists and beanie-wearing activists set up markets and held rallies year-round in the bohemian paradise. Incense and marijuana wafted onto the cracked sidewalks. Beneath an awning, someone strummed a guitar.

Beck trailed behind Jordan as they weaved through the hub of restaurants and bars tucked into the dripping Douglas firs, windows burning orange through the misty night. She never would've guessed Jordan preferred the alternative scene, but it also wasn't the first time the coach surprised her. In fact, she still didn't fully comprehend that they were out together, and that she'd broken her rules in the process. Yet she knew it was too late, knew she didn't stand a chance, when she saw Jordan in her suit, eyes setting the dressing room on fire, smoldering Beck's willpower to dust.

They ended up at the Hubcap, where a bearded man with a nose ring checked their IDs at the door. Jordan ordered pizza and beers and they found a rickety table in the corner as a band set up at the other end of the bar. Rusted car parts, faded concert posters, and surrealist landscapes covered the walls. The comforting aroma of a wood-fire pizza oven infused the air.

"So, is this your usual spot?" Beck asked.

Jordan drank her beer and shook her head. "No. I've been here a few times with Frost. I honestly don't go out much."

"Why's that?"

"I'm busy. When we're not in season, I'm usually on the road recruiting," Jordan said.

The pizza arrived steaming, meat and vegetables piled so generously that they toppled over. Beck peeled off a pepper and popped it into her mouth.

"Enough about me though," Jordan said. "You already had your interview. It's my turn."

"You're going to interview me?" she asked.

"Why not? Can't take the heat?"

"I can handle it." Beck grinned. "Shoot."

"Where were you born?"

"Philadelphia."

"You don't sound like you're from Philly."

"Ah, well, that wasn't exactly encouraged in prep school. You'd have to get me drunk at the Linc for a Birds game to hear that."

"Sign me up." Jordan chuckled. "Are your parents married?"

"Going on thirty-six years."

"What do they do?"

"They're retired now, but my dad was an investigative reporter, and my mom was a morning anchor," Beck said. "I made my first television appearance at two days old."

"They must be happy you joined the family business."

"Not in the way they wanted. My dad knew how hard it would be for me to get a fair shake in sports. My mom can't understand why games and playoffs dictate my schedule."

Beck picked at her pizza, unaccustomed to sharing. She was a pro at prying others open but guarded her own story. When her eyes drifted back up, she found Jordan's gaze set squarely on her, her mouth drawn up in kindness. She blushed, not just at the gentle attentiveness, but the flash of the dream that put the ghost of fingers and lips upon her skin.

"What made you commit to the wonderful world of sports, then?" Jordan asked.

Beck seized the opportunity to ramble in favor of fantasizing. "I grew up cheering for the Eagles, Phillies, Sixers, Flyers—every team in town. I wanted to be part of it somehow. The energy, the fans, the game. My brothers were the first to tell me I'd never play for the Eagles, which was my first real disappointment. But then I saw Lesley Visser, Doris Burke, Erin Andrews. I thought, that's what I can do. That's what I'm going to be."

Behind them, a cymbal crashed as the band warmed up. Beck jolted in her seat, and Jordan patted her hand.

"Sorry," Jordan said over the noise. "I didn't know that—"

The bassist strummed a single chord that screamed through the amplifier. This time Jordan startled, her eyes stretching comically wide.

"I didn't know there would be a band tonight!" she shouted.

Beck laughed as the group tuned and berated their instruments, uncaring because Jordan's hand lingered on hers, long fingers tracing her skin. Beck squeezed on to it.

"Do you want to get out of here?" Jordan asked.

"I can't hear you!"

Jordan moved to the chair closest to her. She brought her mouth inches from Beck's ear, her breath and body a heater in the chilly bar. Beck resisted leaning into the coach while her voice vibrated against her, transforming the flutter in her stomach to a carnal rhythm below her waist. "I'm sorry, I didn't know we'd have a front-row seat to . . . this."

The drummer clashed his cymbals and snare again, and Jordan dropped her head in defeat. Beck snorted and angled closer to her face. "You weren't lying. You really don't get out much."

"This is what I get for trying to be cool." Jordan's lips grazed the shell of her ear for the briefest of seconds. If she hadn't wanted the pass, Beck could've moved, should have moved, but she wanted it and much more. She nearly closed her eyes against the oak and rain drifting from Jordan's skin.

On stage, the lead singer stepped up to the microphone and the small crowd clapped as she strummed another ear-shattering chord.

"I'm Oyster and we are the Angry Botanists," the green-haired woman said. "I dedicate this first song to my ex. It's called 'Eat Shit, Nathan.' "

"Okay, we're taking this to go."

Jordan brushed Beck's shoulder on her way to the bar, shooting fire across her skin. She reminded herself to steer clear. It was time to go home and extinguish the embers. The irreversible tempted them. She didn't need Jordan to say it. Beck was now certain that she wanted it too.

She made light of the tension as they hurried out. "You didn't want to stay for the show? I felt like I was getting to know the real Coach D'Amato."

"You're not going to let me live this down, are you?" Jordan asked.

Beck chuckled. "I don't think so."

They stood under the cramped awning outside. Rain spilled from the gutters and splashed into puddles. There was barely enough space under the cover for the bouncer or the smokers leaning against the building, forcing the two of them to squeeze together to avoid the downpour.

"I'm sorry again. This is not how I pictured this night going," Jordan said.

"How did you picture tonight?" Beck asked as she lost the last threads of better judgment. They stood so close that her shoulder rested against Jordan's chest, her face the only thing she could see.

"I thought it was my turn to ask the questions."

"Alright, Coach. Your interview."

"You know, you can call me Jordan."

"Okay, Jordan." She said it breathier than intended but found it impossible to use the full strength of her voice around the name. It reverberated like something forbidden, like their pressed limbs and whispers. "What's your question?"

The rain swelled. "Do you have a boyfriend? Or a girlfriend? Someone I should know about?"

"No." Beck shivered, but not from the cold. "Why do you want to know?"

"My interview," she said. Beck registered that the smiling, easy Jordan she spent the evening with ceded to the serious and controlled operator that demanded excellence on the court. The same passion of the coach who broke a clipboard, ordered the men fearlessly, competed when others might shrink, oozed from her. "Do you think about me like I think about you?"

"I think I do," she whispered.

Beck braced herself against the wall. This was it. It was happening, and Jordan didn't look away. She never looked away. Not from the start. She waited, eyes like a gas flame in the wind. Jordan inched closer, shielding them against the others seeking refuge from the weather. Her hand traced the small of Beck's back.

"My turn." Beck dissolved the last sliver of space between them. "Are you going to kiss me already?"

The corners of Jordan's mouth twisted, reminiscent of the bashful delight that Beck encountered when she first asked for an interview. Only this time, Jordan didn't deny her. She drew Beck in, introducing her lips delicately, tepid but capable of burning. She kissed like she intended to leave something behind. And she did, searing her mouth, permanently altering Beck's appetites.

When they parted, Beck inhaled sharply above the rain. She shouldn't have kissed her. Not only because it violated every rule she set for herself, but because now she knew how it felt. Now she knew just how desperately she wanted it. And worse, now that she crossed the line, one more kiss no longer seemed a risk. She cradled Jordan's jaw, crushed her lips when they coasted in a second time. Her mouth opened for the coach's tongue, a beguiling stranger she longed to make an acquaintance.

Jordan broke from her first, flushing when she glanced at the nearby strangers. "Should we get going?"

They put up their hoods before stepping into the rain, and Jordan held her hand without so much as a glance, as if they always moved that way. Despite the short walk, they were soaked by the time they scrambled into the car. Rain splattered the windshield. Their breathing rose above the storm, fogging up the windows. Jordan pivoted in the passenger seat to face her, but Beck couldn't move. She throttled the wheel and stared ahead, the brief pause in their kissing enough to push her into panic.

"You okay?" Jordan asked.

Beck nodded but couldn't look at her. In any another instance, she might've shrugged it off as just a kiss and moved on. But this didn't feel like just a kiss. It didn't only linger on her lips but filled the rest of her too. And without it, the emptiness loomed larger, scarier and bolder after discovering its counterpart.

"You know, I like you, Beck, but I understand this might complicate things." Jordan's gentle voice beneath the rain inspired Beck to turn her head and meet her gaze. "I respect you. I respect your career. So, it's okay if we need to stop."

No, it wasn't just a kiss. Not with how Jordan saw and understood her, holding back from more to avoid hurting her. Thunder boomed outside.

"I don't want to stop." Beck swallowed. "But I can't."

"I understand."

An unexpected prickle reached Beck's eyes at wanting someone so badly and being unable to have them. It was losing a crush, sinking those butterflies as quickly as she captured them. "I'm sorry."

"Don't be sorry," Jordan said. "I'll get my bike."

She sighed. "No, don't be ridiculous. I'll take you home."

Their shared desire thickened, became humidity on the drive. Jordan's knee bounced in the passenger seat while she muttered directions. Beck strangled the wheel at each hoarse word. It tickled her skin, inflated the swollen, sensitive beat below.

"This is me," Jordan said.

Beck parked along the curb and glanced up at the modest apartment complex. She didn't know what she expected, but something about it saddened her. Perhaps its seclusion from campus and the city. Its lack of warmth. "Do you live alone?" she asked.

"Yeah. Do you?"

Beck blushed. "No, I have a roommate, which I know, twenty-eight and still living with a roommate—"

"I don't think that," Jordan said.

Beck studied Jordan in the weak light. She wanted to kiss her again, kept roving over that nimble mouth. A heavy, dissatisfied sigh escaped her.

"What?" Jordan asked.

"Nothing." Beck shook her head. "Is it going to be weird now? Seeing each other at games and press conferences?"

"Totally not," Jordan said with a faint laugh.

She smirked. "Liar."

"Well, I better go before it gets any weirder."

"Wait. There was something I wanted to ask you during our interview, but I didn't."

Jordan leaned back and granted her a clear view of her face. "What's that?"

Beck shifted and rested her head on the seat like they weren't in a car, but on a couch, in a bed, in a place just for them. "Who do you talk to after a hard day? Like after that first loss?"

Her mouth slackened. "I guess I don't know."

"I'm sorry." Beck shook her head. "I don't know why I asked."

"I used to talk to Royce." She stared out the window and fiddled with her necklace. "He was kind of a dad, older brother type. Frost is my best friend, but he has two kids under two now, so it changed. Maybe everyone is just growing up except for me." A car passed, throwing yellow squares of light across Jordan's face. Brief twinkles flashed through her irises like falling stars. "Why'd you want to know who I talk to?"

Beck glanced away, unsure if she should share the truth. Their evening, from shopping to dinner to the kiss that left her floating, blurred every line between them, as though giving her license to tell or ask Jordan anything. "Sometimes you look so by yourself out there. I wondered if you ever feel alone."

"Sometimes," Jordan whispered. "But I'm used to it. What about you? Do you ever feel alone?"

"Sometimes." Beck nodded, her heart wobbling at Jordan's

forlorn answer and how badly she wanted to remedy it. She was also rattled by her own confession. Another part of herself she rarely disclosed. "I think that's what happens to people who want something so much. Everything else fades away. It can make you an island."

Jordan's eyes possessed Beck entirely. She thought the coach might kiss her again. She wanted her to.

"I'm not the best at talking, especially when things get tough. I usually put my head down and move forward. But if I had to say who I talk to when it's gotten hard this season, it's you. I like talking to you, Beck." Jordan shrugged. "Even if you're just doing your job. The interview and the way you made me feel better after that first loss. I've never talked to anyone like that before."

"I like talking to you too," she whispered. "And it's not just a job, Jordan. This would be so much easier if it was."

Jordan smiled, a touch glum, but also gleaming, allowing Beck a brief flash of her spirit. "I better go. Thank you for everything and I'm sorry—"

"Don't apologize."

Beck hugged her, and Jordan squeezed back, firm and assured. She wanted to nuzzle into her, nearly wilted at knowing her arms, just as she now knew her lips. Beck rubbed Jordan's back, wished it could somehow express everything she wanted to say. Even though she still wasn't sure of all that might entail.

They kissed when they released. Beck couldn't say for certain who reached first, but Jordan cupped her jaw, thumbs traced her cheeks, and Beck grasped whatever part of her she could reach. The kiss proceeded slower, wetter, and longer than the first. They didn't break for a breath or for the console between them or the downpour ending. They made out in the ecstasy of it being the first time and the desperation of it being the last.

Beck started to moan and broke away. "Okay. Okay, we can't."

"I know." Jordan's chest visibly heaved. "Can we keep that off the record?"

"Strictly off the record." Beck laughed, though her heart thudded to the point of pain.

"I'll see you at the next media availability?"

Her shoulders sagged. "Not this week. I have to write and edit our interview. They want it to air before the Camden game."

"Right." Jordan nodded, crooked one side of her mouth in another innocent tell that Beck melted for. "Well, cut out any parts where I sound stupid."

"That won't leave me much to work with." Beck winked. "I'll be at Sunday's game."

"I'll see you then." Jordan paused and briefly glanced at her lips. Beck nearly leaned in, thought Jordan might too, but then the coach slipped out of the car and slammed the door shut.

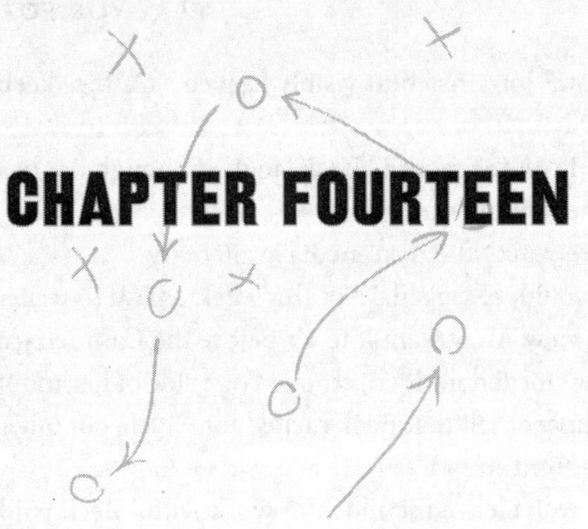

CHAPTER FOURTEEN

She leaned against the wall for support as soon as the apartment door closed behind her. Her breath cycled in ragged intervals. Her cheeks burned, and that burn slid down her neck, her stomach, and groin, which hadn't stopped drumming since the first velvet brush of Beck's lips.

"Shit." Jordan knocked her head back against the plaster. She didn't know what she thought might happen when she invited Beck to dinner. She welcomed the flirting and the talking, and of course, wanted to kiss her, but it wasn't supposed to feel like this. It wasn't supposed to be so desperate and debilitating and complicated. Jordan didn't do desperate or debilitating or complicated.

She admittedly sacrificed relationships, usually avoided intimacy altogether, in favor of basketball. But now, when the game required her greatest focus and commitment, she'd met Beck. The ultimate distraction. The first person that might challenge her devotion to the game.

She paced, raked fingers through her curls, and stared at the door. Worse than the complicated, off-limits nature of her crush was how terribly she wanted Beck anyway. She considered whether the attraction might simply be a case of forbidden fruit, but that had never swayed Jordan before, not with her first girlfriend or the other dalliances that followed. This was entirely different. Beck made her laugh when she didn't think it possible, made her talk when she'd spent a lifetime guarded, and made her forget, for a brief second, the burden of her position.

Jordan scrambled to the shower, plunged into the cold water, and willed herself to straighten out and focus on the team and their next game. Beck's grasp on her arms, her tongue, her hair brushing Jordan's skin, broke up every play and basket. Despite the late hour, Jordan dressed for work. Her night with Beck and another must-win game was a perfect recipe for insomnia. Plus, a bike ride never failed to bring her back to earth. But as she reached the door, she realized her ten-speed remained in a certain reporter's trunk.

"Damn it."

Beck had her off her game.

Badly.

She snatched her car keys and cursed on the drive to campus. Jordan beat her palms on the wheel as sports radio played low. The pundits and analysts brought her back to Beck. She anxiously pondered what the reporter might be thinking. If she'd ever look at Jordan or talk to her again.

Like an answer to her insecurities, her phone rang. Jordan grinned, though her fingers shook as she accepted the call.

"I think I have something that belongs to you," Beck said, competing over the volume of the humming road.

"My heart?"

"You better be joking."

Jordan chuckled, the heat returning despite her damp hair and the freezing temperature. The call soothed her fears. Beck could've texted or waited until she got back to Portland. Instead, she'd reached out less than an hour after their uncertain goodbye.

"Don't flatter yourself," Jordan said. "I'm talking about my bike."

"Wow, I didn't know you had a sense of humor, Coach."

"There's a lot you don't know about me, Caroline."

Beck laughed. "Oh, there's no way you're getting it back calling me that."

"How about I take you to dinner? Fair trade?"

"I think you're breaking up." Beck hissed into the receiver, feigning static. "Horrible reception."

Jordan bit her lip as the campus came into view. While she wanted to speak longer, she played it cool. "I'm pulling up to the arena. I have to go."

"You have a car?" Beck asked.

"I'm full of surprises."

"What are you doing at work this late?"

"Thought I'd get caught up on some game film."

"You should sleep, Jordan."

Beck's tender concern stripped her raw. Not just that, but her name from her lips hitched her breath.

"I'll be alright," she said. "But I still want my bike back."

"How about another interview?"

Jordan chuckled. "Good night, Beck."

"Don't forget to contain Karsten Marks on the perimeter. Seriously. Good night, Jordan."

She frowned at the line going dead despite her insistence on hanging up. The pang intensified at Beck's upcoming absence that week. Jordan secretly looked forward to seeing her in the media scrum before, but didn't depend on it until now. That, coupled with the unknowable future, tempered her spirits by the time she parked, a deflation that allowed her to slip back into her coaching mask and persona, to fixate on winning rather than Beck.

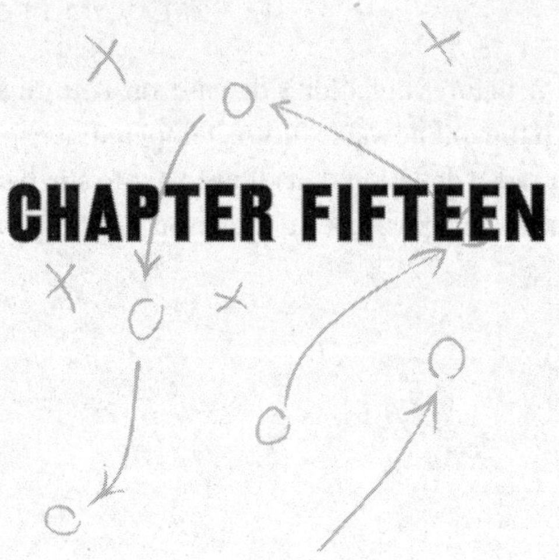

CHAPTER FIFTEEN

In a cruel irony that Beck decided must be the punishment for her transgressions, Jordan filled her week without her stepping foot in the coach's vicinity. Not only did she incessantly ponder their non-date date, but she confronted the complicated source of her affections as she wrote the story she'd nearly begged for.

She'd spent two days reviewing their interview, taking notes, crafting a script, berating herself throughout. After their kiss, she second-guessed her storytelling, scrutinizing it for bias she normally wouldn't have. Should she have asked about Jordan's difficult upbringing? Should she have delved further into her sexuality? Should she have questioned her credentials, her losses, and focused on her doubters?

Beck reassured herself that the piece wasn't meant to stir controversy. The purpose of the sit-down was to introduce Jordan to a curious audience and highlight her place in basketball history. She stuck to the questions that Vince and Nick approved, only straying for follow-ups. Any other journalist with the exclusive would have taken the same liberties, would've framed Jordan just as positively, especially with her recent success.

But Beck didn't just dwell on her reporting. She recognized the obvious magnetism between them. Jordan's gaze twinkled, soft at the corners, the hint of a smile constant during their conversation. A look Beck had never witnessed before on camera. She prayed no one else noticed how she grinned at Jordan's answers, her head tilted to the side, enchanted.

She wanted to scream at their past selves through the edit bay monitor to quit being so damn obvious. Perhaps she only recognized it now because of what she knew. Because of what she discovered in Jordan's arms and lips. Whenever Beck trembled at the memory, she furrowed her brow, crouched closer to the screen, and checked her work for the hundredth time, convinced she'd somehow shown favoritism. Fortunately, both Vince and Nick applauded the piece, okayed the script, and by the time the story aired at prime time, she let herself revel in a job hard earned and well done.

"And now we go to Caroline Beck, joining us in studio with an NWSN exclusive."

The camera swiveled in her direction after Easton's lackluster handoff.

"Thanks, Easton." Beck didn't shy away from the lens as though born for such a moment. "By now, you've read the headlines and seen her on the sidelines. For the first time, a woman is the head coach of a men's D1 basketball team. Making history is never easy, but for Jordan D'Amato, who's leading the David Douglas University Bulldogs this year, pressure is just part of who she is. Comebacks and firsts have defined her career. During our sit-down interview, I had the chance to learn more about what makes the coach tick, how she's won over the team after a rough start, and how she maintains composure in the face of backlash. Her message is simple: it's just about basketball. But for the rest of us, her strength and story inspire much more—a future where she's no longer the only woman with the top job. A future that she says she's fighting for every day."

The story rolled, and she joined Easton at the desk. Beck beamed at the playback monitors. The soundbites, the pace of the interview, and footage of Jordan worked together fluidly. Beck even intermixed video of the coach's playing days in high school and college, and by the end of the eight-minute piece, she imagined viewers walking away with a deeper respect for Jordan, or at the very least a fuller picture.

When the package faded to black, Nick counted her back in, and Beck addressed the camera.

"As for this season, D'Amato says she's taking it one game at a time. Her focus right now is helping the Bulldogs secure their fourth straight conference title."

"Great work, Beck," Easton said, and Beck grinned because she knew it killed him. "Between your interview and time covering the team, what's your take on D'Amato?"

"She's intense. I think it's impossible to fully capture on camera, but it radiates from her. Still, she's calming and approachable." Beck paused for a shred of breath, her admiration of Jordan an Achilles' heel she determinedly hid. "That quality, at least from what I can tell, draws players in. I think a lot of new coaches try to force the team to mold to them. Instead, D'Amato's growing into the team. So far, it's working."

"That will certainly be put to the test this weekend. David Douglas hosts Camden University, who's leading the conference and boasts one of the nation's toughest defenses. We'll see if D'Amato's style can stack up. Isn't that right, Beck?"

He delivered the question like a nudge into the corner, putting her on the spot to reduce her to a nod and smile. Instead, Beck shrugged. "I mean, that's giving Camden a lot of credit, but sure." She volleyed the response as bait. A more modest reporter might have bowed out, might have been happy for their five minutes in the spotlight, but Beck pounced for a sneak attack.

"You must be mistaken," Easton said with a mocking laugh. "Camden is leading the conference in points allowed and their big men gobble rebounds. Please, tell me how that's not a defensive threat to David Douglas."

"You forgot that they're also leading in steals." Beck maintained an easy smile for the camera. She had Easton right where she wanted him. She hadn't intended to go head-to-head, but now he goaded her, invited her to play, expecting her to fail. "I agree, the Cougars are a defensive powerhouse, but I don't think you're taking David Douglas's spread offense into account. It's an absolute nightmare for teams. Brooks McCray executes handoffs like he's in the NBA. The entire squad is a shooting threat. You talk about clogging that post, but that's exactly what the Bulldogs open with their play calls. No one sits in the paint, not even big man Charlie Washington. They work the perimeter, feed the weak side of the court, and annihilate with the backdoor cut."

The monitors flickered with footage of David Douglas to accompany her analysis. Easton grimaced. "While I appreciate the master class in the Bulldogs' offense, it doesn't change the Cougars' efficiency on the defensive end of the ball."

"Master class? Easton, I'm flattered. Get me a whiteboard and I can draw it out for you." She winked and the camera operators in the studio chuckled. "What I'm getting at is Camden's defense hasn't found an answer for the spread. They've faced it twice during the preseason and gave up the most points they have all year, chalking up their worst games defensively. But yes, there's still no doubt that Camden will be a challenge for David Douglas."

Easton grinned artificially under the harsh studio lights. "Interviewer, statistician, analyst, what can't she do?"

"Anchor my own show apparently," Beck said.

"Yeah, you best leave that to the pros, sweetheart." Easton chuckled, and she gritted her teeth, using every ounce of self-control to not shoot him a nasty glance, or worse. "That's it for us on *Fast Break.* Until next time, I'm Easton Prescott. Have a good night."

They sat still as statues at the anchor desk with plastered smiles until Nick confirmed they were off the air. Their mouths drooped to scowls instantaneously.

"Real cute, Beck." Easton sucked his teeth.

"First of all, don't *ever* call me sweetheart on the air again. Second, you asked for my take."

"You know I didn't mean it. You were just showing off."

Beck sighed, disregarding his criticism as she usually did, riding the high of their debate and airing her piece. "What did you think of the story?"

"I think it should have been my interview." Easton unknotted his tie with a sneer. "But it makes sense now that I know she's a dyke. She's probably just interested in you."

"Right, because I can't achieve anything without my looks?" Beck snarked, but her stomach hardened. Guilt ate at her since making out with Jordan, and more than once, she'd wondered the same. If she'd only gotten this break because the coach wanted her.

Easton loomed above. "I hope you enjoyed this, because the next time you steal my story, I won't be so nice."

"Is that a threat?" She glared up at him.

"Try me and find out."

He stomped off, and Beck hated that she strained around a pit in her throat when she swallowed. She refused to let him squash her satisfaction, but he'd stabbed her in a weak spot and inflamed her deepest insecurities. Beck accepted compliments from her other colleagues, but she couldn't shake the shadow. She rejected

Nick's invitation to get drinks with the rest of the gang and trekked to her car, slipping into the driver's seat as her phone buzzed.

Jordan's name flashed across her phone, dispelling her gloom, even though she was also the source of it. But Beck hopelessly longed for her voice, the only one she wanted to hear.

"Hey." The coach's throaty greeting loosened Beck's shoulders.

"Hey. What did you think?"

"It was amazing. You were amazing," Jordan said. "Though it's not fair, you looked so much better than me."

Beck's relief dwindled. "No one was looking at me. They're interested in you."

"I was looking at you. I'm interested in you," Jordan said. She sounded playful, teasing like they usually did, but it prickled Beck in the wrong places.

"Is that the real reason you wouldn't talk to Easton?"

"Yeah, he's a jerk." Jordan chuckled.

Beck squeezed her eyes shut. Her conscience taunted that she wasn't a good journalist; she was a good flirt. It should have been Easton's interview. She was a fraud.

"Hey, I was joking. Are you really worried about that?" Jordan asked. "That's not why I did it. You made me feel comfortable, and I knew you weren't just using me. I respect that you were at every practice and game from the start. You earned it."

Beck chewed her lip, not fully convinced. "Thanks."

"What happened between us after has nothing to do with it. I would've done the interview with you regardless because you fought for it. Don't sell yourself short."

Jordan's kindness, the goodness she'd witnessed on the court and off it, heartened Beck. The Jordan she knew wasn't manipulative enough to trade an interview for a kiss. It assured her not just of her own abilities and worthiness, but of their natural chemistry, of what existed beyond the work that brought them together.

"Are you giving me a pep talk?" Beck asked.

"Wow, I guess I am." Jordan laughed on the other end. "That's embarrassing."

"And a little sweet." Beck chuckled along with her, then withered down to a placated sigh. "It's nice to hear your voice."

"It's nice to hear yours too," Jordan whispered. "Congratulations. Really, the piece was perfect."

"You think?"

"I do," Jordan said. "Thanks for not making me look like an idiot."

"That's impossible. You were great."

"How'd you get those pictures of me? From when I was a kid?"

Beck gritted her teeth. "I called your parents."

"How'd that go?" Jordan asked.

"Well, your dad hung up on me as soon as I said I was a reporter." She faked amusement, attempting to make light of the situation. Since learning of Jordan's scars, Beck couldn't help but despise the ones responsible for them.

"Typical."

"Your mom said she would try to dig something up and emailed me a few photos."

Annette's disinterest in her daughter, the way she had nothing kind to say about her despite her accomplishments, disturbed Beck more than Cash's refusal to speak. Somehow, in those brief interactions, she understood Jordan better than she had anyone, sympathized deeper, felt almost as much of her as she did in their kiss.

"How was she?" Jordan asked.

"Good," Beck lied. "We didn't talk much."

"I, uh, better get back to work." Jordan trailed off. "I just wanted to say thank you and let you know you were fantastic, Beck."

"Thanks for trusting me, Jordan," she said. "Have a good night."

Beck frowned. She wanted to prolong their conversation and absorb its comfort, but she let her go. With the interview behind them, she didn't know what was ahead. If they could afford to see each other again. If their connected but opposing worlds stood a chance.

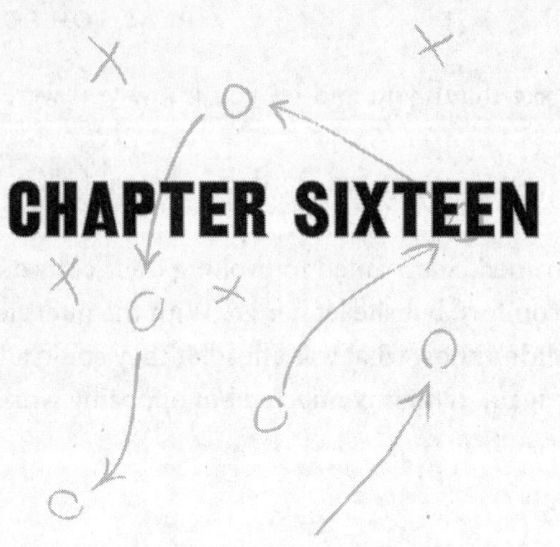

CHAPTER SIXTEEN

While the interview was a turning point for Beck's career, it helped Jordan in ways she never expected. Her phone rang with calls from old teammates, coaches, and friends. Rather than pure hate mail, fanfare from young girls, aspiring athletes, and others poured in. According to Molly, the buzz online was just as fervent. She'd gone from a liability to an inspiration overnight.

The team's response, however, was the interview's greatest reward. Jordan didn't think the guys even watched it until she walked to the locker room before practice and paused at another Leon Torres tirade. She rarely eavesdropped anymore, but this time she couldn't help herself, leaning against the wall out of view.

"Did you know she's . . . you know?"

"An English Lit major?" Charlie asked Leon. "No. But when she quoted D. H. Lawrence, I should've known."

"What the hell are you talking about?" Leon asked.

"D. H. Lawrence. His poem is on the whiteboard this week," Charlie said as he flipped through a thick MCAT study guide. "Crack a book, Leon, it's disturbing."

Jordan covered her mouth to stifle a laugh.

"I'm talking about her playing for the other team," Leon said. "That she's a lesbian."

"Oh, that," Charlie said. "I never assume."

"Am I the only one surprised?" Leon asked his teammates. "I mean, she's fine as hell."

"What does it matter, Leon?" Brooks spoke up.

"It—it doesn't matter," Leon stammered. "I'm just saying."

"Trying to say what? What is there to say?"

An uneasy silence overtook the locker room. Jordan gripped her necklace and waited for the team to settle. Now it would be too awkward to coast in. Fortunately, Charlie's wise baritone defused the tension. "Leon's just upset because he thought he had a chance with her," he said.

"Who says I still don't?" Leon asked with a strut, brushing his shoulder.

"Well, me for starters." Jordan rounded the corner. "You're just really not my type."

The team broke into hysterical, shrieking laughter. Jordan managed a straight face in front of Leon, whose mouth hung ajar. "We were just fooling around, Coach, you know," he said.

"Mr. Torres, I understand you may not have developed object permanence since you were likely dropped on your head as an infant, but just because you cannot see me, doesn't mean I can't hear you."

Charlie chuckled so hard that he fell off the stool in front of his locker. Jordan glanced at the rest of the team.

"If you have any other inquiries or opinions about my personal life, you can ponder them internally until you are no longer curious," she said. "Understood?"

"Yes, Coach," the players echoed, smiling bigger than she'd ever seen them.

"Alright, let's get going." Jordan clapped her hands.

"Okay, but hold up, Coach, I have to ask you something," Leon said.

"Oh God, what, Torres?" she asked, earning more chuckles as the team lingered.

"Do you have a girlfriend or what?"

The locker room fell quiet, except for Frost, who doubled over and snorted. "Sorry," he said, recovering with a fake cough.

Jordan paused before answering because her first instinct brought her to Beck. She wasn't delusional enough to think they were dating, but she couldn't deny her thoughts landed on her each night, and that she'd talked herself out of reaching out more than once. Now, though, confronting the question bluntly, she wished she could call Beck hers.

"Do you think I have time to date while I'm trying to keep this team in line?" she asked. "What about you? What's your girlfriend like, Leon?"

He wiggled his eyebrows. "Which one?"

While the players howled, Jordan rolled her eyes. "You better be careful, Torres. I'm seeing your mother tomorrow."

"Damn, Coach, don't go for his mama," Dominic teased.

"He's going to be calling her step-coach!" Charlie hooted as Leon grabbed him into a headlock.

Jordan broke with a grin. "Okay, okay, that's enough," she said over the hyena-like roar. "Go warm up now, guys, come on."

When the team filed out, Jordan stopped Brooks. She hadn't failed to notice that while his teammates spiraled into jokes and giggles, he didn't crack a smile. "You okay?"

"Are you?" Brooks asked.

Jordan scoffed. "Me? Yeah. That doesn't faze me, but you know I have to humble Leon every chance I get."

He nodded but wouldn't look at her.

"Talk to me, Brooks."

"I'm seeing someone," he blurted.

Jordan smiled. "That's good, right?"

"It's good. But it's getting serious, and I don't think it can go any further if I don't come out, you know?" Brooks dragged hands down his face, hyperventilating through each word. "And I mean, what would the guys say? Would I just be the butt of some joke? They're supposed to be the easy ones to tell."

"Hey, hey, just breathe." Jordan led him to sit and crouched in front of him, aiding with the simple instruction of inhale and exhale. It wouldn't be the first time Jordan helped him through such a panic.

"I just can't right now." Brooks's throat bobbed as he cried. "Not this season. Not when we have a shot. I can't be distracted."

"Stop that." Jordan moved to sit next to him. "This is just basketball. What you're talking about, who you love, how you want to live your life—that's everything, Brooks. That's what matters."

Jordan sank, however, at the parallels to her own situation. That even if she and Beck tried to make things work, they'd be a secret, with no real way forward.

Brooks sniveled. "You said it during the interview."

"What?"

"Did you know she was going to ask that? About your sexuality?"

"I knew it was a possibility." Jordan shrugged. "I considered telling her it was off limits, but then I thought about you and our talk. I thought about other people too. That maybe it does matter, for people to know and see me for who I am."

That, of course, wasn't the entire truth. Jordan didn't just share for Brooks or the other queer fans and young people, but because Beck once again made her feel comfortable in her own skin, no different than the new suit that day in the mall. She scaled her walls. Drew her out and reminded Jordan that there was still room to grow. There was more of herself to give.

"It doesn't happen all at once. You do this on your own time, and I'll be here when you need me," she said.

"Thanks." Brooks wiped tears, rushing to compose himself. "I'm sorry."

"Don't be sorry. Just take a minute."

"What about practice?"

"Frost can handle it. We have all the time in the world." Jordan patted his shoulder. "Why don't you tell me about this boyfriend of yours?"

Brooks beamed. "He's studying to be a psychologist."

Jordan smiled as he rambled, sharing details of his relationship in a way she imagined he never had before. A new triumph, one away from the court, left her soaring. Lending an ear to Brooks, joking with Leon, sharing laughter with the team, fostered a camaraderie that they'd been missing. The better she let them know her, the real her, the easier it was to bond with them. And Jordan knew she had Beck to thank.

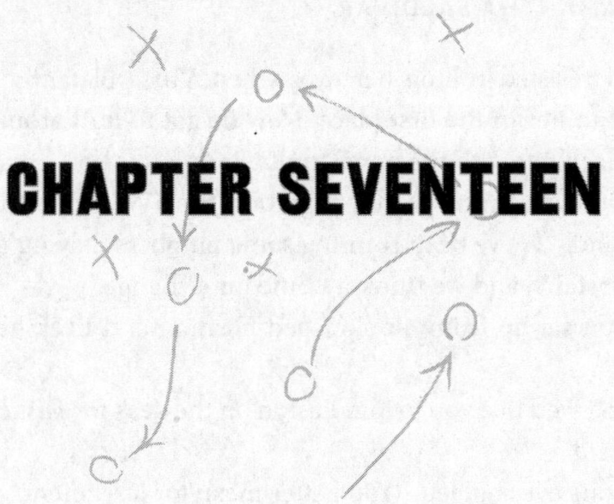

CHAPTER SEVENTEEN

Despite her crisis of conscience over Jordan, Beck reaped the benefits of her story. Congratulatory texts and phone calls inundated her, her followers tripled in days, and her parents expressed rare pride when several national networks aired the story. To top it off, new opportunities flew into Beck's inbox, including a query from Fiona Wandell, a talent scout and agent who claimed to have the power to get Beck to the next level. She pondered her invitation to meet, the launch pad forming sooner and clearer than she ever imagined.

"Beck, do you have a minute?" Nick asked.

She nearly jumped out of her chair. "What?"

"Vince wants to talk to us."

Beck followed him through the bullpen, hating the queasiness that twisted her gut. Vince couldn't possibly know about her and Jordan. She reassured herself of it as she entered his office to find Easton sitting inside.

"What's up?" Beck asked.

"First of all, the interview." Vince grinned. "I knew you'd knock it out of the park."

Beck resisted rolling her eyes when Vince blatantly hadn't given it to her in the first place. Now he got to lord around like he'd graced her with the opportunity.

"Obviously, this is great recognition for NWSN and for you," Vince said. "We've been running some numbers, having discussions upstairs, and we think it's time for a change."

Easton sat up from his slouched position and Beck held her breath.

"Beck, we'd like you to join Easton on the desk for *Fast Break,*" Vince said.

Easton's eyes bulged. "You better mean for a segment."

"As your co-anchor."

Beck's cheeks strained against a grin. "Yes."

"No! Absolutely not!" Easton shouted.

"Her coverage is consistent and we're due for a change," Vince said.

"I won't do it." Easton bolted up and paced. "I refuse."

"That's fine. *Fast Break with Caroline Beck* has a great ring to it," she said.

"That's the other thing." Vince raised his bushy eyebrows. "This is going to mean some rebranding. Marketing's toyed around with a few names, but they settled on *Fast Break with Beck and Prescott.*"

Easton's mouth fell open. "Her name is first!"

"Don't take it personally," Beck said. "It just sounds better, *sweetheart.*"

He snarled at her before pivoting to their boss. "Vince, you know this is bullshit!"

"Beck is recognizable. She's one of our only women, and she's even more known now after the interview. It's the perfect time to elevate her profile with us," Vince said. "Plus, this is going to be great for ratings."

"Fuck the ratings! I'm not doing it. I'll quit."

"That would truly make this the greatest day of my life," Beck said.

"I'm not against it, Vince." Nick rubbed the back of his neck. "But you know they want to kill each other. You expect them to anchor an hour together every night?"

"Like I said, great for ratings." Vince winked as Easton stormed out.

Beck shook her boss's hand. "You won't regret this."

"I know," he said. "Keep up that fire. Take him to the mat."

"Yes, sir."

She sprinted out of the station while Easton screamed profanities in the bullpen. As soon as she reached the parking lot, she pumped her fists and released a feral, unabashed roar of her own.

"Yes! Yes! Yes!"

"What's going on?" Todd asked.

She hadn't noticed the cameraman smoking outside but for once didn't care. "I fucking did it, Todd." She high-fived him so forcefully that he winced.

"Did what?" he asked, shaking out his hand.

"Vince made me Easton's co-anchor. They're calling it *Fast Break with Beck and Prescott.*"

"Good for you." Todd squashed his cigarette. "I'm going to watch Easton burn down the building. I hate that guy."

Beck grabbed her phone to spread the news when an unexpected hurdle blocked her bliss.

She wanted to call Jordan.

In light of the piece's positive reception, she'd already been tempted, but now she wanted to share this too. Because she didn't just want Jordan's story. She wanted Jordan to know hers.

Beck had dated plenty, both seriously and serially at different points in her life, but never longed for this closeness. One that wasn't just built on something physical or fun or interesting. She wanted to give something to Jordan. Something of herself. Something she couldn't afford. Not with her promotion or goals within reach.

She traveled south to the Camden game the next day, torn between the two things she wanted most but never expected to experience at once—advancing her career and understanding her heart. On the ride down, she called Kevin for reinforcements. "Please list every reason that I can't see her again," she asked, and Kevin, with drag brunch roaring behind him, proceeded to drunkenly come up with a half-solid list of why they would never work.

Despite her efforts, when she spotted Jordan across the court, Beck buckled. Of course, on the day she planned to end their dangerous and surely doomed connection, Jordan looked better than ever, magnetic in her new suit. The blazer cut perfectly below her waist, hugging her arms and shoulders, the pants fitting so seductively snug on her thighs and ass that Beck gawked. White sneakers completed the outfit, and Beck didn't know if they made Jordan cute or sexy. She only knew that she loved her like this.

Beck watched her pace the sidelines, yelling, pointing, never sitting, never still. She gestured wildly in the huddle, often with a clipboard, the guys nodding along with her. Jordan was a tall woman, but the players towered above, requiring her to stretch on her tiptoes or them to lean close when she spoke to them. Lately the players listened to her, running the court effortlessly, never slowing the pace or passes. They looked like the team everyone thought they could be. A team that could win the whole damn thing with Jordan D'Amato at the helm.

After beating the Cougars, Jordan entered the postgame press conference with swagger. She smiled as she took her usual seat and, without hesitating, her eyes found Beck's. She clutched her notepad so tight it folded, unable to resist smirking back.

"Coach, not only did you serve Camden their worst loss of the season, but you held them to their lowest points scored," Beck said. "What was the key to tonight's success?"

"Well, for starters, we contained Karsten Marks. That kid was averaging four threes a game, so we knew if we could take those perimeter shots away, we'd shave off crucial points."

Jordan's gaze never veered as she recited Beck's advice. She might as well have written her a love song.

By the time Beck waited outside Jordan's apartment, she wanted to crawl back into her, hold her, and kiss her again. She glared at the handlebars poking up from her back seat. The bike had mocked her all week. "Just give her the stupid thing and then go home. Simple," Beck muttered to herself, fruitlessly gathering willpower.

Jordan tapped on the passenger window, the wind flapping her jacket and hair. She lifted a half smile in the fading light. So much for willpower. "Hey," she said, muffled from outside.

Beck sat motionless in the driver's seat, cheeks flaming. "Hi." She forced herself out of the car and met Jordan at the trunk. "Glad you took my advice. Next time, I won't give it away for free."

"What's your price?" Jordan asked.

The coach hovered a mere sliver from Beck, eyes flicking to her lips. Beck turned and opened the trunk. "You looked good tonight," she said before shaking her head. "I mean, the team. The team looked good."

Jordan hefted the bike out of the car. "Well, I think I owe you another thank-you for that."

"For Karsten Marks? You already had that figured out."

"No, the interview. I think it helped us as a team. I'm not the best at sharing myself with the guys." She beamed. "I think we might actually be bonding."

Beck's heart imploded at Jordan's joy.

"I'm glad," she said. "It helped me too. They're promoting me to anchor."

Jordan's smile stretched even wider, and she enveloped Beck as if on instinct. She shut her eyes when her cheek met the coach's chest. It was a peaceful shelter, so natural that Beck nearly forgot the problem of burrowing there. When they unlatched, Jordan bent to bring her face closer. Beck stepped back.

"I've been thinking." She halted Jordan's momentum with a gentle hand. "I think we need to be careful. I need to be careful."

Jordan's eyes darkened, as if matching the gravity of the statement. "Of course."

"I don't think we should see each other anymore," Beck said. "Outside of a professional, working capacity."

"I totally understand."

"You do?" Beck's mouth fell open.

"Yeah. I've been thinking about it too." Jordan shrugged. "I think it's the right thing to do."

"You do? You're not upset?"

Jordan leveled her with an expressionless stare, as if they were back in a press conference. The detectable shift destroyed Beck's already weak desire for distance. She didn't want to accept that they would exist like this instead.

"I really like you, but we don't make a lot of sense together, do we? I can't tell you about anything private going on with the team because you might report it. And you have to go on TV and critique me when I'm doing a bad job. It seems complicated."

Beck struggled to swallow. "Yeah, yeah. Exactly."

Jordan frowned. "Are you okay?"

"Yeah, I just thought this conversation would be harder."

"You're incredible at what you do. It would be wrong to risk that." Jordan shoved her hands in her pockets and hitched her shoulders against the cold. "Plus, I'm tied up with the guys and recruiting, and we've got some big road games ahead. I probably wouldn't be good at this."

"Right." Beck crossed her arms. "I better let you get on with your night."

Jordan's brow furrowed, her chin crumpling then firming again. She opened her mouth but closed it just as quickly. Beck nearly filled the silence, even though there was nothing left to say except *Fight for me. Please. Show me something.* Instead, Jordan sighed and shifted her gaze to the pavement.

"Well, uh, good luck with the new gig."

"Good luck to you too, Coach."

She climbed back into her car without sparing Jordan another glance. Rather than relief at her easy acceptance, Beck resented it. She didn't want to hurt Jordan, but she'd expected some sort of emotion. Something that told her she wasn't the only one who found turning away torturous. That she wasn't wrong for still longing to take the risk.

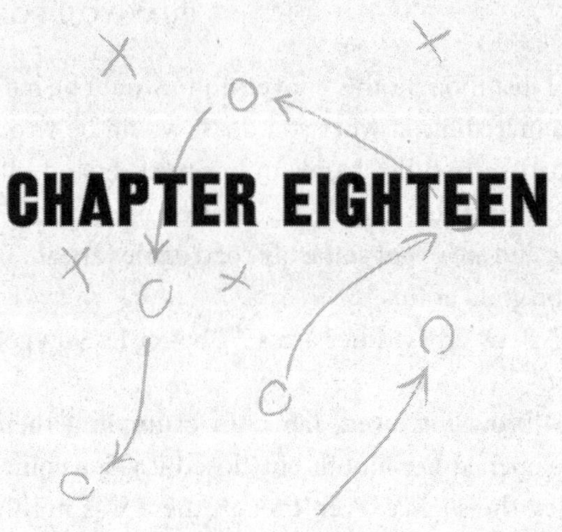

CHAPTER EIGHTEEN

Despite a 5-1 record, a top-ten national ranking, and a hot streak that Jordan once wished for, her problems on the coaching front didn't end. Winning and everything it required comprised only one aspect of her job. Recruiting was another important, if not more important, beast. If she couldn't build a team for the next season and plan for future success, then her time as head coach would be short-lived.

That's why she panicked when Pierce Watson, a top ranked forward out of Texas, decided to attend UCLA. David Douglas had been one of three hats placed in front of the high schooler when he picked the Bruins. Royce made multiple visits during Pierce's junior year and Jordan tagged along for a few. She called him after Royce's departure as she had done with the other recruits, assuring him that nothing had changed, but Pierce clearly wasn't convinced.

"His uncle played for the Bruins," Frost said. "I'm sure that played a factor."

They posted up in the weight room, squeezing in a workout

after practice. Jordan took out her frustration on the bench press while Frost spotted her.

"It's not like they're having a great season." Jordan gritted her teeth and extended the barbell. "Maybe I didn't give him enough personal attention. I should've gone to Texas to see him."

"You've been taking care of business here and bonding with the guys. That's important too."

"I just feel stretched thin. I was hoping winning would be enough to convince some of these kids to come here," Jordan said with a final grunt to finish her set.

"It's one recruit, Jay." Frost eased the bar back onto the rack. "Plus, we still have Hunter Garrick."

Hunter Garrick was a four-star recruit out of southern Oregon. He'd verbally committed to Royce and confirmed he'd stick it out with Jordan. Hanging on to him would make Pierce Watson irrelevant. Still, Jordan didn't like the way the winds changed. She wiped sweat from her forehead before getting into position to spot Frost. "What if it's me?"

"What do you mean?" he asked, struggling through a few reps.

"What if the kids don't want to come here because they don't want to play for me?"

Frost hissed through another extension before his arms started shaking. Jordan swooped in and lifted the rest of the weight onto the rack.

"God, I'm out of shape," Frost wheezed before addressing Jordan. "Listen, these top recruits want to go somewhere that they can win. We keep doing that, the rest will take care of itself."

Jordan nodded, leaning on his optimism. They'd coached together for six years and seen each other through the trials of winning and losing seasons. They were there for each other through the big moments. Jordan introduced him to his wife, stood at his side when they got married and when his twins were born. Frost never doubted or questioned her when she won Royce's favor or took the top job. She considered him family and didn't know how she would manage without him.

"Can I ask you something unrelated?"

Frost nodded as they loaded more weight on the bar. "Shoot."

Jordan glanced at the door before sitting on the bench. "I kind of started seeing someone. I mean, not really. It was a date and a kiss. Okay, a few kisses. And I don't know if it was really a date." She glared at Frost's low chuckle, flopped down, and seized the bar. "It's complicated because of my job."

"Who is she?"

"No one." Jordan huffed through a rep.

Frost furrowed his brow. "Hold on. When have you had time to meet someone?"

"It doesn't matter. She said we should break it off, and I agreed."

"So, what's the problem?"

"She seemed mad at me or something when she decided we shouldn't see each other."

Jordan pushed through the weight like she longed to push through the space between them. The way things ended left Jordan more dejected than she expected. She understood Beck's reservations, held similar ones of her own, and assured herself they avoided heartache by stopping cold turkey. Jordan didn't have time for romance. But losing Beck stung worse than a defeat on the court, and whatever heartache she thought they avoided scorned her anyway.

"What did you say to her?"

"I said she was right and that we don't make sense together." Jordan grunted as her arms locked up. "Help."

Frost threw his head back, aiding her through obnoxious laughter.

"What's so funny?" Jordan asked, catching her breath.

"She probably wanted you to fight for her or show some emotion. I can just imagine you with that blank face of yours."

Jordan contemplated his advice. It wouldn't be the first time her lack of emotion stunted a relationship. Not that she and Beck had one. Not that they were speaking anymore.

"If you really like her, tell her. Better yet, show her," he said.

"I don't really like her."

Frost smirked. "Then why do you care if she's mad at you? Plus, you have never, ever asked me for advice about a girl."

"That's not true." Jordan chucked her towel at him before walking away.

"It's definitely true," he said. "Where are you going?"

"Getting away from you," she said.

"Don't run from your feelings, Jordan!"

XOXO

The last game before winter break pitted the Bulldogs against Redwood State University. The stands weren't nearly as full as students left for the holiday, the guys wanted to get home, and their opponent teetered on the edge of a losing season.

"Don't lose focus today. Don't let them in this game for a second," Jordan said in the locker room.

While she demanded the players maintain their focus, she struggled too, but not because of the holiday. She searched the cameras on the opposite sideline for Beck and frowned when she didn't spot her.

"Are you okay?" Frost asked.

"Yeah," Jordan said, turning back to warm-ups.

Beck slipped in right before the game started and Jordan uncrossed her arms. Her disappointment lessened, but she didn't like that Beck held sway over her mood. Especially as Jordan noticed her friendliness with Wyatt Holt, another beat reporter she recognized from press conferences. Every so often, she ventured a glance to find them laughing or talking close. Jordan gripped her papers tighter, barked at the team louder, even though they led by double digits at halftime.

While Beck's flirtation sparked flames, Redwood State's dirty play stoked a full-blown inferno. Though they dominated through the second half, the Bulldogs contended with their opponent's pushing and violent scraps. Aggressions the refs did nothing to stop. Jordan stifled her temper as her guys got roughed around, but each foul enraged her more than the last.

"Call it both ways!" Jordan stomped a foot when Charlie went down beneath the hoop after an obvious charge. The ref blew the whistle against him, and the arena erupted with boos.

Jordan cracked her knuckles and paced. Her edginess intensified when she risked a glance at Beck happily chatting with Wyatt. The poor officiating and her jealousy steamed like water in a kettle coming to a squeal when the referee blew his whistle two plays later. Leon skidded across the floor in front of Jordan after his defender tripped him.

"That's a technical, on thirty-three." The ref pointed at Leon.

"Are you kidding me?" Jordan stepped toward the ref, but Frost pulled her back.

"That's a warning, Coach!"

"You're calling baseless fouls on my guys while they're getting run over! Are we watching the same game?" she shouted. Fans booed the ref, others screamed and egged Jordan on. She jabbed a finger at the man's chest. "I won't stand for this horseshit!"

"One more word and you're out of here!"

While tension boiled over on the bench, tempers also flared

on the court. Behind the ref, Leon and a Redwood State player squared off. Jordan couldn't hear above the crowd and her screams but would later learn a simple sneer prompted the first shove.

"Get your bitch under control," the Redwood State player said.

It launched Leon into attack mode. He pushed, and the rest blurred. Sean and Frost held the bench players back from the fight, while the Redwood State staff did the same. Brooks yanked someone off Leon, but another player tugged his jersey, starting a second scrap. Jordan, the refs, and the opposing coach entered the mix to break apart the brawl. She waded through a mess of colors, bodies bumping, arms flailing, referees desperately blowing whistles. The crowd jeered at the mayhem.

If not for the noise and chaos, Jordan might have thought twice about coming between Leon and his sparring mate. She grabbed for the Redwood State player right as he cocked back to throw a punch. Unaware of her behind him, he smacked his elbow into her face with a crunch.

"Fuck." Jordan grunted. She knew at the snap, the white flash blurring her vision, and the tears springing into her eyes that he'd broken her nose. She doubled over and covered her face.

"Are you okay?" Charlie steadied her.

Blood drenched Jordan's hands when she removed them from her face. "Shit."

The fight came to a halt as the Bulldogs frantically flocked to her. The referee ejected Leon and two Redwood State players, but the forward didn't care.

"I'll kill 'em." Leon moved to bolt, but Dominic held him back.

"No. You need to go to the locker room and cool down," Jordan said.

Frost forced her to the bench and handed her a towel. "You need to get checked out by Sid."

"No, I'm good." Her nose throbbed, but she could tolerate pain. What she couldn't bear was the guys staring at her in terror.

"I'm not leaving unless you leave," Leon said.

"Why are you always a pain in my ass?" Jordan grunted. She addressed the rest of the squad, who'd surrounded her in a half circle, shielding her from the fans and press. "I'm going to get the bleeding to stop, and I'll be right back. This is nothing, okay? Humiliate them for me."

"We got you, Coach," Brooks said.

Jordan followed Leon and Sidney, the team medical trainer, off the court to a thunder of cheers. The stands rattled and students bellowed down at her. "Hell yeah, Coach! Give 'em hell!"

She stopped when they reached the tunnel. "How bad is it, Sid?"

Sidney shook her head. "Let's get you to the locker room. I can see better there."

"Does it need to be set?" Jordan asked.

Sidney held her chin with gloved hands and evaluated her in the dim light. "It's definitely crooked."

"Then set it."

Leon groaned. "Coach, come on. There's like five minutes left."

"We should let a doctor assess this," Sidney said.

"Just do it," Jordan said. "I don't want the guys to worry or people to see my empty seat. I'm getting back out there."

Sidney contemplated her for a beat while the game started back up behind them. She typically treated cramps and sprained ankles, but Jordan nodded at her in a sign of trust. Sidney sighed. "Fine, but this is not advisable. And it's going to hurt."

"No shit," Jordan muttered.

"Hell no! No way. Are you two actually serious?" Leon covered his mouth when they ignored him. "No. I can't watch. I'm going to throw up."

"Don't be a baby, Torres."

Jordan ate her words when Sidney gripped the side of her face with one hand and her nose with the other. She hissed. Fresh tears sprang. A shooting pain hit the back of her skull and she squirmed on instinct.

"Maybe you should hold her hand," Sidney said to Leon.

"No!" Jordan and Leon blurted.

Sidney recoiled. "Okay, sorry."

"Just hurry up and do it."

"One, two . . ."

Sidney snapped her nose into place and Jordan groaned, thought she might faint before Leon held her up.

"Fuck me." She sucked in an uneven breath. "You went on two."

The brute force against her fractured bones sent her into shock. Tremors rocked her back. Vomit hit her throat, which she promptly swallowed. Tears and snot rolled into the blood on her chin. Sidney muttered soothing nothings as she cleaned and bandaged Jordan's nose, but it was Leon's hand on her shoulder that brought her back.

"You're okay, Coach. You'll be alright." Leon patted her once, twice, then he darted back as if suddenly aware and simultaneously offput by his sympathy. He coughed and looked away, folding his arms across his broad chest. "You're crazy, you know. Wait until I tell Charlie about this."

"I know," she muttered.

"All better," Sidney said as she fixed a cotton swab up Jordan's nostril.

The ache retreated in a flood of numbness, allowing Jordan to straighten up and draw her shoulders back. No tears. Only her mission. "Leon, go to the locker room," she said.

"But Coach—"

"You can't be on the court. What the hell happened out there, anyway?"

Leon frowned. "He called you a bitch."

Her mouth fell open in disbelief. A month ago, Leon despised her. Now he'd swung fists to defend her. "I appreciate you defending my honor, but if I got into a fight every time someone called me that, I wouldn't have a job."

"Sorry." Leon's eyes glistened as he surveyed her face. "I feel like this is my fault."

Jordan sighed. "It's not your fault." She shoved him toward the locker room. "Go rest your legs. You owe me stadium stairs."

He groaned and mumbled curses at the punishment, slamming the door with his typical feistiness. Jordan drew in a breath, nodded at Sidney, and stalked back to the court with blood on her jacket. The crowd clapped as she retook her spot on the bench. The cameras zeroed in and put her image up on the screen despite the game.

"God, you're stubborn," Frost said.

Jordan rolled her eyes. "It's just a little broken nose. I swear, you guys are bigger wimps than I thought."

The Bulldogs routed Redwood State, going on a twelve-point run in the closing minutes, defeating the visiting team by nearly thirty points. Their fallen leader, crimson on her shirt while she barked orders, energized the squad to the point of raw power. For the first time ever, the guys hugged Jordan when the game ended. The embraces reduced the pain to nothing. She felt like she'd earned something. Like they'd reached the final stage of becoming a team.

After fresh bandages and briefly icing, Jordan trekked to the media room. Frost offered to do the presser for her, Sidney bemoaned her being a horrible patient, and while she resembled a defeated boxer, Jordan determinedly took her place, not in a show of toughness but to filch a glimpse of Beck. Even after the blood and commotion, she pathetically longed for the postgame interview simply to see her. She'd taken Frost's advice to heart. She liked Beck and intended to show her. Granted, she wasn't sure how she'd manage under these circumstances.

"How are you feeling, Coach?" Wyatt asked.

Jordan resisted glaring at the man who spent the game in Beck's ear. "I'm okay. This isn't my first broken nose."

"We were surprised you stayed on the court," he said.

"It was important for me to be with my team."

Jordan drifted to Beck. The reporter's shoulders slouched, her mouth drooping in a way that she'd never seen. She didn't know if she was upset or angry, but it unsettled her. When their eyes connected, she didn't emit a flicker and, for the first time since Jordan became head coach, Beck didn't ask a single question.

The presser ran shorter than usual after Molly broke in to tell reporters that Jordan needed to take care of her nose. She glanced over her shoulder to find Beck in the crowd, but she was already gone. Jordan frowned at the missed opportunity. At a door shutting on them. At being too late. Winter break and a pair of road games waited on the horizon, whittling down their rare interactions. In the locker room shower, a pink tinge swirling at her feet, she morosely contemplated what she never feared before. She let a good one get away.

"I hope you take this holiday break seriously for once," Frost said on their way up to her apartment. He'd insisted on driving her home and carrying her bag.

"What do you mean?"

"Taking a break for real. Maybe watch something other than

game film. Come over for Christmas." Frost paused at her front door and grinned. "We're really doing it, Jordan. This isn't a fluke. The guys are on fire. And they care. I mean, Leon defending you like that?"

"Yeah, it is something." Jordan smiled.

"I'll call you tomorrow."

As soon as she shut the door, the agony she'd successfully distracted herself from reared its head. She shut her eyes against the throb. Jordan didn't drink often, having grown up around booze in the worst way, but the painkillers weren't cutting it. She found a rarely touched bottle of bourbon and hissed through a few sips when the doorbell rang.

She assumed Frost decided not to trust her to her own devices.

Instead, she found Beck waiting outside her door.

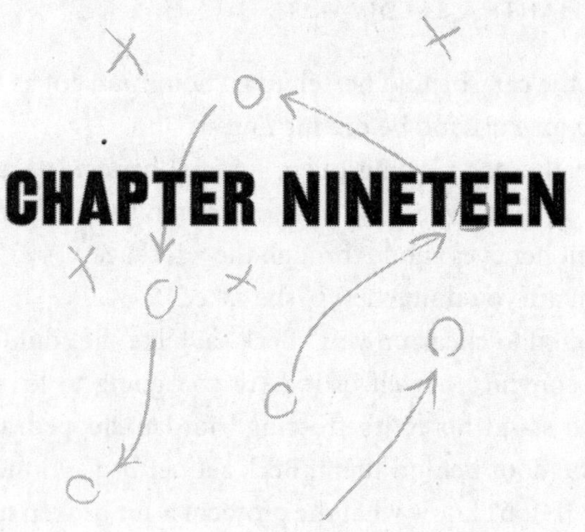

CHAPTER NINETEEN

Beck didn't consider herself squeamish, but when Jordan broke her nose, she thought she might be sick. Her body clenched and nausea filled her gut. She spent the game distracting herself with Wyatt, vindictively using him to ignore Jordan. Whatever spite she mustered, however, dissolved as soon as the coach took a blow.

"What's wrong?" Wyatt asked. Beck couldn't answer as Jordan hobbled off with a red-stained towel over her face. "You don't like blood?"

Beck nodded, perturbed by him patting her shoulder. Blood didn't bother her. What she didn't like, couldn't stand apparently, was Jordan's blood.

By the press conference, she hadn't recovered. She couldn't manage a question. She couldn't ignore Jordan's injury and treat her solely as the head coach of the Bulldogs. Instead, she pictured that precious face in her hands, gentle eyes, balmy skin beneath her fingers. It pitted her to see it tarnished. She halfheartedly filed her story, her resolve to avoid Jordan slipping away. In the car, she told herself to go home and got as far as the on-ramp for Portland before turning around.

When the door swung open, Jordan's battered face startled her. The swelling worsened in just a few hours, the bruise darkening, but her eyes shone through the wreckage.

"What are you doing here?" she asked.

"I wanted to check on you," Beck said like she could simultaneously convince herself of it. "Are you going to let me in or make me stand here? It's freezing." Jordan stepped aside and closed the door behind them. Beck set her bags on the kitchen counter. "I don't know what the protocol is for broken noses, but I got you soup."

Jordan flashed a frail smile. "Thanks. I'm starving."

Beck busied herself by finding bowls and spoons, stopping when she spotted a bottle of whiskey. "You're drinking?"

"Desperate to be numb. Help yourself," she said. Beck slid her bowl across the granite island and Jordan paused. She glanced from Beck to the soup, and back at Beck again. "Am I supposed to know what's going on right now?"

She nervously cleared her throat. "I was worried about you."

"What happened to only seeing each other in a professional capacity?"

"I know." Beck's cheeks flushed. "I just needed to see you."

"Well, I'm glad you're here," Jordan said, inspiring Beck to meet her gaze. "I missed you."

"You did?" Her breath zapped at Jordan's timid nod. "I missed you too."

"I'm sorry if I reacted wrong the last time we saw each other. I'm not the best at . . . this. I thought I was making it better somehow."

"You did nothing wrong. I know I'm making things confusing." Beck fiddled with her spoon, uncertain of what to say, jittery, in such nearness to Jordan despite already kissing her once, twice, however many times before. "It scared me when you got hurt. I wanted to be close to you."

"If a broken nose sent you running here, I'd break it every week," Jordan said, her ears flaming red as she attended to her soup. "Who was that guy you were with tonight?"

"Who?"

"The guy you kept talking to."

"Oh, Wyatt. He's a reporter from another station." She squinted at her. "Why?"

Jordan shrugged. "You two just looked friendly."

"I didn't think you'd care."

Beck relished the hint of jealousy. She used Wyatt in a manipulative, adolescent ploy, admittedly not one of her more upstanding traits, but days ago she believed Jordan set her aside without a second thought.

"I care." Jordan raised an eyebrow. "I care a lot."

The coach's firmness shot a shudder through Beck. One that erased all remnants of rational thought. She shifted to her soup, battling two parts of herself. The objective reporter and the impulsive, lovestruck fool she'd never been before.

They ate quietly as though pondering the implications of another late-night meeting. Jordan gingerly slurped, occasionally flinching, and Beck imagined she pushed through more pain than she'd ever admit.

"You should probably ice," Beck said when they finished.

"I'm fine."

"You know you need to, and I know you're hurting."

Beck tossed her an ice pack from the freezer. While the coach flopped to the couch and flipped on basketball highlights, Beck did what she did best. Meandered, snooped, and picked apart clues to gain insight into her subject. Only Jordan was no longer a subject. She wasn't an interview or even an infatuation. She was a flutter in her lower gut, a smile she failed to suppress, a siren that Beck chased.

The apartment embodied sterile cleanliness. Jordan kept the fridge nearly empty, the counters sparkling as though never touched, her dishware short of a full set. Beck stifled a chuckle at its sensibility. There were few personal touches, confirming what she already knew. Jordan ate, slept, and breathed basketball—even at home.

The living room, however, briefly broke from that pretense. Beck paused at the bookshelves spanning two walls, stretching from floor to ceiling. Countless hardbacks and volumes lined the wood beams, an array of poetry, histories, classics, autobiographies. Beck traced a few spines of the eclectic but thorough mix that left little to be desired.

"You can borrow anything you like," Jordan said from the couch.

Beck eyed the mementos and photos, mostly coaching related, interspersed among the literature. Basketballs functioned as bookends, dated and marked with special milestones. Jordan's first WNBA game. The national championship with Atherton State. The Sweet Sixteen with David Douglas. The most recent was her first win that season.

"You're going to run out of space at the rate you're going," Beck said.

"I hope so," Jordan murmured. She rested her feet on the coffee table, head propped uncomfortably against the cushions while she held ice to her nose.

"Give me that." Beck took the ice pack from a baffled Jordan and plopped down to the other side of the couch. She piled two throw pillows on her thighs and nodded at her. "Come here."

Jordan laid her head across Beck's lap, and she cautiously replaced the ice. "Is this okay?"

She nodded. Jordan's stare rooted into hers, and Beck was relieved that it wasn't that of press conference restraint or sideline stoicism, but open and reaching. Something fragile shone through in a way Beck imagined Jordan rarely permitted. It's what sent Beck running to her door, secretly hoping she was the only one to know the coach this way. She brushed a curl off Jordan's forehead as if to confirm it.

"What are we doing, Beck?" she asked. Just as Jordan no longer exuded coach, Beck no longer wielded her on-camera confidence, faltering and speechless with the precious weight of Jordan's head in her lap. She responded with hands instead. She traced Jordan's cheek, longed for her mouth, currently hidden beneath ice. Jordan put a few fingers to Beck's as if receiving the message. "Can I kiss you now?"

Beck exhaled, but it did little to relieve the pressure in her chest. The same pressure that spread lower and fuller when they kissed. It started slowly, but her timidity quickly faded away because at the first brush of lips, Beck knew exactly what they were doing, and exactly what else she wanted. She widened her mouth for a slip of tongue, looped her arms around Jordan's neck as she shifted to sit up, the ice pack falling to the floor with a thud. Beck hedged closer for more, thoughtlessly pushed her lips in deeper, like the only thing that might counteract the budding pressure inside was more of Jordan. The broken nose became a nonfactor, both plunging in, grabbing between quick intakes of air, before Jordan hissed with a wounded gasp.

"Ah. Ow."

Beck flew back at Jordan's flinching. "I'm sorry."

"No, no, it's okay." She blinked away a few tears. "I broke it before back in college. Played the next day like it was nothing. I guess I'm not as young and pliable anymore."

"You should probably keep icing." Beck gently blotted the damp corners of Jordan's eyes. She longed to ease her pain, to patch the small cut on her nose, and heal the purple splotch beneath her eye.

"I thought the last few days without talking to you were torture." Jordan pushed out a chuckle. "But this might be worse. Having you right here but unable to kiss you."

"At least I'm here now." She sighed, the pause in kissing and Jordan's pain a cold plunge back to reality. "Even if I shouldn't be. Even if it's probably reckless and impulsive and confusing—"

"Maybe it's not any of those things," Jordan said. The discomfort evaporated from her features as she tilted her head to the side. "I keep telling myself that you're the last thing I need too. That you're a distraction, but you're not. You're making me better at my job, in a way I didn't know I needed." She rested a hand above her heart. "You're making me better here."

Beck liquefied—back and shoulders going limp, effectively releasing the final smidge of control she stubbornly believed she still had. It left room for the ballooning in her chest that she usually guarded against. Only now, that raw, tender place didn't scare her. Not in the face of Jordan's honesty, her calmness while she waited, wanting but not entitled to what she sought. A safe landing for Beck's letting go and the endless fall that followed.

She squeezed Jordan's hand to steady herself. "If the school or my station finds out—"

"No one is going to find out."

Beck didn't know if she fully believed her—not because she didn't trust Jordan, but because there were no guarantees in their world. A world where a job well done didn't promise the next game or grant a moment's peace. Not on the court. But here, together, just maybe they might find it.

She swallowed a final pit of fear, clearing the way for a choice she'd made long before that moment on the couch. "I'll have to be objective. I'll have to keep asking you the hard questions."

"I know." Jordan nodded with an amused twinkle in her gaze. She traced her thumbs across Beck's hands, still in hers. "And you can't snoop around for my playbook."

Her cheeks flamed at getting caught, but she also smiled at being known. "I wasn't snooping around for your playbook. But I did peep the trick play on your coffee table."

Jordan grinned and eased into her.

"Careful," Beck said.

But Jordan didn't care for caution. She kissed Beck, tipping her head so that their noses scarcely brushed. Beck stopped herself from putting too much weight into the embrace but there was something satisfying in the restraint, knowing that this was scalp prickling and stomach fluttering and more still waited. A sigh vibrated out of her chest.

When they parted, Jordan brought her mouth to her ear. "Stay with me."

Their eyes locked, and Beck nodded as if pushing her chips to the center of the table. A chip for her career. A chip for her family. A chip for her future. A chip for Jordan's. All neatly piled and counted, for the sake of one hand, one game that now mattered more than the rest. "I'll stay."

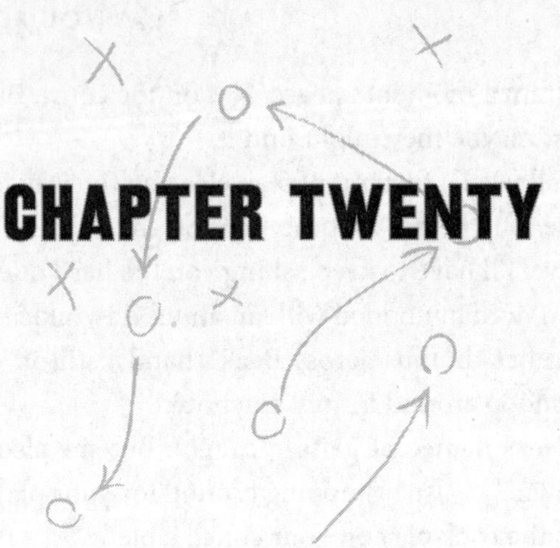

CHAPTER TWENTY

Beck roused her with a whisper in the dead of night. "Jordan, you should go to bed."

She didn't know if the pain finally caught up with her or if Beck soothed her to the point of surrender, but she'd slackened into her lap on the couch, lost to the world. While embarrassed, confused, but quietly elated at waking to Beck, Jordan followed her down the hall. She shuffled blearily but hummed with the same want. Broken bones and fatigue didn't stand a chance against it.

"I'll let you sleep," Beck said when they reached the bedroom.

Jordan flipped on a lamp and glanced at the time. "It's three in the morning. Just rest awhile."

She bit her bottom lip, a blush warming her cheeks as Beck considered the offer with a playful squint. Jordan couldn't remember the last time she suggested someone spend the night, or maybe she never had at all. But once again, Beck inspired boldness, a change from the norm, even if it meant risking her ego in the middle of the night.

"Alright." Beck smirked. "Do you have something I can change into?"

Jordan nodded, unable to speak at the glint of her in shadowed light. She gathered a David Douglas University T-shirt and sweatpants, both of which would undoubtedly swim on a much smaller Beck. Their fingers brushed as she handed them off.

"Can you unzip me?" Beck turned her back to Jordan.

Jordan cleared her throat before daring to grab the zipper. Her fingers trailed along Beck's back, the nape of her neck a temptation that she tensed at. Beck stood straight, unbothered, but her shoulders betrayed her as they heaved with breath. She trailed the zipper down, biting on a gasp when the dress parted to reveal freckled skin.

"Thanks," Beck whispered.

Jordan didn't move. A subtle rattle that started in her heart reverberated to the rest of her. It came with a rush of heat both pleasant and a touch uneasy, only because she didn't know how to think past it. Didn't know how to not let it melt her into Beck for solace, for calm, for release.

She just breathed and hovered and when Beck didn't move either, she inched closer. Streamed three fingers down the constellation of freckles. Brushed a few gold locks off her shoulder. Beck shivered and sighed.

"Okay?" Jordan asked.

Beck didn't turn or answer. She just reached back for Jordan's head, bringing it to her neck. Jordan wrapped her arms around her waist, pulled her closer, inhaled the hair that brushed against her nose. Her knees wobbled at Beck's ass against her, and she pressed for more without thinking. Trailed lips down her neck without coming up for air, slow and methodical, sure to not leave any flesh unkissed.

The low hum of Beck's sighs, the way she came closer to fist her curls, budded want beneath Jordan's skin, but it was the way she turned, a flash of hazel eyes and inviting lips, that sparked a quake between her hips. Jordan always thought Beck beautiful and charming and undoubtedly sexy, but never did she imagine how badly she'd want her with shameless, senseless lust.

They tangled onto the bed, Jordan fast to loop her in her arms, to feel her weight and bring her tight against her. And even still, none of it was close enough. Not the kisses that occasionally bumped and flicked her injured nose. Not the gentle graze of Beck's teeth that drew a moan out of her throat. Not their hips knocking together or the friction of a thigh between legs.

Her fingers trembled when she slipped the dress off Beck's shoulder like she hadn't done such a thing before. She was busy and often neglected her sex life, but it hadn't been long enough for her to forget how to be naked with someone. And still, she nearly gawked at the delicate arch of Beck's collarbone, the cleavage rising beneath her bra, breasts waiting beneath. When Beck tugged at her shirt, demanding its removal, Jordan clumsily yanked it over her head, bumping her nose in haste. She grunted but eagerly plunged down to resume kissing before Beck applied light pressure to her chest, holding her back.

"Hey, careful."

Jordan shook her head. "I'm fine."

"Okay, well then, I need you to be gentle," she said. "Be gentle with me."

Jordan's mouth dropped, the elation deflating at even slightly disappointing the perfect woman beneath her. Despite her desperation, offending Beck would be far worse than not having her. "I'm sorry. I can stop—"

"No, don't stop." Beck kissed her again. Then she cupped Jordan's cheeks. "Just be gentle. Just be here with me."

Jordan nodded, her arousal no less pronounced, but less dizzying. And while it hadn't been long enough for her to forget, Jordan certainly never had sex like this. So much of who she was—her career, the game, her ambitions—required toughness, relentlessness, its own brand of passion. She applied it to almost all aspects of her life, until now. Beck left her vulnerable. Required her to slow down, to be gentle, to venture a different kind of risk. Something intimate. With Beck, she didn't fear giving it.

The softer kisses provoked a stronger flutter. The traces instead of grasps tickled down her inner thigh. Beck's careful breath matching hers built waves in her stomach. Each touch a promise to be present, to give without taking. The lack of thoughtless, horny frenzy brought Jordan to a deeper throb and a sharper edge.

"Can I?" Jordan whispered against the shell of Beck's ear, a hand at her breast, the other lingering at her knee.

Beck grabbed her hand and guided it up her thigh. Jordan sighed at the invitation. Ached when she brushed beneath the last shred of lace at Beck's center and found her drenched. Beck groaned, a sensuous rumbling that reached into the dark corners of the room and left Jordan shuddering. In the same pause, Beck stroked fingers along the slick spot between her legs. Jordan whimpered through the kiss that they'd started several minutes ago, and released her weight into Beck, so that their limbs and curves met in one heave.

They traded in moans and curled fingers, traces along openings and careful circles at sensitive swells. Beck gave in first, threw her head back, and clutched Jordan's shoulders. Her hips moved for more and Jordan followed, pulling Beck closer while she dipped deeper.

The cry that accompanied Beck's orgasm was louder than Jordan anticipated. A raw, uninhibited sound that sent a ripple through her stomach. Her hips stilled, and Beck's breath—shaky and hot—tickled Jordan's neck.

"You okay?" Jordan asked.

Beck's eyes, which had become dilated, caught a shred of lamplight. Her humid cheeks glowed, a few strands of hair stuck to her forehead, and while she lay limp and peaceful in Jordan's hold, a seriousness filled her gaze.

"Let me take care of you," Beck said.

Before Jordan responded, Beck's mouth reached to meet hers, and her fingers returned to assuage the throb. After the gentle kisses, after their skin meeting, after Beck's moans, and her insistence on taking care of her in this way as she had in every other, Jordan might have climaxed from as little as a breath. She basked in the sweetness of Beck's kisses, but it was her hand with deliberate, perfect pressure that she let herself free in.

"Come for me," Beck whispered.

The gentle demand split Jordan into pieces, careening into a place unknown—somewhere between pleasure and deeper. The same intimacy of talking to Beck flourished in something physical, consuming, and carnal. When the climax ebbed, when she could see clearly again, she rested her forehead against Beck's. Her heart slowed and settled. Her breath returned. The most peace she'd felt in weeks. Months. Maybe ever.

They pecked lips just once, quick but sweet like they'd always done it. Just like when they rolled to their backs, their bodies stayed linked as if belonging in such a way. And in the silence, Jordan somehow knew she didn't need to say anything but Beck's name. Beck whispered hers back as a storm pattered across the roof. They sleepily examined each other. Beck outlining the web of tattoos on Jordan's shoulders, usually hidden, but unveiled to her as everything else. Jordan's fingers twisting through her tresses. She rested her lips on her temple and waited for whatever came next.

But there was nothing. And there was also everything. And then there was sleep.

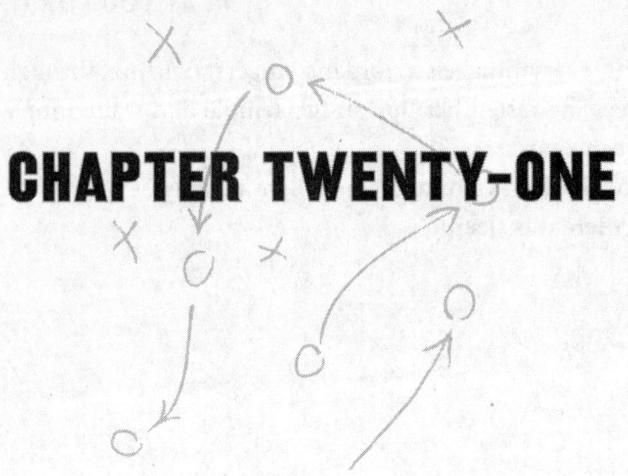

CHAPTER TWENTY-ONE

The guilt that accompanied Beck's crush on Jordan didn't emanate when she woke up beside her. The desire that drove her to bed in the first place didn't dissipate either, unlike the other infatuations that she often fucked free from her system. Instead, when she opened her eyes and comprehended where she rested her head, Beck encountered something entirely new. Steadiness.

She didn't hesitate with Jordan. Didn't stop herself from threading through her curls, from twisting the gold chain around her neck, from tracing the tattoos that she unearthed like treasure. She knew these things existed for months, through interviews and photos and their moments, both charged and casual, but to touch them and know her this way solidified Jordan for Beck. Made her someone she imagined calling hers.

As they huddled together beneath the sheets, safe from the world and winter, Beck's heart teemed with a touch of homesickness for what she didn't yet need to miss. Jordan kissed, held, and burrowed into her as if she too feared the power of their togetherness and that they couldn't exist in bed forever.

"I was worried you might take off." She rested her chin on Beck's head.

Beck ran fingers along her shoulders, outlining the twisting tree limbs pressed in ink. The tattoos were never visible, not even when Jordan wore T-shirts, except for maybe the slightest tease of ink at her biceps or if she turned her neck just right. Beck only knew of them from researching her playing days, when they peeked out from her uniform, sprawled along her back and shoulders.

"You think I'm the kind of girl who just hooks up and runs out?" Beck asked.

Jordan's gravelly chuckle vibrated in her ear. "No. But maybe I'm not who you'd want to wake up next to."

Beck frowned and shifted. She cupped Jordan's cheeks, their legs, stomachs, and centers brushing together, the slightest friction a second awakening on the frigid morning.

"I'm exactly where I want to be."

Beck kissed beneath the purple splotch around her eye. The coach's bruises and crooked nose didn't deter her. In fact, something about the rugged scars endeared Jordan to her further. She used her lips as a balm, landing careful pecks on her face, neck, down her chest.

When she drifted her mouth lower, Jordan pulled her back up. Beck furrowed her brow before whispering, "Let me."

Beck pressed Jordan's wrists back to the pillows with careful weight to render her still. Jordan's bright eyes darkened the same way they had last night, when Beck guided her hand between her thighs.

She loved how vigorously Jordan conveyed her desire in a rash of kisses and certain hands, but also how quickly, with a simple word like *gentle,* that Beck tamed it. Made it hers. She could slow and soften the harried coach, though she already suspected her plenty soft before she ever submitted.

It wasn't just about controlling Jordan, but about how badly Beck wanted to give. A new but equally consuming need that rattled inside, only soothed by Jordan's taste and gasps. She swore that when she came with Beck's mouth in that wet, guarded place, it reverberated in her just as deeply. And when Jordan rolled on top of her, tugging her closer—rougher than before, but safe—and croaked, "My turn," in a crackle that Beck stiffened at, something told her that this would be a game they played too.

The rest of the morning unfurled with the same ease that they uncovered beneath the sheets. Like they'd always shared black coffee and showers and clothes. In fact, rather than insist on an exit as post-coital clarity usually inspired her to, Beck let herself linger. She didn't mention leaving when they settled on the couch to watch basketball. She rested her head against Jordan's shoulder and Jordan's hand drifted across her knee, a shared understanding passing between them, similar to the way they chatted about the game flickering on the screen.

"Is this new for you?" Jordan asked during a commercial.

"What?"

"Being with a woman?"

Beck lifted her head from Jordan's shoulder and raised an eyebrow. "Was I that bad?"

"No! The opposite." Jordan grinned.

"Thank God," Beck said with a chuckle. She looked down and fidgeted with Jordan's long fingers. "You're not the first woman I've been with. There was someone in college. A teammate." She frowned at the memory. "Paige. But I never let it go further, even when I wanted it to."

Jordan squeezed her hand. "Family?"

"Eh, kind of." Beck shrugged. "We're barely Catholic. My parents are liberal, but they kind of have an idea of how everything should be. I don't know if being with a woman fits into that."

"Well, hopefully your happiness does, regardless."

"You're sweet," she whispered. "I shouldn't complain. They want the best for me. They're not like—well, if they knew, they wouldn't, I mean."

"It's okay." Jordan nodded. "I know. They're not like my parents, and that's a good thing."

Beck's mouth crumpled. "I'm sorry."

"Don't be." Jordan wrapped an arm around her, kissed the side of her head. "Are you going to see them for the holiday?"

"Yeah, I'm catching a flight to Philly this afternoon." Beck's frown deepened at the reminder of leaving. "Do you have Christmas plans?"

"I'm staying here. It's an abbreviated break anyway. The kids only have a few days off. I'll probably go to Frost's for dinner," Jordan said. "There's also the Ortega Classic."

"What's the Ortega Classic?"

"It's a charity basketball tournament we put on. The other coaches, faculty, and their families play. And so do local kids. The ones who might not have somewhere to go or something to look forward to on Christmas."

Beck squinted at her. "Why does this sound like your idea hidden behind Royce's name? And that it wouldn't be the first time . . ."

"No comment." Jordan blushed. "I can't be revealing these things to a member of the press. Though you are freakishly good at your job."

"Fine. But I expect game updates. It would be embarrassing if you lost your own tournament."

"Well, Frost and I have a winning record. But it's tradition for the head basketball coach to have Dean Gilchrest on their team, and let's just say I don't think he's been picked anything other than last in his life." Jordan laughed. "Maybe next year I can take you. You'd be a ringer."

"I'd love that." Beck beamed. All of it, Jordan's modesty, her goodness, and allusion to a future, fluttered Beck. The idea of being together not just now, but a year from now, had her nesting back into Jordan. "It sounds more fun than my family Christmas."

"Oh, yeah?"

"Well, we used to have a neighborhood hockey game, but then someone always ended up hurt or getting in a fight. My brother Scottie broke his wrist a few years ago, and we spent Christmas in the emergency room, so no more hockey game."

"Why do I get the feeling you were an instigator in this incident?"

"No comment," Beck said. "And that's rich coming from you, Rocky."

Jordan groaned. "At least Rocky landed a punch."

"That's true. You're more of a Sonny Liston, going down in the first round."

"You're truly a sports almanac."

Beck cringed. "Sorry. You wouldn't be the first to find it annoying."

"Why would I find it annoying?"

"Most guys just think it's a challenge or that I don't know what I'm talking about—"

"In case you haven't noticed, I'm not most guys. And I'm not here to put you down, Beck." Jordan pecked her cheek, quick but sweet. Beck wouldn't get over how often and simply she did it, like it was as natural as breathing. "I actually have something for you."

Beck furrowed her brow as Jordan grabbed her gym bag by

the front door. She rifled through it for a package, which she promptly handed to her.

"You got me a gift?"

"I was going to give it to you after the game yesterday, but then the fight happened." Jordan reddened. "Just, uh, open it."

Beck peeled the newspaper wrapping, smirking at its haphazard corners and tape. She uncovered a worn paperback. *The Old Man and the Sea.* The pages were yellow and worn, well-loved and marked.

"I give it to a player every season. Someone that I think has potential but needs a touch of inspiration or is struggling with doubt."

Beck eyed the list of names on the back cover, many of them professional athletes. "Oh my God, is that . . ."

"It's passed through a lot of hands," Jordan said. "When we talked after the interview aired, it seemed like you were feeling a little unsure about how everything went down. I thought this might be helpful, especially with the promotion." She cleared her throat. "I'm sorry if that sounds weird."

"It doesn't." Beck clutched the book as if Jordan had given her diamonds instead of a tattered novel. "Are you sure you shouldn't give this to one of the players?"

"I'm sure. Honestly, I've been feeling a little different about it lately. I'm worried that this time, I'm the old man and the team's this big fish I'm reeling in. I'm scared I'll end up feeding them to the sharks. Maybe you can give it a read. Tell me what I'm missing."

"I'd be honored. This means so much to me. Thank you."

"Of course."

She sighed. "I should go if I'm going to catch my flight."

Jordan nodded, though her mouth sagged ever so slightly. "I'll miss you."

"I'll miss you too," she whispered. They shared another kiss, held tight, as if they may not get another.

"Let me know when you land."

"I will. Take care of yourself. No more broken bones," she said before a final hug. "Merry Christmas, Jordan."

"Merry Christmas, Beck."

The December chill forced her back to reality. Her heart panged on the way to her car at the uncertainty of their next meeting. Of the logistics and secrets ahead. Of the homesickness that already filled her stomach. Certainty became uncertainty. Beck clung to their kiss, to the near-perfect morning, and to the tattered story in her hand, poised to become part of their own.

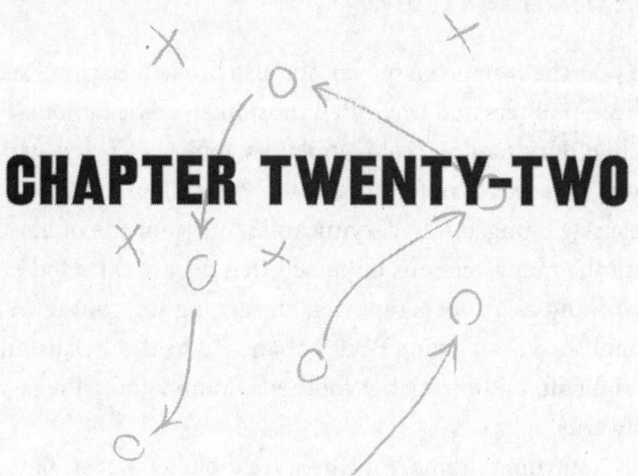

CHAPTER TWENTY-TWO

The Beck family resembled the model image in a new picture frame. Stuart and Candace Beck produced a brood of exquisitely blond children. Their three sons were carbon copies of the handsome Stuart, with dimpled chins, green eyes, and broad shoulders. The differences between the brothers were so comically slight—one taller than the others, one with a more strapping jaw, another with a scar on his cheek—that most struggled to tell them apart. The couple's lone daughter, Caroline, lived up to the expectations of golden locks and beauty laid before her, but failed to inherit her father's height or gregarious smile, her mother's long neck or grace. She was by no means short of stunning, but if one were to name a runt of the litter, it would undoubtedly be Caroline.

She embraced the differences as the sole girl, the shortest, and the only child Candace forced into the upper social circles of Philly's Main Line. Beck compensated by laughing the loudest, sharing the crudest jokes, and playing whatever sport was in season with her brothers after cotillion and charity league. The same year she won prom queen, she also broke the school record for three-pointers and was voted most likely to be famous.

While Beck had no real complaints about her privileged upbringing, she was grateful to leave it behind when the time came. She eagerly plunged into carving an identity outside of her family and the many versions of herself that people expected her to be. Working as a sports reporter, zigzagging the country, easily accomplished that, giving Beck a chance to be a journalist in her own right after admiring her mother's Emmys and father's Murrow awards.

But returning home for the rare holiday never failed to squeeze her back into place. She despised her mother's inquiries about her love life and her father's insistence that she get out of sports and write investigative stories that mattered. Usually, she joked and grumbled through their thinly veiled disappointment, but this year she worried she might not so easily ignore it.

Not with Jordan still setting her aflutter several state lines away. Through the festivities, Beck struggled to find the same gladness she usually did, all of it falling hollow in Jordan's absence. She longed to speak of her, to share the tenderness she'd discovered in the coach, and subsequently herself. She imagined Jordan there, opening gifts, playing with her nephews, sitting next to Beck at dinner. At night, relief came from their phone calls and texts, and the book that she grasped like a piece of her heart.

She trudged through most of the holiday unbothered, her parents usually saving their evaluation of her life until after the thrill of having her home wore off. That blessed time came at Christmas dinner. Her two older brothers were already married and produced carbon copies of their own, as if towheaded little boys simply spawned every few decades. Even Beck's younger brother, Scottie, intended to propose to his girlfriend that spring.

"You too, Brutus?" she hissed at him, following the announcement at dinner.

"I'm sorry, Caro, should I have waited until you found true love?"

"Yes. I'm glad you can see how messed up it is." Beck winked. "Congrats, Scottie."

"Thank you."

"Caroline, are you dating anyone?" Candace asked from the head of the table.

"Right on cue." Beck sighed. "No. I've been busy with basketball season."

"Speaking of which, I wish you wouldn't go by Beck on the air."

"And I wish you hadn't named me Caroline," she muttered.

"It's just not very feminine." Candace shook her head, stiff bottle blond curls bouncing. "Neither is the way you all fight on that show. It's unbecoming."

Beck opted to chug her wine rather than respond.

"Oh my god, Mom," Scottie said.

"What?" she asked.

"Candace, you know that's what they do on those sports shows. Not really journalism if you ask me, but who am I to judge?" Stuart said from the opposite end of the table.

"I think you're judging, Dad, but thanks." Beck rolled her eyes, trying to stay even, especially in front of her napping grandmother, timid sisters-in-law, and the future football captains and fraternity presidents who sprinted in and out from the kids' table.

"Listen, I'm not saying I agree with Mom," Troy, the family's second son, said with a sardonic smile. "But there's no doubt you scare the shit out of guys, Beckster."

"Speak for yourself. I think only you're afraid of her." Conner, the prodigal firstborn, winked.

Beck reached across the table and clinked his glass. "I'll drink to that."

Candace frowned. "I just don't understand why it has to be sports or nothing. How are you ever going to find a husband or have a family with the demands of your job?"

As Beck's cheeks flamed, she realized perhaps she'd drunk more wine than she thought. Just enough to loosen her tongue with a severe enough push. "Who says I need a husband or a family?"

"Oh, you love to say that," Candace sang in a taunting tune. "But eventually you're going to want to settle down."

It was true. Beck threw the argument in her mother's face at least once a year, though now it struck her that maybe she'd meant it beyond the sake of rebellion. With Jordan thudding inside her, a secret on the tip of her tongue, a feeling she longed to make a fixture, she considered taking the leap.

"Fine, maybe I'll want to get married eventually, but who says I need to do that with a man?"

Candace furrowed her brow. "What do you mean?"

"It looks like we could use some more wine." Scottie nudged Beck. "Caro, you want to give me a hand?"

Beck's ears rang in the silence. "No, I don't think I do," she said to him. Her neck burned, but she didn't want to turn back. She didn't know when she'd get this far again. Even if Jordan wasn't a guarantee, this part of herself would always exist. "What do I mean?" She paused under her mother's stare and the attention of the table. "Do you remember Paige Raybourn?"

"Yes, of course. You two were always so close."

"Well, she got married."

"See."

"To a woman." Beck gulped despite her clenched throat.

"Oh, shit," Conner muttered.

"And she wasn't just my best friend. We were together." Beck braced for her mother's gasp, but Candace sat dumbfounded. "I was in love with her. I almost left Grant to be with her, but I was too afraid of what everyone would think."

"What are you saying?" Candace asked.

"I'm not entirely sure." Beck froze. She hadn't planned for this conversation and now found herself in treacherous waters without a paddle. Revealing her relationship with Paige seemed like an easy place to start. The woman's picture sat on the dresser in her childhood bedroom, never failing to revive a slight heartache that lessened over the years but reminded her of the choices she made and the secrets she buried.

"You've dated men. You always date men," Candace said.

Beck's grandmother, Evelyn, stirred at the commotion, snapping out of her nap, shouting to be heard. "What is she saying?"

"Caro experimented with women in college!" Troy yelled at the nearly deaf woman.

"Troy," Stuart scolded.

"She what?" Evelyn asked again.

"She experimented with women!"

"Troy, stop saying that!"

"Are you a lesbian now?" Candace asked Beck, who cringed at the shouting. "Is that what you're trying to tell me?"

"Daddy, I want to experiment," Conner's youngest son announced, skipping around the table.

Conner snorted as he swirled his scotch. "Maybe when you're older, buddy."

"Is this really an appropriate time for this conversation?" Stuart asked.

"Caroline, are you going to answer me?" Candace asked.

"I don't know, okay!" Beck shouted to be heard through family dinner, like she was a teenager once more. "I don't know if I'm a lesbian, but I know it's not straightforward for me!"

Troy snickered next to her. "Pun intended, right?"

"Shut up." Beck punched his shoulder without taking her eyes off their mother. "I'd just appreciate—" She paused as Troy poked behind her ear. "Troy, stop it!" She swatted his hand away. "Mom, I'd just appreciate it if you don't assume I'm going to bring home Mr. Right someday."

Stuart cleared his throat, always the levelheaded patriarch. "I think we should take this conversation into the kitchen."

Candace huffed and barreled ahead.

"No, let's keep talking out here." Troy chuckled. "Dinner and a show. It's not Christmas without it."

Conner chucked a dinner roll at him. "Grow up."

"Bite me."

Beck threw her napkin down, ignoring Scottie's assurances, sure to take her empty wineglass with her. Candace had finished uncorking a fresh bottle of red by the time Stuart and Beck entered. She refilled her own glass and then her daughter's, a truce of sorts at the kitchen island.

"I'm sorry if I ruined dinner," Beck said after a sip. She didn't know what she'd expected. Truthfully, she never thought she'd have to come out. It'd been simultaneously worse and better than what she'd predicted. Her parents weren't throwing her out of the house, but she braced for their raw reaction.

"You didn't ruin anything, honey," Stuart said, eyes gleaming behind his tortoiseshell glasses. "When did you start feeling like this?"

"I think it's always been there." Beck shrugged.

"Are you seeing someone?" Candace asked gently.

Beck shook her head. One secret was enough for tonight. She wasn't quite ready to confront the disdain her parents would have for her dating a source. In fact, she was almost certain in their old-school, hard journalism sensibilities, they would consider that worse than simply dating a woman. "I just had to speak my truth. But there's no one now."

"Good." Stuart nodded.

Beck stiffened. "Good?"

"No, it's just, sorry, I just don't want things to be hard for you," Stuart stammered. "You know the industry, being on television, being a woman in sports specifically, it's already hard enough."

She crossed her arms. "So, you're suggesting I stay in the closet indefinitely?"

"We've seen how awful it can be," Candace said. "We've had beloved co-workers who came out and were completely ostracized. Joan Turner lost her job, and she taught your father everything. One of my best friends couldn't find work again after someone outed him for living with a man. He moved across the country to start over. The hate mail, the disgusting things people said, it was awful. We don't want that to happen to you."

"Things have changed since you two were on the anchor desk. There are plenty of queer television personalities now." Beck's shoulders clenched at the warning to hide herself. "Look at Kevin. He's out."

"And I'm sure he deals with his fair share of hate."

Her father wasn't wrong. Kevin showed her the abhorrent slurs that viewers posted on his social media page, and she knew that was likely just a small fraction. While she'd learned to deal with the scathing remarks about her gender, she didn't know if she could also handle homophobia. She despised that it overshadowed her moment of liberation. Despised that it made a public, open life with Jordan seem even more unlikely.

"We love you." Her father embraced her. "We just want you to make sure you're certain if you decide to share this publicly."

"And you don't have to," Candace said when she hugged her. "Don't do it if you don't have to."

Beck nearly recoiled at her mother's counsel. It struck her as a familiar and insulting nudge into place for the sake of normalcy.

"How's everything going in here?" Scottie plowed into the kitchen. His gaze landed on Beck, but she rolled her eyes and shook her head.

"Everything is fine, Scott. It's just time for pie!" Candace patted her youngest son's cheek. "Caroline, can you grab the dessert plates, honey?"

While their parents returned to the dining room, Scottie lowered his voice. "Are you okay?"

"I'm fine," Beck said, no longer in the mood to discuss her feelings or the countless barriers standing between her and Jordan.

She carried the plates to the table and settled into her spot just as unperturbed as her parents, dismissing the discussion of her sexuality like an unwanted tangent on religion or politics. Even Troy, who she swore was born predisposed to take pleasure in roasting her, didn't broach the subject or make another snide remark. It somehow made her feel worse.

The next twenty-four hours passed in a similar, avoidant fashion. She counted the hours until she could leave, grinding her teeth at her mother's unsubtle mentions of ex-boyfriends and eligible men in the area. Beck nearly jumped for joy when Scottie offered to drive her to the airport on his way to New York, ignoring Candace's tears at her departure and Stuart asking when her next visit would be.

"Jesus." Beck groaned when they finally left Haverford behind and hit the freeway. "That was worse than usual."

"Have to agree," Scottie said. "Way to stick it out."

Plump snowflakes flurried, turning the Philadelphia skyline

into a snow globe out Beck's window. She lost herself in the view, adding it to the endless list of things she wished to share with Jordan.

"So, who is she?" Scottie asked.

Beck twitched. "What?"

"The woman that you're seeing." He raised an eyebrow. "I know I'm your punk little brother, but I wasn't born yesterday."

Rather than clam up, Beck dared to let him in. "There's someone. But it's not a big deal." She hesitated to divulge the details, determined to protect Jordan's identity, and unclear about their future. But just sharing that she was seeing someone unburdened her chest.

"Not a big deal? You came out for her," Scottie said.

"It felt much less brave than that." Beck stared at her lap, unsure if she'd accomplished anything with her dinner revelation. "I don't know if we can make things work in the real world."

"Well, if it's enough to inspire you to say what you did, then it's probably worth trying. What's she like?"

Beck pursed her lips, unable to fight a smile. "She's really smart and driven. A little tough but always sweet," she said, her eyes prickling. "I don't think I've ever been so in awe of someone. I just wish it was easier."

She blushed like she'd unloaded at a sleepover, half expecting girlish shrieks and a pillow fight to follow. Scottie instead took one hand from the wheel and squeezed her shoulder. "I hope I get to meet her one day."

"Me too." Beck's heart pattered with hope, clinging to her brother's optimism, the kindest Christmas gift he could have given her.

When they got to the airport and said goodbye in the snow, she squeezed him a little tighter. "Thanks for driving me. I'm sorry you have to go to work so soon."

"Oh, I don't have to work. I just wanted to have you to myself." Scottie grinned.

"How did I get so lucky in the little brother department?"

"Come on, you were always my hero, Caro. You were the one who stuck up for me. Remember, you bit that kid when he stole Teddy? He was twice as big as you."

She chuckled. "If you hadn't carried that bear around until you were eight, I wouldn't have spent elementary school as your personal bodyguard."

"Well, it's my turn to have your back."

Beck hugged him before he finished speaking. "Thank you."

"I want you to be happy," Scottie said when they parted. "I love you."

"I love you too."

She hung on to his kindness as the plane coasted down the runway. The flight after Christmas always felt like more than just travel, but like airborne transformation. Beck took off with one name and landed with another, took off from family and landed without kin, and now for the first time took off lonely to land in reach of love.

Dusk greeted her outside PDX, the air so cutting it burned, but she hardly processed it when she spotted Jordan on the curb. The coach waved and Beck's mouth fell open. She almost didn't recognize her in street clothes and a stocking cap, but her bright eyes welcomed her like a home she'd always known. Beck abandoned her suitcase, ran the few strides between them, and launched herself into Jordan's arms.

"You have no idea how glad I am to see you," she said into Jordan's thick coat.

"I missed you." Jordan's lips pressed to the top of Beck's head, her raspy voice dissolving the remainder of her hometown blues.

Beck inhaled the chill from Jordan's chest, wishing she could become small enough to disappear inside her. "Did you have a good Christmas?" Beck asked.

"Yeah." Jordan smiled. "You?"

Beck nodded. She didn't intend to tell Jordan about her half confession. Not with Philly long behind her, transforming her back to the Beck she liked best. She traced Jordan's face, pleased to find the bruises fading yellow.

"It's healing," she said, melting at the way Jordan leaned into her touch. "I thought you'd be tied up with practice."

"I gave the guys an extra day off. I thought I'd take a little break of my own," Jordan said. "If you'll have me."

Beck's pulse skipped. "Of course."

Jordan moved in to kiss her when she abruptly stopped. She stared up at the clouds and Beck did the same. "Looks like you brought something back from Philly."

Sparse, tiny snowflakes drifted from the sky, landing on Jordan's eyelashes and amused cheeks. Snow wasn't common in the city, but the novelty didn't entrance Beck. Instead, her gaze stayed on Jordan in the white winter drift, certain that even with the holiday behind them, this was how she'd always remember Christmas.

CHAPTER TWENTY-THREE

"And welcome back to *Fast Break*. If you're just joining us, we're recapping the whirlwind month of January college basketball and assessing where the chips have landed with less than a month until the national tournament."

Beck would never tire of the anchor desk. The quickness and showmanship suited her better than beat reporting. She welcomed the camera like a friend and sparred with her co-host like she was back at the family dinner table, unafraid and unfiltered.

"Well, Beck, a lot can happen in a month. We know that firsthand. But one storyline we've kept an eye on is the David Douglas Bulldogs. They've somehow, against all odds, clung to a top-ten ranking nationally, they're first in their conference, and tied the school record for longest win streak before suffering just their second loss of the regular season a week ago," Easton said. "So, on paper, they look like a threat."

"*Are* a threat," Beck said.

Offending and correcting Easton might as well have been written into her contract. As predicted, their antagonistic relationship enthralled viewers. They tried to play it chummy at first, but it usually spiraled into bickering. Even their promotional shoot captured the hostility. When the photographer gave up on getting them to stand together and smile, marketing embraced a different approach. The billboards and advertisements portrayed them as battling foes on the basketball court, Beck blocking Easton's shot at the rim.

Easton leaned back in his chair, prepared to lure her into another debate. "Right. But it brings us back to the one blemish they face every year—strength of schedule," he said.

"And every year, I remind you they're a mid-major. Their conference simply doesn't have the firepower of other D1 conferences."

"Which begs the question, can a mid-major win a national title?"

"Is this a trivia question?" she asked.

"Do you know the answer?"

"UNLV 1990—they were part of the Big West Conference," Beck said. "Is that the best you can do?"

Easton rolled his eyes. "I'm not trying to single the Bulldogs out, but their best competition in the Pacific Coast Conference is Vardell, and they haven't cracked the top twenty nationally."

"The Bulldogs rely on the preseason for strength of schedule. They faced multiple top-ten teams before the regular season started. They beat Duke, Kansas, and UCLA. The losses to Baylor and Virginia were close, and those two are considered favorites for the title."

"Yes, they played some great competition earlier this year, but with one important caveat: Royce Ortega was still their head coach. Jordan D'Amato hasn't been at the helm for that level of competition."

"But she was still there coaching. She didn't have a paper bag over her eyes."

"I'm sure some of our viewers would say the paper bag is still there."

"Some of our viewers also believe in lizard people," Beck said.

Easton smiled smugly. "My point is those wins are tallied in the Ortega column. We haven't seen D'Amato tested."

"I think you underestimate her contributions under Ortega. And Ortega isn't God. I mean, he's getting a real wake-up call in Seattle right now."

"We're not talking about Ortega, Beck."

"Nick, can we get a replay of Easton bringing up Royce Ortega exactly one minute ago?" She tapped her earpiece for effect, smirking at the laughter echoing from the control room. "The point is that this is D'Amato's team too. That first year as an assistant, she was the one who observed practice from the greats like Kerr, D'Antoni, and Popovich. She spent a summer in Italy studying the league there and came back to write the playbook. And she's had a major hand in player development too. She recruited and championed Brooks McCray when Ortega wanted to bench h-him." Beck choked on the last word as she remembered these details didn't come from soundbites or interviews. This information came from the comfort of the bedroom. She cleared her throat. "Anyway, it's not like D'Amato wasn't there or didn't have a hand in the team's success before. That's like saying I just wandered off the street and became your co-anchor with no reporting experience."

"Well, you said it first, Beck, but I'm glad you brought it up," Easton said. "Because some days it feels like that's true."

"Must be the days that you don't look at our phenomenal ratings." Beck grinned, despite clenching a fist beneath the desk.

"Oh, and look at that. We are out of time. I think this is the tenth straight episode of us not agreeing on anything."

"But day eleven of you not trying to run me over with your car in the NWSN parking lot. Baby steps."

"For the record, it was late, and your dress was very dark," Easton said before squaring his shoulders to the camera. "For *Fast Break*, I'm Easton Prescott."

"And I'm Caroline Beck. Have a great night."

They waited with rigid smiles and exhaled when the "On Air" light turned off.

"Good show," Beck said, pulling her earpiece out.

"You too. I thought I might get you with the UNLV question." Easton scrolled through his phone. They'd made at least some headway at being cordial. Hatred was exhausting, especially when partially performative. They had a truce, of sorts. Some necessary downtime to recover when they weren't rolling. "How'd you know all that about D'Amato?"

Beck shrugged. "Just from our interview. It didn't make the cut for air."

"Right." Easton narrowed his brow. "Also, maybe don't tell people I tried to run you over."

"I mean, you revved your engine, squealed your tires, and then rolled down your window after I jumped out of the way to say, *'Oh damn, I missed.'* It just felt kind of intentional, you know?"

"I was only trying to scare you." Easton unbuttoned his collar.

Beck gathered her things to leave the studio. "Do you think that maybe you're a sociopath?"

"Maybe."

"You know, you can get a diagnosis. I'm sure it's covered by our health insurance."

"Great. But only if when I'm done, you get diagnosed as a narcissist."

"Deal," Beck said over her shoulder. "Let's have the cameras follow us. I can pitch it to Nick."

"I'm game," he called after her.

For all the success and thrill of work, Beck stopped short of being fulfilled thanks to one missing piece. Anchoring *Fast Break* during weekdays cut her time at David Douglas in half. She attended home games but rarely afforded appearances at practices or media availability, which wouldn't have mattered to her if those opportunities didn't include Jordan.

Over the last month, they'd made it work as painlessly as possible. Jordan's coaching and recruiting schedule left little time, but they settled for scraps. Phone calls, texts, and the shuttle back and forth. In the past, it would've been enough of an inconvenience for Beck to call it quits almost immediately. But the promise of Jordan, the anticipation between each rendezvous, minimized that doubt.

More important than the promise of their next meeting was a promise they never spoke of; the promise that they were both achieving something great thanks to the game they loved. An opportunity they wouldn't steal from the other, but one they risked with each kiss and secret meeting. A dangerous game within the game that they both intended to win.

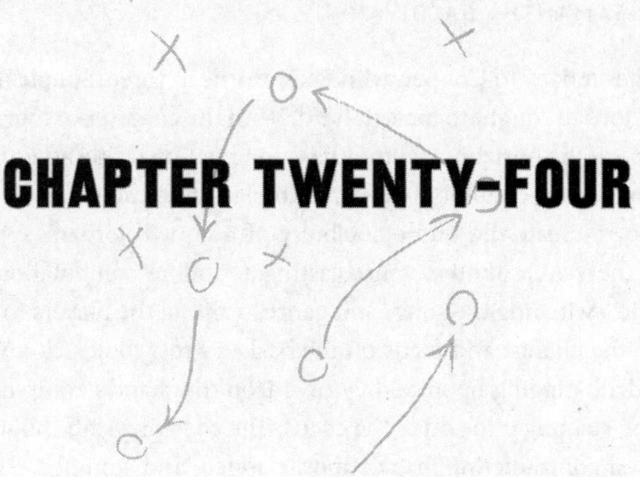

CHAPTER TWENTY-FOUR

Metallica, Vivaldi, George Strait, Bocelli, and Black Sabbath blasted out of the arena speakers at varying, unpredictable intervals in Jordan's latest coaching scheme. When Maria Callas's soprano echoed from the rafters, the team collectively groaned.

"This is cruel and unusual punishment!" Leon whined.

"This isn't punishment, Torres. We are preparing you for distraction," Jordan said. "Now, let's do it again! Cooper's Play, run it!"

She pivoted to the freshman, who gulped from the other end of the court. She devised "Cooper's Play" after the shooting guard lost his nerve, passing his open three-pointer to Charlie in double coverage, resulting in the Bulldogs' second loss of the season. Fortunately, Mark didn't fire Jordan after, but she spent the entire flight back from the road game on edge, prepared to be terminated. When that didn't happen, she resolved to turn Cooper Sloane's weakness into a strength.

Cooper's Play was simple. An inbound from Brooks to Cooper, Cooper back to Brooks to take it to the top of the key, Brooks pitches it back to Cooper, who takes the deep three. Simple. Except Jordan sought to make it hard. With the conference tournament on the horizon, and the chase for a national title after that, she needed the Bulldogs prepared to play under pressure.

To re-create the unpredictability of a crowd, Jordan tapped into the WAC sound system, blasting a random combination of music, switching the songs and genre, training the players to ignore the change and focus on the basket. Frost took sick joy in the drill, digging up an old cymbal from the band's equipment room, striking it to add to the chaos. The coaching staff shouted, barked contradicting instructions, clapped, and stomped. Anything that might throw Cooper off his game. If that wasn't enough pressure, the team depended on his success. For every missed shot, the guys ran sprints while Cooper watched.

Jordan could admit it might have been a touch excessive.

As Brooks pitched the ball to Cooper, Frost beat the cymbal mercilessly, and Jordan changed the music to shrieking death metal that had the rest of the team covering their ears. Cooper winced as he took the shot behind the three-point line. His sweat-beaded baby face crumpled when it shanked off the rim.

"On the baseline!" Jordan shouted.

"Sorry, guys." Cooper frowned.

Dominic clapped his shoulder as he passed. "You got the next one."

Frost blew the whistle, and the team charged through sprints while Cooper watched. Jordan sidled up next to him. "What are you thinking about when you take the shot?"

"Of making it," Cooper said with hands on his hips.

"Sorry, I mean, what are you feeling?" Jordan asked. Cooper shrugged, avoiding her eyes. "The reason I chose you for this play, Coop, is because I know you can make the shot. I saw you make it time and time again during your high school career. Everyone knew they were screwed when you had the ball out deep."

Cooper smirked. "Yeah."

"You weren't afraid. When they put more people on you, you just took the shot from further out." Jordan patted his back as the team finished their sprints. "I want you to feel like you're on the high school court, no fear, no worries. Don't think about it going in, focus on feeling like it already has. Do you know what I'm trying to say?"

"Yes, Coach."

"Again!" Jordan stepped back as the music flipped to an up-tempo jazz drum solo, a cacophony of snares and kick drums and cymbals, which Frost added to, and Leon scowled at.

"Interesting tactic," Mark Fellner said behind her.

She jumped at his sly arrival, brow furrowing. The athletic director had stopped lurking at practices, but his presence never inspired confidence. "What's up, Mark?"

"I thought I'd see how things are going."

The team exploded with cheers as Cooper sank a perfect three-pointer. "Yes, Coop! Yes! Run it again!" Jordan yelled. She shifted back to Mark. "Things are good. Unless you're about to tell me otherwise."

Mark crossed his arms, his ever-grim face sagging lower. "I'm getting intel that Hunter Garrick and his family have been meeting with other programs."

Jordan sighed. "I've been trying to get down there for a visit, but every time I call, his dad stonewalls me. Says it isn't a good time."

"Well, I think you best find a way to make it happen. And fast." Mark narrowed his gaze. "This recruiting issue isn't something we can take lightly, Jordan. The boosters are concerned. I'm trying to keep them calm, but if we lose Garrick, I don't know how much I can do."

"Don't worry yourself, Mark. You've been nothing but helpful," Jordan muttered.

He shook his head. "You can paint me as the bad guy, but I'm looking out for the future of this team," he said over the roar of another successful three-pointer from Cooper.

Jordan bit her tongue, the looming pressure returning, identical to that of her first weeks on the job. "I'll do everything I can to retain Garrick's verbal commitment," she said. "You have my word."

"Good." Mark clenched his jaw before stalking off. "And turn down the music."

Jordan smiled and turned it up louder, skipping to a track that spurred the players into a dance-off. Mark pivoted at the door and glared. She shrugged back in defiance, but inside she shrank.

XOXO

The recruiting difficulties and Mark's veiled threat of termination typically would've consumed Jordan's night, had her begging the Garricks for a meeting, lying on her office floor and scheming to make it right. Instead, she left a message for the family after practice and returned home, because she was no longer typical Jordan. No longer single Jordan. Though even in relationships of the past, she hadn't been this Jordan either.

This Jordan battled a hissing skillet, her rarely used kitchen a mess of sauce, herbs, and meat. This Jordan squinted through recipes as though searching a defensive scheme for holes, which she found much easier than browning and searing. This Jordan counted the minutes until Beck arrived, chest aflutter despite a month of seeing the reporter in secret.

"Since when do you cook?" Beck asked, entering with her own key.

"All the time." Jordan left the stove to meet her.

Beck chuckled and pecked at her lips. "No, you don't."

"How do you know?"

Beck hopped on one of the few clean areas of the counter, sitting there like she belonged. Like it was her home too. "I know because you don't think about anything other than basketball."

Jordan slid over to meet her, rooted between her parted knees. "Basketball and you." She rested her hands on the counter, hedging Beck in. "I wanted to do something nice."

"Thank you. I love . . ." Beck flushed and cleared her throat. "I love that you did that."

Jordan's mouth quirked to the side, her pulse sputtering at that single word. The one they still hadn't said to each other. Not yet. "Well, I love doing it."

Beck wrapped her arms around Jordan's neck. "Really? You love cooking?"

"Yes. Can't get enough."

"What are you making?"

Jordan traced Beck's thighs. "Spaghetti and meatballs. You said you liked Italian."

"I was mostly referring to you." Beck smirked. "This is pretty ambitious."

Beck cupped the sides of Jordan's head and snaked fingers through her hair. The light scratch along her temples, the caress of hands, relieved the leftover anxiety Jordan harbored from the day. "I'm very, very ambitious."

She leaned in and kissed her. Beck squeezed her thighs around Jordan's hips, dragged her tongue in a tease of what else she might conquer with it. Jordan hooked her arms around Beck's waist and lifted her from the counter.

"Hey, Jordan," she panted.

"Hmm?"

"It's burning."

Jordan jerked her head up from Beck's neck and promptly set her down. "No, it's not. Well, maybe. It's normal to smell like that, right?"

Beck winced. "I don't think so."

The boiling pasta water sloshed out of its pot, sizzling as it hit the burner. Jordan scrambled to turn down the heat when the smoke alarm blared above. "Shit." She yanked her sorry excuse for meatballs from the oven. Smoke effused from the charred pieces. "Damn it."

Beck snorted while she waved a towel beneath the smoke alarm until it stopped screeching. She settled beside Jordan, who hovered over the ruined dinner.

"It was a good effort. You'll get the next one."

Jordan turned to her. "Please tell me you're better at this. Do you know how to cook?"

"No. I'm afraid we might be a takeout couple."

"I suppose there are worse things." Jordan grabbed two beers from the fridge and handed one to Beck.

"How was work?" Beck asked.

The question stopped her mid-drink. "Good."

"That didn't sound convincing."

"Everything's fine. What do you think about Chinese?" Jordan turned away and checked her phone. Still nothing from Hunter Garrick. She sighed. She wanted to tell Beck but worried it might be too tempting. Worried that while sleeping together and tiptoeing toward the next step, Jordan faced a reporter in her kitchen. She wanted to trust Beck and, for the most part, did trust Beck. But it also wouldn't be the first time that what she said to her in private made its way into the public sphere.

"Thinking of a career change I don't know about?" Beck asked.

Jordan looked up from her phone. "What?"

"Studying for the MCAT?" She lifted a thick study guide from the edge of the counter.

"Oh no." Jordan shook her head. "Charlie is, though."

"Are you going to take it for him too?"

"No. I've just been helping him prepare a little."

"Do most coaches do that?"

Jordan squinted at her. "I don't know. Does it matter?"

"You just do a lot for them off the court. You take any call or problem. Extra one-on-one sessions, studying." Beck shrugged. "It's just hard to share you sometimes."

"They need me. And they're not just my team. They're family too."

"Right."

Jordan chewed her lip. While she wasn't staying at the gym until midnight anymore, she couldn't deny the game snuck up even with Beck. She left the bed more than once to take phone calls at night, woke up before dawn to train with Leon, and postponed meeting with Beck in favor of easing Brooks's fears. It had never seemed like a problem before. But now, with someone besides the team needing and wanting her, she encountered a rare inkling of guilt.

"It's not like you're much easier to pin down." Jordan cleared her throat. "Speaking of, I caught the show yesterday. Interesting insight you had on me."

Beck's face fell. "Sorry." She looked down at the floor. "It just slipped out."

"It's okay," she said. In the grand scheme, it was innocent enough. "Just as long as nothing else slips out."

"Like what?"

Jordan eased into her, longing to return to their uncomplicated bubble. “Like my favorite postgame ritual.”

“Oh, would that be me?” Beck grinned at Jordan’s nod. “Well, that’s certainly not suitable for air. This little cooking incident, however . . .”

She scoffed. “I can hear the critics now—back in the kitchen where she belongs.”

Beck assessed the burnt scraps. “Well, you certainly don’t belong here. No offense.” She kissed her, then held her face, and launched her eyes into Jordan’s. “I’m sorry about the show. I’ll be more careful.”

“I’m sorry about dinner.”

“No, this was unexpectedly perfect.” Beck nestled into her, and the tension evaporated from Jordan’s shoulders. “I know you only had practice today, but now that you mention that postgame ritual . . .”

“It’s not just restricted to games, actually.”

“Good,” Beck whispered before slinking down the hall. “Why don’t you order that Chinese and I’ll meet you back here?”

She gulped and nodded as she checked her phone. No texts from the team. No texts from Hunter either. As she considered the takeout menus, she wondered if she could afford to let herself fully be *this* Jordan. Not simply the coach that belonged to the team, but the Jordan that belonged to Beck.

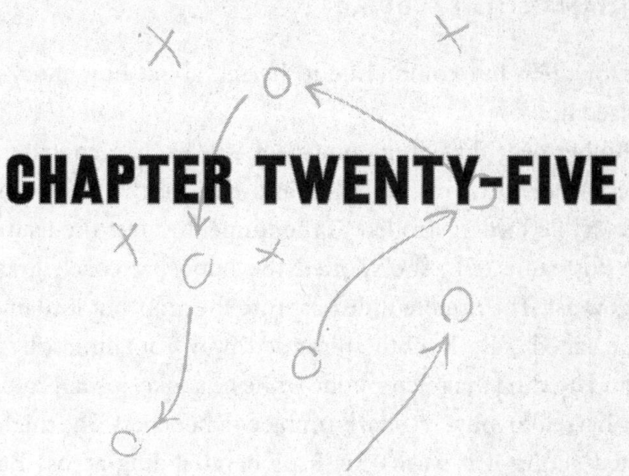

CHAPTER TWENTY-FIVE

The band fired up the school fight song after another Saturday night trouncing, trumpets and drums thundering across the WAC with the final buzzer. Jordan shook hands with Vardell's coaches and players, who slumped after the twenty-point loss. In a few weeks, the Bulldogs would chase their fourth straight conference title. While Jordan's future wasn't guaranteed, she knew her guys were locked in and primed to compete with anyone in the country.

Rather than dart off to avoid fans and the press, she lingered on the court. She smirked at Leon chatting up the cheerleaders, Brooks signing autographs, and the other players hugging their friends and families. She also discreetly observed Beck interviewing Vardell's aging head coach.

While Jordan swelled with pride, admiring her composure in front of the camera, tuning in to *Fast Break* nightly, she also sank with a shred of disappointment. Disappointment at not being able to embrace Beck after a victory like the other coaches did with their wives or families. She always knew this hurdle would exist for them but couldn't lie to herself about how much she despised it.

Mulling over that disappointment was likely a contributing factor in her next misstep. That and Kip Keating's wandering hand. While Jordan strolled to the tunnel to meet the team for their postgame talk, she spotted the opposing coach grazing Beck's waist. The camera didn't capture the grab, but Jordan did.

She halted as Beck subtly shimmied away from him, still smiling, and holding the microphone while he spoke. Jordan couldn't bring herself to move. A snarl rumbled in her chest. She might've resisted acting if it wasn't for Kip's hand sliding across Beck's back a second time.

Jordan waited for the interview to end before stalking over.

"Thanks, Coach." Beck nodded at him.

"Always a pleasure." He winked and caressed her shoulder as Jordan arrived.

"Really, Kip?" Jordan kept her voice low but had half a mind to publicly embarrass him.

His mouth fell open. "What?"

"I saw that. You need to watch your hands."

"Please don't," Beck muttered.

"What the hell is wrong with you, D'Amato?" Kip glared.

"You can't touch her like that." Jordan inched up to meet him when a hand pressed her chest.

"Jordan, stop it." Beck nudged her back from Kip and put herself between them.

"But—"

"Go. Now." Beck glared so severely that it took her aback. It was enough to make clear that she wasn't mad at Kip; she was pissed at Jordan. Her cameraman, Todd, gaped, and Kip folded his arms across his chest. Jordan turned away to avoid additional attention or more of Beck's wrath, grinding her teeth when she heard the reporter syrupy sweet behind her. "I'm so sorry about that, Coach. Have a good night."

"What the hell was that about?" Frost ran to catch her in the tunnel.

"Nothing."

"What did you say to Keating?" he asked. Jordan shook her head, neck smoldering. "Does this have something to do with, you know?"

"With what?" Jordan reddened when he raised an eyebrow in response. She plowed into the locker room, hissing over her shoulder in futility, "It was nothing."

XOXO

An hour later, Jordan paced her office, twisting her necklace. Beck spent the press conference staring daggers at her, and she didn't know if it would be better or worse if they met for their postgame rendezvous. So, she hid out at the arena rather than go home, not expecting the pending fight to find her anyway.

"What is wrong with you?"

Jordan looked up from her desk, eyes bulging at Beck standing in the doorway. "What are you doing here?" She scrambled to pull her inside and lock the door.

"Are you out of your mind?" Beck asked.

"Are you?"

"You can't *ever* do what you did tonight."

"I'm sorry, okay? I'm sorry." Jordan surrendered, flinching at Beck's rage. "I shouldn't have drawn attention to us like that."

"That's not the problem, Jordan! I mean, it is a problem, but that's not the main problem! I can take care of myself. Do you understand me?"

"But the way he grabbed you—"

"Do you think that's the worst I've dealt with from guys like him?" Beck's jaw clenched. "I don't need a protector. I can handle myself and I can handle what comes with the job."

"Well, I don't like that asshole coaches or players can grope you whenever they please." Just saying it reawakened Jordan's rage, her hands clenching in fists that she would've happily slugged at Kip or anyone who dared to make a pass at Beck.

"That's such an exaggeration!"

"I don't care! I don't like it!"

"Too bad!" Beck's chest nearly puffed into hers. "I don't care if you like it, you don't get to put your nose in my business or make me look weak like that in front of sources or my co-workers! And if you can't handle that, then maybe you can't handle me."

"Don't tell me what I can't handle." Jordan gritted her teeth.

"Oh, you mean like you did to me tonight?"

"It's not the same."

"Why not?"

"Because you're mine!" Jordan huffed, bringing herself down to a simmer. "I know you can handle yourself. And I'm sorry. I messed up. I just can't bear to see anyone touch you like that. Because I want you to be mine. For real. Not just in secret."

Beck instantly shed her scowl. "I am yours, Jordan," she said so softly that Jordan strained to hear it.

Her tensed shoulders buckled. "I'm yours too," she whispered at the floor. "Sometimes I wish people knew, even though I understand why they can't."

"It's hard for me too." Beck squeezed her hand.

Jordan glanced up. "Really?"

She nodded, then folded into Jordan's chest. "I can't believe you did that. I forget you have a temper." Beck chuckled against her.

"I always knew you had one. I just never thought I'd be on the receiving end."

"Is this our first fight?"

"I guess so," Jordan said. "Also, how did you get in here?"

"I'm really good at my job." Beck pulled back from her. "And campus security is subpar. I'm a little concerned for your safety."

"I think you're the only crazy reporter I have to worry about sneaking back here."

"I better be."

Jordan bit her lip, dragged her gaze across Beck's. "Well, since you're here." She kissed her gently. "Maybe we could, you know . . . Something about being in my office—"

Beck's mouth dropped. "Oh, you think I'm going to forgive you that easily?"

"I was hoping so."

She shook her head. "You're going to have to earn it."

"How might I do that?" Jordan smiled.

Beck swiped a basketball from the sofa and thrust it at her. "Play me for it." She gathered her bag at the door. "I'll see you on the court."

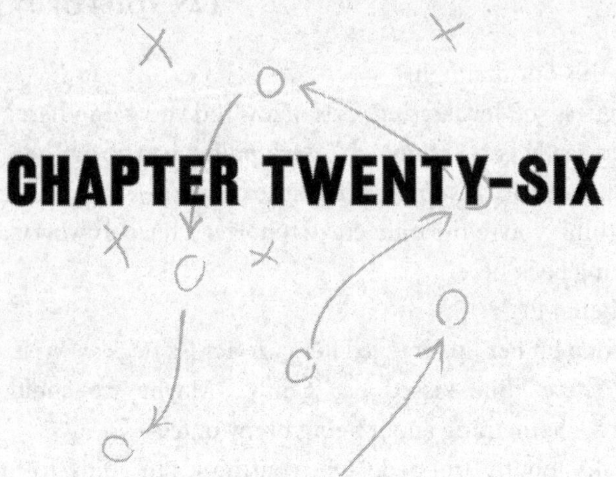

CHAPTER TWENTY-SIX

It was getting serious. More serious than Beck expected. Not because she didn't want it, but because she'd never experienced it. Still, they avoided titles or references to a relationship. They never talked about what it meant or what came next.

They pretended the apartment key Jordan gave Beck was sensible. That Beck leaving clothes and a toothbrush was practical and Jordan clearing a drawer and buying new hangers the polite thing to do. They deemed the hours-long, nightly phone conversations natural, as if Beck prepping Jordan for interviews and updating her wardrobe wasn't suggestive of the girlfriend label.

They counted the nights that didn't amount to sex in that same "just seeing each other" category. Like the night Beck fell ill—rather than driving home feverish as she would've with anyone else, averse to leaving herself vulnerable, she let Jordan take her keys. She obeyed when she said, "Let me take care of you." And when Jordan sniffled with the same cold on the sidelines a few days later, Beck didn't just pretend to not notice. She pretended that willingly sharing germs wasn't among the intimate, revolting signs of a relationship that she usually steered clear of.

They didn't use the words "partner" or "girlfriend" to each other and certainly not around anyone else, but it was there beneath the rest. While Beck didn't mind it—in fact, she cherished Jordan and wanted more—it presented one problem. That problem being that the closer they got, the more they risked. More weaknesses and lapses in judgment. The kind that had Jordan ready to punch Kip Keating. The same one that had Beck sneaking into Jordan's office.

The stakes were getting higher and the game more dangerous. Rather than turn away, however, Beck suited up. Because while partner and girlfriend lurked beneath the surface, so did a more blinding weakness they also pretended didn't exist. Love.

"Coast is clear. The janitorial staff went home, and I locked the doors," Jordan said as Beck stepped onto the court.

She furrowed her brow. The typically abrasive arena lights glowed a gentle gold, the same hue of candles at night. A mellow ballad droned from the speakers. "What's this? Mood lighting and music?"

Jordan grinned as Beck joined her at midcourt. "Dominic showed me how to hack the sound system so we could practice a new play."

"Is the play to seduce the other team?"

"No." Jordan's raspy laugh made her smile. "It's called Cooper's Play. Here, I can show you." She dribbled to the baseline like a kid excited for show-and-tell. "You be Brooks. I'm Coop."

Beck played along as Jordan walked her through the play, chattering about each nuance and move. The coach's eagerness lightened Beck, especially as she called for the last pass.

"Then Coop takes the three." Jordan sank a shot from behind the arc. "And the crowd goes wild!" She threw up her arms to the whoosh of fake cheers.

Beck laughed. "I can imagine the call now." She lowered an

octave to her broadcaster's voice. "There's the pass to Sloane . . . puts it up . . . Yes!"

"What is that?" Jordan wrapped her arms around Beck's waist.

"Kentucky and Duke for the Final Four, 1992. Verne Lundquist on the call for the buzzer beater. Instant classic."

"I love when you speak in basketball trivia." Jordan kissed her cheek, then grazed her lips down Beck's neck.

She sighed and fought the urge to melt into her. "Hey, you're still in the doghouse." Beck backed away. "I didn't suit up for nothing."

"Okay, what are we playing?"

"How about a little one-on-one? First to twenty-one wins."

"You sure?"

Beck bounced the ball to her. Jordan checked it back. After setting her feet with a single dribble, Beck lofted a basket and posed with her shooting hand in midair. "1–0."

Jordan pulled off her sweatshirt and tossed it aside. "Okay, I see you."

"It's a lot easier when I'm not wearing a dress." Beck sported running tights, tennis shoes, and a David Douglas shirt she'd stolen from Jordan. While she played in a lower division of competition during college, she intended to give the coach a run for her money. She checked the ball again. This time Jordan crouched into a defensive stance and swiped at Beck's dribble. Beck pump faked, spun around her, then finished with a layup. "2–0. You better not be taking it easy on me, D'Amato."

"I wouldn't dare." Jordan crooked her mouth to the side. "You just forget I'm older and slower than you."

"Excuses, excuses."

The game plugged along in easy rhythm. Jordan inevitably made a comeback, effortlessly blocking Beck's attempts, showing off with behind-the-back dribbling, fadeaways, and hook shots.

Beck reveled in challenging her, sweating, swiping, nudging. The game broke up for kisses and laughter, then devolved into joking, pulled shirts, Beck jumping on Jordan's back to stop her. In return, Jordan faked knee pain to freeze her and sneak a basket.

Beck didn't just love playing but also the chance to forget everything tugging at them from the outside. A rare interlude where they weren't reporter and coach, but simply Beck and Jordan.

"Okay, game point." Jordan wiped her brow.

Beck checked the ball to her, bent her knees into a defensive position. Jordan expertly dribbled, bobbed her head, faked a shoulder, and powered past. Before she could completely slip away, Beck cut in and hip checked her, knocking the ball loose.

"Foul!" Jordan chuckled. "Foul! Cheater!"

Beck scooped up the ball but never had a chance for a shot as Jordan picked her up and spun her away from the basket. She playfully flailed, called for her own foul as Jordan carried her away. Beck tripped backward when Jordan set her down, and they tumbled to the court, heaving and snorting as the ball rolled away.

"Okay, okay, I surrender." Jordan breathed through laughter.

Beck rolled onto her and playfully kissed her for the nonexistent crowd. When she pulled away, Jordan firmly drew her back. She buried fingers into her hair as she suckled her lower lip, tongue filling Beck's mouth so that her placated sigh stayed trapped in her skipping chest.

"Am I forgiven?" Jordan whispered when they broke for a breath of humid air.

Beck bit her lip and nodded as she traced a finger down Jordan's cheek. "I think there's one more thing you might have to do for me."

Jordan's face lit up with a smile that reached her twinkling gaze. She ghosted her hands down the small of Beck's back, moving to bring her closer, when her phone buzzed. Beck groaned as Jordan fumbled away from her to reach it. "Can you just ignore it?"

Jordan didn't look up while she texted. "Dom jammed his fingers tonight. Just want to make sure he's been icing—"

"Isn't that what the medical staff is for? Let Sidney handle it."

Jordan finished texting and set her phone aside in surrender. "I'm done, okay? See?" She lay back down next to her.

Beck shook her head. "You need boundaries. They can't text or call for every little thing. They depend on you too much." She paused, considering what she'd suspected for the last month. That Jordan clung to the team to unconsciously keep distance between them. A wall Beck couldn't breach. "Or maybe vice versa."

"Hey, come on. I'm sorry." Jordan pulled her back to her chest and pecked the side of her head. "It'll be easier once the season's over. I'll be able to make more time outside of recruiting and summer workouts."

Beck's ears perked up. While they needed to finish their talk about boundaries and Jordan's overcommitment, her own equal obsession with work won out. "How is recruiting going, by the way?"

"I don't know if I can say."

"Oh, come on. I know as much as everyone else. You've lost a few big ones, but Hunter Garrick is still on the hook with a verbal commitment—right?"

"Yeah, I mean, that's pretty much it."

"You can trust me."

"Can I?"

Beck shot up. "What does that mean?"

“I mean, there was the whole Charlie story.” Jordan sat up next to her.

“That was a fluff piece.” She rolled her eyes. The short profile of the senior focused on his medical school aspirations. Beck even interviewed his parents—Dr. Charles Washington Jr. and Dr. Naomi Washington—about what it meant for their son to become a third-generation doctor while juggling his commitments as a basketball player. “Honestly, Molly should thank me for the story. It’s nothing but positive press.”

“Right, but it was based on a tip you got from me.”

“It wasn’t much of a tip.” Beck scoffed. “Charlie’s major is listed as premed on the roster. Anyone can look it up.”

“You just didn’t happen to until I mentioned he was taking the MCAT last week.”

Beck’s stomach hardened. The interlude had ended. No more Beck and Jordan. They were once again reporter and coach.

“What are you getting at?”

“I don’t know.” Jordan shook her head. “It’s stupid. I guess I wanted to make sure you’re not just doing this with me for a story.”

“Really?”

“Well, you’re asking me about recruiting, and you know I can’t talk to the media about that right now,” Jordan said. “You don’t think I want to tell you? You don’t think I want to tell you all the ins and outs, the stress, or how I’m still scared for my job? That I don’t want to say off the record to the one person I want to tell everything to?”

“Well, I’m sorry that you decided to sleep with a reporter. I think I’m more insulted that you think I’m trading what we have for cheap tips. And that you apparently can’t trust me.” Beck stood and Jordan scrambled up to meet her.

The subtle guilt that always tormented Beck, the fear that she was doing something wrong to get ahead, needled her. But it was never to get ahead. If anything, Jordan was a risk to her career. An unavoidable by-product of her heart.

"Please, I'm saying this wrong. I do trust you." Jordan scrubbed a hand down her face. "You want the truth? Recruiting is a concern. It's not going great. I have a meeting with Hunter and his family, but I don't know if he wants to play for me. I don't know if anyone wants to play for me."

Beck's heart thundered. For as offended as she was by Jordan suggesting she used her for stories, now she struggled to not prove her right. Part of her sympathized, but another part of her was absolutely electrified, blood pumping at the prospect of an inside scoop.

"I know I don't have to ask you to not share that," Jordan said. "I'm sorry for what I said about Charlie. For the shit I pulled with Kip. I trust you to handle yourself *and* us."

Beck accepted Jordan's hug, the woman's head dropping meekly to her shoulder. Despite her misgivings, Beck rubbed her back, staring off with her thoughts in a tangle. As much as she adored and was growing to love Jordan, she didn't know how the hell she was going to sit on this story.

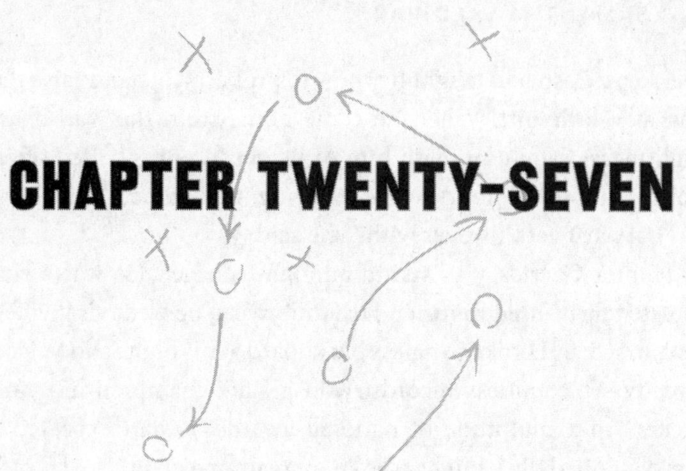

CHAPTER TWENTY-SEVEN

As if Hunter Garrick's home visit didn't carry enough weight, it brought Jordan flashbacks of a childhood best forgotten. The homegrown talent hailed from southern Oregon, a region substantially more rural than its northern counterparts. The modest downtown gave way to sprawling fields that stretched until they reached emerald hills. Jordan and Frost drove into the countryside, until the asphalt turned to gravel and then to dirt, the car dipping and kicking up dust until they found a mailbox labeled GARRICK.

Despite their living in the middle of nowhere, the Garrick property included vast, cow-dotted acreage, a horse stable, and a mansion complete with several luxury SUVs, a boat, a guesthouse, and a full basketball court. Jordan's eyes widened. "So much for simple living."

Frost gulped at the towering flagpole in the middle of the driveway. An enormous American flag, a Marine Corps flag, and finally a Gadsden "Don't Tread on Me" flag flapped in the wind. "Are we safe out here?" he murmured.

Jordan shivered at the display, reminiscent of the one her father kept. Cash had taught her how to properly fold and raise the flag as a little girl. When he came home from the war, if his nightmares caught up with him or he got too drunk, he'd often hoist it in the wee hours of the morning, waking her for help.

"Let's just get this over with," she said.

Hunter Garrick was a kind enough teenager. He was a six-foot-ten farm-bred monster. His junior year, he went viral when he dunked and broke the glass backboard at his high school. He'd already set countless records, won a state championship, and racked up a multitude of national awards. Jordan expected a cocky, spoiled diva, but he was an unassuming giant. No, Hunter Garrick absolutely wasn't the problem. It was his parents that made Jordan wary.

"David Douglas University. It's kind of a liberal hippie school, isn't it?" Randy Garrick asked. He was large, though not as large as his son, with a thick beard and lumbering cadence.

Jordan and Frost sat on the couch opposite him in a living room that resembled a hunting lodge. "I think most college campuses maintain a culture of free self-expression." Jordan flashed a disingenuous smile. She didn't know how Royce made recruiting visits seem so easy. She'd joined him on many of the trips but never mastered his charisma or sales tactics.

"Well, the world is changing, isn't it? I mean, we have women coaches now. Isn't that something?" Randy asked. Jordan guessed he didn't consider it a welcome change.

"What does your husband think of you coaching?" Melanie Garrick had scarcely said two sentences since bringing out a tray of iced tea, but this piqued her interest.

Jordan shook her head. "Oh, no, ma'am, I'm not married."

"And there certainly won't be a husband in the picture, will there?" Randy asked as he swirled his glass, clinking ice. "I saw your interview on NWSN."

Jordan's jaw tightened. She fought the instinct to hide within herself. The insecurity and fear from adolescence crawled out of her chest as if always lying in wait for a moment like this. A moment with a man as demeaning and bigoted as her father.

"Dad, come on." Hunter's pale cheeks reddened.

"What?" Randy threw his hands in the air. "I want to make sure my boy gets the best. The best team, the best school, the best coach. That's what he deserves."

"I completely agree with you," Jordan said, though it scalded her tongue.

"That's why we're here," Frost added.

"I have to ask you." Randy leaned back, addressing Frost. "Why didn't they make you head coach?"

"Me?" Frost raised his eyebrows. "Well, sir, because Jordan is one of the sharpest minds in college basketball. There's no one I trust more to do the job. This season speaks for itself—and we're just getting started."

Jordan smiled at Frost, not only for his support, but his convincing delivery. She was ready to name him director of recruiting right then and there.

Randy cleared his throat. "And the players and parents feel the same way?"

"What do you mean?" Jordan asked.

"Well, it's just an odd decision, don't you agree? I don't see any other women head coaches on the men's side, and that's probably for a reason."

"We don't make decisions based on gender, race, religion, or sexuality at David Douglas University. Though that should be the standard everywhere, don't you agree?"

"What are you trying to say?"

"I'm trying to say that I can't change who I am. Yes, I'm a woman. And yes, as you've already alluded to, I am a lesbian."

Jordan nearly rolled her eyes at Melanie's gasp. "But what matters right now, for Hunter, is that there's nothing I'm more dedicated to than my team. And there is nothing I care more about than winning. Except ensuring that the young men I coach go on to succeed at life, whether that takes them to the NBA or a profession off the court."

Randy folded his arms across his chest. Jordan struggled to maintain eye contact with him, mostly because she struggled to not imagine Cash. To not shake like the teenager he whipped when he found her in bed with her girlfriend. The same teenager he hit when she told him she wouldn't and couldn't change. That she wasn't afraid of him or God.

She shifted her focus to Hunter, who sat between his parents. "This season we're going to win the conference title. After that, we're going all the way. We're going to go further than this school has ever gone in the national tournament. Next year when you come to play for me, Hunter, we're going to do it again. And again, and again, until we cut down that net and bring back a national championship." Jordan rubbed her hands together. "I'm not naïve. I know you've been talking to other schools. I get it. You all have to make the best decision for Hunter's future. I just hope you don't choose those other teams because you don't want your son to be coached by a woman. You should choose the best program, where he can grow and achieve greatness. I believe, I know, that place is with me and Frost at David Douglas."

The living room dropped into dead air. Jordan didn't move, though sweat pooled beneath her shirt. She squeezed her hands, hiding just how badly they shook. Hunter gulped and shifted to stare at the floor, and Jordan knew that she'd already lost him.

"That's quite the little speech," Randy finally said. "But the truth is, we can't sign with you." He stroked his beard. "I want my son coached by a man who's played in the NBA. I want my son to learn to be a powerful man from powerful men. You understand? While I appreciate your passion, we invited you here as a courtesy, to let you know that we're going to pull Hunter's verbal commitment if another school can make a competitive offer."

"I think that would be a major mistake." Jordan's throat wrenched around her words.

"Well, having him play for you is a risk I just can't let my son take." Randy stood and offered her a handshake. "Good luck with the rest of your season."

"Thank you." Jordan shook his hand, wishing to spit in it instead.

Frost and Jordan spent the first ten minutes of the drive back in silence. She didn't know if she was more shocked, devastated, or enraged by Garrick's rejection. If she wasn't clinging to a pathetic shred of hope that Hunter might not back out, she would've screamed in Randy's face, would've torn him down just like he did to her.

"Did that really just happen?" she finally asked.

Frost nodded. "Yeah." He clenched the steering wheel and peered over at her. "I don't think he's coming."

"No shit," she said with a chuckle. She flopped her head back into her seat. "It seems right, though, you know? Like that's just our luck. Just our fucking luck."

When they returned to campus, Jordan turned down Frost's offer to grab a drink, hopped in her own car and hit the road north. It was late, and she didn't bother with a phone call, but Jordan only wanted to see Beck. She didn't care that it meant another hour in the car. In fact, she would've driven all night, even with the company of her anxieties mocking her the entire way.

Unfortunately, when she knocked on Beck's apartment door, she quickly came to regret her impulsiveness. Rather than find the woman she sought for comfort, she came face-to-face with a curly-haired man who gawked at her.

"Uh, hi." Jordan rubbed her neck as they stood on opposite sides of the doorway. "I'm looking for Beck."

He nodded, and a peculiar squeak escaped him.

"Is she here? I'm Jordan."

"I know, yeah, uh, she's here." He cleared his throat. "Beck! Beck, get out here!"

Jordan rocked on her toes. "You must be her roommate, the meteorologist. Kevin, right?"

"Kevin Weathers," he said as they shook hands.

"Weathers? Is that your real name?" she asked.

"All the greats have stage names. Rihanna. Lady Gaga. Drake."

"Right, but you're a weatherman."

Kevin's nostrils flared and Jordan cringed as he yelled louder into the apartment. "Beck!"

"I'm here. Stop screaming," she said from inside.

"You have a visitor." Kevin opened the door wider.

Jordan waved. "Hey. Sorry I didn't call."

Beck's usually welcoming gaze flickered dark. Much like Jordan misread and struck out with the Garricks, she now misjudged their relationship. She'd misjudged how serious of a secret she was and that they hadn't quite reached the point of spontaneity. It threw another stone down the expanding well in her gut.

Jordan pretended to examine the two-bedroom apartment despite her desire to flee. Mahogany floors, high ceilings, modern appliances, a vibrant couch, plants, and bohemian artwork. Even though Beck shared the space with Kevin, Jordan thought she detected Beck in the details. In the geometric rugs, in the collection of antique cameras, in the typewriter and bold vases, excess pillows and chunky blankets. Portland's skyline blinked across the river. Soft but bold, composed but colorful, everything just right. Just like Beck.

"I'm sorry again. I shouldn't have shown up like this."

"You don't have to keep apologizing." Beck handed her a mug of coffee and joined her on the couch. Kevin had awkwardly bowed out, mouthing an unsubtle *"What the fuck is going on?"* before Beck handed him his jacket and slammed the door in his face. "You just surprised me."

"I didn't realize Kevin didn't know about us." Jordan frowned.

Beck stared into her mug. "It's best for both of us to keep this quiet."

"Does anyone know? I understand maintaining secrecy at work, but does anyone know you're seeing someone?"

She didn't meet her eyes. "I just don't think now is the time for that."

Jordan wanted to ask Beck when the time would be. She wanted to ask if Beck thought a reality existed where they could be out and together, but she also didn't want to know the answer. Jordan's shoulders dropped. In just twenty-four hours, she'd been wedged back into the closet, as if her truth required hiding.

"Are you going to tell me what's going on?" Beck asked.

"I don't know if I can say. I'm sorry, this was a bad idea. I'm not thinking straight lately."

"Come here." Beck opened her arms and Jordan fell into them. "Stop apologizing for being here. Stop worrying about us. Nothing's changed."

"Are you sure?" Jordan released a tense breath.

"Talk to me." She raised a brow. "Off the record."

Jordan hated those three words and how they gatekept her ability to speak freely but shared anyway.

"I met with Hunter Garrick and his parents today. I don't think it went well." She grimaced. "His dad wasn't my biggest fan."

Beck frowned. "What happened?"

"He was kind of sexist. He asked Frost why he wasn't head coach. And he alluded to my sexuality thanks to our sit-down interview." Jordan twisted her necklace as she stared off.

"I'm sorry."

"Don't be."

"Did they pull Hunter's commitment?"

Jordan wanted to trust her. She wanted to tell her that Hunter was a lost cause. Wanted even more to tell her of Mark's warning, of the concerned boosters, and the increasing likelihood that she might get axed. But something inside her screamed no. No matter how sweet Beck's affections or calming her presence, Jordan couldn't risk it. Didn't fully trust her. Especially not while she was a secret.

"They haven't pulled it," Jordan said. It wasn't a lie, but she omitted Randy's warning that it was only a matter of time and that the visit was just a courtesy slap in the face before they made it public.

"That's good, right?" Beck grabbed Jordan's hand, threading their fingers together. "It's going to be okay. You looked so worried when you came here. I thought someone died."

"I'm just tired." Jordan swallowed the pit in her throat. "Please, don't mention any of this. Not the visit or Randy Garrick being an asshole."

"I won't." Beck's voice rose in a pitch that made Jordan second-guess her. Before surveying her face for signs of insincerity, the reporter drew her into another hug. "You did what you could, Jordan. It'll be okay."

She hated that while in Beck's arms, she saw the end. The end of her career at David Douglas. The end of their relationship. The end of everything she'd fought for. She clung tighter and burrowed into Beck's chest, determined to enjoy it for just a second longer.

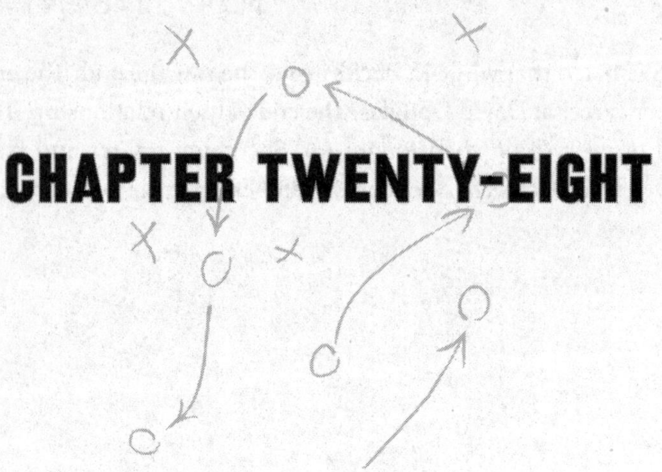

CHAPTER TWENTY-EIGHT

A feeble whimper startled Beck in the darkness. It took her a moment to detect that the tormented cries stirred from Jordan beside her, thrashing in the sheets, eyes stitched shut.

"Jordan," Beck whispered. "Jordan, wake up."

The coach's incoherent mumbles and whines endured. Beck shook her, first gingerly, but then more firmly when her attempts failed.

"Jordan, you're dreaming."

The last nudge jolted her awake. Jordan gasped as she sat up, the glisten of her eyes visible in the gray wash of dawn. "Beck?"

"It's okay." Beck embraced her despite rattling inside. But it wasn't the abrupt wake-up that jarred her. Jordan's whimpers gnawed at her core, wore her spirit down to threads, pushed her into fight or flight, not for her own safety but to restore the woman's peace. "It's okay. I've got you."

"I'm sorry," Jordan said over and over, so hoarse that Beck didn't stop hushing her.

"You're okay." Beck pressed her lips to the top of her head, shocked at the usually stoic Jordan shaking uncontrollably. "What were you dreaming about?"

"Nothing," she whispered.

Beck hugged her tighter. She didn't need an answer. Deep down, she knew. More importantly, deep down, she shattered at Jordan's brokenness. The overwhelming empathy nearly reduced her to tears. It swelled beyond the ache that arose when Jordan broke her nose or the adoration that burst when she watched her coach. When her mouth parted, the words didn't just escape but surged. "I love you."

And Jordan, without missing a beat, said it back like a vow. "I love you too."

Beck's doubts, the ones that troubled her hours earlier, vanished. The resentment she felt at not being able to report on Jordan's leads, the shame at not being out, the worry that choked her over their forbidden romance, dwindled. Comforting Jordan mattered. Living her truth mattered. Not stories. Not making her family or the world comfortable. She was in love with someone, willing to take risks for someone, and that night with Jordan, nothing seemed more precious or important. They would make it work. There wasn't a world in which they wouldn't.

Unfortunately, the afterglow of "I love you" lasted less than twenty-four hours.

Beck rode the high into work that morning. Her heart sprouted wings when Jordan kissed her forehead and whispered the same sweet three words before departing. A wake-up that Beck could commit months, years, a lifetime to.

She coasted with fresh confidence. She'd tell Kevin first, as if the night hadn't spoken for itself, and go from there. She'd tell her family and her friends. Maybe word would get around. Maybe it wouldn't. She absolutely didn't care. She was too busy picturing Jordan at her side each morning. Too busy fantasizing about what it would be like to introduce her to Scottie in New York or bring her home for the holidays.

"Good afternoon, co-host," Easton greeted her when she entered the studio.

Beck furrowed her brow as she clipped on her mic. "You seem happy. What did you do, make a small child cry?"

"Oh, even better." Easton grinned, rubbing his hands together. "You're in for a big, big surprise, Caroline."

Her saccharine stupor faded in the wake of his near manic joy. "What surprise?"

"Let's just say I'm back in it, baby. You're not the only one who can scoop a story."

Before she could respond, the show intro video played, the camera tally lights flashed red, and the floor director counted them in. "Good afternoon and welcome to *Fast Break*. I'm Caroline Beck."

"And I'm Easton Prescott." He swiveled to a one-shot as a script that Beck didn't recognize rolled in the teleprompter. "We start with breaking news in the college basketball world. Four-star recruit Hunter Garrick has withdrawn his verbal commitment to David Douglas University. His family told me *exclusively* that they met with coach Jordan D'Amato yesterday and informed her that it wasn't the right fit."

Beck was thankful the camera wasn't on her because her mouth hung ajar. Her first thought was the story should've been hers. The second, that Jordan lied to her.

"This is a major loss on the recruiting front for the Bulldogs. They've already lost Pierce Watson, but this is a new low for D'Amato. If things keep going as they are, she's poised to have David Douglas's worst recruiting class in a decade. You have to wonder what that's about, Beck?"

She snapped into focus after zoning out for much of Easton's report. "Well, we've talked about it before. D'Amato lacks experience as a head coach. For some players and parents, that's a red flag." Especially for the sexist ones, she resisted adding. Another secret insight, lost in the mess of their relationship.

And that's when the glow of love lost out to her hunger to be the best. Just as quickly as she drew up their eminent future, she erased it. Her work couldn't survive, her journalistic instincts couldn't flourish, with those three sweet words in her ear. Not when they competed with three other bittersweet ones—*off the record.*

"How'd you get that scoop?" Beck asked Easton after the show.

"I have my sources too." Easton cracked his knuckles. "Game on, sweetheart."

"Game on, asshole," she muttered under her breath. Beck's frustration became a sour pill she struggled to swallow. In the face of the camera and studio lights, she couldn't afford to love Jordan D'Amato.

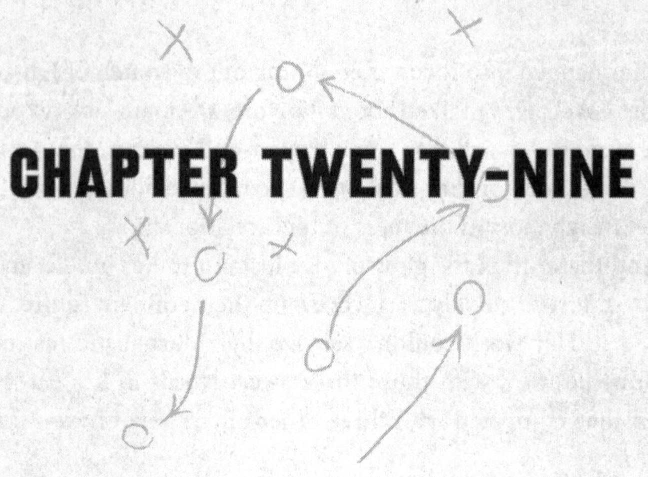

CHAPTER TWENTY-NINE

The Bulldogs crushed Tempe State University in another Saturday blowout, securing an automatic berth into the conference tournament semifinals, but Jordan couldn't bring herself to smile. She coached stoically, calling plays on autopilot, shaking hands after the win no differently than she would have after a loss. During the press conference, she stared off as if prepared to face the electric chair.

"Coach?" Brooks nudged her.

"What?"

"She asked you a question," he said.

Jordan's cheeks flushed as she refocused on the cameras. "I'm sorry, what?"

"I asked how it feels to be going to the semifinals of the conference tournament," Beck said, her brow raised.

"It feels good." Jordan nodded as she sat between Brooks and Leon. She knew she should say more, knew that the reporters expected more, but she couldn't bring herself to.

"Coach is so locked in, it's hard to get her to crack a smile," Leon teased.

"That's because the journey is just getting started, Torres," Jordan said.

"That's right. And we're going all the way," Brooks added.

"Any message for your opponents?" Beck asked.

"Yeah, I have one." Leon leaned closer to the mic. "Look out. We're coming for you."

Jordan left the presser in a trance, breezing past Beck when she tried to speak to her. She couldn't afford to talk. Not when Mark Fellner predictably waited for her. "Jordan, a word?" He might as well have been wearing black robes and brandishing a scythe.

She trudged up to his office. She always thought this day would come. Even on that rainy afternoon in Mark's office with Royce, she imagined at some point she'd end up sitting across from him again, unworthy and disgraced.

"Jordan, it pains me to say this, but we're letting you go."

Her ears stopped ringing. The air stilled. "Can I ask why?"

"You know why," Mark said. "I warned you that the recruiting situation was fragile. The boosters agree. You've done a good job here, but it's just not going to work in the long term."

Jordan shook her head. "You've been waiting for this to happen all along."

"That's not true," he said. "I took a chance on you when most others wouldn't have."

"No. No, I'm so sick of hearing that." Jordan clenched a fist. "Took a chance on me? You know why you say that? To cover your ass. To continue to propagate this idea that I can't do the job because I'm a woman. That I'm going to eventually fail because I don't have the balls to do this." The words sprang from her mouth before she comprehended them. But they'd always been there, growing whenever she lay on her office floor in a panic, whenever the team trailed and she prepared to be fired, the pressure always looming, never giving her a moment's peace so that she might enjoy her job instead of fearing for it. "You have never, ever believed in me. So, you've treated me like a chance, an experiment, a charity project. I'd bet good money that you won't call the next man you hand the keys to a chance but an obvious choice, a smart decision, a true leader among men. Someone you can stand behind instead of waiting to watch fall."

Mark pursed his lips like he'd eaten something bitter. "I never wanted you to fail. I want what's best for this team and for this school!"

Jordan smacked his desk. "Well, in that case, I've led them to one of their best seasons. I have fought for this team! I've literally spilled blood for this team! And for what? What more could I do?"

"That's the problem! You can't do anything else." He glared. "The decision has been made. That's it. You can kick and scream all you want, but it's done."

Jordan scrubbed a hand down her face and lowered her voice. "Who's taking over?"

"Sean Reilley. We'll start the interview process after the season is over, but this signals to prospective recruits that we're making a change."

"That's bullshit."

Mark sighed. "I understand you're upset."

"No. I'm fucking pissed." Jordan stood. She considered kicking over her chair, screaming in his face, ripping down the plaques in his office, but resisted. Never let them see you sweat. Never let them see you cry. "Is that all?"

"We're releasing a statement and telling the team tomorrow morning. I'd appreciate if you kept this quiet until then."

Jordan stiffened her chin. "Anything for you, Mark."

She slammed the door, rattling the photos that adorned the

hall. Jordan sniffled, but tears didn't fall. She charged for her office, locked the door, and paced. She didn't want the players to see her, the other coaches, not even Beck.

After everyone left, she changed into joggers and a T-shirt. Her hands shook, the pit in her throat throbbed, but not a droplet of self-pity streamed. She flipped the arena lights on and rolled a cart of basketballs to the arc, desperate to calm herself.

But the ball felt wrong in her hand.

It didn't bounce quite right.

Every shot rattled the rim.

"Fuck," she said when a fifth ball missed. She swiped another off the cart, but instead of taking the shot, she hurled it into the stands. She took another and did the same. "Fuck!" She punted the next ball into the rafters with a grunt. "Fuck! Fuck! Fuck!" She kicked the cart over, and the remaining balls scattered and rolled away.

Jordan panted and covered her face with her hands. No tears, but the disappointment, the betrayal, the futility of her efforts became raw heat beneath her fingers.

"Hey."

Jordan jumped, spinning to find Beck behind her. "Hey. What are you doing here?"

"We need to talk." Beck scanned the mess of basketballs but didn't mention them.

"I told you I can't right now." Jordan barely managed words through her secret anguish.

"Well, this isn't working for me."

Beck's edge brought Jordan back, putting a pause on her termination's fallout. "What isn't working?"

"You lied to me."

Her mouth fell open. "What?"

"I asked you if Hunter was pulling his commitment and you

said no," Beck said as the unmistakable scarlet flush of her fury crawled from her chest to her cheeks.

"Because he officially hadn't."

"But his dad told you it was happening. He told Easton that."

"Okay, yeah. What does it matter?"

"That should have been my story! I should've broken that news!" Beck shouted.

"Even if I told you the truth, we were off the record!"

Beck threw her head back. "I'm so sick of off the record!"

"You don't think I'm sick of it too?" Jordan shouted. "What do you expect? Am I supposed to just give you intel because we're sleeping together?"

"No! I don't know!" Beck pressed her temples and paced. "It's not like that. It's just that I'm so wrapped up in you and trusted you so much that I didn't pursue my own leads. I was too distracted to keep chasing the story. And what's worse, the real rub, is that even if I did, I don't want to report something that would reflect poorly on you." She stopped pacing and frowned when she met Jordan's gaze. "This is exactly why I never do this."

"Well, what do you want to do? What are you trying to say?" Jordan's head pounded, her stomach whirled, and she wasn't sure if she could handle a breakup the same night she got fired. She wanted to drop to her knees and sob to Beck about her termination. She wanted to drop to her knees and beg her not to leave. Instead, she stood as she had in Mark's office, determined to take the next blow on her feet.

But it didn't come. Beck's chin quivered. Her mouth opened, but then shut.

Jordan ventured closer. "Beck?" She whispered it like she did in the dark. Whispered it like she whispered love. "I'm sorry about the story."

"I'm sorry." Beck sniffled. Her eyes glistened, and she shook her head.

Jordan knew the apology wasn't about the story. The apology was a goodbye she wasn't ready to accept.

A phone call broke through the torment. She took it on the second ring, not only to prolong the inevitable with Beck, but because of the name that flashed across her screen. "I need to take this."

"Jordan." Beck huffed.

"What?"

"You always do this! You always take it. We're in the middle of something—"

"Just hold on," she said before answering. "What's up?"

Charlie Washington spoke gravely in her ear, eclipsing everything else. Getting fired and their unfinished quarrel didn't matter against his strained voice. She gulped down pride and pain to give a steady assurance with strength she didn't know she still had. "I'll be right there. Just send me the address. You did the right thing by calling." She hung up and darted down the tunnel.

Beck followed her. "What's going on?"

"Uh, it's Charlie. Something's wrong." Jordan plowed into her messy, half-packed office. She swiped her jacket and then gritted her teeth at her bike. It didn't exactly lend itself to urgency. "Shit."

"What?"

"I should've brought my car."

"I'll drive you."

"I'll get a ride."

"Jordan." Beck said her name in the way she could never resist. "I'll take you."

"Okay." Jordan nodded. She would keep her team in one piece if it took everything she had. Even Beck. Even if neither were hers anymore.

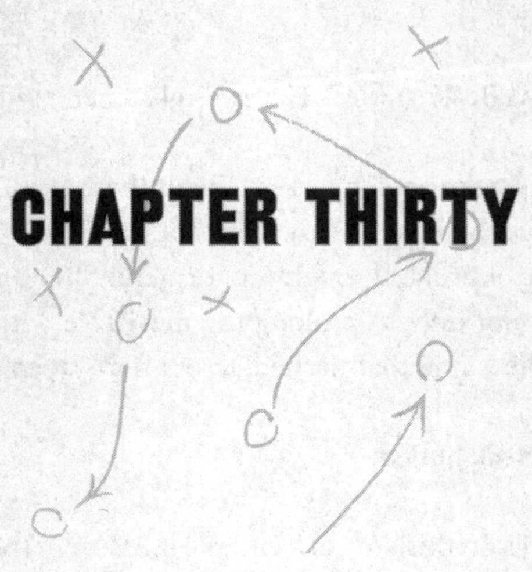

CHAPTER THIRTY

The windshield wipers worked overtime as Beck weaved across town, splashing through puddles. Jordan didn't elaborate on the emergency. In fact, they hadn't spoken since leaving campus except for directions. While they waited at a stoplight, Beck thought to bring up the conversation they'd started in the gym, but it wasn't the time. Not just that, but she didn't want to finish it. When she stared into Jordan's eyes, she couldn't say it.

"This is it," Jordan said when they reached a rundown college house. Music thumped above the downpour. Dozens of students smoked and drank on the front porch, and she presumed plenty more gathered inside. "I'll be right back."

Beck bounded out too. "What's going on?"

"Beck, damn it, just wait in the car," Jordan said as they started up the walk.

"What? So, you can lie to me again?"

When they reached the front steps, Jordan smacked a plastic cup away from the first person within reach, sending beer splattering to the concrete. Beck's mouth dropped as the young man yelped. "What the fuck!"

"Cops are on the way. Party's over." Jordan deftly plucked a cigarette out of another student's mouth, threw it to the ground, and squashed it without stopping on her way inside.

"Fucking bitch," the kids hissed after her.

Beck's stomach somersaulted. Only Jordan could impress her when she was trying to break up with her.

"Party is over! Everyone out!" Jordan's game-worn voice failed to carry over the drunk students and music. "I said get out! Now!"

Beck trailed her through the jammed hallway, the musky odor of booze, sweat, and weed transporting her back to her partying days of long ago. Plastic cups covered every surface as people cheered for games and clinked shots. The dancing, shouting, and bumping became so aggressive that Jordan grabbed Beck's hand to not lose her.

"Is that the coach?"

"Holy shit, that's Jordan D'Amato!"

"Yo, Coach! You here to party? Take a shot with us!"

The crowd tightened as more students recognized Jordan.

"Party's over! Everyone out!" Her shouting hardly disrupted the chaos.

When they reached the kitchen, Beck brought her thumb and index finger to her mouth and whistled. Much of the crowd, including Jordan, startled at the high pitch, and she took advantage of the temporary lull.

"The cops have been called! Everyone needs to get out now!" Beck bellowed.

"She's not kidding! Get out or I'm taking names to the dean." Jordan raised a playful eyebrow at Beck as the students dispersed. Beck smirked back.

"Coach!" Charlie appeared wide-eyed and frantic.

"Where is he?" Jordan asked. Charlie led them deeper into the house as streams of people plowed for the exits. They passed the living room, where Cooper Sloane slept with a mustache drawn on his lip and a pacifier in his mouth. Beck suppressed a snort, but Jordan growled. "Who did that to Coop?"

"I think we have bigger problems, Coach," Charlie said as they reached a door that Leon and Dominic hovered outside of. They straightened up at Jordan's arrival, likely inebriated if the party's rowdiness was any indication of how the night had been going. "He won't come out. Did you really call the cops?"

"Of course not. How long has he been in there?" Jordan asked.

"Like an hour. We tried to get everyone to leave," Leon said. His eyes flicked over to Beck. "What's she doing here?"

"Brooks! Brooks, open the door!" Jordan knocked and jiggled the door handle. She pressed her ear to the worn paneling. "Brooks, open up. It's me."

"Come on, man, the party is clear now," Charlie said.

"What happened?" Beck couldn't resist asking. Just as she couldn't resist entering the house even if it blurred professional boundaries and risked her journalistic integrity.

"He was upset about something. Crying. I don't know what he was saying," Leon said.

"Aren't you that hot reporter?" Dominic slurred.

"Obviously." Leon licked his lips and offered his hand to Beck. "I'm Leon. Leon Torres, but you already know that. Just thought we should start with a proper introduction."

"Guys, knock it off," Jordan said before pounding the door again. "Brooks, let me in. Let's talk. Everything is going to be alright."

The group froze as a weak voice wafted through the barrier. "Is everyone gone?" Brooks asked.

"Just me and the guys now," Jordan said. "We're here for you, Brooks."

The handle rattled, and when the door swung open, Beck's face pinched with sympathy. The young man's eyes were puffy and red, and his sobs resumed as he collapsed into Jordan's arms. She held him up as he wept on her shoulder.

"He left me," Brooks whimpered. "He left."

"It's okay. It's okay." Jordan struggled under his weight and the two of them lowered to the tile floor in front of the tub. The rest of the players watched, and Beck stepped back, observing with a hand on her chest.

"I just couldn't do it," Brooks sniveled.

"Couldn't do what, man?" Leon asked.

Brooks wiped at his cheeks, snot spilling down his lips. He shook his head.

Jordan squeezed his shoulder. "No one here is judging."

"I couldn't tell my parents." Brooks cracked. "I couldn't tell the team. He wanted to hold my hand on campus. He wanted to kiss me after a game. But I couldn't do it. So, he broke up with me."

Beck nearly drew blood from biting her lip to stave off tears. The young man's desolation was heartbreaking, but his secret, so much like Beck's, nearly split her in half. When she caught Jordan's gaze, their own struggles roared like an unseeable monster standing between them.

The guys stood so still that Cooper's snores rippled through the quiet.

Leon's brow pinched together. "So, you're like . . ."

"I'm gay." Brooks sniffled. "Is that okay with you?"

Another beat of cringeworthy silence. Beck nearly turned away in it.

"How long have you known?" Charlie finally asked. "I mean, wasn't there that girl freshman year?"

"Stella. She was hot," Leon said.

"I think I've known since high school, but it wasn't until I got away from my family and tried to date girls that I understood why it never felt right." Brooks frowned. "It's always been there. It's always been my biggest secret."

Leon tilted his head to the side. "So, in the locker room . . ."

"It's not like that." Brooks glared.

"So, you're not attracted to me?"

"No!"

"Why not?"

"Hey, enough. It's not a joke." Jordan's reprimand had the boys sheepishly staring at the floor. "Do you think this is easy for him? For anyone?"

Brooks shook his head. "No. No, it's okay. I get it. I'm sorry if this changes things for you guys." His eyes welled again. "If it makes me less of a captain or basketball player to you."

Charlie's mouth fell open. "Why would it do that?"

"Come on. What's more masculine than the NBA? And you guys know who my dad is."

"You don't need to be your dad, Brooks. You're our captain no matter what. This doesn't change that."

Leon nodded. "And you deserve all that shit. Holding hands, kissing whoever you want. Fuck everyone else. Don't be sorry for it." He nudged Dominic off the doorframe. "Say something nice to him."

"My uncle is gay." Dominic hiccupped.

"No. Say something actually nice."

"Okay, well, I love you, man," he said. "Just, you know, not like that—"

"Dom!" The group booed and shoved him, but Brooks didn't waver. In fact, his dimples spread with a smile.

"Maybe we should stop bungling this with words." Charlie, all long legs and arms, squeezed in to sit on the other side of Brooks, taking up the remaining space in the small bathroom. "Everyone, bring it in."

Jordan laughed. "I don't think more of you can fit in here."

Leon and Dominic closed in anyway, forming a cramped circle around their teammate, hugging him with an acceptance that choked Beck up. She absorbed the image. The image of Jordan on the floor with her players, of the guys responding with compassion, of the embrace that emitted pure love, a closeness that Beck knew came from Jordan. From the work she'd done and the trust she built. Beck loved her more in that moment than she ever had before. A love that didn't align with her ambitions and the accompanying doubt, the one that had her ready to walk away for good.

She retreated to the sticky kitchen. Desperate to settle her nerves, she rummaged for a clean cup and grimaced as she sniffed several dirty ones in a row. She considered taking a straight pull from a bottle of cheap tequila when a beer cracked open behind her. Leon smiled in the doorway, a clean, cold beverage in hand. Beck snatched it from him.

"Thank you," she said after a long chug.

"My pleasure." Leon leaned against the kitchen counter and grinned. "So, you came here with Coach?"

"She needed a ride." Beck started emptying plastic cups in the sink.

"Are you two together?" he asked.

Beck shook her head. "That's none of your business."

"I can't help but be curious. I mean, a beautiful woman like you with Coach late at night . . ."

She crossed her arms and leaned on the counter across from him. "Leon, I think it's best you forget about me being here and drop this conversation."

"Why?"

"Because I know for a fact that Jordan will run you until you do." She took a drink before raising her eyebrows. "How many sprints do you think it will take?"

Leon just grinned wider. "How about I promise to forget if you go on a date with me?"

"How about I agree to not break your fingers and ruin your senior season?"

"I think I'm in love with you."

"Get out of here, Torres." Jordan entered, unamused by the forward's antics.

"Coach, can I just say, well done." Leon bowed to her.

Beck smirked at Jordan, who shook her head. "One more word and I'll drag you out of bed tomorrow for wind sprints."

"Told you," Beck said to Leon.

"Let's go." Jordan grazed the small of her back on their way out. "Good night, Torres."

He grinned as they departed. "Good night, Coach. Good night, Mrs. Coach."

"Leon!"

"What? I think it has a nice ring to it." Beck winked.

Jordan smiled sheepishly, but the same dreariness that surfaced after the Garrick visit remained. Beck noticed it in her sunken gaze, in the way her smile didn't quite lift. She'd been withdrawn at the press conference and at the game she barely glanced at her. Beck was so caught up with breaking up with her that she hadn't paid it much thought. Now the scattered basketballs on the empty court and half-packed boxes in her office struck her as peculiar.

"Jordan, what happened tonight?" Beck asked once they were back in her car.

The windshield wipers wailed while she navigated a maze of

dark neighborhood streets that she wasn't sure she wanted to escape. Escape meant confronting their own problems and future.

Jordan stared out the window. "I told you not to go in there."

The bitterness, the one that momentarily lifted in light of Brooks's crisis, reemerged. Beck hitched her jaw. "Can you blame me? After you hid the Garrick story from me—"

"You're unbelievable." Jordan shook her head. "Not everything is a story, Beck! You shouldn't have been there. The last thing Brooks needed in that moment was a reporter hovering."

Beck's mouth fell open. "Oh, so I'm just a reporter now?"

"You mean like I'm just a source?" A red sheen cast over Jordan's face as Beck stopped at a light.

"I wasn't hovering and it's not like I'd report it." She frowned. "Do you really think that little of me? That I'd out someone to get ahead?"

"I suppose not, since you won't come out yourself. I mean, not even to Kevin, really?"

"You know it's complicated." Beck tightened her grip on the steering wheel. "It's not like you're perfect either or make this relationship easy. The team asks you to jump and you ask how high. You take every call. I'll always take a back seat to that."

"It's my job!"

"Showing up to a house party? I know Brooks needed your help, but Jordan, this is what I'm talking about! Boundaries."

"Yeah, you're great at those—with us." Jordan glowered. "But God forbid it's a lead story."

"It's not that simple. It's not just coming out for me. It's sleeping with a source." Beck's cheeks flamed as she pulled into Jordan's apartment complex. She threw the car into park. "I've fought to be where I am. I've worked my fucking ass off."

"Like I haven't?"

"It won't ruin your career!"

"Ruin my career? What career?" Jordan chuckled so maliciously that Beck shuddered. "Here's a story for you, Beck—I got fired tonight. There's your lead. You can be the first to break it. I don't give a shit anymore." She got out and slammed the car door.

Beck hardly had time to comprehend the news as she jumped out into the storm. "What do you mean, fired? What happened? When?"

"After the press conference. Mark told me that if I didn't retain Garrick that it wouldn't be good. He canned me because I'm a shit recruiter, I guess. Because these kids don't want to play for me."

The oddities of the last few weeks threaded neatly together. Jordan always stopping short in their conversations, her surprise appearance in Portland, her restlessness and sorrow. She'd been on the verge of the end and Beck hated that she'd faced it alone.

"I'm so sorry." Beck reached for her, but she backed away.

"No, don't." Waves thrashed in her eyes, but the only water cascading down her cheeks came from the rain. "I'm surprised you're not pissed at me for not telling you sooner, so you could report it. I mean, you were about to break up with me over what happened with Garrick. Weren't you?"

Beck frowned. "I was wrong."

"No, you were just being honest. And that's the problem with this. With us." Jordan mournfully tilted her head. "I can't be honest with you about the team. And you can't be honest about who you are or what we are. What kind of relationship is that?"

They considered the question, silent and soaked.

"I love you. I do. Even when we fight." Beck sniffled. "I know it's not fair, and I know our situation isn't easy, but we can figure it out. You don't have to do everything alone."

"But I can't do it with you either." Jordan stood drenched, hands out at her sides. "I love you too. But there's no figuring this out. You have to do your job. You have to get up tomorrow and report on me getting fired while I figure out how to swallow it. So, let's just keep things uncomplicated like we should have from the start. It'll be easier this way."

"It won't be easier." Beck didn't want it to end. It was happening too fast, too reasonably, even though she knew where they were headed. Even though an hour ago she was prepared to drown them. Now she fought to stay afloat. "What if I play you for it?" It was a pathetic request, but she'd do anything to stay, even stall a moment longer.

"Not this time." Jordan lifted a pitiful half smile. "It was a good run, though, right?"

"The best," she whispered beneath the rain.

Jordan went straight for her, but Beck froze. Tender lips pressed her forehead, the hands she whimpered for cupped her jaw, and before she could muster the strength to reach for her, the kiss was over, and Jordan was gone. Beck staggered toward the stairs to the apartment but then paused, deciding in the downpour to stop chasing their story.

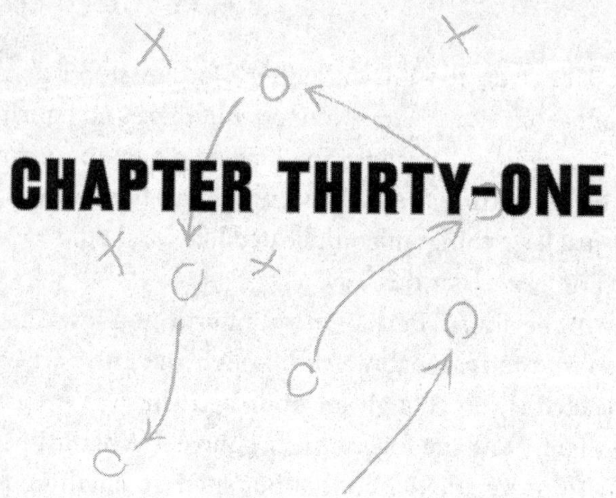

CHAPTER THIRTY-ONE

For the first time in thirty-four years, or at least since she could remember, Jordan D'Amato languished in self-pity. She didn't shower, she didn't clean up the takeout cartons that littered the living room, and she ignored her phone. She let the loss of the team and Beck bury her.

On the first day, she didn't get out of bed. She stared at the ceiling and mourned how close she'd come. The conference championship. A run at the national title. All of it within reach. And then there was Beck. She knew she'd been naïve to think they could make it, but they got damn far too. Far enough for love. Far enough to keep Jordan down for the count when it ended.

On the second day, she took Brooks's call.

"This is bullshit. They can't do this to you."

"Brooks, it's okay. I'm okay." Jordan gnawed her lip to avoid unloading her own resentment at Mark and the school. Brooks wasn't the one to vent to. "I need you to focus on basketball. On winning."

"This isn't right."

"That doesn't matter. What matters is that you do what's right for the team. That's what being a leader is. Even when it's hard."

When they hung up, she considered Beck's missed phone calls but didn't let herself listen to the voicemails. It would be too much. Hit her too deep. She glanced at her last text message.

Please just talk to me. I love you.

Jordan turned off her phone.

XOXO

On the third day, she groaned at a knock on her door. "Go away!"

The next thump landed like a battering ram, and Jordan froze. She'd know that brute force anywhere.

"Come on, Jordan, don't make me break this thing down. You know I'll do it!"

She hurried to fling open the door, her mouth falling when she laid eyes upon her mentor.

"Royce. What are you doing here?"

"Are you kidding? I got you into this mess." Royce crushed her into one of his bear hugs, the kind that eased the strapped sensation in her chest. If she wasn't so accustomed to withholding tears, this embrace might have been the place Jordan freed them.

Instead, she sighed. "The mess was all mine."

"I doubt that." Royce released her.

"I can't believe you're here. What about Seattle? Don't you have a game tomorrow?"

"A long drive helps clear the head. It's been a rough season for me too." Royce shrugged. "Plus, some things are worth stepping away for."

Jordan's heart twinged. Beck's charge that she overcommitted to the team still taunted her. She shook it from her head and frantically tidied up her kitchen and living room, which lay in rare disarray beneath takeout cartons, laundry, and empty beer bottles.

"The recruiting excuse is bullshit," Royce said as he held open a garbage bag for her.

Jordan shook her head. "I don't know. I'm not like you. I should've been more convincing." She threw a bottle into the trash. "I got distracted. It was my fault." Jordan wound up to toss another bottle when Royce grabbed her hand in midair.

"Hey." He narrowed his brow. "Let's sit for a minute, okay?"

Jordan huffed onto the couch and pinched the bridge of her crooked nose. The cushions shifted with Royce's weight next to her. "I'm sorry I let you down," she said. "After you fought for and believed in me all this time."

"You didn't let me down. You changed the game, just like I hoped for." He patted her shoulder.

"I don't know. I think the game changed me this time."

"It's supposed to, Jordan. We're supposed to change. That's why not everyone gets to do this forever. We're the lucky ones," he said. "I'm going through growing pains too. My first losing record in a decade. I hear the boos and calls for my head."

"I never asked you how you do it." Jordan swallowed through a pit at the memory of Beck's question in the mall that night. Her eyes pleading to know more of her. "How do you deal with the pressure?"

"I have more than just the game. A wife, kids, a family, a home." He smiled. "I know basketball is your safe place, but you need more. You can't be everything to the team and the team can't be everything to you. You have to keep something for yourself and the people that love you. Because the game can go away in an instant."

"Well, I messed that up too."

Royce waited, and when she didn't elaborate, rolled his eyes. "You going to tell me how?"

"There was someone." Jordan fiddled with her necklace. "But the team came first. Every call. Every problem. It makes it hard to let someone in all the way."

She paused. Not only had she replayed their fight endlessly, cringing and berating herself for each failing, she replayed the rest too. The insecurities and disappointments that kept her from forming deeper intimacy. She'd gotten close with Beck, but knew it wasn't just their careers that stunted her trust.

Jordan couldn't look at Royce, cheeks burning through her next confession. "You know I leave tickets for them. Like they might show up one day?"

He emitted a subtle growl. "Your folks are idiots, Jordan. What would you tell a player if they were in your position? If they can't appreciate what you've achieved and who you are, do you really want them in the stands? Do they even deserve to be?"

Jordan shook her head. She knew he was right, but after Beck's interview aired, after the mention of her parents, that same lonesome teenager inside longed for their acceptance. The same one that shook inside her at the Garrick house. She didn't know why she held on to hope or the need to win their approval, except that maybe without that pathetic longing, she had nothing left of them.

"I don't know about the person you let go, but if they can understand you and this crazy game, it might be worth the risk to trust them. The game, the boys, can't be your only family." Royce's phone rang and he smirked. "Speaking of . . . the wife wanted me to tell her you were still hanging in there."

"Tell her hi for me," she said as she stood to finish cleaning.

"Hey, Jordan, hold on," Royce said shortly after answering the phone. "Turn on the TV."

"Why?"

"It's about the team. Hurry up."

Jordan scrambled for the remote. Since getting fired, she'd avoided television. Not only were the headlines unbearable, but she didn't have enough self-restraint to not torture herself by watching Beck. But when she appeared on-screen that afternoon, it wasn't torturous. Jordan's heart fluttered at the sight of her. And the news about the team wasn't a reminder of her loss. It was a flicker of hope.

"I'm outside the Walton Athletic Center where the men's basketball team has walked out of practice," Beck reported as the camera zoomed past her shoulder. The players stood with their arms linked—Brooks, Leon, Charlie, Dominic, Cooper, and the others—outside the arena doors. "The team says they won't play until Jordan D'Amato is reinstated as head coach."

Jordan covered her gaping mouth. She may have been fired, she may have broken up with Beck, but it wasn't a complete failure. Perhaps she'd chalk up one more win after all. More important, perhaps that person was still in her corner.

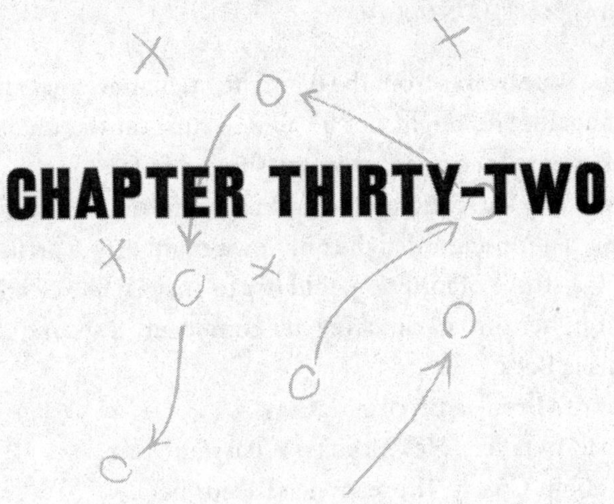

CHAPTER THIRTY-TWO

"Sorry about your little girlfriend."

Of the countless insults, harassment, and hate mail she'd long ago learned to endure, the comparably mild jab from Easton made Beck's lower lip quiver violently enough to send her into hiding. She glared at the bathroom mirror. Of course, it'd been building to this. Each time she had to say Jordan's name on air, each time she had to talk about her termination like it didn't personally affect her, deepened her sorrow.

Beck wanted to curl up in a ball and cry but didn't get the chance. The breaking news out of David Douglas thrust her into work, into the studio, into press conferences that made her miss Jordan even more. She never revealed a shred of grief on camera. Never lost a beat on the desk as they debated the woman's career, abilities, and failures, as if Beck didn't know there was so much more to it. Her heart broke for losing Jordan, but also for Jordan losing the team. And she couldn't express any of it.

She withstood the shitstorm of her own making alone. She was too ashamed to turn to Kevin. Too ashamed to turn to her family. She thought of calling Scottie, but also feared that if she freed the waterworks from the dam, she might never get ahold of herself again. She might not be able to turn on the unaffected, objective, witty persona that viewers tuned in for.

Before she surrendered to the first cathartic cry, her phone rang. Beck almost ignored the unknown number, but an unusual instinct, a stroke of intuition, told her to answer. She cleared the tears from her throat, clutching her composure a second longer. "Hi, this is Beck."

"Hey. It's Brooks. Brooks McCray."

She stood taller. "Hey, Brooks. What's up?"

"It's about Coach. The team needs your help."

Beck didn't need further convincing. She sprinted out of the bathroom before Brooks finished sharing his plan. She narrowly avoided Easton, tripping to her desk as she shouted over her shoulder. "Todd, get your shit! We're going to David Douglas."

"What's going on?" Nick asked.

"Let me guess, semiannual sale at the mall." Easton poked her ankle with his baseball bat and spoke in a mocking high pitch. "She can't possibly get the good stories in last season's heels."

Beck yanked on her jacket. "I'll explain when I get down there, but be ready for me to go live." She rolled her eyes at Todd, who sat gawking with a meatball sub in hand. "Todd, camera, now. We don't have much time."

"But my lunch."

"Just eat in the truck!" She snatched the sandwich from him.

Nick narrowed his brow. "What about the show?"

"This is going to be the show," she said, shaking marinara from her fingers and rifling for a napkin.

"No way. You can't just let her run out." Easton shook his head. "What the hell is the story?"

"I'm not saying until it's confirmed and I'm there. That's the only way we can have it first. And I don't trust you to keep it quiet."

"Smart girl." Todd chuckled.

Easton glared. "Shut up."

"Nick, please, trust me. I haven't led us wrong yet. I promise, this is going to be worth it." Beck clasped her hands at the producer in a plea, Todd's lunch hostage between her palms.

Nick sighed. "You're going to go even if I say no, aren't you?"

"Isn't it nice that I'm asking you, though?"

"Call me when you get there."

Beck dragged Todd and his sandwich out the door, ignoring Nick's parting instructions. They arrived at the WAC with little time to spare. Leon snuck them through a side door, wearing jeans and his letterman's jacket. Brooks and Charlie met them in a discreet corner of the arena, also in street clothes, though practice started in less than twenty minutes.

"Thanks for coming," Brooks said.

In just moments, the players planned to walk out to support Jordan. They'd written a letter to Mark Fellner, demanding he bring her back. Brooks called Beck to help spread the word, and she was more than willing to answer.

"You sure you want to do this?" she asked. As much as she admired the young men's willingness to put everything on the line, she worried they didn't fully comprehend the risk.

The three of them nodded. "Coach told me to do what's best for the team in her absence. This is what's best for the team right now," Brooks said.

"And if it doesn't work?" Beck asked.

"Then our season's over," Leon said coolly.

Beck nodded. "Good luck then. Thanks for trusting me with this."

"If Coach trusts you, we do too."

Beck frowned. If only that was still the case. If only Jordan had trusted her enough to keep trying, if only she'd been less selfish in her own ambition. She wanted to call her and let her know what was about to happen. She could only hope that it would reach her. That she would know how much the players cared, and how much Beck cared too.

The camera rolled as the Bulldogs exited the arena, twelve players filing out behind Brooks. Leon ceremoniously chained and locked the main doors before the team stood outside with their arms linked in unity. The power of the image left static across her skin.

After setting the stage, Beck dove into live interviews. "I'm here with Brooks McCray Jr., team captain. Brooks, tell me about what's happening here today and what this means?"

"We've asked that Jordan D'Amato be reinstated as head coach. Until she is, this team has taken a unanimous vote—we won't take the court again for practice or games. We've called on the athletic director and dean to bring her back."

"The team is ranked eighth in the country. You're weeks away from the conference tournament. Are you truly willing to risk that? Some people might call your bluff."

"We're not bluffing. I dare anyone who thinks that to try us." Leon glared into the lens.

Students gathered, filming and taking photos.

"Are you concerned about how this could affect your seniors? This is your last chance to chase a national title. Maybe the school's best chance."

"Coach D'Amato is our best chance," Brooks said. "We're not doing it without her."

Beck stiffened when she spotted Mark Fellner, Sean Reilley,

and Molly Liu speed walking toward them with campus security in tow.

"It's been speculated that the university let Coach D'Amato go because of recruiting struggles. What do you have to say to young players on the fence right now?"

"If this isn't enough proof that she's the real deal, then you don't deserve to come play here," Leon said.

"Okay, that's enough." Molly pushed through the students and grabbed Beck. "You can't be filming right now."

"They're not doing anything wrong," Brooks said.

"This is absolutely uncalled for." Mark shoved Todd's camera down. "You two need to leave. Now."

"Hey!" Todd barked as campus security grabbed him.

"Don't touch him!" Beck tugged at the security guard, only to have another grab her shoulders. "Let go of me! Jerk!"

"Leave them alone," Leon snarled, and while Beck hated getting driven away, she also prayed the notorious hothead wouldn't worsen the situation.

"This is free speech!" Brooks yelled.

"This is not how we do things at this school. One more word, and you're all facing a suspension," Mark said.

"You can't force us on the court, and you can't make us silent!"

Beck glowered as security and Molly boxed them out from the confrontation and escorted them away. "You know this is bullshit," Beck said.

"You know you're not supposed to be here like this," Molly said. "Who told you this was happening? Was it the players?"

Beck swallowed. She didn't know what would come of disclosing Brooks's call but wouldn't risk it. "I can't reveal my sources."

"Was it Jordan? Did she put them up to it?" Molly stepped

closer and lowered her voice to a whisper. "Beck, there are rumors that the team threw a house party and you and Jordan showed up. Is that true?"

She twisted her face in disbelief, despite her gut hurtling off a phantom cliff. A secret relationship with a coach was one thing, but perceived socializing with players, some of whom were underage, another. While nothing happened at the party, the optics, let alone journalistic ethics, were murky at best.

"Why would I be at a house party? Are you hearing yourself?"

"Just tell me the truth and we can chalk it up as a mistake. If you don't, I'm going to have to revoke your press credential for the next game." Molly squeezed her eyes shut in exasperation. "Please, don't make me do this."

The next game, much like the entire season, would be another major story. Either Jordan would return, or the team would stay on the sidelines. Fans and critics alike would tune in. Beck painfully considered what felt like an impossible choice—giving up the story or giving up Jordan. Only it wasn't impossible anymore.

"I don't know what you're talking about. There was no house party. And we just happened to be in the neighborhood for the walkout."

"Lucky you then," Molly said. "But NWSN will have to send another reporter for Saturday."

She clenched her teeth. "I thought we were cooler than this, Molly."

"It's one game. I'm just trying to keep my job, Beck. Now you have your story. Please go," Molly said before leaving them with security.

Todd's mouth dropped. "Do you think I'm banned too?"

"I think you're innocent in this one, Todd." Beck rolled her eyes. "Are you okay? They kind of manhandled you back there." She grabbed the tripod from him.

"Yeah. Are you?"

Beck nodded, her adrenaline surging from the scuffle and narrowly dancing past the truth.

"She really brings something out in you, doesn't she?" Todd asked.

Beck did her best to not react. "Who?"

"D'Amato."

"What do you mean?" Beck clenched the tripod like her life depended on it.

"I just know. I mean, I can tell." Todd stopped both his sentence and steps. Beck swore she might pass out as she peered up at him. "You're doing good work, Beck. That's what I mean to say."

She swallowed so hard she almost choked. "Oh. Thanks, Todd. You too. You were great back there."

"The school's just embarrassed that we blasted this over the airwaves and they're taking it out on our best reporter. That's all the boss needs to know, right?" He winked. "I'm going to take a smoke break. Then, what do you say we find a spot where the gestapo can't stop us? You may be off the next game, but we still have this story for the night."

"Yeah. Yeah, sounds good," Beck said as he walked off. She squeezed her eyes shut, unsure if she'd gotten lucky or if he knew her secret. Whatever the case, she was safe for now.

Beck frowned at her phone. In the heat of the walkout, she'd hoped that Jordan might contact her. She might see the team, might see Beck, and might return for another chance. The continued silence struck deeper. So, much as she had before Jordan and now after, she clung to what she did have—a story. Perhaps one that might still be theirs.

CHAPTER THIRTY-THREE

You will never do anything in this world without courage. It is the greatest quality of the mind next to honor.
—Aristotle

Jordan stared at the quote on the locker room whiteboard as if she'd stumbled upon gold. She rested a finger next to Charlie's penmanship and, like so many other times, didn't know if the words better applied to the team or herself.

The last forty-eight hours since the walkout were chaos. The press predictably hounded her, and the situation with Mark became more precarious than ever. When he called her into his office the next day for a private meeting, he accused her of putting the players up to the protest.

"That was all them, Mark. I would never encourage them to risk their season," Jordan said.

"It's too bad you couldn't encourage them to get back on the court."

"I think they've made themselves pretty clear. But if you want to play chicken with them, that's on you. I'm not going to force my way back in or beg."

Mark sneered. "You must be enjoying every minute of this."

"It never had to be this way." Jordan stood. "Good luck with the rest of the season."

She kept her shoulders back as she went for the door, smirking when Mark frantically blurted behind her. "Jordan, wait." He loosened his tie like he was giving up on a noose. "Give me twenty-four hours. I need those boys on the court tomorrow. Will you be ready?"

"That depends. Are you going to be breathing down my neck, waiting to pull the plug, or are you going to give me a real shot?"

"It's a real shot, Jordan." His gray eyes softened and the creases in his forehead unfixed themselves. "The team needs you."

She nodded. "Then I'll be ready."

The school didn't announce Jordan's return ahead of the last home game, staving off the media circus for as long as possible. She biked to campus undetected, sunglasses and a beanie on in the overcast February light, pedaling through slicked backstreets and side roads to avoid the various news vans and reporters champing at the bit to see if the team would take the court or continue their protest.

Despite being out of the job for less than a week, Jordan soaked up the WAC with new appreciation. The drone of lights, the musk of sneakers, sweat, and freshly cleaned hardwood, the echo of her footsteps, even her small office, offered the serenity of home. It had always been home, the only one she'd ever known. But for the first time, its welcoming embrace fell short. Short of Beck.

"Coach?"

Jordan pivoted from the whiteboard to receive Brooks's hug. He lifted her off her feet while the rest of the team joined behind them, hooting and smacking high fives.

"Welcome back." Frost beamed.

"Thank you," Jordan said when the welcoming party settled. "Thank you for what you did. Though I don't know if I would've advised risking the season like that."

"You've fought for us. It was our turn to fight for you." Leon smiled.

"Well, the fight isn't over." Jordan cleared the emotion from her throat. "We've put a lot on the line to get here. Now we show everyone why. Tonight is a new beginning. So, suit up, lock in, and forget about the noise that we've made, and they've made. It all goes away when we step on that court."

But the noise wasn't easy to ignore. The crowd roared louder than ever as the players jogged out of the tunnel, and when Jordan stepped out after them, the cheers turned to thunder. Her eyes widened at the deafening show of support, the seats full to the rafters, moving like a wave as people rose to their feet. Jordan's heart rattled in her ears as she scanned the crowd, searching for the one person she wanted in her corner. But Beck wasn't there. Her grin faded in the fanfare.

The cheers built to a crescendo when the game started, but rather than distract the Bulldogs, it fueled them. Brooks and Cooper showered threes, Leon owned the paint, and Charlie set a personal record for rebounds. Dominic hustled so hard that he nearly plowed Jordan over to keep a ball inbounds, leaping over the bench like a gazelle. The guys competed like it was for the title and not an absolute demolition in conference play. When the final score glowed, the drama of the last week disappeared in the power of their performance.

Reminiscent of Jordan's first days at the helm, reporters squeezed into the media room for the postgame press conference. And much like the other times she confronted a sea of cameras, she sought Beck. While she never glimpsed her on the sidelines, she hoped that just maybe she'd be here. Instead, Easton Prescott took her usual place in the front.

"Coach, tell us what the last two days mean. The walkout and now this win," he asked.

"I couldn't be more grateful to be back on the court with these young men." Jordan nodded at Brooks and Leon at her sides. "They risked everything to keep our team together and bring me back. I'm honored and I'm humbled."

"Any message for the athletic director or school for firing you in the first place?"

Jordan shook her head. "No comment," she said flatly, though the empty response radiated with an unmistakable *fuck you.*

The reporters broke into an uproar. Jordan dodged and weaved through the presser as usual, keeping her answers brief. She scrambled out after the last question before the cameras stopped rolling and paced the hall while she waited for Molly to exit the media room. "Where's Beck?"

"Oh God." Molly groaned and stalked past her. "It wasn't a rumor, was it?"

"What?"

"The house party? You and Beck were there."

Jordan flushed but didn't speak. Molly's heels stopped clicking when they reached her office door.

"She didn't say anything." Molly shook her head. "I asked her point-blank, and she covered for you and the guys, even after I threatened her press credential. She covered for the walkout too. Brooks confessed to Mark that he called her."

"Then you shouldn't have banned her from the game. I don't see what the big deal is. She didn't do anything wrong."

"Because there are rules for a reason. Reporters are supposed to go through me if they want to talk to you or the players. They can't just show up on campus or at a house party or wherever else. She knows that. It protects the team, and it protects the press too." Molly raised a brow. "She's lucky she only got a one-game suspension. Mark wanted to ban her from the conference tournament too. He's afraid she knows too much."

"Or he wants to punish her over the walkout because he can't punish me." Jordan clenched her jaw.

Molly sighed. "Just be careful, Jordan. I wouldn't advise fraternizing with a member of the press."

"But she'll be in Las Vegas?"

"As far as I know." She rolled her eyes. "You two are going to be the death of me, aren't you?"

Jordan's forehead crumpled as Molly stomped off. While the media director warned against trusting Beck, this proved the opposite. Beck gave up the game and a story for Jordan. For the team. Jordan didn't just miss her, but as she looked at the path ahead, she didn't want to face any of it, not one more game, without her.

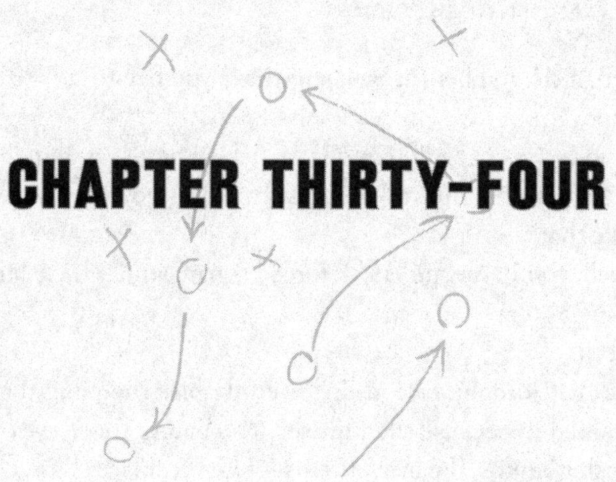

CHAPTER THIRTY-FOUR

The neon lights, jingle of video poker, stale cigarettes and regret on the casino floor, strippers, gamblers, drunkards, and high rollers alike did nothing to distract Beck from basketball. She was so dedicated to reporting on the Pacific Coast Conference tournament that she often forgot she was even in Sin City until she walked outside to find herself on the strip. She and Easton hosted every pregame and postgame show of the week-long tournament from the MGM Grand Arena. Despite her fatigue from the work that went into coverage, Beck flourished in the spotlight, and admittedly, the distraction.

Until she spotted Jordan in the hotel elevator.

It'd been two weeks since their breakup. Two weeks since they spoke at all. While she convinced herself she was over the heartbreak, when the doors peeled open and Jordan stood next to her, Beck clung to the railing to hold steady.

"Hey," Jordan said, so hoarse that Beck barely made it out.

"Hi." Beck focused on the countdown of elevator floors, knowing full well if she spared Jordan a glance, she'd blush, or worse, let the prickle behind her eyes grow to a wistful glisten.

Jordan cleared her throat. "How have you been?"

"Fine. You?"

"Good." Her gaze fluttered over Beck. She felt it, but she refused to turn. "Thank you for what you did—covering the walk-out like that."

"Well, you know me." Beck forced a grim smile. "I can't resist breaking a story."

"Beck."

She met Jordan's face, didn't even despise the pang that accompanied it, because she'd missed it so badly. Those eyes. That sheepish twinkle. The briefest twist of her necklace.

"I'm sorry. I should've never said that to you." Jordan frowned. "Molly told me what happened. You gave up covering the last game to protect the team. To protect me."

"It was nothing. I always protect my sources."

"Right."

The elevator doors opened to let on another herd of people, not just interrupting their conversation, but reminding Beck why they never worked out. The secrecy. Even if she proved herself trustworthy, even if Jordan said sorry, and their mournful glances suggested they missed each other, the conflict of interest and need for discretion hadn't changed.

They charged off their separate ways, and while Beck put on a steady face for the semifinals, her mind never stopped drifting to Jordan. The ache tormented her by the time she and Easton signed off for the night, leaving her without the distraction of work she so desperately needed.

"Beck, you're a hard woman to track down." A stout woman with cat-eye spectacles and a sequined suit jacket stopped her before she left NWSN's perch above the court.

Beck backed away, certain that a crazed viewer had wandered in from the casino. She grimaced to find Easton and the crew had left her behind. "Uh, yeah, we're just done here. Have a good night."

"I'm Fiona Wandell. I've left you a dozen voicemails," the woman said in a rich southern drawl.

Beck's eyes bulged. "You have?"

"Well, I thought I did. Hold on, I need my readers." Fiona swapped her glasses to read her outstretched phone, rattling off a number that wasn't Beck's. "Oh, shit. Well, we're here now. I watched your tapes. I've seen your recent work, and I want to represent you."

Fiona's abrasiveness caught Beck off guard. Especially as she stood in an outfit with enough sparkles to rival Elton John.

"I'm sorry. Did you come all the way here to see me?"

"No, I have another client covering the tournament and I never pass up an excuse to hit the casino," Fiona said. "Listen, NSBC is interested."

"You work for NSBC?" Beck's heart thundered. She'd grown up watching the National Sports Broadcasting Channel and dreamed of sitting at its anchor desk.

"No, I'm an agent at CTI. But I work closely with the network's talent scouts. I have other clients associated with them. Let's just cut to the meat and potatoes here—I can get you an audition."

"You can get me an audition with NSBC?"

"God, honey, you sound so much smarter on TV. Yes, read my lips. I can get you in front of the people that matter." Fiona chuckled and Beck blushed. "Walk with me. I'm going to be late to Cirque du Soleil."

They waded through the arena mezzanine, dodging throngs of basketball fans waving foam fingers and sloshing beer.

"If NSBC is interested in me, why do I need you?"

"Ah, you are in there." Fiona smirked. "One, I can get you out of the slush pile and into the front of the line. And two, you don't want to keep going in this business without representation. I used to be in your shoes, believe it or not. I'm sure I don't have to tell you, the industry has changed, but not that much."

Beck nodded. "Well, no one lets me forget I have tits, that's for sure."

Fiona clapped her hands. "And that's the spunk I like. Your reporting and feature stories are original and human. But it's that personality and banter you bring to the desk that they're desperate for."

"It helps that my co-anchor is insufferable."

"Ha! Trust me, we can find you insufferable at NSBC." Fiona handed her a business card. "Shoot me your best reel, I'll put together some paperwork, and I'll get you to Los Angeles."

"Just like that?"

"Well, I can get you to the audition. You have to do the rest." Fiona shook her hand. "Want to join me for a steak?"

"No, I need to get ready to cover the finals tomorrow. It was nice to meet you," Beck said in a daze as Fiona waddled off.

Her mind charged a million miles a minute. She didn't know what to do first. Rush upstairs to edit her reel, look up whether Fiona was legit, or call her parents for advice. All that ran through her head was *NSBC, audition, Los Angeles. Los Angeles.* Dread knocked her back.

Los Angeles meant no Jordan.

Not that she had Jordan. That didn't stop her throat from clenching when she passed the coach's floor in the elevator. And as she dug through her bag for her editing gear, she froze when her fingers brushed across a threadbare paperback. The book Jordan gave her. The one that now had her own underlines in the musty pages and name on the back cover.

Beck put it beside her laptop, glaring at it every so often as though the Pulitzer Prize winner might open its jaws and bite her. She determinedly spliced through her work until it came time to edit her sit-down interview with Jordan. She paused at the snippets. At her gentle glances and the voice that steeped her skin in heat. Beck groaned.

She slammed her laptop shut and grabbed the hotel stationery. She didn't have Jordan, and while Los Angeles was still just a dream, though one she might now achieve, the prospect of losing either left her spinning. So, Beck scrambled to do what she did best. Make sense of one more story.

She finished the letter just before midnight, though the strobe lights and crowds outside created the illusion that it wasn't late at all. Beck didn't have a solid plan for returning the book, nor did she consider the implications that might follow, but that was always par for the course with Jordan. Only she could send her lurking through the corridors of a Las Vegas hotel in the middle of the night.

"Oh, Caroline!" The obnoxious high pitch of a Miss Piggy impersonator assaulted her ears as her door slammed shut. She glared at Easton and Wyatt stumbling down the hall. "Oh, fair maiden, your prince has been looking for you!"

"Shut up." Wyatt shoved Easton before nodding at Beck. "Why didn't you join us?"

"I had work to do," she said.

Easton rolled his eyes. "Of course you did."

"Where are you going?" Wyatt asked.

The two men reeked of liquor and too much time at the craps table.

"I was just going to grab some food." Beck walked away, but they followed.

"What if I come in and we order room service?" Wyatt's eyes were bloodshot, and Beck inched away from him.

"No, that's okay."

"I have a better idea." Easton glowered. "How about I take you in there and teach you a lesson?"

"And what lesson would that be?" Beck tensed. Sober Easton was unbearable, but drunk Easton frightened her. It wasn't lost on her that both men towered above her, that they staggered with her every step, and that no one was around to help.

"Depends on your willingness to learn," Easton slurred with a self-satisfied smirk.

The hair on the back of her neck stood. Despite her back against the wall, she held firm, taking up as much space as possible like you were supposed to when confronting a bear.

"Let me guess, it lasts eight seconds too?" she asked, and Wyatt snorted. "This is harassment."

Easton smacked his hand to the wall near her head and leaned closer. "You'll know when it's harassment, sweetheart."

She bumped past them and stormed to the elevator. "You're a real stand-up guy. You too, Wyatt."

"Beck, it's a joke."

"It's not funny." She punched the down button. Wyatt walked toward her, but Beck put up a finger. "Don't."

When the elevator doors slid shut, she caught a shaky breath. She hated her rattling pulse, hated that they scared her, and hated that alluding to fucking and assaulting her was nothing more than a punch line. It wasn't the first time and wouldn't be the last that she was harassed, and while over the years she considered filing a dreaded HR report, she'd always stopped short. Something in her suggested it would make it worse, or that it wasn't that bad or that it was simply how men spoke. The reasons always echoed in her mother's voice, Candace Beck ruing the industry but the first to encourage silence.

She rode the elevator down to the casino floor. The run-in

sufficiently sobered her, and Beck lost all motivation to find Jordan. She fingered the note in the book's front cover, flipping through the pages. At the very least, Jordan deserved to get it back, and with Los Angeles threatening to end their connection for good, Beck needed to know how this might end.

She pulled out her phone. He answered on the first ring.

"Hey, Brooks, it's Beck. Can you be discreet? I was hoping you could do me a favor."

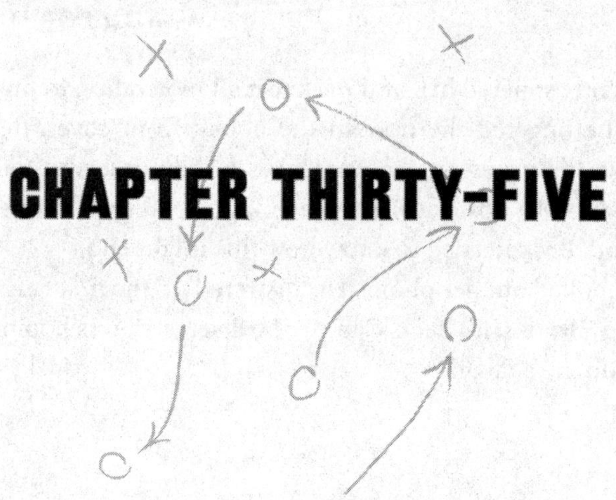

CHAPTER THIRTY-FIVE

Jordan puked before the Pacific Coast Conference finals. Fortunately, there weren't any cheerleaders to witness her nerves. Nerves that sprang not from her desire to win, but the expectation that came with her success. In the beginning, the critics and fans doubted she could hack it. Now they demanded a trophy.

Winning the PCC Championship in Las Vegas meant the Bulldogs would enter the national tournament as a top seed. It was a formality, really, after their performance during the regular season. But while they easily trounced St. Anthony University in the semifinals and were primed to cut down the net that evening, Jordan faltered.

She faltered just as she had for two weeks, battling insomnia, pondering a call that she'd never make. Faltered like she did in the elevator when she finally encountered Beck, her presence spurring such unbearable homesickness that she nearly bolted the first chance she got. Faltered like she did when she spotted her a day later, reporting on the sidelines.

"Jordan, did you hear me?" Frost asked from his seat in the stands next to her. They were supposed to be scouting their opponents with the team, but she spent most of the time staring at Beck.

Leon snorted. "I don't think she's watching the game, man."

"I don't blame you, Coach." Dominic gawked at Beck on the court below. "I can't take my eyes off her."

"You wish, Dom," Leon said through a mouthful of popcorn. "You wouldn't know what to do with her."

"Knock it off." Jordan flicked Dominic's ear and smacked the popcorn out of Leon's hands.

"Hey! That's my popcorn!" Charlie shouted.

While the boys roughhoused, Jordan chanced a last look. Her insides twisted with familiar longing, and she knew, as she had for weeks, that admiring from afar simply wouldn't do. Of course, the must-win conference championship left little time to mourn or remedy the distance. The lone glimmer in the darkness, however, was the finals required Beck report on the Bulldogs.

All tournament long, Easton slid in for press conferences in place of her, while she covered the other games. Jordan tried not to take it personally, but it stung. Now it came down to this. A necessary step to chase a national title, and maybe the last time Jordan might ever glimpse Beck on the sideline.

She splashed water on her face and straightened her jacket before leaving for the team locker room. Her brow furrowed when she found Brooks in the hall. "What are you doing out here?"

"I believe this belongs to you," he said.

Jordan's heart crawled into her throat as he outstretched her copy of *The Old Man and the Sea*. "How did you get this?"

"Beck asked me to give it to you." Brooks smirked. "What was it you told me earlier this season? This is just basketball. Who you love and how you want to live your life—that's everything."

"Brooks, there's nothing—" Jordan stopped. She couldn't conceal her frown. "There's nothing now."

"Maybe there is." He nodded at the book. Jordan opened it and found a note tucked behind the front cover. Brooks cleared his throat. "I didn't read it. I just grabbed it from the front desk for you."

"Thank you," she mumbled.

"I'll meet you in there." Brooks patted her shoulder and slipped into the locker room.

Jordan inhaled and didn't release it as she leaned against the wall. Her shaking fingers struggled to unfold the letter. Beck's looping penmanship, the ink she put to paper just for her, reached out like a hand cupping her cheek.

Jordan,

The team was never the big, impossible fish.

The team is the boy in awe of the fisherman, eager to help and learn from him, despite the odds of success.

But you were right about one thing. You are certainly the old man, which sounds incredibly unromantic but is the highest of compliments. You are just as admirably dogged and determined, unafraid of the endless ocean or favored fishermen, and gently poetic about life in a way I've come to cherish almost as much as your eyes that hold the vastness of the sea. But perhaps the thing you have most in common is a turtle heart that beats long after death. Though maybe that heart makes me like the old man too. Because even when we part, my heart will still thunder for you.

This season is yours to take, and so am I.

Love,
Beck

Jordan exhaled and closed her eyes. Her heart galloped as though attempting to break free from the confines of her chest. She read the note again before putting it in her pocket, though she would've read it a hundred times over, holding it with the same reverence as she did the Greeks and Romans, the Nobel laureates, poets, and playwrights. She opened the book to the back cover, a smile digging trenches in her cheeks at the precious addition to the list: *Caroline Beck*.

The simple name, the paper in her pocket, infused her with a love that eclipsed her obsession with victory and its ill side effects. She stood straighter. Clean, calm energy rolled in her veins and vividness returned to her vision. She entered the locker room with war drums keeping rhythm in her heart.

"We are what we repeatedly do. Excellence then is not an act, but a habit." Jordan examined her players. They twitched in their navy uniforms, teeth bared, bouncing on the balls of their feet. The air in the room thinned, laced with adrenaline. "Anyone remember who said that?"

"Aristotle," Leon said, as he nudged Charlie. "See, I can crack a book too, Doc."

Jordan nodded, her jaw stiff enough to slice. "You know exactly what to do. So go out there and be excellent. Let's take what's ours."

The team marched out without smiles or laughter, without so much as a blink. An unspoken fortitude overtook them as they became warriors, reflecting the ferocity of their chief. They warmed up with gravitas, transforming the court into their battleground.

When Jordan spotted Beck, she didn't wave or nod. She walked straight for her.

"I got your note." Jordan resisted lingering long enough to take her in, though she wanted to. She didn't pause for Beck's irises flecked with gold or stare at her parted lips. She delivered her message in a whisper, though the roaring crowd, the music, and bouncing basketballs provided an ample shield. "My heart's still beating too, Beck."

She pivoted back to the court before anyone could think more of their exchange than a simple hello. But it was enough to bring relief. Not just for Jordan, but she detected it in Beck too. In her loosening shoulders, in her smirk and nod after Jordan peeled away.

Then, with the letter lining her pocket, with the war drums thumping, Jordan coached her fucking ass off. She'd led and commanded the floor before, but nothing compared to the way this game molded under her like she wasn't coaching but sculpting clay. She paced with each pass, clapped, and pointed with every play, yelled ceaselessly at both her players and the referee when they didn't conform to her vision. The score and clock didn't matter. The fans and cheers never impeded her focus. She communicated plays with a simple nod or look.

It wasn't until Cooper screened for Brooks, who spun and threw a ball up for Leon to dunk, that the roar finally hit her ears, that the numbers meant something again, that she emerged from her trance. The minutes slipped to seconds.

"This is it. Take it in, Jordan!" Frost shouted to her over the crowd.

The fans stood. A head rush forced her to squat on the sideline while she held her breath. Karsten Marks tossed a desperate three-pointer in the fading seconds. Jordan screamed, *"Rebound!"* before it hit the rim, but Charlie was already there in a swarm of elbows to secure the ball. The buzzer wailed. Brooks chucked the ball into the stands, the bench players stormed the court, and Jordan shut her eyes. She'd won her first conference championship and a shot at a national title.

The celebration came in snippets. In fact, Jordan didn't fully comprehend the win as she shook hands with Camden's coach, as she congratulated her players at midcourt, as navy and white confetti fell, and cameras circled her. It wasn't until she found Beck that the feat burst in brilliant color.

"Coach, congratulations!" Beck shouted over the cheers and shrieking players. She swayed but never lost her spot in the swarm. Her eyes reflected the light bouncing off the hardwood. They never veered from Jordan, and Jordan, despite the other microphones vying for her, chose Beck. Would always choose Beck. "How does it feel to win your first conference championship as head coach?"

The question barely reached her through the celebration. "I, uh—" Jordan stopped. Her answer hitched in her throat, and without warning, the strangled sensation of tears took hold. She couldn't say for certain where they came from. The win. Or her. "I, um . . ."

"It's okay. Take a minute." Beck subtly grazed her back.

Jordan took hold of her advice like a safe harbor. She cast her stare out, first at the cameras and dozens of reporters awaiting her answer. Her eyes traveled up to the stands filled with adoration, then to the fluttering confetti drifting like snow.

"We've been through hell, you know?" Jordan answered, winded against her locked lungs. "This team could've given up so many times and they didn't."

Beck's hand lingered on Jordan's back as she leaned down to hear her. "*You* also never gave up. You've faced countless critics. You've been fired and brought back. People never stopped saying that you can't do the job. And you're still here. In just a few minutes, you're going to raise that trophy. Tell us how that feels."

"Like I pulled in that impossible fish," Jordan said with a grin that Beck mirrored back. "It's the guys who did the work, though. It's the guys who make this job worth every challenge."

As if on cue, Brooks threw an arm around her, and Charlie hugged her from behind, carrying her away. Jordan lost sight of Beck in the embraces, in the presentation of the trophy, in the cutting of the net, in the photos and interviews, but her mind never drifted far from her. Because the win wasn't yet complete.

After a water fight in the locker room that left her soaked, after an hour-long press conference, after hugs and team dinner, Jordan knew exactly where she needed to go. She took rare advantage of her fame, agreeing to autographs and selfies with the hotel's front desk workers in exchange for Beck's room number, though she imagined she would have somehow found the door anyway. Like gravity would've sucked her there no matter where she stumbled.

Before knocking, she turned off her phone for the first time in months. It buzzed with texts from the team and dozens of others. Leon was calling to ask her to extend curfew, but she sent him to voicemail. This time, she'd put the game aside. This time, when she took Beck, she wouldn't let her go again.

The door swung open, and Beck smirked as if expecting her. "Big win tonight." She leaned against the doorframe like Jordan's personal Aphrodite, curls in a waterfall down her shoulders, her eyes a magnetic pool, the slightest glimpse of skin at the vee of her sweater a tease that Jordan could hardly stand.

"It is now." She smiled. "You going to let me in?"

Beck grabbed her by the basketball net that still hung around her neck and pulled her inside.

Both of them oblivious to Wyatt Holt lingering in the hallway.

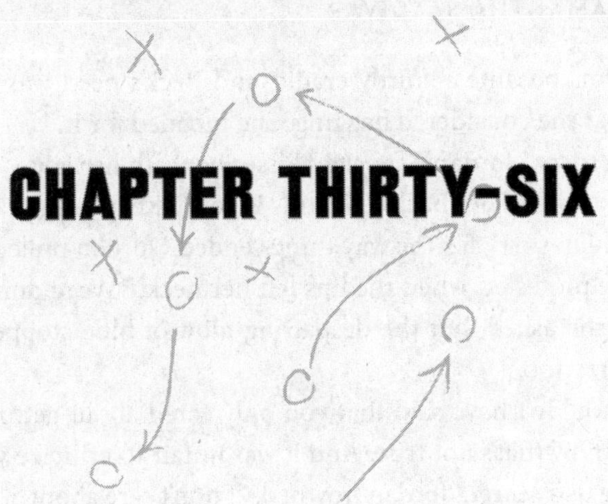

CHAPTER THIRTY-SIX

Beck and Jordan's reunion lacked hasty lust or words. They simply held each other. Beck shut her eyes, clinging on as if she could express her passion, her pride, and pain through osmosis. She didn't know how long they stayed like that, but minutes must have passed because her vision blurred, and her legs were numb when they parted.

"Can I kiss you now?" Jordan tucked a lock of hair behind Beck's ear. Her eyes glowed richer than Beck remembered, or perhaps she simply wasn't used to them anymore.

"Yes." She clutched Jordan's jaw when her lips swept into her own. Beck relished the sway of her tongue. She ran her fingers through Jordan's curls, down her neck, across her shoulders. The kiss, one she'd gone too long without, left her dizzy. Rather than fight it, she opened wider, grasped Jordan closer, shut her eyes in willing submission.

She didn't care for air. Every break of Jordan's lips, however brief, was like being chucked into a blizzard. Each time she returned, Beck waned beneath her heat. Their hips adjoined on the bed, arms became a sturdy cradle, and Beck's need was so fervent that she considered begging. She moaned for it.

"I'm sorry." Jordan deposited kisses beneath her jaw.

Beck rubbed her back. "No, this is good. Keep going."

"No. I'm sorry for the way things ended." Jordan pulled back.

Beck protested when the lips left her neck. "We're doing this now?" she asked, but the despairing glint of blue stopped her. "I'm sorry too."

"I shouldn't have said that you only cared about getting stories. I know that's not true. And it was unfair to criticize you for keeping us a secret." Jordan frowned. "I don't care about any of it. I love you."

Beck swallowed. "I love you too." She held Jordan's cheeks, brushed them with her thumbs. "I shouldn't have gotten so wrapped up in the recruiting story. This, us, is what matters to me."

"Me too." Jordan pulled her down to her chest, and they lay in easy silence. So much waited beneath the surface, so much to be said and solved, but it wasn't daunting. Not here. Not with Jordan's heart beating beneath her ear. "Your letter. That was everything."

Beck traced a finger across Jordan's chest. "I meant it. I just thought you deserved to know. Even if we were over."

"It was more than I deserved."

"Stop." Beck shifted and met her face. "You deserve love, Jordan. You deserve to not go it alone."

The corners of Jordan's mouth crumpled. "I've just been by myself for so long. Not just coaching, you know? Growing up. Constantly moving army bases. Riding out the crossfire of my parents." Her throat bobbed. "I think maybe it affected me more than I realized."

Beck's throat tightened. "I know," she whispered.

"I still leave tickets for them at games. Even today, which I know is pathetic."

"It's not pathetic. We all want our parents' approval." She sighed. "I didn't tell you, but I tried to tell mine about us over Christmas. Or at least, I told them I was attracted to women."

Jordan's eyes widened. "Was it okay?"

"It wasn't horrible. But they asked if I was seeing anyone, and I backed out. It just seemed complicated with you being someone I report on," Beck said. "Their recommendation was that I stay in the closet unless necessary."

Jordan held her closer. "I'm sorry."

"No, I'm sorry I didn't follow through. It's not like I don't want to—"

"I trust you, and if we have to be a secret that's okay with me." Jordan traced circles along her arm. "You were right. It's not like I've made anything easier. I know I let the team take over. I thought the game might be all I needed, but that was wrong. Even when I got reinstated, it wasn't the same. It's not home anymore. Not without you."

The worried voice in Beck's head finally fell quiet. Despite their closeness before, she could never shake a lingering separateness. The unbreachable wall that held them apart as reporter and coach. While they were still those things, for the first time, it didn't feel like all of them. It slid away in the equal sacrifice, the vows to change for this place away from the court and cameras.

Beck kissed her, slowly, without hurry or uncertainty, because she didn't fear the future or their careers or secrecy. Not now.

"Does that mean you want to get back together?" Jordan whispered.

She chuckled. "Yes."

Jordan grinned just as wide as she did when she raised the trophy that night. "It's probably a good thing we waited until after the tournament to make up."

"Why?"

"Because it took everything in me to not kiss you after we won."

"Well, that makes two of us." Beck smiled but also bore an unexpected pang. The pang that she couldn't be the one to embrace Jordan after triumph. That she couldn't peck her lips in the confetti. She settled for the less passionate but still satisfying task of interviewing Jordan after. She'd never forget the way she glowed, the way the win overwhelmed her. "I thought you might cry. Though I just realized I've never actually seen you cry."

Jordan shrugged. "Never let them see you sweat. Or cry. The last thing I need to be is the blubbering woman in the huddle."

"You don't always have to be so tough."

"I'm not that tough."

Beck pecked Jordan's cheek, the ripples inside turning to waves. She found her lips, seized them like they never stopped belonging to her. When they parted, she pressed her mouth to the shell of Jordan's ear, with every intention of sending equal currents through her. "Did you just come here to say sorry, or did you come here to celebrate?"

"That depends," Jordan said, unhooking Beck's bra with two lithe fingers. "Is this off the record?"

Beck grinned against her lips and slid hands to her waist. "There's no more record, Jordan."

They made love like it was a promise. With Jordan on her lips, Jordan inside her, Jordan's name a song, Beck didn't just give herself but would have begged to be taken. But she didn't need to beg. Jordan took her with mercy, with tenderness, with love. And each time she hit the edge, she landed safe and fulfilled. It confirmed what she already knew in her bones. She could leave, she could run, she could never see her again, but she would never be free from Jordan. And she didn't want to be.

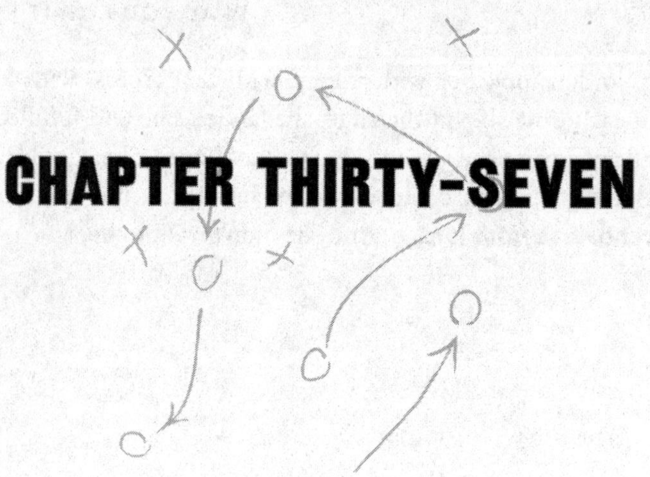

CHAPTER THIRTY-SEVEN

Ten days after Las Vegas, the first two rounds of the NCAA National Tournament came to Portland. Winter rainstorms cleared for brighter spring showers. Greenery bloomed along the waterfront, people shed their layers, and the clouds broke each afternoon. With the city hosting the games, the David Douglas Bulldogs essentially enjoyed a home court advantage.

Leading up to the chase for a championship, Jordan buckled down, dedicating additional hours to practice. She often worked late into the night after Beck nodded off or left before sunrise, peppering her with kisses before departing. But while unflappably concentrated, perhaps more determined than Beck had ever seen her, it was no longer all of her. She turned her phone off when she left the arena. She left the study sessions to the tutors and the injuries to the team medical staff.

They talked more than ever before. Jordan no longer cut her sentences short when it came to the team. She no longer prefaced her words with *off the record.* She shared the goofy anecdotes and jokes from the players that made her laugh, sparking Beck with identical joy. She told her of her concerns and plans on the coaching front and even asked for advice as they curled up to watch game film. Beck took pride in her own observations, smitten with Jordan's arm draped around her shoulder.

And Beck changed too. Not once was she tempted to report any of Jordan's schemes or team secrets. She hit the desk for analysis, attended press conferences, and reported on the sidelines without the inclination to share or the desire to. During those ten days, Beck wholeheartedly believed that a world existed where they could do it. They could handle their jobs and be together.

Until game one of the tournament.

"The city of Portland is buzzing with college basketball fans from around the country. This afternoon kicks off the first round of the national tournament. Oregon's own David Douglas Bulldogs come in as a number three seed in the west region, taking on fourteen-seed South Atlantic University. Beck, the cards are stacked in David Douglas's favor for round one."

Beck nodded at Easton as they stood on the Moda Center pavilion for the pregame show. Foot traffic bustled on the dry, overcast day. Fans waved and jumped at the camera as they passed behind them.

"You're going to see a lot of navy and white in the stands supporting the Bulldogs. They're coming in hot after a dominant performance in the Pacific Coast Conference tournament, and frankly, they were primed and clicking on all cylinders before that. The question, of course, is if they're peaking at the right time because anything can happen during this tournament. Sometimes it's scary to even have a lead."

"Let's talk about some of the firepower on this squad. Point guard Brooks McCray Jr. was named the PCC Player of the Year. He's a finalist for several national awards and he's been named an all-American along with Leon Torres. Torres is another major threat. He's known to have a temper on the court, but this team absolutely depends on him. He's a defensive force, leading in offensive boards, but he's even more fearsome driving through the paint. He's like a young Scottie Pippen."

"Or Dennis Rodman, depending on the day," she added.

"And we'd be remiss to not mention head coach Jordan D'Amato. I could go down the list of history she's already made, but that PCC tournament win truly solidified her place. I'll be the first to admit I had my doubts, but she's done something special at David Douglas."

Beck smirked ever so slightly. "She's mastered the spread offense, but more importantly, won the team over. The players are loyal, they respond to her, and during the walkout just weeks ago, they emphasized they want to win the national title with her."

"Despite that, a slight snub earlier this week, when she didn't win PCC Coach of the Year."

"I mean, in her debut season she won the conference tournament and boasted the best record in the league. I think we'd be surprised if any coach with that résumé didn't win it." Beck had been more furious than Jordan at the obvious slight. Jordan's fellow conference coaches voted for the award, so they'd sent her a pointed message: you're still not wanted. "Of course, when asked about it after practice earlier this week, D'Amato shrugged and said maybe next year."

"A woman of few words." Easton chuckled.

"I'm sure she'll let her team's performance do all the talking."

The arena vibrated at tip-off. Beck slid into a spot on the packed press row to observe the game, take notes, and fire updates on social media. She allowed herself glimpses of Jordan, intuitively reading her expression for satisfaction or stress. While she always secretly rooted for the Bulldogs, even before they started a relationship, now her heart thundered with every basket. On press row, one wasn't permitted to cheer or boo or show their allegiance, but with the stakes higher than ever, a loss ending a team's season, Beck pulled for Jordan and the team with secret ardor.

Fortunately, the Bulldogs answered her silent cheers and telepathic hope for a win, stunning the much lower ranked SAU. They thrived off the crowd, were faster and bigger than the fourteen-seed foe. At halftime, they led by fifteen and piled on points through the second half.

Beck swelled at witnessing Jordan succeed on a larger scale, in a bigger arena, with the nation's attention. Fumbling the first round, despite her success, would've tarnished everything she accomplished. The critics would have punished her, Beck included, and she wouldn't be surprised if the school turned on her as well. So, with just three minutes left and a twenty-two-point lead, she breathed a little easier, let her back unclench, until Wyatt tapped her shoulder.

"Hey, Beck, do you have a minute?" he asked.

They'd passed each other multiple times since Las Vegas, but the usually eager Wyatt hadn't said more than hello. Beck assumed his behavior in the hotel rightfully embarrassed him.

"What's up?" she asked, still suctioned to the court.

"Can I talk to you privately?"

"Uh, sure." Beck furrowed her brow. If the game wasn't an absolute blowout, she would've denied him. He led her to the mouth of their section, where they could monitor the game but avoid unwanted ears. "What's going on? Is this about Las Vegas? Because I'm just trying to bury it."

His eyes widened. "You saw me too?"

"Uh, yeah, you and Easton were plastered. Do you not remember?"

"That's not what I'm talking about," Wyatt said, though his cheeks turned scarlet.

"Oh, I thought you might want to apologize."

His brow hardened. "I saw D'Amato go into your room after the finals."

Beck wished to transform to stone, to not react or twitch, but she knew her face crumpled before she could help it, certain she didn't just flush but fade of color. "What?"

"I saw Jordan D'Amato go into your hotel room," Wyatt said.

She shook her head. "No."

"I'm positive."

The crowd roared with another deep shot down on the court. Beck could barely breathe in the face of her worst fears. "It's not what you think."

"I think it is." Wyatt frowned. She denied him again, but he spoke over her. "Listen, you know how much I like you, Beck. I'm not going to say anything. But whatever is going on with you and D'Amato, you need to be careful. If someone else saw that, I think they'd come to the same conclusion I did."

Easton rounded the corner with a grin. "Oh, what an interesting conversation this is . . ." He slinked behind them and clapped a hand on both of their shoulders.

Beck jerked away, teeth clenched as she leveled Wyatt with a glare. "You're wrong. I don't know what you think you saw."

Easton snickered. "I am going to have so much fun with this."

"Dude, don't be like that." Wyatt shook his head.

"Really, you still have the hots for her even though she's D'Amato's plaything?"

Beck's world spun at a nauseating velocity. She didn't know what to say or do. It was already too late. Easton would run with it, even if it was a lie. Even if Wyatt had been wrong. And that was the worst part. He wasn't. The more she denied it, the more she sounded like a guilty cliché.

"What's she like, Beck?" Easton hissed into her ear. "Actually, don't tell me. I'd rather use my imagination."

Beck turned to slug him, but the arena's cheers gave way to a fearful coo. They pivoted to the court. A gut-wrenching scream rang out below as a Bulldog lay limp beneath the basket.

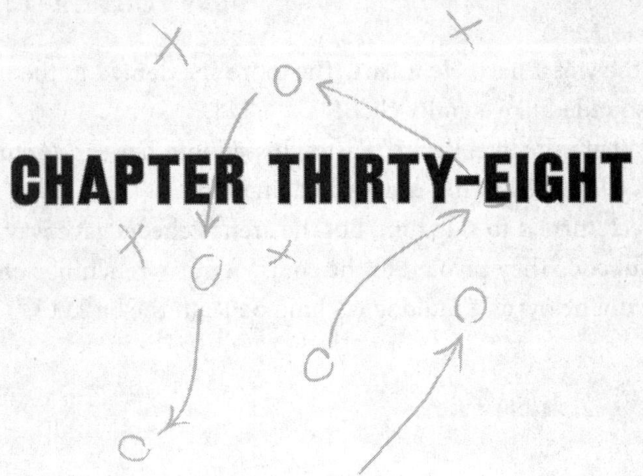

CHAPTER THIRTY-EIGHT

Jordan knew Leon Torres's season was finished, his entire basketball career potentially over, when he landed wrong after an ambitious but unnecessary layup. The horrifying angle of his leg as it broke would haunt her for many nights, in fact, even several years later. A wounded, guttural cry, more animal than human, ruptured from the forward when he buckled to the ground with the lower half of his right leg twisted in the wrong direction.

Players from both teams backed away in horror. Charlie buried his head in his hands and Brooks broke into tears. Jordan trailed the medics and trainers who ran to him, her stomach curdling at his disfigured leg. She kneeled at his head and forced her voice steady. "It's going to be okay. You're going to be okay. Just breathe."

"No, no, no." Leon's cries echoed to the rafters. Players and coaches from both teams took to a knee.

Jordan hushed him as she pulled off and folded her suit jacket, placing it under his head. "Just breathe. You're going to be fine."

"No, Coach. No." Leon wailed into his hands. "I can't be done. I can't be done."

Her heart shattered. Leon, who dreamed of the NBA, realized it was over. She knew he sobbed not just because of physical agony but crushed dreams. Dreams of providing for his family, dreams of running out of an NBA tunnel, dreams of basketball glory.

He wept and Jordan, who couldn't remember the last time she cried, nearly sobbed with him. "Hold my hand. Hold it," she demanded, and Leon grabbed on. "You're not done. You always have a place on this team. You understand? You're not done."

They clutched hands even as the gurney rolled out. The fans cheered for Leon when he raised an arm in a sign of fortitude. Jordan hugged him before he departed and allowed herself a single exhale, a brief second with her eyes closed. Then she scooped her jacket off the floor and rejoined the team.

She'd never seen the guys so despondent. Many of them wiped tears. Others cast their gazes a thousand miles away. She spoke gently, hiding her shaking hands behind her back. "He's going to be okay. I promise. Come on. Bring it in here."

The huddle tightened into a group hug.

"Leon would want you to go out there and finish strong. We're going to get through this," she said. "Charlie, you want to lead us in a prayer?"

He nodded, and the players closed their eyes as his soothing baritone took over. Jordan's religious trauma didn't make her one for prayer, but she never kept her teams from it. She usually waited with her eyes open in the background until they finished. But in this moment, she knew they needed to hear Charlie, needed to feel like they could do something, and more than that, she needed this prayer too. She shut her eyes and thought of Leon, her favorite pain in the ass.

The Bulldogs pushed through the last minutes to secure the win. The fans respectfully clapped when it ended, and both teams exchanged well wishes. Jordan wanted to hide in her devastation but couldn't avoid the network sideline reporter at the tunnel. She rolled her eyes when the woman asked if Leon was out for the tournament. "You saw it. Of course he is."

She trudged into the postgame press conference alone, determined at the very least to shield the rest of the team from the press. She sat in a daze in front of the cameras, offering brief answers. To make things worse, Beck unleashed friendly fire.

"I know this is a tough question, but you were up by twenty-six points with a few minutes left. Do you regret that he was on the court?" Beck asked.

Jordan inhaled slowly. "I take full responsibility for what happened to Leon. It's my job to protect the players. I didn't do that."

Beck frowned and Jordan longed to collapse in her arms, but it would be many more hours until she would get to. After getting the team settled at the hotel, she went to the hospital to sit with Wanda Torres. She held the woman's hand as the doctors informed them Leon sustained compound fractures in his tibia and fibula. The kid was on enough painkillers to tranquilize a horse, but Jordan knew the news would crush him later. The injury meant at least a year-long recovery. His shot at the pros wasn't just unlikely, but nearly impossible.

After assuring Wanda that she'd pay for her hotel room for as long as she needed, Jordan rode the hospital elevator down in a stupor. She hadn't eaten, showered, or had the chance to process anything. So, when she spotted Beck in the lobby, her legs nearly gave out.

"Are you okay?" Beck jumped to meet her. Jordan squeezed onto her. "It's alright. You're alright."

"Fuck." Jordan breathed raggedly, as though catching up with the shock of the day. When she regained control, Beck took her by the hand and led her to sit.

"You want to talk about it?"

Jordan smirked. "Have you ever asked anyone that question? I thought you usually just start badgering people."

"Shut up," Beck said with a weak chuckle. She rubbed Jordan's back, graveness returning when she caught her gaze. "How is he?"

"Fractured tibia and fibula. It was awful." Jordan dragged hands down her face. "I don't know how we're going to get through the next game. I don't even know who we're playing."

"Creighton. They just beat Camden by five. They were sloppy. Sixty percent at the free throw line, thirty-six percent outside the arc. Nearly a dozen turnovers. Camden just couldn't get their shit together," Beck said, and Jordan could've kissed her. "I'm sorry about that question at the press conference. I hope you don't really blame yourself."

"I might a little." Jordan swallowed the knot in her throat. Leon's mutilated leg and his whimpers ran on an endless loop in her head. "But not because of your question. You were just doing your job." But Beck sighed uneasily. Jordan furrowed her brow. "I promise it's fine."

"It's not that." Beck fidgeted with her fingers. "I hate to do this to you with everything going on, but we might have a problem."

Jordan's shoulders sank. "What's wrong?"

"Wyatt saw you go into my hotel room in Vegas." Beck's eyes glassed over. "He confronted me about it at the game, and Easton overheard."

"Shit." Jordan clutched her hand. "I'm so sorry."

"Don't be. I'll deal with this. But in case something comes out, you should be prepared."

"We'll just deny it, right?" Jordan asked.

Beck nodded half-heartedly. "I'll try. I have been. I don't know what will happen. I don't know if he'll tell our boss or if I'll lose my job."

"Oh, Beck," she whispered. Shame hardened in her gut like cement. She hadn't protected Leon. And she hadn't protected Beck.

"I don't want you to worry. I have some dirt of my own on those guys, so if they want to bring me down, two can play at that game."

"What dirt?"

"Just Easton and Wyatt harassing me at the hotel." She said it casually, but Jordan's vision flashed red.

"I swear to God." She stood with clenched fists and teeth, though she had no idea where she intended to go before Beck yanked her back down to sit.

"Jordan, don't. Just let me handle myself. You handle yourself." Beck leveled her with the same glare that flickered after her confrontation with Kip Keating.

It wasn't lost on Jordan that berating Keating on Beck's behalf played at least some part in her losing coach of the year, as rumors spread that he rallied the votes against her. Not that she was about to tell Beck or that she regretted it. She only regretted not fully unleashing on him to make his petty revenge worthwhile. The same desire flooded her now. Only Easton was a much more worthy and satisfying target.

"You need to focus on winning." Beck wrapped her hand around Jordan's, bringing her rage to a low simmer. "You look terrible. You should come home with me."

Jordan sighed. "I should get back to the hotel."

"I don't trust you to feed yourself or sleep right now."

Truthfully, Jordan didn't trust herself either. With fried nerves and the day's events a reel of horror, the simplest tasks daunted her. But she wasn't about to offload that on Beck.

"I should get ready for Creighton."

"You'll be useless if you don't rest, Jordan. Hey." Beck lifted her chin and forced her to look up. "Come home with me."

Jordan didn't know how she would've gotten through the night without her. Sweeter than her help, however, was everything left unspoken. Beck didn't pester with questions or even speak while they ate. When Jordan flopped to the bed, she simply opened her arms to hold her. And when Jordan insisted she wake up at four that morning to get back to work, Beck didn't protest. She woke her with kisses. "It's time for you to go," Beck whispered, her body a cocoon that Jordan didn't want to leave.

"You sure? I swear I just closed my eyes," Jordan said.

"I'm sure." Beck swept back her hair, kissed beneath her ear. "I want you to stay, but you need to get ready for Creighton."

Jordan brushed her lips across Beck's, drawing strength from them like a cure to her weariness. "I love you."

"I love you too, Coach."

Despite her fatigue, the trauma of Leon's injury, and the drama of being found out, Jordan ventured into the dark morning revived. Royce's counsel struck true. It was in these moments that she needed people beyond the court. While she never considered what it would be like to have an equal at her side during the game's trials, she realized all along it'd been Beck. It would always be Beck.

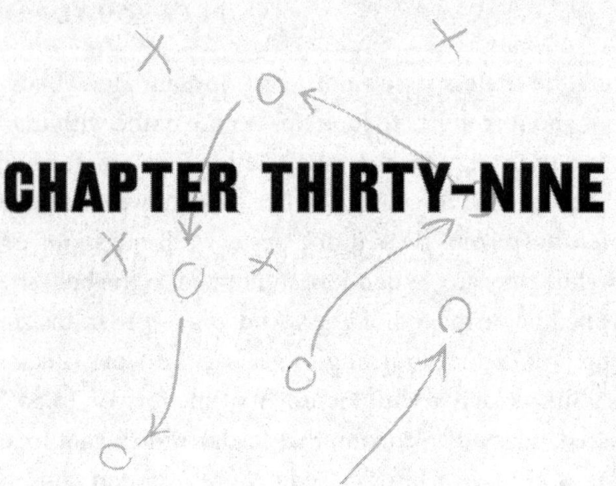

CHAPTER THIRTY-NINE

Regardless of what she told the media or her team going into the second round of the national tournament, Jordan didn't know if the Bulldogs could survive the loss of Leon. He didn't just rack up points, but invoked fear in opponents, his energy a catalyst for the entire team. Without him, the locker room lapsed into eerie silence.

"Come on, guys, look alive." Jordan bounded into the center of the room.

She was dead on her feet after devising a strategy, preparing the players with a brief practice, and visiting Leon at the hospital. It's part of what made the chase for a title so taxing. Just a day to prepare for an unknown opponent while recovering from the previous game.

"Let's go, we don't have time to wallow!" Jordan clapped to spur them, but nothing changed. "What's going on? Do you think we're going to lose? Because that's what you all look like right now and we haven't even hit the court. What a shame that would be."

"Leon should be here." Brooks frowned.

"He should." Jordan nodded. "But you guys can do this without him. You're going to have to. I mean, what do you think he would say right now?" When no one answered, she lowered her voice for a lousy impression of the forward. "If you don't stop looking like someone beat your ass, I'll do it myself."

The guys chuckled, shoulders loosening the slightest bit.

"I'm heartbroken too. But I saw Leon yesterday, and he's in good spirits. He wants us to win this." Jordan chewed her lip. "Creighton doesn't feel sorry for you. No one feels sorry for you. And that's the crux of hardship in the arena and out of it. No one is going to stop because you're down or take it easier on you because you're hurting. The game doesn't stop. Life doesn't stop. You know this. So, let's stop wasting time feeling sorry for ourselves." Jordan surveyed their faces. "Everyone thinks you're down. Everyone thinks you're out already. Let's take advantage of that. Let's shock the world like we've been doing all season."

The team left the tunnel with more confidence, but Jordan twisted the chain around her neck, doubts bubbling a sour film in her gut. She'd rotated Nolan Carter, a junior, into Leon's spot, but while he was their best bench player, she knew he wouldn't fill the hole left behind. Instead, she turned to Dominic, who'd spent his entire sophomore season in Leon's shadow.

"This is your time, Dom," Jordan said to him. "Embrace it."

But Dominic's time and the team's waned in Creighton's stampede. Jordan cursed under her breath at their valiant three-pointers, at the way they smartly double-teamed Brooks, at their perfect read of their game.

During the breaks and time-outs, Jordan struggled to know what to say. She struggled to find a gap and tell her team what they were doing wrong, except missing shots and getting outmaneuvered by a team that decided to play their best game of the year in front of a roaring crowd. With Brooks's miraculous Steph

Curry–like threes out of commission, she advised the team to drive through the paint, earn a simple layup, or draw the foul. It wasn't their usual game, which relied on crisp passes and endless ball movement, but this wasn't their usual team. They battled, but the spark wasn't there. Leon wasn't there. Without him, she'd have to create the spark herself.

Jordan ripped off her suit jacket to start the second half and pushed her sleeves up. When Creighton sank a deep three, increasing their lead to twelve, she turned to Frost.

"Give me your clipboard," she said to him.

"What?"

"I have an idea."

Frost's eyes flashed. "Oh, hell no, use your own clipboard."

She ripped it out of his hand, and the next time Dominic hit the floor from taking a blow on defense, Jordan snapped the clipboard in half. She tossed it to the ground and bellowed at the referee. "Make the call! Are you kidding me!"

The referee blew a whistle at her. "Watch yourself, Coach!"

"Yeah, that's right, come here! Let's talk!" Jordan waved him over as the crowd rumbled. "You got money on Creighton? Call it both ways!"

They pointed fingers in each other's faces, spewing nonsense like feuding auctioneers. Jordan didn't care about what he said or she said. She only cared that her team saw her fighting.

"That's it! Technical!" the referee shouted as the crowd booed.

"Good! If it'll get you to watch the game!" Jordan turned to her stunned players. She addressed Dominic first, grabbed him by his jersey, and put her nose inches from his. "Are you going to keep getting pushed around, Dom, or am I going to have to get thrown out of here?"

His eyes stretched to saucers. "No, Coach!"

"Then take what's yours!" She released his jersey, completely winded. She turned to the huddle. "And the rest of you! Are you going to let your brother get pushed around? Or are you going to fight for him? Fight for each other! You've got fifteen minutes to get back in this or it's over! You hear me! Fight!"

The Bulldogs roared back. The next ten minutes turned into a back-and-forth of baskets, David Douglas creeping in one layup at a time, one rebound, one free throw. On defense, Dominic turned into a gnat, never giving his man breathing room. With Brooks in tight coverage, Cooper slotted in crucial baskets that launched them into contention.

Then, with less than a minute left and trailing by one, Jordan called for a trick play, named after none other than her father. The players believed the scheme was called "Cash" because it depended on a perfectly timed alley-oop pass landing right on the money. In reality, Jordan named it after him because it started with an argument.

Brooks dribbled the ball up court, shaking his head in confusion at Jordan as she shouted.

"What are you doing?" She threw up a few fingers for a fake play to sell it.

"What?" Brooks screamed back, dribbled a little slower, and bulged his eyes at her.

And just as Creighton stalled, frozen by their confused performance, Brooks tossed up a perfect alley-oop pass without casting a glance at the hoop. Dominic sprinted in from the corner of the court, past his flat-footed defender, and met the ball in midair for a dunk and the lead. The arena exploded as he swung from the rim, the trick play executed like a masterpiece.

Creighton sprinted down the court, hurried to make a quick two points, but it was over. After a missed basket and only ten seconds left, they fouled. Brooks made his free throws, and with nothing left to do, Creighton threw a desperate half-court shot that hit the backboard as the buzzer rang. Jordan nearly dropped to her knees. She caught Beck across the court, beaming.

They were going to the Sweet Sixteen.

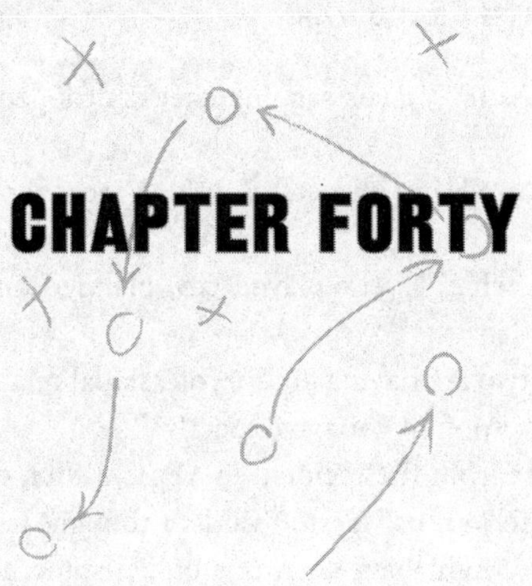

CHAPTER FORTY

Despite bracing for the worst, Easton surprised Beck when he didn't immediately try to ruin her. He waited until after David Douglas beat Creighton, though he tortured her with smirks and off-color remarks while they reported on the second round. It got so bad that Beck left press row to observe the game alone. She worried that him saying nothing, simply holding it over her head, might be worse than having to come clean.

But she was wrong about that too.

"Beck, do you have a moment?" Vince asked her after *Fast Break* the next day.

It'd finally caught up with her. Jordan, the gamble of their courtship, fell like a tower of cards, her chips swiped from the table. Easton sat in front of Vince's desk, and, for some reason, Todd was there too. Beck's stomach hardened. Easton didn't just have Wyatt's accusations. He was bringing witnesses.

"What's this about?" Beck asked.

"I was asking the same thing," Todd said.

"Easton came to me with some troubling news, and I think it's best we discuss it." Vince's sagging cheeks drooped into a deep frown.

Easton cleared his throat. "I told Vince about you and D'Amato."

"Told him what?" Beck played coy, planned on denying as long as possible.

"That you two are having an unprofessional relationship."

"And what proof do you have exactly?"

"Well, aside from the incident in Vegas, I took the liberty of asking Todd to join us," Easton said. "I thought he might have some insight. Might have seen or noticed something between you and D'Amato."

Beck's throat tightened. When she imagined this moment, it didn't include a trial by fire. In her nightmares, some tired woman from human resources took her into a back room to unveil black-and-white photos of her and Jordan, as if the station had the money for a private investigator. She didn't expect a humiliating open court with Easton as judge, jury, and executioner.

"Vince, how are you entertaining this? You're going to let him go on a witch hunt?" she asked.

"This isn't a witch hunt. You know it's a conflict of interest, Beck," Vince said.

"For the record, I haven't seen anything." Todd folded his arms across his mustard-stained shirt. "We go down there, shoot the game or presser, and get our story. Beck doesn't talk with D'Amato any more than the other reporters. This is out of line, Vince."

Beck could've hugged the cameraman.

"Wyatt Holt from KASE saw D'Amato go into Beck's room the night of the conference championship and didn't see her come out. I mean, for another station to see that, Vince, it's embarrassing." Easton shook his head.

"Oh, so we're just listening to every rumor? How about the fact that you and Wyatt were so drunk, you threatened to take me into my hotel room and teach me a lesson?"

"That was a joke, Beck."

"It's harassment. And if we're going to just start accusing each other of things without evidence, I actually have plenty." The years of torment boiled up inside her. She remembered every crude one-liner, every sneer and snicker, every time she entered a room and encountered the vile stares of being unwanted in the workplace but wanted in bed. "All the offensive remarks, sexism, and not to mention the disgusting things you've said to me over the last few days since you and Wyatt stirred up some rumor!"

"Don't deflect this. These are the facts—D'Amato goes to your hotel room, and everything suddenly makes sense. Your constant inside scoop and the tip about the walkout. No wonder they banned you from the last home game. And don't get me started on the one-on-one interview."

"She didn't want to do the interview with you! And I was protecting my sources after the walkout. I'd do it again. This is uncalled for, and I'm going to HR."

Easton scoffed. "Fine. I'll take matters into my own hands, let viewers decide."

"Easton, Beck, please, let's try to be civil." Vince's face was so bloated and red that Beck thought he might double over with a heart attack. In her rage, it didn't strike her as a bad thing.

"If you try to take me down, I will take you down with me. I'll take this whole fucking station down." Beck took aim at Vince next. "The toxic workplace, the constant harassment, the opportunities you passed me over for again and again. Then I finally get something, and you pull me into your office and allow my co-worker to make malicious, unfounded allegations?"

Vince held up his hands. "Let's just take a time-out. This is complicated. We should get HR involved. Until then, Beck, you're off David Douglas and you're off the desk."

"No." She shook her head, a sob clogging her throat. "What about Easton?"

"He's not accused of sleeping with a source."

"You're going to regret this." Beck glared at Easton. "I'll make sure I ruin everything for you before it's over."

She stalked out of Vince's office, ignoring his demands to wait. Beck swiped her car keys from her desk as commotion stirred in the bullpen among the other reporters and producers, who murmured about the mayhem. Leaving wasn't ideal, but she didn't know what she might do if she stayed. She might explode, she might cry, she might even confess to the truth.

Before she could make a clean break, Easton swooped in like a predator, starved for another bite. "That's right, run away, Beck."

He twirled his prop of a baseball bat, and she eyed it like an evil metronome, keeping time with the hell he unleashed on her daily. Beck snatched the bat from his grasp before she fully comprehended what her shaking hands were reaching for. She had enough sense to not hit him with it, though she wanted to. Enough sense to not destroy any irreplaceable NWSN property, though that would've been satisfying as well. Instead, with rage pumping in her veins, she grunted and swung the bat into an innocent filing cabinet, denting the metal and provoking gasps from their idle co-workers.

"Oh, relax, sweetheart." Easton sniggered.

Beck held the bat out like a sword to thwart him. "Stay the hell away from me."

Easton's brow hardened, and he ripped the bat from her grasp, chucking it to the floor with a clatter. He devoured the inches separating them, so close that spit hit Beck's cheeks. "You never belonged here. You're nothing but a dirty, fucking slut."

A fist flew over Beck's shoulder, colliding with Easton's face, knocking him on his ass. Todd stepped in front of her, hand still clenched. "Don't talk to her like that, prick."

"Holy shit, Todd." Beck covered her mouth as the bullpen broke into an uproar.

Easton dabbed at his bloody lip. "You are so done, you sack of shit!"

"Oh, bite me. I'm retiring after this season."

"For real this time?" Beck asked.

"I told you, Mary and I finally got the RV. We're hitting the road." Todd grinned as he rubbed his knuckles. Beck frowned at not paying better attention to him during their time together. For not noticing that he'd had her back all along. "Forty years filming highlights and that might be my best shot yet."

"What the hell is going on in here?" Vince's eyes widened as Easton picked himself up from the floor and clutched his bleeding mouth.

"An HR nightmare," Beck said. "Please tell me someone filmed that."

Three different people, including two interns who Beck mentored, raised their hands.

"Okay, we're having a station meeting, right now." Vince braced himself on the dented filing cabinet, a hand on his chest.

"Nah, screw that. I quit," Todd said.

Beck nodded. "Me too." She said it before truly grasping what it meant. Said it without a plan. Said it without being sure that she truly wanted to leave NWSN.

"Beck, let's just go into my office and talk," Vince said breathlessly. "There's no reason for you to quit like this."

She hurriedly gathered some of her things but left most of them behind. Todd put his bear-sized palm on her shoulder as they left in the awed silence of their co-workers. He flipped Vince the bird before leading them out the side door.

Beck released a jagged breath outside. "What did I just do?"

"The right thing." Todd lit a cigarette. "You can't work in a place that would do that to you. But you've been talking to Fiona, right?"

Beck's mouth dropped. "How do you know that?"

"I told her you were the real deal. I used to be her cameraman back in the day." Todd smirked. "She had it as bad as you. Worse probably. But you have that same spunk. You should call her. I've been doing this a long time and I know you have the stuff, Beck. Just maybe leave out the part about dating D'Amato."

He said it so casually as he tapped his cigarette that Beck choked. "Why didn't you say anything?"

Todd shrugged his heavy shoulders. "Maybe I'm just a hopeless romantic. That's what Mary would say," he said through a laugh that turned into a cough. "I mean, I never saw anything definite, but after the one-on-one interview, I thought there's no way these two aren't crazy about each other. It's never hindered your reporting. And it's not like you're the first to have a relationship with a coach or player."

Beck hugged Todd, unbothered by his sweaty hold. "Thank you."

"Of course, kiddo." Todd smiled when they released. "You know what you have to do?"

"I know exactly what I have to do," she said, unafraid as she braced for her next shot.

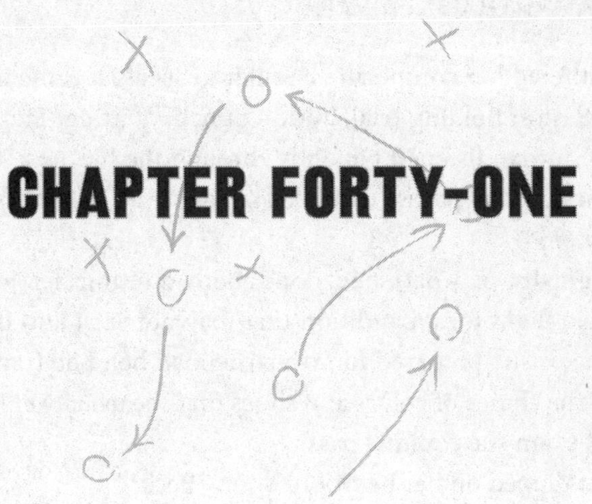

CHAPTER FORTY-ONE

The same evening Beck walked away from NWSN, she made two phone calls. The first to Fiona Wandell. While she'd sent her a reel after their meeting in Las Vegas, she hadn't followed up in the blissful bubble that formed after reuniting with Jordan. Now, with it unceremoniously popped, Beck contacted her like someone possessed.

"You still want to be my agent?" she asked as she drove to her apartment. "I'll sign whatever you want. I'm coming to Los Angeles, and I want an audition with NSBC."

"Well, I don't have one booked for you. There's a process. People to talk to."

"Either way, I'll be there tomorrow, and we'll figure it out."

Rather than scold Beck's persistence, Fiona broke into a rich laugh. "Okay, Ms. Beck. Let me see what I can do."

She called Jordan next and despite her rage, a sob ruptured the second the coach answered. When it became clear that Beck couldn't explain and equally clear what happened anyway, Jordan stayed on the line, cooing assurances and love, apologizing as though responsible for the cracks that left her broken. When

Beck gathered her composure enough to speak, it came in fragments. Easton holding trial, Todd's punch, quitting, Fiona, Los Angeles. Jordan listened patiently through the hiccups, and offered one constant phrase that Beck no longer believed: "It's going to be okay."

The gravity of what she'd done, both quitting her job and booking a flight for an audition that may not exist and if it did exist, she wasn't prepared for, overwhelmed her. She frantically packed, the choice of colors and shoes that she usually enjoyed a dreaded exam she couldn't pass.

Kevin rapped on her bedroom door. "Beck?"

She cleared her throat, hating this level of hysteria, the kind that provoked crying no matter what was said. "Yeah?" she asked so weakly that she didn't recognize herself.

"I heard about what happened," Kevin said. "Can I come in?"

Beck couldn't answer through her tears. In a flash, Kevin entered and looped her into a hug. She sniffled into his shoulder. Kevin had been the one to warn her of Jordan and the risks, the one who knew and disapproved. The one with the greatest reason to say I told you so.

Beck shook her head. "I'm sorry. I know I'm an idiot."

"Not an idiot. I mean, maybe an idiot in love."

"What are people saying?"

"The rumors are that Easton unloaded on you, Todd punched him in the face, and then you both quit," he said.

Beck rubbed her eyes, somewhat relieved that the details stopped there. Gossip among the city's journalists spread like wildfire. "That's all true. Easton accused me of sleeping with Jordan and tried to get me fired."

"I had a feeling, so I started spreading a few rumors of my own." Kevin winked.

"What?"

"I said that Easton was in love with you and jealous that you liked Wyatt better," he said.

Beck snorted. "Who's going to believe that?"

"There's a fine line between love and hate. Plus, it's more believable than my other rumor, which is that you and Todd are secret lovers, and he finally had enough of Easton's chauvinism." Kevin grinned as Beck laughed harder. "Every man in this city is in love with you and you choose the one woman you're not supposed to be with."

"Just the last part is true." Beck turned to the pile of clothes on her bed and apathetically picked through dresses.

"She's the real thing, isn't she?"

Beck met his gaze and nodded, a few tears spilling. "Yeah. She is."

"Is that why you're packing? Running off into the sunset?"

"No. I'm going to L.A. to meet with an agent. I don't know if she's my agent actually or if I have an interview or audition, but I'm going. I'm not giving up. I want Jordan, but I want both. I want to have both, Kev."

"You will." He assessed the mess on her bed and shook his head. "But not like this. What kind of friend would I be if I let you go to L.A. without an outfit that screams network?"

"You're already a better friend than I deserve." She wrapped an arm around his waist and rested her head on his shoulder.

Kevin squeezed her back before pillaging through her shoes. "You'd do the same for me, Becky."

She studied that night for her non-interview. NSBC wasn't just a regional station covering a handful of teams like NWSN. She'd have to be ready for anything. Professional baseball, football, basketball, hockey, golf, tennis, fucking cornhole. She didn't care what it was. She wanted in. She'd do it all. She'd grind it out and start from the bottom if she had to.

When she rolled her suitcase to the curb the next morning to catch a ride to the airport, she should have expected Jordan. The coach had a knack for showing up just when Beck needed her. But her breath still hitched, especially when Jordan crushed her in a hug. She kissed Beck with a tenderness reserved for apologies and long-awaited reunions. As if the embrace wasn't just a press of lips, but a last chance to speak.

"What are you doing here?" Beck's eyes prickled.

"Kevin texted me," Jordan said. "Though I don't know how he got my number."

"He has a talent for breaking into people's phones." Beck managed a weak laugh. She noticed dark half-moons under Jordan's eyes, knew she must not have slept to make it to Portland in time to take her to the airport. "Aren't you supposed to be catching a flight to Phoenix?"

"I get the distinct feeling the team won't leave without me." Jordan winked. "Some things are worth stepping away for. You're worth stepping away for."

The endless sea rolling from Jordan's gaze glowed heavenly in the sunrise, and a pacified sigh slipped from Beck's lips. In the last twenty-four hours, a sliver of her came to resent Jordan. She tossed and turned that night, despising the consequences of keeping her. She despised that it cost her a job, and that love ended up being so damn hard. But encountering her now, standing in front of her as if her own looming commitments were nothing, washed away those same doubts.

They held hands on the way to the airport, Beck resting against her shoulder, breathing in as much of her as she could. She knew she should ask Jordan how she planned to get past a number-two-seed Texas, but she didn't have the energy. Jordan didn't ask her about Los Angeles either, or what the hell was going to happen with her job. They marinated quietly, as if gaining strength in each other's proximity before the daunting tasks ahead.

Beck clutched Jordan at the airport, her chest thudding, though she didn't know who exactly the heartbeat belonged to. "It feels wrong to not be there for the biggest game of your career."

"Sounds like this is going to be a pretty big moment for yours too," Jordan said.

Beck's throat bobbed. The nerves of her trip resurfaced along with the disappointment of not covering the game. "I was supposed to go."

"No, you're supposed to do this." Jordan nodded. "You've earned this."

"So have you."

"I guess we make a pretty powerful pair then." Jordan's mouth quirked with unshakable optimism. "It's your turn now. Take your shot. Don't look back."

She said it so certainly that Beck's heart quaked. "Okay."

They kissed long and hard, holding on before the icy plunge that always shocked Beck at their departure. They exchanged whispers of love, and when her lower lip trembled, Jordan touched it ever so gently and shook her head. Beck steadied herself and nodded, using the last threads of her fortitude to not look back.

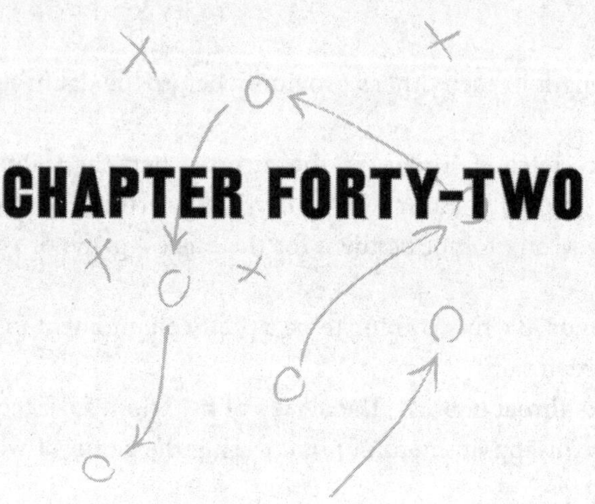

CHAPTER FORTY-TWO

While Beck couldn't make it to Phoenix for the Sweet Sixteen, Jordan still had a piece of her. Since the conference championship, she hadn't coached a game without Beck's letter in her pocket, and while she told anyone who asked that she wasn't superstitious, whenever the game was on the line, simply brushing a finger across the folded paper restored her poise.

She gripped it so tight her knuckles faded white as the minutes to tip-off slipped away. The war drums thundered in her chest, keeping time with the bouncing basketballs and her frenetic breathing. For the first time since her run as head coach, since the team started winning, since she started making history and headlines, the weight of what she'd accomplished collapsed on her.

She'd made it. The Bulldogs had never advanced past the Sweet Sixteen, so she'd reached as high as anyone, as high as Royce, higher than hundreds of other teams in the nation, and far beyond expectations—except of course her own. Not once had she allowed herself to really feel it. But gazing out at the court, a sentimental pull threatened to overtake her stoicism.

"Team looks like shit without me," Leon said behind her.

Jordan spun around and hugged the young man balancing on crutches. "You made it." Seeing him standing again, after the pain she witnessed, healed something inside her she didn't know had broken.

"Wouldn't miss it." Leon waved at his teammates, who smiled at his arrival, but his lower lip trembled. "I just thought it would be me out there."

"It still is. You always have a place on this team." She jostled his shoulder. "You going to help us win today?"

His dark eyes glassed over as he nodded. "Hell yeah, Coach."

XOXO

Fiona got Beck an interview the day after she landed in Los Angeles, and she signed a contract with the agent on the spot. "So, you going to tell me what the hurry is?" Fiona asked at the hotel bar.

"I'm just excited to advance my career."

"That bad, huh?" Fiona downed the olives from her martini. "Will NWSN give us trouble?"

"I think it's going to be beneficial for all parties if we split amicably. But if you must know, I have my insurance." Beck showed Fiona the video on her phone of Easton screaming at her and Todd punching him in the face.

"Oh, Todd's always been a knight in shining armor." Fiona chuckled. "Do I want to know what led up to that?"

"Do you need to?"

Fiona chewed her lip, studying the marble bar top for a beat. "You know, I left the business because of men like Easton Prescott. Sometimes I wish I'd stuck it out, but that's why I do this. To make sure women like you get a fair shot." She waved for another drink. "I don't need to know your personal life. Let's just get you in the door."

While Fiona assured her it didn't matter, the truth haunted Beck from afar the night before her interview. She constantly checked her phone for rumors from Easton or to find the video circulating. It wasn't just the fear of getting found out that kept her awake, but that Fiona reminded her of another distant voice. The weight of it became too much as she tossed and turned, and while she could have called Jordan, she dialed the one person she both dreaded talking to and needed to hear.

"Caroline, is everything okay?" Candace answered on the first ring, even though it was after midnight in Philadelphia.

A knot of emotion filled Beck's throat, making it difficult to speak. "I, uh. Yeah. I'm sorry, I know it's late."

"What's wrong?"

"I'm okay. I just . . . I messed up, Mom." Beck gulped, prepared for a scolding, though the tightness in her chest lessened with the confession. "I don't know what to do."

Beck detected a lamp clicking on and her father's murmuring in the background. She imagined them both in the same bed she once jumped on, wearing the same pajamas she found them in after the countless times she broke curfew, bearing identical, grim frowns.

"What happened?" Candace asked.

"You remember what I told you this Christmas?" Beck barely knew how to say the rest, so she kept it short. "It's Jordan."

Candace sighed on the other end, and Beck cringed. Tears tickled her throat. And while she waited in the lull, she considered all the others who endured the same. Brooks crying to his teammates at the party after his boyfriend left him. Jordan getting kicked out and sent couch surfing at just seventeen years old. What a cruel rite of passage to live in one's truth. And while it hurt, she also embraced this step, waiting for her mother's answer in the dark.

"The coach," Candace finally said.

"Yeah. Someone found out, and I quit NWSN. I don't know what's going to happen." Beck rambled to hurry through her shame, but then paused, hating her usually outspoken mother's silence. "I messed up. You and Dad taught me better than to get involved with a source, but I just . . . I fell really hard. It's real to me." She frowned, rubbing her forehead. "I'm sorry. I know I'm always disappointing you—"

"You've never disappointed us," Candace said.

Beck's eyes widened. "I haven't?"

"No. Not now, not ever."

It landed more like a reprimand than an assurance, so much so that Beck nearly apologized again. "I just always thought you didn't want me to do this, because it wasn't enough. I'm not as good as you two and this just proves it."

"That's not why I didn't want you to become a journalist. I knew what you might miss out on. What we missed out on. Birthdays because of breaking news. All the holidays and school performances because I was on the anchor desk, or your father was chasing a story."

"Are you kidding? I thought you two were superheroes." Beck realized then that she'd never told her mother that either. Her shoulders fell. "I love the game, but why else do you think I chose this?"

She swore a sniffle crackled through the static, but she wasn't sure.

"I just don't want you to miss out on anything. Not a family or whoever you love." Candace's voice wavered ever so slightly. "And it's okay to love who you love. I'm sorry for making you feel like you couldn't."

Now Beck fell quiet, letting it wash over her. She could breathe again in a way she hadn't been able to in months. The warmth in her gaze didn't stem from fear or shame, but the desire to hug her mother through the phone.

"Honestly, I was more scared I'd never get a call like this at all," Candace said.

"What do you mean?"

"A call that you were in love."

Beck blushed and barely resisted a chuckle. "I never said that."

"I'm your mother. You don't have to." Candace sighed. "I had a feeling over Christmas. I should've said it then."

"Well, you say that now. I really backed myself into a corner with the whole follow-my-heart thing." Beck picked at the starched comforter. "I have an interview tomorrow with NSBC. I'm really nervous."

"Don't be. You're ready," Candace said, providing another boost of confidence that Beck didn't expect. "But think about what you want. Really. People only get a chance like this once."

"For their dream job?"

"For their dream *life,* honey. Don't miss out."

Beck swallowed. Even if she landed her dream job, it didn't guarantee a future with Jordan. And as she sat in the dark, she didn't know if she'd want either without the other.

"I love you," Candace said.

"I love you too, Mom. Tell Dad too."

Sleep didn't come any easier that night, but her heart steadied, soaring from her mother's support. She didn't need her approval to love Jordan, but it wrapped around her like a security blanket, had her standing straighter when she arrived at NSBC's massive headquarters the next morning. Beck wanted the job, stood in awe of the journalists' photos that lined the hallways, but a new calm soothed her nerves. Even if she didn't get it, she had Jordan. She had her family. She swore they all stood behind her as she met the network's director of talent, Lindsay Rork.

"I'll be honest, I rewatched your tape more than once. You're witty and have a great memory for stats. So glad we could make this work," Lindsay said.

"Me too," Beck said.

The two-hour interview flowed effortlessly. They discussed the ups and downs of Beck's career, traveling across the country for jobs, her vision for her future. But they also talked about life. Lindsay wasn't much older than Beck, with a similar education and family in New England. Beck nearly pinched herself at how easy it was. But the true test came in the form of an audition.

"I know you can report and do long-form pieces. That's not what we're worried about," Lindsay said as she led her to the bullpen. It was nearly triple the size of NWSN, with countless desks and dozens of monitors showing games around the country. "We need to add more women to our analysis and debate shows. It's kind of my personal mission. Are you familiar with *Keeping Score*?"

"Yes." Beck gulped. The audition was supposed to just be highlights and a few on-camera reads.

"Well, since he's here today, we'd like to do a screen test with you and Speck," Lindsay said as they stopped at the infamous man's desk.

Without missing a beat, he offered a hand. "Marty Spector, but please, for the love of God, call me Speck."

She'd spent years watching the redheaded king on camera and barely tempered her excitement. "Caroline Beck, but only my mother calls me Caroline."

"Speck and Beck. Sounds like we already have a show." He grinned, vibrant yet fatherly in his loosened tie, dark jeans, and spectacles. Beck always thought of him as the type of guy you could grab a beer with when she watched his show, but television personalities rarely held up in real life. Speck, however, seemed to be the real deal, unthreatened and welcoming in a way Beck seldom experienced in a male anchor.

"Is it that easy? I would've booked my flight much sooner." Beck smiled.

"No, they're going to make us perform like monkeys first, aren't you?" Speck said, nudging Lindsay's shoulder. He winked at Beck. "The secret is, just make me look good."

"Where's the fun in that? You can get a plucky sidekick anywhere."

"I like her. Where'd you find her?" Speck asked Lindsay.

But Beck's attention drifted. Her eye caught the nearest television, her shoulders clenching as Texas sank a three-pointer against David Douglas. "Shit."

"What?"

Beck cringed. "I'm sorry. The game."

"Ah, did you take David Douglas too?" Speck watched with her. The Bulldogs led by eight in the first half. "They always let me down in the Sweet Sixteen."

"They start strong, but once teams squash the pick and roll and their perimeter shots go cold, they flounder. Ortega could never innovate in the second half."

"That's something D'Amato brings. The trick play last week—we must've run that a hundred times. I'm a big fan of hers," Speck said.

Beck refused to react even though it killed her to catch the game in glimpses, to deal with not only her own nerves about the audition, but a separate anxiety for Jordan. During her interview, she'd been tempted to check her phone for a score before remembering Jordan's parting words at the airport. She wouldn't turn back. Not right now.

"She's a good role model for my daughters. My oldest is looking to play college ball," Speck said.

"I played a little college ball myself."

"That's good. The last part of the audition is a pickup game."

"That's why I wore my comfortable heels."

Lindsay laughed. "Alright, I have a feeling this could go all day. Shall we go to the studio?"

"After you," Speck said. Beck followed Lindsay, stealing a last glimpse of the score. David Douglas up by six.

XOXO

Despite not playing a single minute, Jordan dripped with sweat at halftime. The Bulldogs maintained a slim lead, but it was no easy task. Texas put up a fight at every turn. Jordan sketched out a few plays during the break, but mostly let the guys breathe. Let herself breathe too.

She leaned against the whiteboard, next to her X's and O's, and rubbed Beck's letter in her pocket. She wondered what was happening in Los Angeles, wishing she could send her a telepathic message. *You got this.*

"Are you hearing this?" Frost sidled up next to her and nodded at Leon.

"Oh yeah. He might be a natural," she said.

They observed Leon sharing the nuances of offensive rebounds with Nolan and Dominic, who stared at him as if receiving scripture. Jordan smiled. As he rattled off tips, hands flailing, she was reminded of her first year of coaching after her injury. A year that launched her to this very moment.

An official popped his head into the locker room. "Two minutes, Coach."

"Thanks." She cleared her throat, and the team's attention settled on her. "This is it. It's going to come down to inches and seconds. This is why we conditioned. You're in better shape than them."

"Coach, maybe you should break a clipboard, just in case." Dominic chuckled.

"Not all of us are that superstitious," Jordan said, though she traced the note in her pocket. "This is going to be a fight. I can't do it for you. But I'm with you. I trust you. Right now, we put our trust in each other."

She paused on a few faces and briefly considered that it might be the last time. Much like her second game with a win necessary to keep her job, this too threatened a final curtain call. Only now she didn't beg or fight for their respect. Now they depended on her. Now she could depend on them.

"This is one of those moments. You're going to remember this game for the rest of your lives—no matter how it ends. So, hold nothing back."

"Amen." Charlie nodded.

Brooks clapped, bounced up and down in the huddle. "Let's go!"

"It's now, okay? We've been down-and-out." Jordan raised her voice with each declaration. "We've broken noses and bones."

"Let's go!" Leon barked.

"We've been humiliated and torn apart, but it never mattered. We're here anyway." Jordan nodded at Brooks. "It's now."

"It's now!" The team captain pushed Charlie. Nudged Dominic too who nudged him back. The team nodded, bounced, jostled each other in the circle. "Coach said it's now. It's now!"

"It's now!" they barked back at Brooks.

"Now on three!"

"One . . . two . . . three . . . Now!"

Now came down on them like a war.

The Bulldogs entered the second half at full tilt, but Texas met their ferocity. They knocked the Bulldogs on their heels with a six-point run, taking the lead in a matter of minutes. Jordan and

Frost shifted the defense to a full-court press, the Phoenix crowd an obstacle of its own to scream above.

Brooks tracked his man to the sidelines at a sprint, a hand sweeping in for the steal. The ball fumbled loose out of bounds. Brooks chased it down and crashed into the scoring table. Jordan gritted her teeth. "Shit."

He groaned as he staggered back up, clutching his ribs in agony. "I can play, Coach," he said with tears in his eyes.

Leon flashed in her head. So did the long fifteen minutes ahead. Jordan shook her head, hoping she wasn't making a blunder. "Rest up, Brooks. Game's not over."

XOXO

Keeping Score with Speck was NSBC's most popular debate show. Speck hosted, rotating in panelists, reporters, and analysts from the network and outside of it, for a conversation about sports' biggest headlines and a little ribbing. As much as Beck despised Easton, she now considered their time at the desk together with gratitude. In his chiding, obnoxious way, he'd unintentionally prepared her for Speck's show perfectly.

After analyzing highlights at breakneck speed, she returned every one of his serves on players, injuries, trades, and the post-season outlook. She was locked and loaded with quips, never caught off guard by Speck's unexpected tangents. "And that leads us to our final segment—overtime. Beck, you know how to play?" he asked after fifteen minutes of back-and-forth.

"I know all about overtime, Speck. I grew up watching the Flyers." Beck kept a calm air in front of the cameras, though the lights were brighter, the desk massive, the studio crafted with metallic beams, and monitors everywhere, so imposing that Beck's mouth dropped when she first entered.

"That's right, you're a Philly girl. Flyers had the longest NHL overtime in the modern era. You got the numbers?"

"Five overtimes, ninety-two minutes, all past my bedtime."

Speck chuckled. "Oh, now you're making me feel old."

"I'm sorry, just compensating for feeling inferior." Beck paused for a grin. "What with you being at the longest overtime, one hundred and thirteen minutes in 1936."

"I actually reported on that game." Speck winked. "Alright, thirty seconds on the clock for your last shot. The question is—what do you think about moving to Los Angeles?"

For the first time in their banter, Beck stuttered. "Wh-what?"

"That's not for you to decide, Speck," Lindsay said from behind the camera where she'd been observing. "That's well past the air check we needed. Truly, Beck, fantastic job."

"A pleasure." Speck shook her hand. "I hope the eggheads upstairs are smart enough to welcome you to the team."

Beck nodded, at a loss for words. "Thanks, thank you," she stammered.

"Come on, there are a few people I'd like you to meet," Lindsay said as they walked out of the studio.

Beck had been so locked in for the audition that she briefly lost her grip on reality, like going toe-to-toe with Speck in the NSBC studio was an elaborate dream. But out in the bullpen, with everyone on staff crowding around television screens, she plummeted back.

"What's the score?" Speck asked.

"Texas up by five, with a minute and a half to go. You missed it. McCray went down, but D'Amato kept him out so long it might be too late. She could've lost the whole thing for them."

Beck chewed her lip, her heart roaring. The camera zoomed in on Jordan, screaming in the huddle. The players nodded along, drenched and breathless. She knew by the straining tendons in Jordan's neck, by the intensity of her stare, the way she pointed at each man in front of her, that this was the moment she laid everything on the line.

"You coming?" Lindsay asked.

"Just let her watch," Speck said.

Beck slid in next to him and held her breath.

XOXO

The second half of David Douglas versus the University of Texas would become an instant classic, a test of wills and innovation. With Brooks on the sidelines for a prolonged break, their opponents steadily climbed, expanding their lead to double digits. The Bulldogs hustled valiantly, the long hours of conditioning paying off as they maintained man-to-man coverage, sprinting baseline to baseline, double-teaming in a full-court press. While they needed Brooks and trailed without his shooting power, Jordan had learned a crucial fact after Leon's injury. They were survivors that didn't depend on one star.

So, despite Texas's lead and her guys battling exhaustion, she kept Brooks on the bench longer than necessary. Even Frost asked what the hell she was doing. Still, she waited. And when she put him back in with only minutes to go, his return to the hardwood was a punch that Texas wasn't ready for.

Living up to every expectation put on him since birth, Brooks floated across the floor. The first ball in his hands, he dropped in for a deep three. Then, with the arena vibrating, he sprinted back on defense to avenge his missed steal, swiped the ball from Texas, and turned a quick layup. "Let's go!" he shouted, waving his arms up to the screaming fans.

It wasn't just Brooks carrying the load during those final, fateful minutes. Every player wearing navy made a difference. Charlie sprinted faster than Jordan knew possible to block a Texas fast break. With the double-team on Brooks, they executed an isolation play for Cooper, who went on a tear of twelve points in that second half. Dominic went to the foul line for two crucial free throws in the last ninety seconds. Texas called time-out to ice him, but he didn't waver. He sank both shots, the most important free throws of his career, to bring them within victory.

And just like that, with slivers on the clock, David Douglas faced the end.

"Time-out! Time-out!" Jordan shouted.

She already knew what she was going to say. Could already see it happen in her head. A vision of their victory. They were down by one, Texas had the ball, and while they needed just two points for the win, Jordan had been waiting for this moment all season.

"When they miss, when they miss this, it's our time." She couldn't hear herself over the shrieking and shaking stands. "Cooper's Play!" The freshman didn't balk, and the players didn't question. "Cooper's Play! We're going for the win."

Frost shot her bug eyes when the huddle broke, and she nodded at him. Texas took the ball up court slowly, but they wouldn't be able to run out the clock. They'd draw the foul. When they did, Jordan clenched her teeth and turned away from the court for just a moment. Texas made their first free throw, putting them up by two. She gulped. The second shot rattled off the rim, and she exhaled in relief.

With seven seconds left and no time-outs, Cooper inbounded the ball to Brooks. Six seconds. Two points would tie it. They could survive in overtime. Jordan was sure of it. But they'd already committed. Already given Cooper the nod. Their fate now rested with the freshman. Five seconds. Texas jammed the paint. They rushed Brooks, but no one suspected Cooper out deep. Four seconds. Brooks pitched the ball to the shooting guard.

Cooper was further outside the arc than Jordan would've wanted. Too far. But he lined up for the shot anyway. Three seconds.

The ball lofted off Cooper's hands, and while people around the country held their breaths, doubting the decision to go for three when two would do, Jordan knew it was over. She'd seen Cooper make the basket a hundred times. Before it spliced through the net, before the buzzer, before making school history, Jordan grinned.

XOXO

The NSBC bullpen erupted when Cooper Sloane sank the game winner. Speck high-fived Beck, who stood with her mouth hanging ajar.

"Cooper's Play," she muttered.

She remembered Jordan eagerly walking her through it months ago. It made her smile so big that her cheeks ached nearly as bad as her chest. She couldn't pull herself from the screen as the players tackled Cooper to the court, as Jordan threw her hands in the air, as Frost picked her up. A mix of pride, love, and sadness that she couldn't celebrate with Jordan seized her. Even as she shared the excitement with those around her, she couldn't share how personal it was, that it wasn't just a win on her bracket or a thrilling finish.

The conflicting joy and disappointment followed her through the next hour at NSBC's headquarters. Lindsay introduced her to executive producers and the vice president of programming, all of them equally kind and happy to meet her. She should've been screaming inside at how well things were going, but when Lindsay walked her out to the lobby, her stomach swirled with the same guilt that haunted her for weeks. For months, since she started hiding herself and who she really loved.

"I can't say anything official yet, but you should consider if you can see yourself in Los Angeles." Lindsay grinned. "Speck has a lot of pull, but beyond that, I know you'd be a great fit."

Beck's heart rattled. This was it. This was the nod. The break she'd been fighting for. "I want to be here. I'll start in the edit bay cutting highlights if I have to. This is what I want."

Lindsay shook her hand. "I don't think you're going to be starting in an edit bay," she said. "I'll be reaching out soon, and I'll loop Fiona in on contract discussions."

"A contract." Beck repeated it like an idiot but was too stunned to care.

"Yes." Lindsay nodded. "It was nice to meet you."

"You too." Beck gaped as the woman turned on an expensive heel. It was done. All she had to do was stay quiet. All she had to do was keep hiding. "Lindsay, wait a second."

Her breath hitched as the woman returned. She didn't want to lose her nerve. She didn't want to lose this chance either. But she couldn't take only having half of Jordan, half of a relationship, half of a dream life that she wanted as much as this turning point in her career. Of all people, it was her mother who chimed in her ear, urging her to take a stand. *Don't miss out.*

"I have to be completely transparent with you." Beck worked past the pulse that filled her ears. "I might have a conflict of interest."

Lindsay raised an eyebrow, slipping hands into the pockets of her slacks. "What would that be?"

"I'm involved with someone associated with a college basketball team," Beck said. It sounded more cryptic than she intended. "A coach."

"I see." Lindsay revealed nothing.

"And it's not a man." Beck internally cursed herself for volunteering the information. But she kept going. "I'm not out, and I'm not trying to come out publicly right now. It won't hinder my reporting. It hasn't. But I want to be honest with you and NSBC, because this is my dream." Beck kept her chin high. "If that ruins this chance for me, it'll crush me. But I think it would be worse to miss out by not being myself a second longer."

Lindsay stared at her for a beat before nodding. "I appreciate your honesty," she said, glancing around the empty lobby. "I can't guarantee anything, but working for a national network is much different from working for a regional station like NWSN. If you were to continue this relationship and work here, I imagine the conflict of interest will be minimal. College basketball is a small fraction of our coverage, as you well know."

Beck nodded, a pit growing in her throat. "Right."

"As for your sexuality, that's not a problem. I agree. You shouldn't have to hide yourself." Lindsay raised an eyebrow. "But my advice, if I were to give it to a friend in your position, would be that maybe this relationship didn't start until after you started working here. Maybe you met on the job at NWSN but struck things up later. It'd be one thing if you weren't great at what you do, but since you are, why jeopardize it?"

"Yeah," Beck whispered.

"Alright. Have a safe trip back and I'll let you know."

Beck lingered, as if she'd launched her own buzzer beater without the satisfaction of knowing whether it went in.

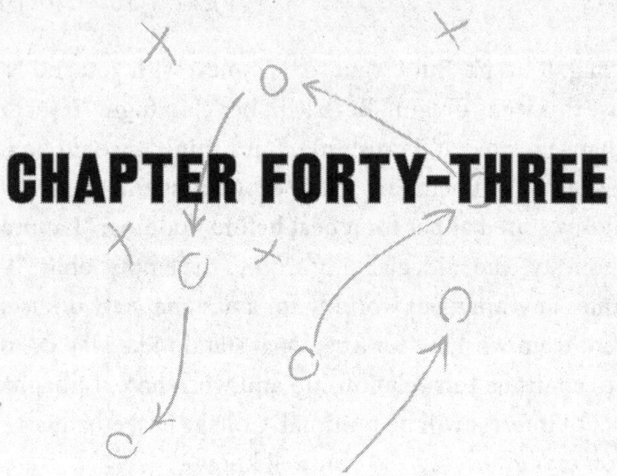

CHAPTER FORTY-THREE

Despite the anxiety of waiting for a call from NSBC, Beck coasted on the bliss of liberation. If she got the job, there would be no more hiding. A slight change to the story of their courtship, sure, but a chance to be together emboldened Beck, made the revelation worthwhile. And even if she didn't get the job, at least she'd started the delicate path of living in her truth. Plus, not getting the gig had its own possibilities. The possibility of watching Jordan from the stands instead of working on the sidelines.

She took advantage of that rare opportunity during the quarterfinals. Rather than return to Portland, she booked a flight to Phoenix. She congratulated Jordan over the phone, rehashed bits and pieces of the audition that felt frail compared to the team's win, but the coach hung on every word. When she told Beck she'd get her a ticket for the game, which hadn't occurred to her as a possibility until the invitation, something blossomed inside her. The same liberation she felt after speaking with her mother and Lindsay. The liberation in choosing Jordan. In fully embracing what they were.

The arena crawled with people that afternoon. Beck was almost unsure of what to do as a spectator. It'd been so long since she arrived at a game without a camera, without work to do, without hurrying straight for press row in heels and a dress, that she felt awkward, almost naked in her jeans and sneakers.

"I'm picking up a ticket under D'Amato," Beck said at will call.

"Caroline Beck?" the woman working the counter asked.

Beck furrowed her brow. "Uh, yeah."

"Going to need some ID."

She fished out her license. "How'd you know it was me?"

"You're the only one on the list."

"Are you sure?" Beck's eyes widened. "There's no Annette? Or, uh, Cash D'Amato?"

The ticket attendant shook her head. "No. Is that a problem?"

"No. No problem at all."

Beck dipped back into the crowd, her heart caught between sympathy and relief. Sympathy that Jordan's parents never came around or appreciated who their daughter became. And relief that Jordan let them go. She didn't need their approval. Not that she ever should have. Beck's chest swelled at how much she'd achieved without them and so many others in her corner. And now she wouldn't have to.

Beck stopped as she reached the section for her seat, a sting breaching her gaze when she spotted Jordan on the court. She'd seen her coach dozens of times, but always through the lens of a reporter. Now she witnessed Jordan in a new light. As her partner. As someone who knew all of her and Beck knew right back.

It stunned her, had her bursting into modest tears, like seeing the world in color for the first time. The beauty of witnessing Jordan doing exactly what she was meant to. Dominant, confident, but kind. Exactly who she was supposed to be. Exactly who Beck loved.

She composed herself before finding her seat next to a small brunette who grinned at her arrival. "Beck, right?"

She swallowed, unsure if she was supposed to know her. "Yeah, hi."

"Julie Frost. I'm Elliott's wife." She shook her hand and Beck smiled. Julie prattled on with gusto, as if they hadn't just met. "It's so great you could make it. The Elite Eight, I can hardly stand it. Elliott hasn't lost this much sleep since our kids were born."

"Yeah, Jordan hasn't slept a wink either." Beck fluttered at speaking about her so openly.

"Well, I'm sure she's happy you're here." Julie patted her hand. "Hopefully, this is just the start."

"Hopefully." Beck grinned, taking in Jordan from afar as the team prepared for tip-off. She wanted the job at NSBC. She wanted to report on the game. But for the first time, more than both of those things, she wanted to be exactly where she was.

CHAPTER FORTY-FOUR

What you leave behind is not what is engraved
in stone monuments, but what is woven
into the lives of others.
—Pericles

After months of stoicism, after unkind words, and roaring doubts endured without a single tear, Jordan D'Amato cried after the Elite Eight. She couldn't remember the last time she cried, the tears foreign intruders on her cheeks, but it happened as if someone threw a splitting hammer into her stone heart.

David Douglas University had never made it to the Elite Eight before and, for what felt like the hundredth time, Jordan made history with the feat. But it was finally the history she wanted to make. Not just history because of her gender, but history in her own right. History for the school, regardless of her sex. She'd summited a mountain and thrown her flag at the top. As the Bulldogs faced UConn, she hoped to do it once more. When she glanced up at the stands and spotted Beck, she thought for sure they would. But the game didn't bounce in their favor.

The Sweet Sixteen left the guys understandably beat up. Brooks hissed through cracked ribs. Dominic strained his shoulder. Charlie and Nolan fought cramps and fatigue, but never stopped boxing out or snagging rebounds, even as they limped.

Leon never stopped cheering or giving pointers from the bench. After he made the best basket of the tournament, carried off in glory, Cooper's range ran cold.

It just wasn't their time. Jordan coached as passionately as ever, but in her gut, she knew they'd fallen. There wasn't a trick or buzzer beater that could save them. She wasn't mad, could never be mad, as her players licked their wounds and put themselves on the line. So instead, she savored the seconds, even as UConn piled on the points. She savored each time she screamed across the court, savored each basket, savored the rare chance to glance at Beck in a seat rather than the sidelines. She savored it even when the final score glowed, and the team crumpled in disappointment.

The end of the season and their unprecedented run arrived with tears. Not her tears at first, though Charlie and Leon hugging each other and weeping, Brooks sitting on the floor with damp cheeks as UConn celebrated, Dominic lowering his head as if the loss was his fault, nearly destroyed her.

She went to Brooks and offered him a hand. He grabbed her into a hug after she hauled him up. Unwanted cameras hovered to capture the moment, but they ignored them.

"Thank you," Jordan said to him. "We couldn't have done this without you, Brooks." She reflected on their long journey together. From his scared freshman year to the day she'd asked for his support as she stepped up to lead the team. She burned with pride for the young man who came out to his teammates when other athletes might have balked. The man she knew would continue to make waves in the NBA. "*I* couldn't have done this without you."

"We couldn't have done this without you either." He sniffled, wiping his eyes when they released. "I couldn't be who I am without you."

Jordan didn't let it break her. She just patted his shoulder and went to Charlie next, who shook with tears. "I wanted it for us. But most of all, I don't want it to end," he blubbered as she hugged him.

"It was a good run, Charlie. Be proud, bud." Jordan swallowed the lump in her throat.

She didn't want it to end either. Didn't want to accept that after this day, their family would split apart. They'd always be a team, yes, but the seniors would leave for greater pastures, and the feeling they brought, more important than their skill, would never be re-created. Jordan had coached dozens of teams, but never had it felt like such a family, one she didn't want to let go.

The scene in the locker room felt like a funeral, but Jordan didn't scold them for long faces. She took the center of the room through the sniffles, ignoring the crippling knowledge that this would be the last time she looked out to see Brooks, Charlie, and Leon.

"I've never been prouder," she said. Still no tears, just a gnaw in her chest that left her raw. "Of anything I've ever done in my life, this is the best. And it's because of you. You didn't have to take this road with me, but you did. You're the type of men this world needs. While we might never step on the court together again, what we've done is worth more than rings and glory. So, enjoy this moment. Even if it hurts. It hurts because we did something special. It hurts because we love each other. And that's a beautiful thing."

Jordan got through the press conference without crying. She expressed gratitude and pride in the boys one last time. She instinctually searched for Beck, her heart tightening without her in the crowd. Because Beck was the other part of the season that made it worthwhile. The part she'd never forget. The part she refused to lose.

Threads held Jordan's composure together when she left the media room, ambling down the hall to the women's locker room.

"Hey, Coach?"

She stopped in her tracks, unsure if the call was real, but instead of charging forward as she had all season, Jordan turned around. Beck stood waiting, the faintest smile lifting her lips and crinkling the edges of her eyes. Much like Jordan thought of her first moments with Brooks, she thought of her first moment with Beck. Of the day the reporter charged into her life and never left.

That's when the tears finally spilled. Jordan staggered for her, the first sob launching before she could stop it, caught by Beck's open arms. She cried every cry she had never allowed herself before. Tears for the end of the road, tears for her last game with the seniors she loved, tears for Leon and his broken bones, tears for being fired, tears for humiliation, tears for the anxiety, lost sleep, all of it spilling as she clung to Beck, who never stopped soothing her. They rocked as if her tears became an ocean.

"I'm sorry." Jordan hiccupped, ashamed of her weakness and the damp mess on Beck's sweater.

"Shhhh. I've got you. You did so good. You did so good."

"I wanted it. I wanted it for me, and I wanted it for them." Jordan cried.

"I wanted it for you too," Beck whispered, kissing the side of her head as Jordan buried herself in her shoulder. "I wanted it for you so bad. But I'm so glad I'm here for this too. Maybe more so."

When Jordan could breathe again, removing her dense weight from Beck's frame, they sat together in the hall, uncaring of those who passed. Jordan shook her head. "I'm sorry for losing it." She tried to hide her surely pathetic face, but Beck brushed her tears, didn't flicker with anything but love.

"So much for never seeing you cry."

Jordan smirked, so depleted from sobbing that she didn't

know how she'd get back up from the floor again. Not that she wanted to. With Beck's hand twined with hers, she would've been satisfied taking permanent residence there.

"Any word from L.A.?" Jordan asked.

This time, Beck's gaze glossed over, a few fat tears filling her eyes. "I got it."

Jordan laughed hoarse but happy as she kissed her forehead, then her lips, then her forehead again. "I knew you'd do it."

"Well, it's good for us too. The director of talent said she made sure to call me during halftime," Beck said.

"Why?"

"Because I told her about us. Well, not entirely, but I think she put the pieces together." Beck smiled as she swiped a tear. "It won't be a problem now. Not with me covering mostly professional sports anyway."

The news pushed fresh emotion into Jordan's throat. She'd felt guilty for her part in jeopardizing Beck's career. While she agreed to live in shadows and silence, it wasn't the life she wanted. Wasn't what she envisioned for a future with the person she loved. But she'd been willing to do it. She just hadn't expected Beck to put it on the line for her.

"I love you," Jordan whispered.

"I love you too." Beck sniffled and rested her forehead against Jordan's. "I just wish L.A. wasn't so far. Part of me felt so happy in the stands today, supporting you for real, instead of figuring out how to grill you after. Being here right now means everything to me. If you're coaching and I'm in Los Angeles, even if we can be out, how can we be together?"

Jordan smirked. "How about I play you for it?"

Beck pulled back, her eyes dancing playfully. "You win, I stay?"

"I win, you go." Jordan ran a thumb down the reporter's cheek.

"You have to do this, Beck. You're meant to do it as much as I'm meant to coach."

"You're sure?"

"Positive. Besides, who knows what will happen with the team. I'm sure the school will come up with some bullshit reason to fire me again." Jordan chuckled weakly.

"I don't think that's going to happen this time," Beck said.

They sat in the hall, trainers and officials passing intermittently, the arena thundering with the next game, content as they stared at an abandoned basketball drifting across the way.

"What a season," Beck whispered.

Jordan kissed the top of her head. "What a season."

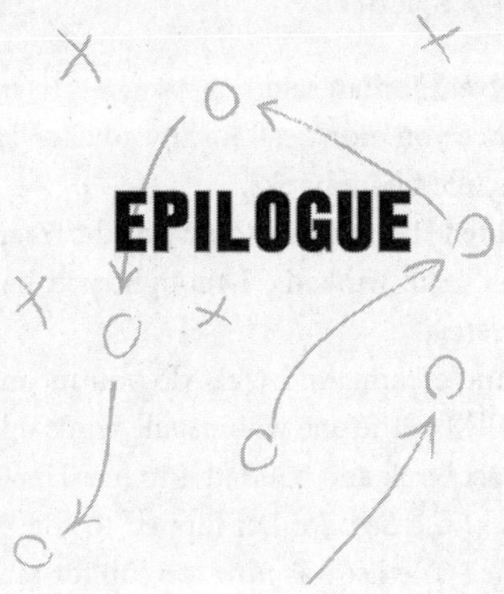

EPILOGUE

Mark Fellner begged her to stay when she turned in her letter of resignation. More plaques hung in his office, sunlight twinkling across the gold adornments. Jordan shook her head, and he conceded a rare smile.

"You were always the choice," he said. "We're going to miss you."

"I'll miss it here too." Jordan accepted his hand.

"You're sure we can't sweeten the deal for one more season?"

She smiled as she remembered Royce's advice, still a reliable guide despite the years and distance. "No. I think it's time for me to step away."

Her office, the one with the door always open and the floor she never stopped lying on, required little packing, but she accepted help anyway.

"So, have you decided?" Brooks slinked in behind her.

They embraced among the cardboard boxes. He was sturdier, his jaw strapping, arms more defined than the last time he'd stepped into the small room, but he was still the same Brooks to Jordan. She recognized the same spirit in his dimpled smile.

"No decision yet," Jordan said.

"I figured, since you didn't call for my advice." He helped her clear the shelves filled with books.

"Well, I doubted the former Rookie of the Year would have time for my call." She winked. "I thought you had to shoot a shampoo commercial."

"It's for shaving cream. And what do you mean I don't have time for your call? I'm the one who usually ends up calling you." He swiped the last book and handed it to her. Her worn copy of *The Old Man and the Sea.* Jordan flipped to the back cover to admire the names. The list was now too full for any others. "So, what's it going be? UCLA? USC? The NBA? WNBA?"

Jordan shrugged. "You'll be the first to know when I decide."

"I'm certain someone else will get that inside scoop." Brooks paused at the display behind her desk and grabbed one of two trophies for Pacific Coast Conference Coach of the Year. "You know, it's not too late for me to put in a good word with the front office. The Clippers would be lucky to have you. Plus, I wouldn't mind playing for you again."

"You're doing fine without me," Jordan said. "Though your perimeter defense is weak. They get you with the screen on your left side every time. Have you been doing those footwork drills?"

"See, this is why we need you."

"Please, if we go to the NBA, it'll be the Lakers." Leon strolled in and slapped Brooks in a hug.

Brooks shook his head at Jordan. "I can't believe you're actually taking him with you."

"Me neither," she said.

"Oh, come on. You think we'd have all this hardware without Coach Torres?" Leon gestured to the awards.

"Yeah, I'm still not used to hearing that." Brooks chuckled. He nodded at the line of basketballs taking up another shelf, all marked with special dates and milestone games. "These weren't here when I was, were they?"

Jordan stood next to him to admire them. "No. I just started running out of room at home."

Brooks took one down. "This is when we went to the Elite Eight?"

"Yep." Jordan took the ball from him and spun it on a finger. That last game would always be bittersweet. The tears on the court. Beck in the stands. The hardest and most rewarding season of her coaching career.

Brooks pulled down another. "National championship?"

Leon thrust out his left hand to show off a clunky piece of gold and silver. "That's when we got our rings."

Jordan glimpsed the jewelry on her own finger. While her second year coaching at David Douglas resulted in a sophomore slump, the team falling in the Sweet Sixteen, her third year proved a charm. With Dominic a senior, Cooper a junior, and recruits pounding at the door to get on the team, she finally brought home the title.

"What game was this?" Brooks grabbed the last ball from the shelf, dated just a month after the national championship.

"That's when I got my ring." Beck smiled from the doorway.

Jordan's mouth dropped as she spun around to meet her. "I thought you had the show tonight."

"Speck can handle it," Beck said. "Plus, he owes me for two straight weeks of playoff coverage. My hair still smells like champagne."

Jordan swooped in to kiss her. After three years of long distance, they'd grown accustomed to texts and phone calls, weeks between visits, Beck watching games from the road, and Jordan tuning in to *Keeping Score* each night. While they undoubtedly preferred the nights together, what gave them their start kept them from growing apart—chasing the game they loved. Only now, with Jordan's sights set on Los Angeles, they'd finally get to do it together.

Leon groaned through their kiss. "Get a room."

"Grow up, Torres," Jordan said when they parted.

"Have you two set a date?" Brooks asked. "We better be invited."

Beck shook her head. "Not yet, but you will be."

Jordan already had a blank basketball ready for the occasion. She set it aside the same night they hoisted the trophy for the title, after nearly proposing to Beck amid the cheers and confetti. Despite telling NSBC of the conflict of interest, the network insisted on having Beck on the sideline for the championship game. Mostly because to both their surprise, rather than a liability, their relationship had blossomed into pleasant, positive PR. Beck kept the questions professional during the postgame interview on the court, but when it ended, Jordan couldn't resist kissing her in a sports moment that would become infamous, muffled "I love yous" picked up by the microphones.

"Forget about the wedding date. When are you going to interview me?" Leon asked Beck.

"Once you do something interesting," she said.

His mouth fell open as he gestured to Brooks. "Oh, what, he's gay, so you give him an hour at prime time? Big deal. I'm plenty interesting."

"Leon, I've covered amateur golf tournaments more interesting than you," Beck said.

More than that. In three years, she'd reported on the sidelines for every major sport, in prime-time slots, playoffs, World Series, and Super Bowls. When the Olympics came to Los Angeles, she'd be there too. And after successfully sparring but never smiting Marty Spector, she enjoyed a permanent place on the coveted desk for a show now known as *Keeping Score with Speck and Beck.*

"I thought I heard trouble." Frost entered with a grin.

"Me or her?" Leon asked.

"Definitely her." He embraced Beck. "We're just missing Charlie now."

"I talked to him the other day. He's trying to do his residency in L.A. We could have the whole gang back together," Brooks said. "You sure you can't come with us, Frost?"

"Nah, someone's got to stay here and defend our title." He winked. "Speaking of, am I good to move in?"

"You're taking this office?" Beck asked.

"Of course. It's good luck." Frost clapped Brooks's and Leon's shoulders. "Come on, you two give me a hand."

Jordan took advantage of their departure, looping her arms back around Beck for another kiss. "I can't believe you're here."

"I wanted to surprise you." Beck played with Jordan's necklace. "Plus, I might be a little sentimental about this place. It's where everything started for us."

"Me too." Jordan sighed at the brief pang in her chest. David Douglas had been her home for years. But somewhere along the way, despite her love for the team, it stopped. It stopped because she couldn't have this.

"What do you say we give it a proper sendoff?" Beck asked.

"I mean, they're going to be back in a few minutes."

"Not like that."

She chuckled. "I know."

Jordan rolled a cart of basketballs to the empty court with Beck in tow.

"You know, Brooks is right. We need to set a date. Mom won't stop badgering me," Beck said as they stopped at the three-point arc, arena lights humming above. "Are you sure we can't elope?"

"Candace would never forgive me."

"Oh God, you just love that she likes you more than me."

Jordan grinned. "She does not."

"She literally started watching basketball because of you, even though I've been reporting on it for how many years?" Beck rolled her eyes. "She asked me if you'd coach the Sixers, so we can be closer to home."

"Oh, I know."

"How?"

"Scottie texted me this morning," she said. Beck beamed at her. "What?"

"Nothing."

The path to a public relationship formed slowly. Beck followed Lindsay's advice after starting at NSBC. She didn't hide Jordan, but didn't make a public announcement either. They both valued their privacy. So, it happened quietly. Jordan staying with Beck during the summer when she wasn't recruiting, meeting her co-workers, Beck attending games whenever possible. Word circulated gradually, and when it became known, the world didn't end. Not even when Beck brought her home that first Christmas.

Jordan swiped a ball and sank it from behind the three-point line.

"Oh, you've been practicing?" Beck asked.

"Practice? I don't need practice."

Beck grabbed a ball, dribbled to the foul line, and made a basket of her own. "I've been thinking about something." She eased closer. "I know you're determined to win another national championship or coach in the NBA or do something else historic and overachieving, but I have another idea."

Jordan licked her lips as she stared down at her. "And what's that?"

"Now that you're going to be in Los Angeles permanently, you should consider being a color analyst for NSBC." Beck smiled. "Can you imagine me and you broadcasting games together?"

"I think we might single-handedly ruin the sport of basketball."

"How about I play you for it?" she asked slowly.

Jordan found her lips before her answer, stealing a kiss on the hardwood like she once longed to three years ago. When they released, she reveled in Beck's hazel spell, the smile that reached the corners of her eyes, the ring glinting on her finger, and grinned. "Bring it on, Beck."

She snatched a ball from the cart, pivoted her back to the basket, closed her eyes, and lofted a backward shot with her left hand. When it went in, Beck's mouth dropped. "You have been practicing!" She hopped on her back. "And you learned that trick from me!"

"Your shot," Jordan said, not interested in victory, simply satisfied to play the sweetest game of all.

ACKNOWLEDGMENTS

Over the years as a journalist, writer, and athlete, I've had the pleasure of working alongside and being inspired by countless strong women in front of and behind the camera, on fields and sidelines, making waves in arenas where they were only recently welcomed—and sometimes not welcomed at all. Thank you to the coaches, athletes, reporters, producers, trailblazers, and dreamers, in sports and beyond, who push that line every day. We're all better for it.

Thank you to my agent, Jo Ramsay, for their belief in this book. I truly could not have made it to the finish line without your guidance and support. I'm eternally grateful to have you in my corner.

Thank you to Dell Romance, Penguin Random House, and my editor, Alicia Clancy, for making this book sing. Your enthusiasm and understanding of this project made for such an enjoyable journey. It was a pleasure getting to collaborate with you and bring this to life.

Thank you to my family and friends for their constant support, especially my parents. My mom didn't live to see this publication, but this book is a true testament to the power of her love and belief in me. Thank you to my dad, who carried the torch from where she left off. Thank you for being my biggest fan whether I was on the field or in the booth, and now as I embark on my writing career.

And finally, the biggest thank-you of all to my wife, Emily. Thank you for being my safe place but also the swift kick in the ass I sometimes need. This book absolutely would not have seen the light of day without you encouraging me to quit hiding in my writing and try again. Thank you for dreaming with me. I love you.